Classic
CHRISTMAS
STORIES

This text was originally published in the UK
in the years 1867-1896. The text is in the public domain.
The edits and layout of this version are Copyright © 2022
by Moncreiffe Press. This publication has no affiliation with the
original Author or publication company. The publishers have made
all reasonable efforts to ensure this book is in the Public Domain in
any and all territories it has been published, and apologise for any
omissions or errors made. Corrections may be made to
future printings or electronic publications.

MONCREIFFE
— PRESS

Classic CHRISTMAS STORIES

By
LOUISA MAY ALCOTT

1867 - 1896

UNITED STATES

Contents

A MERRY CHRISTMAS 1

KATE'S CHOICE 13

THE QUIET LITTLE WOMAN 29

    I. HOW SHE FOUND IT 31

    II. HOW SHE FILLED IT 36

TILLY'S CHRISTMAS 45

WHAT THE BELLS SAID AND SAW 53

A COUNTRY CHRISTMAS 65

ROSA'S TALE 93

A CHRISTMAS TURKEY AND HOW IT CAME 105

THE ABBOT'S GHOST: A CHRISTMAS STORY 117

    CHAPTER I. DRAMATIS PERSONAE 119

    CHAPTER II. BYPLAY 126

    CHAPTER III. WHO WAS IT? 134

    CHAPTER IV. FEEDING THE PEACOCKS 141

    CHAPTER V. UNDER THE MISTLETOE 148

    CHAPTER VI. MIRACLES 156

    CHAPTER VII. A GHOSTLY REVEL 165

    CHAPTER VIII. JASPER 174

LOUISA MAY ALCOTT BIOGRAPHY 181

A MERRY CHRISTMAS

Excerpt from 'Little Women'

1868

JO WAS THE FIRST TO WAKE in the gray dawn of Christmas morning. No stockings hung at the fireplace, and for a moment she felt as much disappointed as she did long ago, when her little sock fell down because it was crammed so full of goodies. Then she remembered her mother's promise and, slipping her hand under her pillow, drew out a little crimson-covered book. She knew it very well, for it was that beautiful old story of the best life ever lived, and Jo felt that it was a true guidebook for any pilgrim going on a long journey. She woke Meg with a "Merry Christmas," and bade her see what was under her pillow. A green-covered book appeared, with the same picture inside, and a few words written by their mother, which made their one present very precious in their eyes. Presently Beth and Amy woke to rummage and find their little books also, one dove-colored, the other blue, and all sat looking at and talking about them, while the east grew rosy with the coming day.

In spite of her small vanities, Margaret had a sweet and pious nature, which unconsciously influenced her sisters, especially Jo, who loved her very tenderly, and obeyed her because her advice was so gently given.

"Girls," said Meg seriously, looking from the tumbled head beside her to the two little night-capped ones in the room beyond, "Mother wants us to read and love and mind these books, and we must begin at once. We used to be faithful about it, but since Father went away and all this war trouble unsettled us, we have neglected many things. You can do as you please, but I shall keep my book on the table here and read a little every morning as soon as I wake, for I know it will do me good and help me through the day."

Then she opened her new book and began to read. Jo put her arm round her and, leaning cheek to cheek, read also, with the quiet expression so seldom seen on her restless face.

"How good Meg is! Come, Amy, let's do as they do. I'll help you with the hard words, and they'll explain things if we don't understand," whispered Beth, very much impressed by the pretty books and her sisters' example.

"I'm glad mine is blue," said Amy. and then the rooms were very still while the pages were softly turned, and the winter sunshine crept in to touch the bright heads and serious faces with a Christmas greeting.

"Where is Mother?" asked Meg, as she and Jo ran down to thank her for their gifts, half an hour later.

"Goodness only knows. Some poor creeter came a-beggin', and your ma went straight off to see what was needed. There never was such a woman for givin' away vittles and drink, clothes and firin'," replied Hannah, who had lived with the family since Meg was born, and was considered by them all more as a friend than a servant.

"She will be back soon, I think, so fry your cakes, and have everything ready," said Meg, looking over the presents which were collected in a basket and kept under the sofa, ready to be produced at the proper time. "Why, where is Amy's bottle of cologne?" she added, as the little flask did not appear.

"She took it out a minute ago, and went off with it to put a ribbon on it, or some such notion," replied Jo, dancing about the room to take the first stiffness off the new army slippers.

"How nice my handkerchiefs look, don't they? Hannah washed and ironed them for me, and I marked them all myself," said Beth, looking proudly at the somewhat uneven letters which had cost her such labor.

"Bless the child! She's gone and put 'Mother' on them instead of 'M. March'. How funny!" cried Jo, taking one up.

"Isn't that right? I thought it was better to do it so, because Meg's initials are M.M., and I don't want anyone to use these but Marmee," said Beth, looking troubled.

"It's all right, dear, and a very pretty idea, quite sensible too, for no one can ever mistake now. It will please her very much, I know," said Meg, with a frown for Jo and a smile for Beth.

"There's Mother. Hide the basket, quick!" cried Jo, as a door slammed and steps sounded in the hall.

Amy came in hastily, and looked rather abashed when she saw her sisters all waiting for her.

"Where have you been, and what are you hiding behind you?" asked Meg, surprised to see, by her hood and cloak, that lazy Amy had been out so early.

"Don't laugh at me, Jo! I didn't mean anyone should know till the time came. I only meant to change the little bottle for a big one, and I gave all my money to get it, and I'm truly trying not to be selfish any more."

As she spoke, Amy showed the handsome flask which replaced the cheap one, and looked so earnest and humble in her little effort to forget herself that Meg hugged her on the spot, and Jo pronounced her 'a trump', while Beth ran to the window, and picked her finest rose to ornament the stately bottle.

"You see I felt ashamed of my present, after reading and talking about being good this morning, so I ran round the corner and changed it the minute I was up, and I'm so glad, for mine is the handsomest now."

Another bang of the street door sent the basket under the sofa, and the girls to the table, eager for breakfast.

"Merry Christmas, Marmee! Many of them! Thank you for our books. We read some, and mean to every day," they all cried in chorus.

"Merry Christmas, little daughters! I'm glad you began at once, and hope you will keep on. But I want to say one word before we sit down. Not far away from here lies a poor woman with a little newborn baby. Six children are huddled into one bed to keep from freezing, for they have no fire. There is nothing to eat over there, and the oldest boy came to tell me they were suffering hunger and cold. My girls, will you give them your breakfast as a Christmas present?"

They were all unusually hungry, having waited nearly an hour, and for a minute no one spoke, only a minute, for Jo exclaimed impetuously, "I'm so glad you came before we began!"

"May I go and help carry the things to the poor little children?" asked Beth eagerly.

"I shall take the cream and the muffings," added Amy, heroically giving up the article she most liked.

Meg was already covering the buckwheats, and piling the bread into one big plate.

"I thought you'd do it," said Mrs. March, smiling as if satisfied. "You shall all go and help me, and when we come back we will have bread and milk for breakfast, and make it up at dinnertime."

They were soon ready, and the procession set out. Fortunately it was early, and they went through back streets, so few people saw them, and no one laughed at the queer party.

A poor, bare, miserable room it was, with broken windows, no fire, ragged bedclothes, a sick mother, wailing baby, and a group of pale, hungry children cuddled under one old quilt, trying to keep warm.

How the big eyes stared and the blue lips smiled as the girls went in.

"Ach, mein Gott! It is good angels come to us!" said the poor woman, crying for joy.

"Funny angels in hoods and mittens," said Jo, and set them to laughing.

In a few minutes it really did seem as if kind spirits had been at work there. Hannah, who had carried wood, made a fire, and stopped up the broken panes with old hats and her own cloak. Mrs. March gave the mother tea and gruel, and comforted her with promises of help, while she dressed the little baby as tenderly as if it had been her own. The girls meantime spread the table, set the children round the fire, and fed them like so many hungry birds, laughing, talking, and trying to understand the funny broken English.

"Das ist gut!""Die Engel-kinder!" cried the poor things as they ate and warmed their purple hands at the comfortable blaze. The girls had never been called angel children before, and thought it very agreeable, especially Jo, who had been considered a 'Sancho' ever since she was born. That was a very happy breakfast, though they didn't get any of it. And when they went away, leaving comfort behind, I think there were not in all the city four merrier people than the hungry little girls who gave away their breakfasts and contented themselves with bread and milk on Christmas morning.

"That's loving our neighbor better than ourselves, and I like it," said Meg, as they set out their presents while their mother was upstairs collecting clothes for the poor Hummels.

Not a very splendid show, but there was a great deal of love done up in the few little bundles, and the tall vase of red roses, white chrysanthemums, and trailing vines, which stood in the middle, gave quite an elegant air to the table.

"She's coming! Strike up, Beth! Open the door, Amy! Three cheers for Marmee!"cried Jo, prancing about while Meg went to conduct Mother to the seat of honor.

Beth played her gayest march, Amy threw open the door, and Meg enacted escort with great dignity. Mrs. March was both surprised and touched, and smiled with her eyes full as she examined her presents and read the little notes which accompanied them. The slippers went on at once, a new handkerchief was slipped into her pocket, well scented with Amy's cologne, the rose was fastened in her bosom, and the nice gloves were pronounced a perfect fit.

There was a good deal of laughing and kissing and explaining, in the simple, loving fashion which makes these home festivals so pleasant at the time, so sweet to remember long afterward, and then all fell to work.

The morning charities and ceremonies took so much time that the rest of the day was devoted to preparations for the evening festivities. Being still too young to go often to the theater, and not rich enough to afford any great outlay for private performances, the girls put their wits to work, and necessity being the mother of invention, made whatever they needed. Very clever were some of their productions, pasteboard guitars, antique lamps made of old-fashioned butter boats covered with silver paper, gorgeous robes of old cotton, glittering with tin spangles from a pickle factory, and armor covered with the same useful diamond shaped bits left in sheets when the lids of preserve pots were cut out. The big chamber was the scene of many innocent revels.

No gentleman were admitted, so Jo played male parts to her heart's content and took immense satisfaction in a pair of russet leather boots given her by a friend, who knew a lady who knew an actor. These boots, an old foil, and a slashed doublet once used by an artist for some picture, were Jo's chief treasures and appeared on all occasions. The smallness of the company made it necessary for the two principal actors to take several parts apiece, and they certainly deserved some credit for the hard work they did in learning three or four different parts, whisking in and out of various costumes, and managing the stage besides. It was excellent drill for their memories, a harmless amusement, and employed many hours which otherwise would have been idle, lonely, or spent in less profitable society.

On Christmas night, a dozen girls piled onto the bed which was the dress circle, and sat before the blue and yellow chintz curtains in a most flattering state of expectancy. There was a good deal of rustling and whispering behind the curtain, a trifle of lamp smoke, and an occasional giggle from Amy, who was apt to get hysterical in the excitement of the moment. Presently a bell sounded, the curtains flew apart, and the *operatic tragedy* began.

"A gloomy wood," according to the one playbill, was represented by a few shrubs in pots, green baize on the floor, and a cave in the distance. This cave was made with a clothes horse for a roof, bureaus for walls, and in it was a small furnace in full blast, with a black pot on it and an old witch bending over it. The stage was dark and the glow of the furnace had a fine effect, especially as real steam issued from the kettle when the witch took off the cover. A moment was allowed for the first thrill to subside, then Hugo, the villain, stalked in with a clanking sword at his side, a slouching hat, black beard, mysterious cloak, and the boots. After pacing to and fro in much agitation, he struck his forehead, and burst out in a wild strain, singing of his hatred for Roderigo, his love for Zara, and his pleasing resolution to kill the one and win the other. The gruff tones of Hugo's voice, with an occasional shout when his feelings overcame him, were very impressive, and the audience applauded the moment he paused for breath. Bowing with the air of one accustomed to public praise, he stole to the cavern and ordered Hagar to come forth with a commanding, "What ho, minion! I need thee!"

Out came Meg, with gray horsehair hanging about her face, a red and black robe, a staff, and cabalistic signs upon her cloak. Hugo demanded a potion to make Zara adore him, and one to destroy Roderigo. Hagar, in a fine dramatic melody, promised both, and proceeded to call up the spirit who would bring the love philter.

> Hither, hither, from thy home,
> Airy sprite, I bid thee come!
> Born of roses, fed on dew,
> Charms and potions canst thou brew?
> Bring me here, with elfin speed,
> The fragrant philter which I need.
> Make it sweet and swift and strong,
> Spirit, answer now my song!

A soft strain of music sounded, and then at the back of the cave appeared a little figure in cloudy white, with glittering wings, golden hair, and a garland of roses on its head. Waving a wand, it sang...

> Hither I come,
> From my airy home,
> Afar in the silver moon.
> Take the magic spell,
> And use it well,
> Or its power will vanish soon!

And dropping a small, gilded bottle at the witch's feet, the spirit vanished. Another chant from Hagar produced another apparition, not a lovely one, for with a bang an ugly black imp appeared and, having croaked a reply, tossed a dark bottle at Hugo and disappeared with a mocking laugh. Having warbled his thanks and put the potions in his boots, Hugo departed, and Hagar informed the audience that as he had killed a few of her friends in times past, she had cursed him, and intends to thwart his plans, and be revenged on him. Then the curtain fell, and the audience reposed and ate candy while discussing the merits of the play.

A good deal of hammering went on before the curtain rose again, but when it became evident what a masterpiece of stage carpentry had been got up, no one murmured at the delay. It was truly superb. A tower rose to the ceiling, halfway up appeared a window with a lamp burning in it, and behind the white curtain appeared Zara in a lovely blue and silver dress, waiting for Roderigo. He came in gorgeous array, with plumed cap, red cloak, chestnut lovelocks, a guitar, and the boots, of course. Kneeling at the foot of the tower, he sang a serenade in melting tones. Zara replied and, after a musical dialogue, consented to fly. Then came the grand effect of the play. Roderigo produced a rope ladder, with five steps to it, threw up one end, and invited Zara to descend. Timidly she crept from her lattice, put her hand on Roderigo's shoulder, and was about to leap gracefully down when "Alas! Alas for Zara!"she forgot her train. It caught in the window, the tower tottered, leaned forward, fell with a crash, and buried the unhappy lovers in the ruins.

A universal shriek arose as the russet boots waved wildly from the wreck and a golden head emerged, exclaiming, "I told you so! I told you so!" With wonderful presence of mind, Don Pedro, the cruel sire, rushed in, dragged out his daughter, with a hasty aside...

"Don't laugh! Act as if it was all right!"and, ordering Roderigo up, banished him from the kingdom with wrath and scorn. Though decidedly shaken by the fall from the tower upon him, Roderigo defied the old gentleman and refused to stir. This dauntless example fired Zara. She also defied her sire, and he ordered them both to the deepest dungeons of the castle. A stout little retainer came in with chains and led them away, looking very much frightened and evidently forgetting the speech he ought to have made.

Act third was the castle hall, and here Hagar appeared, having come to free the lovers and finish Hugo. She hears him coming and hides, sees him put the potions into two cups of wine and bid the timid little servant, "Bear them to the captives in their cells, and tell them I shall come anon." The servant takes Hugo aside to tell him something, and Hagar changes the cups for two others which are harmless. Ferdinando, the 'minion', carries them away, and Hagar puts back the cup which holds the poison meant for Roderigo. Hugo, getting thirsty after a long warble, drinks it, loses his wits, and after a good deal of clutching and stamping, falls flat and dies, while Hagar informs him what she has done in a song of exquisite power and melody.

This was a truly thrilling scene, though some persons might have thought that the sudden tumbling down of a quantity of long red hair rather marred the effect of the villain's death. He was called before the curtain, and with great propriety appeared, leading Hagar, whose singing was considered more wonderful than all the rest of the performance put together.

Act fourth displayed the despairing Roderigo on the point of stabbing himself because he has been told that Zara has deserted him. Just as the dagger is at his heart, a lovely song is sung under his window, informing him that Zara is true but in danger, and he can save her if he will. A key is thrown in, which unlocks the door, and in a spasm of rapture he tears off his chains and rushes away to find and rescue his lady love.

Act fifth opened with a stormy scene between Zara and Don Pedro. He wishes her to go into a convent, but she won't hear of it, and after a touching appeal, is about to faint when Roderigo dashes in and demands her hand. Don Pedro refuses, because he is not rich. They shout and gesticulate tremendously but cannot agree, and Rodrigo is about to bear away the exhausted Zara, when the timid servant enters with a letter and a bag from Hagar, who has mysteriously disappeared. The latter informs the party that she bequeaths untold wealth to the young pair and an awful doom to Don Pedro, if he doesn't make them happy. The bag is opened, and several quarts of tin money shower down upon the stage till it is quite glorified with the glitter. This entirely softens the stern sire. He consents without a murmur, all join in a joyful chorus, and the curtain falls upon the lovers kneeling to receive Don Pedro's blessing in attitudes of the most romantic grace.

Tumultuous applause followed but received an unexpected check, for the cot bed, on which the dress circle was built, suddenly shut up and extinguished the enthusiastic audience. Roderigo and Don Pedro flew to the rescue, and all were taken out unhurt, though many were speechless with laughter. The excitement had hardly subsided when Hannah appeared, with "Mrs. March's compliments, and would the ladies walk down to supper."

This was a surprise even to the actors, and when they saw the table, they looked at one another in rapturous amazement. It was like Marmee to get up a little treat for them, but anything so fine as this was unheard of since the departed days of plenty. There was ice cream, actually two dishes of it, pink and white, and cake and fruit and distracting French bonbons and, in the middle of the table, four great bouquets of hot house flowers.

It quite took their breath away, and they stared first at the table and then at their mother, who looked as if she enjoyed it immensely.

"Is it fairies?" asked Amy.

"Santa Claus," said Beth.

"Mother did it." And Meg smiled her sweetest, in spite of her gray beard and white eyebrows.

"Aunt March had a good fit and sent the supper," cried Jo, with a sudden inspiration.

"All wrong. Old Mr. Laurence sent it," replied Mrs. March.

"The Laurence boy's grandfather! What in the world put such a thing into his head? We don't know him!" exclaimed Meg.

"Hannah told one of his servants about your breakfast party. He is an odd old gentleman, but that pleased him. He knew my father years ago, and he sent me a polite note this afternoon, saying he hoped I would allow him to express his friendly feeling toward my children by sending them a few trifles in honor of the day. I could not refuse, and so you have a little feast at night to make up for the bread-and-milk breakfast."

"That boy put it into his head, I know he did! He's a capital fellow, and I wish we could get acquainted. He looks as if he'd like to know us but he's bashful, and Meg is so prim she won't let me speak to him when we pass," said Jo, as the plates went round, and the ice began to melt out of sight, with ohs and ahs of satisfaction.

"You mean the people who live in the big house next door, don't you?" asked one of the girls. "My mother knows old Mr. Laurence, but says he's very proud and doesn't like to mix with his neighbors. He keeps his grandson shut up, when he isn't riding or walking with his tutor, and makes him study very hard. We invited him to our party, but he didn't come. Mother says he's very nice, though he never speaks to us girls."

"Our cat ran away once, and he brought her back, and we talked over the fence, and were getting on capitally, all about cricket, and so on, when he saw Meg coming, and walked off. I mean to know him some day, for he needs fun, I'm sure he does," said Jo decidedly.

"I like his manners, and he looks like a little gentleman, so I've no objection to your knowing him, if a proper opportunity comes. He brought the flowers himself, and I should have asked him in, if I had been sure what was going on upstairs. He looked so wistful as he went away, hearing the frolic and evidently having none of his own."

"It's a mercy you didn't, Mother!" laughed Jo, looking at her boots. "But we'll have another play sometime that he can see. Perhaps he'll help act. Wouldn't that be jolly?"

"I never had such a fine bouquet before! How pretty it is!" And Meg examined her flowers with great interest.

"They are lovely. But Beth's roses are sweeter to me," said Mrs. March, smelling the half-dead posy in her belt.

Beth nestled up to her, and whispered softly, "I wish I could send my bunch to Father. I'm afraid he isn't having such a merry Christmas as we are."

KATE'S CHOICE

1896

"WELL, WHAT DO YOU THINK OF HER?"

"I think she's a perfect dear, and not a bit stuck up with all her money."

"A real little lady, and ever so pretty."

"She kissed me lots, and don't tell me to run away, so I love her."

The group of brothers and sisters standing round the fire laughed as little May finished the chorus of praise with these crowning virtues.

Tall Alf asked the question, and seemed satisfied with the general approval of the new cousin just come from England to live with them. They had often heard of Kate, and rather prided themselves on the fact that she lived in a fine house, was very rich, and sent them charming presents. Now pity was added to the pride, for Kate was an orphan, and all her money could not buy back the parents she had lost. They had watched impatiently for her arrival, had welcomed her cordially, and after a day spent in trying to make her feel at home they were comparing notes in the twilight, while Kate was having a quiet talk with mamma.

"I hope she will choose to live with us. You know she can go to any of the uncles she likes best," said Alf.

"We are nearer her age than any of the other cousins, and papa is the oldest uncle, so I guess she will," added Milly, the fourteen-year-old daughter of the house.

"She said she liked America," said quiet Frank.

"Wonder if she will give us a lot of her money?" put in practical Fred, who was always in debt.

"Stop that!" commanded Alf. "Mind now, if you ever ask her for a penny I'll shake you out of your jacket."

"Hush! she's coming," cried Milly, and a dead silence followed the lively chatter.

A fresh-faced bright-eyed girl of fifteen came quietly in, glanced at the group on the rug, and paused as if doubtful whether she was wanted.

"Come on!" said Fred, encouragingly.

"Shall I be in the way?"

"Oh! dear, no, we were only talking," answered Milly, drawing her cousin nearer with an arm about her waist.

"It sounded like something pleasant," said Kate, not exactly knowing what to say.

"We were talking about you," began little May, when a poke from Frank made her stop to ask, "What's that for? We were talking about Kate, and we all said we liked her, so it's no matter if I do tell."

"You are very kind," and Kate looked so pleased that the children forgave May's awkward frankness.

"Yes, and we hoped you'd like us and stay with us," said Alf, in the lofty and polite manner which he thought became the young lord of the house.

"I am going to try all the uncles in turn, and then decide; papa wished it," answered Kate, with a sudden tremble of the lips, for her father was the only parent she could remember, and had been unusually dear for that reason.

"Can you play billiards?" asked Fred, who had a horror of seeing girls cry.

"Yes, and I'll teach you."

"You had a pony-carriage at your house, didn't you?" added Frank, eager to help on the good work.

"At grandma's,—I had no other home, you know," answered Kate.

"What shall you buy first with your money?" asked May, who *would* ask improper questions.

"I'd buy a grandma if I could," and Kate both smiled and sighed.

"How funny! We've got one somewhere, but we don't care much about her," continued May, with the inconvenient candor of a child.

"Have you? Where is she?" and Kate turned quickly, looking full of interest.

"Papa's mother is very old, and lives ever so far away in the country, so of course we don't see much of her," explained Alf.

"But papa writes sometimes, and mamma sends her things every Christmas. We don't remember her much, because we never saw her but once, ever so long ago; but we do care for her, and May mustn't say such rude things," said Milly.

"I shall go and see her. I can't get on without a grandmother," and Kate smiled so brightly that the lads thought her prettier than ever. "Tell me more about her. Is she a dear old lady?"

"Don't know. She is lame, and lives in the old house, and has a maid named Dolly, and—that's all I can tell you about her," and Milly looked a little vexed that she could say no more on the subject that seemed to interest her cousin so much.

Kate looked surprised, but said nothing, and stood looking at the fire as if turning the matter over in her mind, and trying to answer the question she was too polite to ask,—how could they live without a grandmother? Here the tea-bell rang, and the flock ran laughing downstairs; but, though she said no more, Kate remembered that conversation, and laid a plan in her resolute little mind which she carried out when the time came.

According to her father's wish she lived for a while in the family of each of the four uncles before she decided with which she would make her home. All were anxious to have her, one because of her money, another because her great-grandfather had been a lord, a third hoped to secure her for his son, while the fourth and best family loved her for herself alone. They were worthy people, as the world goes,—busy, ambitious, and prosperous; and every one, old and young, was fond of bright, pretty, generous Kate. Each family was anxious to keep her, a little jealous of the rest, and very eager to know which she would choose.

But Kate surprised them all by saying decidedly when the time came,—

"I must see grandma before I choose. Perhaps I ought to have visited her first, as she is the oldest. I think papa would wish me to do it. At any rate, I want to pay my duty to her before I settle anywhere, so please let me go."

Some of the young cousins laughed at the idea, and her old-fashioned, respectful way of putting it, which contrasted strongly with their free-and-easy American speech. The uncles were surprised, but agreed to humor her whim, and Uncle George, the eldest, said softly,—

"I ought to have remembered that poor Anna was mother's only daughter, and the old lady would naturally love to see the girl. But, my dear, it will be desperately dull. Only two old women and a quiet country town. No fun, no company, you won't stay long."

"I shall not mind the dulness if grandma likes to have me there. I lived very quietly in England, and was never tired of it. Nursey can take care of me, and I think the sight of me will do the dear old lady good, because they tell me I am like mamma."

Something in the earnest young face reminded Uncle George of the sister he had almost forgotten, and recalled his own youth so pleasantly that he said, with a caress of the curly head beside him,—

"So it would, I'm sure of it, and I've a great mind to go with you and 'pay my duty' to mother, as you prettily express it."

"Oh, no, please don't, sir; I want to surprise her, and have her all to myself for a little while. Would you mind if I went quite alone with Nursey? You can come later."

"Not a bit; you shall do as you like, and make sunshine for the old lady as you have for us. I haven't seen her for a year, but I know she is well and comfortable, and Dolly guards her like a dragon. Give her my love, Kitty, and tell her I send her something she will value a hundred times more than the very best tea, the finest cap, or the handsomest tabby that ever purred."

So, in spite of the lamentations of her cousins, Kate went gayly away to find the grandma whom no one else seemed to value as she did.

You see, grandpa had been a farmer, and lived contentedly on the old place until he died; but his four sons wanted to be something better, so they went away one after the other to make their way in the world. All worked hard, got rich, lived splendidly, and forgot as far as possible the old life and the dull old place they came from. They were good sons in their way, and had each offered his mother a home with him if she cared to come. But grandma clung to the old home, the simple ways, and quiet life, and, thanking them gratefully, she had remained in the big farm-house, empty, lonely, and plain though it was, compared to the fine homes of her sons.

Little by little the busy men forgot the quiet, uncomplaining old mother, who spent her years thinking of them, longing to see and know their children, hoping they would one day remember how she loved them all, and how solitary her life must be.

Now and then they wrote or paid her a hasty visit, and all sent gifts of far less value to her than one loving look, one hour of dutiful, affectionate companionship.

"If you ever want me, send and I'll come. Or, if you ever need a home, remember the old place is here always open, and you are always welcome," the good old lady said. But they never seemed to need her, and so seldom came that the old place evidently had no charm for them.

It was hard, but the sweet old woman bore it patiently, and lived her lonely life quietly and usefully, with her faithful maid Dolly to serve and love and support her.

Kate's mother, her one daughter, had married young, gone to England, and, dying early, had left the child to its father and his family. Among them little Kate had grown up, knowing scarcely any thing of her American relations until she was left an orphan and went back to her mother's people. She had been the pet of her English grandmother, and, finding all the aunts busy, fashionable women, had longed for the tender fostering she had known, and now felt as if only grandmothers could give.

With a flutter of hope and expectation, she approached the old house after the long journey was over. Leaving the luggage at the inn, and accompanied by faithful Nurse, Kate went up the village street, and, pausing at the gate, looked at the home where her mother had been born.

A large, old-fashioned farm-house, with a hospitable porch and tall trees in front, an orchard behind, and a capital hill for blackberries in summer, and coasting in winter, close by. All the upper windows were curtained, and made the house look as if it was half-asleep. At one of the lower windows sat a portly puss, blinking in the sun, and at the other appeared a cap, a regular grandmotherly old cap, with a little black bow perked up behind. Something in the lonely look of the house and the pensive droop of that cap made Katy hurry up the walk and tap eagerly at the antique knocker. A brisk little old woman peered out, as if startled at the sound, and Kate asked, smiling, "Does Madam Coverley live here?"

"She does, dear. Walk right in," and throwing wide the door, the maid trotted down a long, wide hall, and announced in a low tone to her mistress,—

"A nice, pretty little girl wants to see you, mum."

"I shall love to see a young face. Who is it, Dolly?" asked a pleasant voice.

"Don't know, mum."

"Grandma must guess," and Kate went straight up to the old lady with both hands out, for the first sight of that sweet old face won her heart.

Lifting her spectacles, grandma looked silently a minute, then opened her arms without a word, and in the long embrace that followed Kate felt assured that she was welcome to the home she wanted.

"So like my Anna! And this is her little girl? God bless you, my darling! So good to come and see me!" said the old lady when she could speak.

"Why, grandma, I couldn't get on without you, and as soon as I knew where to find you I was in a fidget to be off; but had to do my other visits first, because the uncles had planned it so. This is Dolly,

I am sure, and that is my good nurse. Go and get my things, please, Nursey. I shall stay here until grandma sends me away."

"That will never be, deary. Now tell me every thing. It is like an angel coming to see me all of a sudden. Sit close, and let me feel sure it isn't one of the dreams I make to cheer myself when I'm lonesome."

Kate sat on a little stool at grandma's feet, and, leaning on her knee, told all her little story, while the old lady fed her hungry eyes with the sight of the fresh young face, listened to the music of a loving voice, and felt the happy certainty that some one had remembered her, as she longed to be remembered.

Such a happy day as Kate spent talking and listening, looking at her new home, which she found delightful, and being petted by the two old women, who would hardly let Nursey do any thing for her. Kate's quick eyes read the truth of grandma's lonely life very soon; her warm heart was full of tender pity, and she resolved to devote herself to making the happiness of the dear old lady's few remaining years, for at eighty one should have the prop of loving children, if ever.

To Dolly and madam it really did seem as if an angel had come, a singing, smiling, chattering sprite, who danced all over the old house, making blithe echoes in the silent room, and brightening every corner she entered.

Kate opened all the shutters and let in the sun, saying she must see which room she liked best before she settled. She played on the old piano, that wheezed and jangled, all out of tune; but no one minded, for the girlish voice was as sweet as a lark's. She invaded Dolly's sacred kitchen, and messed to her heart's content, delighting the old soul by praises of her skill, and petitions to be taught all she knew. She pranced to and fro in the long hall, and got acquainted with the lives of painted ancestors hanging there in big wigs or short-waisted gowns. She took possession of grandma's little parlor, and made it so cosey the old lady felt as if she was bewitched, for cushioned arm-chairs, fur foot-stools, soft rugs, and delicate warm shawls appeared like magic. Flowers bloomed in the deep, sunny window-seats, pictures of lovely places seemed to break out on the oaken walls, a dainty work-basket took its place near grandma's quaint one, and, best of all, the little chair beside her own was seldom empty now.

The first thing in the morning a kiss waked her, and the beloved voice gave her a gay "Good-morning, grandma dear!" All day Anna's child hovered about her with willing hands and feet to serve her, loving heart to return her love, and the tender reverence which is the beautiful tribute the young should pay the old. In the twilight, the bright head always was at her knees; and, in either listening to the stories of the past or making lively plans for the future, Kate whiled away the time that used to be so sad.

Kate never found it lonely, seldom wished for other society, and grew every day more certain that here she could find the cherishing she needed, and do the good she hoped.

Dolly and Nurse got on capitally; each tried which could sing "Little Missy's" praises loudest, and spoil her quickest by unquestioning obedience to every whim or wish. A happy family, and the dull November days went by so fast that Christmas was at hand before they knew it.

All the uncles had written to ask Kate to pass the holidays with them, feeling sure she must be longing for a change. But she had refused them all, saying she should stay with grandma, who could not go anywhere to join other people's merry-makings, and must have one of her own at home. The uncles urged, the aunts advised, and the cousins teased; but Kate denied them all, yet offended no one, for she was inspired by a grand idea, and carried it out with help from Dolly and Nurse, unsuspected by grandma.

"We are going to have a little Christmas fun up here among ourselves, and you mustn't know about it until we are ready. So just sit all cosey in your corner, and let me riot about as I like. I know you won't mind, and I think you'll say it is splendid when I've carried out my plan," said Kate, when the old lady wondered what she was thinking about so deeply, with her brows knit and her lips smiling.

"Very well, dear, do any thing you like, and I shall enjoy it, only don't get tired, or try to do too much," and with that grandma became deaf and blind to the mysteries that went on about her.

She was lame, and seldom left her own rooms; so Kate, with her devoted helpers, turned the house topsy-turvy, trimmed up hall and parlors and great dining-room with shining holly and evergreen, laid fires ready for kindling on the hearths that had been cold for years, and had beds made up all over the house.

What went on in the kitchen, only Dolly could tell; but such delicious odors as stole out made grandma sniff the air, and think of merry Christmas revels long ago. Up in her own room Kate wrote lots of letters, and sent orders to the city that made Nursey hold up her hands. More letters came in reply, and Kate had a rapture over every one. Big bundles were left by the express, who came so often that the gates were opened and the lawn soon full of sleigh-tracks. The shops in the village were ravaged by Mistress Kate, who laid in stores of gay ribbon, toys, nuts, and all manner of queer things.

"I really think she's lost her mind," said the post-master as she flew out of the office one day with a handful of letters.

"Pretty creter! I wouldn't say a word against her, not for a mint of money. She's so good to old Mrs. Coverley," answered his fat wife, smiling as she watched Kate ride up the village street on an ox-sled.

If grandma had thought the girl out of her wits, no one could have blamed her, for on Christmas day she really did behave in the most singular manner.

"You are going to church with me this morning, grandma. It's all arranged. A close carriage is coming for us, the sleighing is lovely, the church all trimmed up, and I must have you see it. I shall wrap you in fur, and we will go and say our prayers together, like good girls, won't we?" said Kate, who was in a queer flutter, while her eyes shone, her lips were all smiles, and her feet kept dancing in spite of her.

"Anywhere you like, my darling. I'd start for Australia to-morrow, if you wanted me to go with you," answered grandma, who obeyed Kate in all things, and seemed to think she could do no wrong.

So they went to church, and grandma did enjoy it; for she had many blessings to thank God for, chief among them the treasure of a dutiful, loving child. Kate tried to keep herself quiet, but the odd little flutter would not subside, and seemed to get worse and worse as time went on. It increased rapidly as they drove home, and, when grandma was safe in her little parlor again, Kate's hands trembled go she could hardly tie the strings of the old lady's state and festival cap.

"We must take a look at the big parlor. It is all trimmed up, and I've got my presents in there. Is it ready, Doll?" asked Kate, as the old servant appeared, looking so excited that grandma said, laughing,—

"We have been quiet so long, poor Dolly don't know what to make of a little gayety."

"Lord bless us, my dear mum! It's all so beautiful and kinder surprisin', I feel as ef merrycles had come to pass agin," answered Dolly, actually wiping away tears with her best white apron.

"Come, grandma," and Kate offered her arm. "Don't she look sweet and dear?" she added, smoothing the soft, silken shawl about the old lady's shoulders, and kissing the placid old face that beamed at her from under the new cap.

~ 22 ~

"I always said madam was the finest old lady a-goin', ef folks only knew it. Now, Missy, ef you don't make haste, that parlor-door will bust open, and spoil the surprise; for they are just bilin' over in there," with which mysterious remark Dolly vanished, giggling.

Across the hall they went, but at the door Kate paused, and said with a look grandma never forgot,—

"I hope I have done right. I hope you'll like my present, and not find it too much for you. At any rate, remember I meant to please you and give you the thing you need and long for most, my dear old grandma."

"My good child, don't be afraid. I shall like any thing you do, and thank you for your thought of me. What a curious noise! I hope the fire hasn't fallen down."

Without another word, Kate threw open the door and led grandma in. Only a step or two—for the old lady stopped short and stared about her, as if she didn't know her own best parlor. No wonder she didn't, for it was full of people, and such people! All her sons, their wives and children, rose as she came in, and turned to greet her with smiling faces. Uncle George went up and kissed her, saying, with a choke in his voice, "A merry Christmas, mother!" and everybody echoed the words in a chorus of good-will that went straight to the heart.

Poor grandma could not bear it, and sat down in her big chair, trembling, and sobbing like a little child. Kate hung over her, fearing the surprise had been too much; but joy seldom kills, and presently the old lady was calm enough to look up and welcome them all by stretching out her feeble hands and saying, brokenly yet heartily,—

"God bless you, my children! This *is* a merry Christmas, indeed! Now tell me all about it, and who everybody is; for I don't know half the little ones."

Then Uncle George explained that it was Kate's plan, and told how she had made every one agree to it, pleading so eloquently for grandma that all other plans were given up. They had arrived while she was at church, and had been with difficulty kept from bursting out before the time.

"Do you like your present?" whispered Kate, quite calm and happy now that the grand surprise was safely over.

Grandma answered with a silent kiss that said more than the warmest words, and then Kate put every one at ease by leading up the children, one by one, and introducing each with some lively speech. Everybody enjoyed this and got acquainted quickly; for grandma thought the children the most remarkable she had ever seen, and the little people soon made up their minds that an old lady who had such a very nice, big house, and such a dinner waiting for them (of course they had peeped everywhere), was a most desirable and charming grandma.

By the time the first raptures were over Dolly and Nurse and Betsey Jane (a girl hired for the occasion) had got dinner on the table; and the procession, headed by Madam proudly escorted by her eldest son, filed into the dining-room where such a party had not met for years.

It would be quite impossible to do justice to that dinner: pen and ink are not equal to it. I can only say that every one partook copiously of every thing; that they laughed and talked, told stories, and sang songs; and when no one could do any more, Uncle George proposed grandma's health, which was drunk standing, and followed by three cheers. Then up got the old lady, quite rosy and young, excited and gay, and said in a clear strong voice,—

"I give you in return the best of grandchildren, little Kate."

I give you my word the cheer they gave grandma was nothing to the shout that followed these words; for the old lady led off with amazing vigor, and the boys roared so tremendously that the sedate tabby in the kitchen flew off her cushion, nearly frightened into a fit.

After that, the elders sat with grandma in the parlor, while the younger part of the flock trooped after Kate all over the house. Fires burned every where, and the long unused toys of their fathers were brought out for their amusement. The big nursery was full of games, and here Nursey collected the little ones when the larger boys and girls were invited by Kate to go out and coast. Sleds had been provided, and until dusk they kept it up, the city girls getting as gay and rosy as Kate herself in this healthy sport, while the lads frolicked to their hearts' content, building snow forts, pelting one another, and carousing generally without any policeman to interfere or any stupid old ladies to get upset, as at home in the park.

A cosey tea and a dance in the long hall followed, and they were just thinking what they would do next when Kate's second surprise came.

There were two great fireplaces in the hall: up the chimney of one roared a jolly fire, but the other was closed by a tall fire-board. As they sat about, lasting after a brisk contra dance, a queer rustling and tapping was heard behind this fire-board.

"Rats!" suggested the girls, jumping up into the chairs.

"Let's have 'em out!" added the boys, making straight for the spot, intent on fun.

But before they got there, a muffled voice cried, "Stand from under!" and down went the board with a crash, out bounced Santa Claus, startling the lads as much as the rumor of rats had the girls.

A jolly old saint he was, all in fur, with sleigh-bells jingling from his waist and the point of his high cap, big boots, a white beard, and a nose as red as if Jack Frost had had a good tweak at it. Giving himself a shake that set all the bells ringing, he stepped out upon the hearth, saying in a half-gruff, half-merry tone,—

"I call this a most inhospitable way to receive me! What do you mean by stopping up my favorite chimney? Never mind, I'll forgive you, for this is an unusual occasion. Here, some of you fellows, lend a hand and help me out with my sack."

A dozen pair of hands had the great bag out in a minute, and, lugging it to the middle of the hall, left it beside St. Nick, while the boys fell back into the eager, laughing crowd that surrounded the new-comer.

"Where's my girl? I want my Kate," said the saint, and when she went to him he took a base advantage of his years, and kissed her in spite of the beard.

"That's not fair," whispered Kate, as rosy as the holly-berries in her hair.

"Can't help it,—must have some reward for sticking in that horrid chimney so long," answered Santa Claus, looking as roguish as any boy. Then he added aloud, "I've got something for everybody, so make a big ring, and the good fairy will hand round the gifts."

With that he dived into his bag and brought out treasure after treasure, some fine, some funny, many useful, and all appropriate, for the good fairy seemed to have guessed what each one wanted. Shouts of laughter greeted the droll remarks of the jolly saint, for he had a joke about every thing, and people were quite exhausted by the time the bottom of the sack was reached.

"Now, then, a rousing good game of blind man's buff, and then this little family must go to bed, for it's past eleven."

As he spoke, the saint cast off his cap and beard, fur coat, and big boots, and proceeded to dance a double shuffle with great vigor and skill; while the little ones, who had been thoroughly mystified, shouted, "Why, it's Alf!" and fell upon him *en masse* as the best way of expressing their delight at his successful performance of that immortal part.

The game of blind man's buff that followed was a "rouser" in every sense of the word, for the gentlemen joined, and the children flew about like a flock of chickens when hawks are abroad. Such peals of laughter, such shouts of fun, and such racing and scrambling that old hall had never seen before. Kate was so hunted that she finally took refuge behind grandma's chair, and stood there looking at the lively scene, her face full of happiness at she remembered that it was her work.

The going to bed that night was the best joke of all; for, though Kate's arrangements were peculiar, every one voted that they were capital. There were many rooms, but not enough for all to have one apiece. So the uncles and aunts had the four big chambers, all the boys were ordered into the great play-room, where beds were made on the floor, and a great fire blazing that the camping out might be as comfortable as possible. The nursery was devoted to the girls, and the little ones were sprinkled round wherever a snug corner was found.

How the riotous flock were ever got into their beds no one knows. The lads caroused until long past midnight, and no knocking on the walls of paternal boots, or whispered entreaties of maternal voices through key-holes, had any effect, for it was impossible to resist the present advantages for a grand Christmas rampage.

The girls giggled and gossiped, told secrets, and laid plans more quietly; while the small things tumbled into bed, and went to sleep at once, quite used up with the festivities of this remarkable day.

Grandma, down in her own cosey room, sat listening to the blithe noises with a smile on her face, for the past seemed to have come back again, and her own boys and girls to be frolicking above there, as they used to do forty years ago.

"It's all so beautiful I can't go to bed, Dolly, and lose any of it. They'll go away to-morrow, and I may never see them any more," she said, as Dolly tied on her night-cap and brought her slippers.

"Yes, you will, mum. That dear child has made it so pleasant they can't keep away. You'll see plenty of 'em, if they carry out half the plans they have made. Mrs. George wants to come up and pass the summer here; Mr. Tom says he shall send his boys to school here, and every girl among them has promised Kate to make her a long visit. The thing is done, mum, and you'll never be lonely any more."

"Thank God for that!" and grandma bent her head as if she had received a great blessing. "Dolly, I want to go and look at those children. It seems so like a dream to have them here, I must be sure of it," said grandma, folding her wrapper about her, and getting up with great decision.

"Massy on us, mum, you haven't been up them stairs for months. The dears are all right, warm as toasts, and sleepin' like dormice, I'll warrant," answered Dolly, taken aback at this new whim of old madam's.

But grandma would go, so Dolly gave her an arm, and together the two old friends hobbled up the wide stairs, and peeped in at the precious children. The lads looked like a camp of weary warriors reposing after a victory, and grandma went laughing away when she had taken a proud survey of this promising portion of the rising generation. The nursery was like a little convent full of rosy nuns sleeping peacefully; while a pictured Saint Agnes, with her lamb, smiled on them from the wall, and the firelight flickered over the white figures and sweet faces, as if the sight were too fair to be lost in darkness. The little ones lay about promiscuously, looking like dissipated Cupids with sugar hearts and faded roses still clutched in their chubby hands.

"My darlings!" whispered grandma, lingering fondly over them to cover a pair of rosy feet, put back a pile of tumbled curls, or kiss a little mouth still smiling in its sleep.

But when she came to the coldest corner of the room, where Kate lay on the hardest mattress, under the thinnest quilt, the old lady's eyes were full of tender tears; and, forgetting the stiff joints that bent so painfully, she knelt slowly down, and, putting her arms about the girl, blessed her in silence for the happiness she had given one old heart.

Kate woke at once, and started up, exclaiming with a smile,—

"Why, grandma, I was dreaming about an angel, and you look like one with your white gown and silvery hair!"

"No, dear, you are the angel in this house. How can I ever give you up?" answered madam, holding fast the treasure that came to her so late.

"You never need to, grandma, for I have made my choice."

THE QUIET LITTLE WOMAN

1878

I.

HOW SHE FOUND IT

Patty stood at one of the windows of the Asylum, looking thoughtfully down into the yard, where twenty girls were playing.

All had cropped heads, all wore brown gowns and blue aprons, and all were orphans like herself. Some were pretty and some plain, some rosy and gay, some pale and feeble, but all seemed happy and having a good time in spite of many drawbacks.

More than once one of them nodded and beckoned to Patty, but she shook her head decidedly, and still stood, listlessly watching them, and thinking to herself with a child's impatient spirit,—

"Oh, if some one would only come and take me away! I'm so tired of living here I don't think I can bear it much longer."

Poor Patty might well wish for a change; for she had been in the Asylum ever since she could remember; but though every one was kind to her, she was heartily tired of the place, and longed to find a home as many of the girls did.

The children were nursed and taught until old enough to help themselves, then were adopted by people or went out to service. Now and then some forlorn child was claimed by relatives who had discovered it, and once the relatives of a little girl proved to be rich and generous people, who came for Katy in a fine carriage, treated all the other girls in honor of the happy day, and from time to time let Katy visit them with hands full of gifts for her former playmates and friends.

This event had made a great stir in the Asylum, and the children were never tired of talking it over and telling it to new comers as a modern sort of fairy tale. For a time, each hoped to be claimed in the same way, and stories of what they would do when their turn came was one of the favorite amusements of the house.

By and by Katy ceased to come, and gradually new girls took the place of those that left, and her good fortune was forgotten by all but Patty. To her it always remained a splendid possibility, and she comforted her loneliness by visions of the day when her "folks" would come for her, and bear her away to a future of luxury and pleasure, rest and love.

But no one came, and year after year Patty worked and waited, saw others chosen and herself left to the many duties and few pleasures of her dull life. The reason why she was not taken was because of her pale face, her short figure, with one shoulder higher than the other, and her shy ways. She was not ill now, but looked so, and was a sober, quiet little woman at thirteen.

People who came for pets chose the pretty little ones; and those who wanted servants took the tall, strong, merry-faced girls, who spoke up brightly and promised to learn and do any thing required of them.

The good matron often recommended Patty as a neat, capable, gentle little person, but no one seemed to want her, and after every failure her heart grew heavier and her face sadder, for the thought of spending her life there was unbearable.

Nobody guessed what a world of hopes and thoughts and feelings was hidden under that blue pinafore, what dreams the solitary child enjoyed, or what a hungry, aspiring young soul lived in that crooked little body.

But God knew; and when the time came He remembered Patty and sent her the help best fitted for her needs. Sometimes, when we least expect it, a small cross proves a lovely crown, a seemingly unimportant event becomes a life-long experience, or a stranger changes into a friend.

It happened so now; for as Patty said aloud with a great sigh, "I don't think I *can* bear it any longer!" a hand touched her shoulder, and a voice said, gently,—

"Bear what, my child?"

The touch was so light and the voice so kind that Patty answered before she had time to feel shy.

"Living here, ma'am, and never being chosen out like the other girls are."

"Tell me all about it, dear. I'm waiting for a friend, and I'd like to hear your troubles," sitting down in the window-seat and drawing Patty beside her.

She was not young, nor pretty, nor finely dressed, only a gray-haired woman in plain black; but her face was so motherly, her eyes so cheerful, and her voice so soothing, that Patty felt at ease in a minute, and nestled up to her as she told her little woes in a few simple words.

"You don't know any thing about your parents?" asked the lady.

"No, ma'am; I was left here a baby without even a name pinned to me, and no one has come to find me. But I shouldn't wonder if they did yet, so I keep ready all the time and learn as hard as I can, so they won't be ashamed of me, for I guess my folks is respectable," and Patty lifted her head with an air of pride that made the lady ask, with a smile,—

"What makes you think so?"

"Well, I heard the matron tell a lady who chose Nelly Brian that she always thought *I* came of high folks because I was so different from the others, and my ways was nice, and my feet so small,—see if they ain't,"—and, slipping them out of the rough shoes she wore, Patty held up two slender little feet with the arched insteps that tell of good birth.

Miss Murry laughed right out at the innocent vanity of the poor child, and said, heartily, "They are small, and so are your hands in spite of work, and your hair is fine, and your eyes are soft and clear, and you are a good child I'm sure, which is best of all."

Pleased and touched by the praise that is so pleasant to us all, yet half ashamed of herself, Patty blushed and smiled, put on her shoes, and said, with unusual animation,—

"I'm pretty good, I believe, and I know I'd be much better if I only could get out. I do so long to see trees and grass, and sit in the sun and hear birds. I'd work real hard and be happy if I could live in the country."

"What can you do?" asked Miss Murry, stroking the smooth head and looking down into the wistful eyes fixed upon her.

Modestly, but with a flutter of hope at her heart, Patty told over her domestic accomplishments, a good list for a thirteen-year-older, but Patty had been drilling so long she was unusually clever at all sorts of house-work as well as needle-work.

As she ended, she asked, timidly,—

"Did you come for a girl, ma'am?"

"My sister did; but she has found one she likes, and is going to take her on trial," was the answer that made the light fade out of Patty's eyes and the hope die in her heart.

"Who is it, please?"

"Lizzie Brown, a tall, nice-looking girl of fourteen."

"You won't like her I know, for Lizzie is a real ——;" there Patty stopped short, turned red, and looked down, as if ashamed to meet the keen, kind eyes fixed on her.

"A real what?"

"Please, ma'am, don't ask; it was mean of me to say that, and I mustn't go on. Lizzie can't help being good with you, and I am glad she's got a chance to go away."

Miss Murry asked no more questions; but she liked the little glimpse of character, and tried to brighten Patty's face again by talking of something she liked.

"Suppose your 'folks,' as you say, never come for you, and you never find your fortune, as some girls do, can't you make friends and fortune for yourself?"

"How can I?" questioned Patty, wonderingly.

"By taking cheerfully whatever comes, by being helpful and affectionate to all, and wasting no time in dreaming about what may happen, but bravely making each day a comfort and a pleasure to yourself and others. Can you do that?"

"I can try, ma'am," answered Patty, meekly.

"I wish you would; and when I come again you can tell me how you get on. I think you will succeed; and when you do, you will have found a fine fortune, and be sure of friends. Now I must go; cheer up, deary, your turn must come some day."

With a kiss that won Patty's heart, Miss Murry went away, casting more than one look of pity at the little figure in the window-seat, sobbing, with a blue pinafore over its face.

This disappointment was doubly hard to Patty; because Lizzie was not a good girl, and deserved nothing, and Patty had taken a great fancy to the lady who spoke so kindly to her.

For a week after this she went about her work with a sad face, and all her day-dreams were of living with Miss Murry in the country.

Monday afternoon, as she stood sprinkling clothes, one of the girls burst in, saying, all in a breath,—

"Somebody's come for you, and you are to go right up to the parlor. It's Mrs. Murry, and she's brought Liz back, 'cause she told fibs, and was lazy, and Liz is as mad as hops, for it is a real nice place, with cows, and pigs, and children; and the work ain't hard and she wanted to stay. Do hurry, and don't stand staring at me that way."

"It can't be me—no one ever wants me—it's some mistake"— stammered Patty, so startled and excited, she did not know what to say or do.

"No, it isn't. Mrs. Murry won't have any one but *you*, and the matron says you are to come right up. Go along; I'll finish here. I'm *so* glad you have got a chance at last;" and with a good-natured hug, the girl pushed Patty out of the kitchen.

In a few minutes Patty came flying back, all in a twitter of delight, to report that she was going at once, and must say good-by all round. Every one was pleased, and when the flurry was over, the carriage drove away with the happiest little girl ever seen inside, for at last some one *did* want her, and Patty *had* found a place.

II.

HOW SHE FILLED IT

For a year Patty lived with the Murrys, industrious, docile, and faithful, but not yet happy, because she had not found all she expected. They were kind to her, as far as plenty of food and not too much work went. They clothed her comfortably, let her go to church, and did not scold her very often. But no one showed that they loved her, no one praised her efforts, no one seemed to think that she had any hope or wish beyond her daily work, and no one saw in the shy, quiet little maid-servant, a lonely, tender-hearted girl longing for a crumb of the love so freely given to the children of the house.

The Murrys were busy people; the farm was large, and the master and his eldest son were hard at it all summer. Mrs. Murry was a brisk, smart housewife, who "flew round" herself, and expected others to do likewise. Pretty Ella, the daughter, was about Patty's age, and busy with her school, her little pleasures, and all the bright plans young girls love and live in. Two or three small lads rioted about the house, making much work, and doing very little.

One of these boys was lame, and this fact seemed to establish a sort of friendly understanding between him and Patty, for he was the only one who ever expressed any regard for her. She was very good to him, always ready to help him, always patient with his fretfulness, and always quick to understand his sensitive nature.

"She's only a servant, a charity girl who works for her board, and wears my old duds. She's good enough in her place, but of course she can't expect to be like one of us," Ella said to a young friend once, and Patty heard her.

"Only a servant"—that was the hard part, and it never occurred to any one to make it softer; so Patty plodded on, still hoping and dreaming about friends and fortune.

If it had not been for Miss Murry I fear the child would not have got on at all. But Aunt Jane never forgot her, though she lived twenty miles away, and seldom came to the farm. She wrote once a month, and always put in a little note to Patty, which she expected to have answered.

So Patty wrote a neat reply, very stiff and short at first; but after a time she quite poured out her heart to this one friend who sent her encouraging words, cheered her with praise now and then, and made her anxious to be all Miss Jane seemed to expect. No one took much notice of this correspondence, for Aunt Jane was odd, and Patty used to post her replies herself, being kindly provided with stamps by her friend.

This was Patty's anchor in her little sea of troubles, and she clung to it, hoping that some time, when she had earned such a beautiful reward, she would go and live with Miss Murry.

Christmas was coming, and great fun was expected; for the family were to pass the day before at Aunt Jane's, and bring her home for the dinner and dance next day. For a week beforehand, Mrs. Murry flew round with more than her accustomed speed, and Patty trotted from morning till night, lending a hand at all the least agreeable jobs. Ella did the light, pretty work, and spent much time over her new dress, and the gifts she was making for the boys.

Every thing was done at last, and Mrs. Murry declared that she should drop if she had another thing to do but go to Jane's and rest.

Patty had lived on the hope of going with them; but nothing was said about it, and they all trooped gayly away to the station, leaving her to take care of the house, and see that the cat did not touch one of the dozen pies stored away in the pantry.

Patty kept up bravely till they were gone; then she sat down like Cinderella, and cried, and cried until she couldn't cry any more, for it did seem as if she never was to have any fun, and no fairy godmother came to help her. The shower did her good, and she went about her work with a meek, patient face that would have touched a heart of stone.

All the morning she finished up the odd jobs left her to do, and in the afternoon, as the only approach to a holiday she dared venture, she sat at the parlor window and watched other people go to and fro, intent on merry-makings in which she had no part.

One pleasant little task she had, and that was arranging gifts for the small boys. Miss Jane had given her a bit of money now and then, and out of her meagre store the affectionate child had made presents for the lads; poor ones, but full of good-will and the desire to win some in return.

The evening was very long, for the family did not return as early as they expected to do, so Patty got out her treasure-box, and, sitting on the warm kitchen hearth, tried to amuse herself, while the wind howled outside and snow fell fast.

There we must leave her for a little while, quite unconscious of the happy surprise that was being prepared for her.

When Aunt Jane welcomed the family, her first word, as she emerged from a chaos of small boys' arms and legs, was "Why, where is Patty?"

"At home, of course; where should she be?" answered Mrs. Murry.

"Here with you. I said '*all come*' in my letter; didn't you understand it?"

"Goodness, Jane, you didn't mean bring her too, I hope."

"Yes, I did, and I'm so disappointed I'd go and get her if I had time."

Miss Jane knit her brows and looked vexed, as Ella laughed at the idea of a servant's going pleasuring with the family.

"It can't be helped now, so we'll say no more, and make it up to Patty to-morrow, if we can." And Aunt Jane smiled her own pleasant smile, and kissed the little lads all round, as if to sweeten her temper as soon as possible.

They had a capital time, and no one observed that Aunty now and then led the talk to Patty, asked a question about her, caught up every little hint dropped by the boys concerning her patience and kindness, and when Mrs. Murry said, as she sat resting, with a cushion at her back, a stool at her feet, and a cup of tea steaming deliciously under her nose,—

"Afraid to leave her there in charge? Oh, dear no! I've entire confidence in her, and she is equal to taking care of the house for a week if need be. On the whole, Jane, I consider her a pretty promising girl. She isn't very quick, but she is faithful, steady, and honest as daylight."

"High praise from you, Maria; I hope she knows your good opinion of her."

"No, indeed; it don't do to pamper up a girl's pride by praising her. I say, 'Very well, Patty,' when I'm satisfied, and that's enough."

"Ah, but *you* wouldn't be satisfied if George only said, 'Very well, Maria,' when you had done your very best to please him in some way."

"That's a different thing," began Mrs. Murry, but Miss Jane shook her head, and Ella said, laughing,—

"It's no use to try and convince Aunty on that point, she has taken a fancy to Pat, and won't see any fault in her. She's a good child enough; but I can't get any thing out of her, she is so odd and shy."

"I can; she's first rate, and takes care of me better than any one else," said Harry, the lame boy, with sudden warmth, for Patty had quite won his selfish little heart by many services.

"She'll make mother a nice helper as she grows up, and I consider it a good speculation. In four years she'll be eighteen, and if she goes on doing so well, I shan't begrudge her wages," added Mr. Murry, who sat near by, with a small son on each knee.

"She'd be quite pretty if she was straight, and plump, and jolly. But she is as sober as a deacon, and when her work is done, sits in a corner, watching us with her big eyes, as shy and mute as a mouse," said Ned, the big brother, lounging on the sofa.

"A dull, steady-going girl, just fitted for a servant, and no more," concluded Mrs. Murry, setting down her cup as if the subject was ended.

"You are quite mistaken, and I'll prove it!" and up jumped Aunt Jane so energetically, that the boys laughed and the elders looked annoyed. Pulling out a portfolio, Aunt Jane untied a little bundle of letters, saying impressively,—

"Now listen, all of you, and see what has been going on under Patty's blue pinafore this year."

Then Miss Jane read the little letters one by one, and it was curious to see how the faces of the listeners woke up, grew attentive first, then touched, then self-reproachful, and finally how full of interest, and respect, and something very like affection for little Patty.

These letters were pathetic to read, as Aunty read them to listeners who could supply much that the writer generously left unsaid, and the involuntary comments of the hearers proved the truth of Patty's words.

"*Does* she envy me because I'm 'pretty and gay, and have a good time?' I never thought how hard it must be for her to see me have all the fun, and she all the work. She's a girl like me, though she does grub; and I might have done more for her than give her my old clothes, and let her help dress me when I go to a party," said Ella, hastily, as Aunt Jane laid down one letter in which poor Patty told of many "good times and she not in 'em."

"Sakes alive, if I'd known the child wanted me to kiss her now and then, as I do the rest, I'd have done it in a minute," said Mrs. Murry, with sudden softness in her sharp eyes, as Aunt Jane read this little bit,—

"I *am* grateful, but, oh! I'm so lonely, and it's so hard not to have any mother like the children. If Mrs. Murry would only kiss me good-night sometimes, it would do me more good than pretty clothes or nice victuals."

"I've been thinking I'd let her go to school a spell, ever since I heard her showing Bob how to do his lessons. But mother didn't think she could spare her," broke in Mr. Murry, apologetically.

"If Ella would help a little, I guess I could. Anyway, we might try a while, since she is so eager to learn," added his wife, anxious not to seem unjust to sister Jane.

"Well, Joe laughed at her as well as me, when the boys hunched up their shoulders the way she does," cried conscience-stricken Bob, as he heard a sad little paragraph about her crooked figure, and learned that it came from lugging heavy babies at the Asylum.

"I cuffed 'em both for it, and *I* have always liked Patty," said Harry, in a moral tone, which moved Ned to say,—

"You'd be a selfish little rascal if you didn't, when she slaves so for you and gets no thanks for it. Now that I know how it tires her poor little back to carry wood and water, I shall do it of course. If she'd only told me, I'd have done it all the time."

And so it went on till the letters were done, and they knew Patty as she was, and each felt sorry that he or she had not found her out before. Aunt Jane freed her mind upon the subject, and they talked it over till quite an enthusiastic state of feeling set in, and Patty was in danger of being killed with kindness.

It is astonishing how generous and kind people are when once waked up to a duty, a charity, or a wrong. Now, every one was eager to repair past neglect, and if Aunt Jane had not wisely restrained them, the young folks would have done something absurd.

They laid many nice little plans to surprise Patty, and each privately resolved not only to give her a Christmas gift, but, what was better, to turn over a new leaf for the new year.

All the way home they talked over their various projects, and the boys kept bouncing into Aunt Jane's seat, to ask advice about their funny ideas.

"It must have been rather lonesome for the poor little soul all day. I declare I wish we'd taken her along," said Mrs. Murry, as they approached the house, through the softly-falling snow.

"She's got a jolly good fire all ready for us, and that's a mercy, for I'm half frozen," said Harry, hopping up the step.

"Don't you think if I touch up my blue merino it would fit Patty, and make a nice dress for to-morrow, with one of my white aprons?" whispered Ella, as she helped Aunt Jane out of the sleigh.

"Hope the child isn't sick or scared; it's two hours later than I expected to be at home," added Mr. Murry, stepping up to peep in at the kitchen window, for no one came to open the door, and no light but the blaze of the fire shone out.

"Come softly and look in; it's a pretty little sight, if it is in a kitchen," he whispered, beckoning to the rest.

Quietly creeping to the two low windows, they all looked in, and no one said a word, for the lonely little figure was both pretty and pathetic, when they remembered the letters lately read. Flat on the old rug lay Patty fast asleep; one arm pillowed her head, and in the other lay Puss in a cosy bunch, as if she had crept there to be sociable, since there was no one else to share Patty's long vigil. A row of slippers, large and small, stood warming on the hearth, two little nightgowns hung over a chair, the tea-pot stood in a warm nook, and through the open door they could see the lamp burning brightly in the sitting-room, the table ready, and all things in order.

"Faithful little creature! She's thought of every blessed thing, and I'll go right in and wake her up with a good kiss!" cried Mrs. Murry, making a dart at the door.

But Aunt Jane drew her back, begging her not to frighten the child by any sudden demonstrations. So they all went softly in, so softly that tired Patty did not wake, even though Puss pricked up her ears and opened her moony eyes with a lazy purr.

"Look here," whispered Bob, pointing to the poor little gifts half tumbling out of Patty's apron. She had been pinning names on them when she fell asleep, and so her secret was known too soon.

No one laughed at the presents, and Ella covered them up with a look of tender pity at the few humble treasures in Patty's box, remembering as she laid back what she had once called "rubbish," how full her own boxes were of the pretty things girls love, and how easy it would have been to add to Patty's store.

No one exactly knew how to wake up the sleeper, for she was something more than a servant in their eyes now. Aunt Jane settled the matter by stooping down and taking Patty in her arms. The big eyes opened at once and stared up at the face above them for a moment, then a smile so bright, so glad, shone all over the child's face that it was transfigured, as Patty clung to Aunt Jane, crying joyously,—

"Is it really you? I was so afraid you wouldn't come that I cried myself to sleep about it."

Never had any of them seen such love and happiness in Patty's face before, heard such a glad, tender sound in her voice, or guessed what an ardent soul lay in her quiet body.

She was herself again in a minute, and, jumping up, slipped away to see that every thing was ready, should any one want supper after the cold drive.

They all went to bed so soon that there was no time to let out the secret, and though Patty *was* surprised at the kind good-nights all said to her, she thought it was because Miss Jane brought a warmer atmosphere with her.

Patty's surprises began early next day, for the first thing she saw on opening her eyes was a pair of new stockings hanging at the foot of her bed, crammed full of gifts, and several parcels lying on the table.

Didn't she have a good time opening the delightful bundles? Didn't she laugh and cry at the droll things the boys gave, the comfortable and pretty things the elders sent? And wasn't she a happy child when she tried to say her prayers and couldn't find words beautiful enough to express her gratitude for so much kindness?

A new Patty went down stairs that morning,—a bright-faced girl with smiles on the mouth that used to be so sad and silent, confidence in the timid eyes, and the magic of the heartiest good-will to make her step light, her hand skilful, her labor a joy, and service no burden.

"They do care for me, after all, and I never will complain again," she thought, with a glad flutter at her heart, and sudden color in her cheeks, as every one welcomed her with a friendly "Merry Christmas, Patty!"

It *was* a merry Christmas, and when the bountiful dinner was spread and Patty stood ready to wait, you can imagine her feelings as Mr. Murry pointed to a seat near Miss Jane and said, in a fatherly tone that made his bluff voice sweet,—

"Sit down and enjoy it with us, my girl; nobody has more right to it, and we are all one family to-day."

Patty could not eat much, her heart was so full; but it was a splendid feast to her, and when healths were drank she was overwhelmed by the honor Harry did her, for he bounced up and exclaimed,—

"Now we must drink 'Our Patty, long life and good luck to her!'"

That really *was* too much, and she fairly ran away to hide her blushes in the kitchen roller, and work off her excitement washing dishes.

More surprises came that evening; when she went to put on her clean calico she found the pretty blue dress and white apron laid ready on her bed "with Ella's love."

"It's like a fairy story, and keeps getting nicer and nicer since the godmother came," whispered Patty, as she shyly looked up at Aunt Jane, when passing ice-cream at the party several hours later.

"Christmas is the time for all sorts of pleasant miracles, for the good fairies fly about just then, and give good-luck pennies to the faithful workers who have earned them," answered Miss Jane, smiling back at her little handmaid, who looked so neat and blithe in her new suit and happy face.

Patty thought nothing farther in the way of bliss could happen to her that night, but it did when Ned, anxious to atone for his past neglect, pranced up to her, as a final contra-dance was forming, and said heartily,—

"Come, Patty, every one is to dance this, even Harry and the cat," and before she could collect her wits enough to say "No," she was leading off and flying down the middle with the young master in great style.

That was the crowning honor; for she was a girl with all a girl's innocent hopes, fears, desires and delights, and it *had* been rather hard to stand by while all the young neighbors were frolicking together.

When every one was gone, the tired children asleep, and the elders on their way up to bed, Mrs. Murry suddenly remembered she had not covered the kitchen fire. Aunt Jane said she would do it, and went down so softly that she did not disturb faithful Patty, who had gone to see that all was safe.

Aunt Jane stopped to watch the little figure standing on the hearth alone, looking into the embers with thoughtful eyes. If Patty could have seen her future there, she would have found a long life spent in glad service to those she loved and who loved her. Not a splendid future, but a useful, happy one; "only a servant," yet a good and faithful woman, blessed with the confidence, respect and affection of those who knew her genuine worth.

As a smile broke over Patty's face, Miss Jane said, with an arm round the little blue-gowned figure,—

"What are you dreaming and smiling about, deary? The friends that are to come for you some day, with a fine fortune in their pockets?"

"No, ma'am, I feel as if I'd found my folks, and I don't want any finer fortune than the love they've given me to-day. I'm trying to think how I can deserve it, and smiling because it's so beautiful and I'm so happy," answered Patty, looking up at her first friend with full eyes and a glad, grateful glance that made her lovely.

TILLY'S CHRISTMAS

✦ ━ ✦ ⬦ ✦ ━ ✦

1892

'I'M SO GLAD TO-MORROW IS CHRISTMAS, because I'm going to have lots of presents.'

'So am I glad, though I don't expect any presents but a pair of mittens.'

'And so am I; but I shan't have any presents at all.'

As the three little girls trudged home from school they said these things, and as Tilly spoke, both the others looked at her with pity and some surprise, for she spoke cheerfully, and they wondered how she could be happy when she was so poor she could have no presents on Christmas.

'Don't you wish you could find a purse full of money right here in the path?' said Kate, the child who was going to have 'lots of presents.'

'Oh, don't I, if I could keep it honestly!' and Tilly's eyes shone at the very thought.

'What would you buy?' asked Bessy, rubbing her cold hands, and longing for her mittens.

'I'd buy a pair of large, warm blankets, a load of wood, a shawl for mother, and a pair of shoes for me; and if there was enough left, I'd give Bessy a new hat, and then she needn't wear Ben's old felt one,' answered Tilly.

The girls laughed at that; but Bessy pulled the funny hat over her ears, and said she was much obliged but she'd rather have candy.

'Let's look, and maybe we *can* find a purse. People are always going about with money at Christmas time, and some one may lose it here,' said Kate.

So, as they went along the snowy road, they looked about them, half in earnest, half in fun. Suddenly Tilly sprang forward, exclaiming,—

'I see it! I've found it!'

The others followed, but all stopped disappointed; for it wasn't a purse, it was only a little bird. It lay upon the snow with its wings spread and feebly fluttering, as if too weak to fly. Its little feet were benumbed with cold; its once bright eyes were dull with pain, and instead of a blithe song, it could only utter a faint chirp, now and then, as if crying for help.

'Nothing but a stupid old robin; how provoking!' cried Kate, sitting down to rest.

'I shan't touch it. I found one once, and took care of it, and the ungrateful thing flew away the minute it was well,' said Bessy, creeping under Kate's shawl, and putting her hands under her chin to warm them.

'Poor little birdie! How pitiful he looks, and how glad he must be to see some one coming to help him! I'll take him up gently, and carry him home to mother. Don't be frightened, dear, I'm your friend;' and Tilly knelt down in the snow, stretching her hand to the bird, with the tenderest pity in her face.

Kate and Bessy laughed.

'Don't stop for that thing; it's getting late and cold: let's go on and look for the purse,' they said moving away.

'You wouldn't leave it to die!' cried Tilly. 'I'd rather have the bird than the money, so I shan't look any more. The purse wouldn't be mine, and I should only be tempted to keep it; but this poor thing will thank and love me, and I'm *so* glad I came in time.'

Gently lifting the bird, Tilly felt its tiny cold claws cling to her hand, and saw its dim eyes brighten as it nestled down with a grateful chirp.

'Now I've got a Christmas present after all,' she said, smiling, as they walked on. 'I always wanted a bird, and this one will be such a pretty pet for me.'

'He'll fly away the first chance he gets, and die anyhow; so you'd better not waste your time over him,' said Bessy.

'He can't pay you for taking care of him, and my mother says it isn't worth while to help folks that can't help us,' added Kate.

'My mother says, "Do as you'd be done by;" and I'm sure I'd like any one to help me if I was dying of cold and hunger. "Love your neighbour as yourself," is another of her sayings. This bird is my little neighbour, and I'll love him and care for him, as I often wish our rich neighbour would love and care for us,' answered Tilly, breathing her warm breath over the benumbed bird, who looked up at her with confiding eyes, quick to feel and know a friend.

'What a funny girl you are,' said Kate; 'caring for that silly bird, and talking about loving your neighbour in that sober way. Mr. King don't care a bit for you, and never will, though he knows how poor you are; so I don't think your plan amounts to much.'

'I believe it, though; and shall do my part, any way. Good-night. I hope you'll have a merry Christmas, and lots of pretty things,' answered Tilly, as they parted.

Her eyes were full, and she felt so poor as she went on alone toward the little old house where she lived. It would have been so pleasant to know that she was going to have some of the pretty things all children love to find in their full stockings on Christmas morning. And pleasanter still to have been able to give her mother something nice. So many comforts were needed, and there was no hope of getting them; for they could barely get food and fire.

'Never mind, birdie, we'll make the best of what we have, and be merry in spite of every thing. *You* shall have a happy Christmas, any way; and I know God won't forget us if every one else does.'

She stopped a minute to wipe her eyes, and lean her cheek against the bird's soft breast, finding great comfort in the little creature, though it could only love her, nothing more.

'See, mother, what a nice present I've found,' she cried, going in with a cheery face that was like sunshine in the dark room.

'I'm glad of that, dearie; for I haven't been able to get my little girl anything but a rosy apple. Poor bird! Give it some of your warm bread and milk.'

'Why, mother, what a big bowlful! I'm afraid you gave me all the milk,' said Tilly, smiling over the nice, steaming supper that stood ready for her.

'I've had plenty, dear. Sit down and dry your wet feet, and put the bird in my basket on this warm flannel.'

Tilly peeped into the closet and saw nothing there but dry bread.

'Mother's given me all the milk, and is going without her tea, 'cause she knows I'm hungry. Now I'll surprise her, and she shall have a good supper too. She is going to split wood, and I'll fix it while she's gone.'

So Tilly put down the old tea-pot, carefully poured out a part of the milk, and from her pocket produced a great, plummy bun, that one of the school-children had given her, and she had saved for her mother. A slice of the dry bread was nicely toasted, and the bit of butter set by for her put on it. When her mother came in there was the table drawn up in a warm place, a hot cup of tea ready, and Tilly and birdie waiting for her.

Such a poor little supper, and yet such a happy one; for love, charity, and contentment were guests there, and that Christmas eve was a blither one than that up at the great house, where lights shone, fires blazed, a great tree glittered, and music sounded, as the children danced and played.

'We must go to bed early, for we've only wood enough to last over to-morrow. I shall be paid for my work the day after, and then we can get some,' said Tilly's mother, as they sat by the fire.

'If my bird was only a fairy bird, and would give us three wishes, how nice it would be! Poor dear, he can't give me any thing; but it's no matter,' answered Tilly, looking at the robin, who lay in the basket with his head under his wing, a mere little feathery bunch.

'He can give you one thing, Tilly,—the pleasure of doing good. That is one of the sweetest things in life; and the poor can enjoy it as well as the rich.'

As her mother spoke, with her tired hand softly stroking her little daughter's hair, Tilly suddenly started and pointed to the window, saying, in a frightened whisper,—

'I saw a face,—a man's face, looking in! It's gone now; but I truly saw it.'

'Some traveller attracted by the light perhaps. I'll go and see.' And Tilly's mother went to the door.

No one was there. The wind blew cold, the stars shone, the snow lay white on field and wood, and the Christmas moon was glittering in the sky.

'What sort of a face was it?' asked Tilly's mother, coming back.

'A pleasant sort of face, I think; but I was so startled I don't quite know what it was like. I wish we had a curtain there,' said Tilly.

'I like to have our light shine out in the evening, for the road is dark and lonely just here, and the twinkle of our lamp is pleasant to people's eyes as they go by. We can do so little for our neighbours, I am glad to cheer the way for them. Now put these poor old shoes to dry, and go to bed, dearie; I'll come soon.'

Tilly went, taking her bird with her to sleep in his basket near by, lest he should be lonely in the night.

Soon the little house was dark and still, and no one saw the Christmas spirits at their work that night.

When Tilly opened the door next morning, she gave a loud cry, clapped her hands, and then stood still; quite speechless with wonder and delight. There, before the door, lay a great pile of wood, all ready to burn, a big bundle and a basket, with a lovely nosegay of winter roses, holly, and evergreen tied to the handle.

'Oh, mother! did the fairies do it?' cried Tilly, pale with her happiness, as she seized the basket, while her mother took in the bundle.

'Yes, dear, the best and dearest fairy in the world, called "Charity." She walks abroad at Christmas time, does beautiful deeds like this, and does not stay to be thanked,' answered her mother with full eyes, as she undid the parcel.

There they were,—the warm, thick blankets, the comfortable shawls, the new shoes, and, best of all, a pretty winter hat for Bessy. The basket was full of good things to eat, and on the flowers lay a paper, saying,—

'For the little girl who loves her neighbour as herself.'

'Mother, I really think my bird is a fairy bird, and all these splendid things come from him,' said Tilly, laughing and crying with joy.

It really did seem so, for as she spoke, the robin flew to the table, hopped to the nosegay, and perching among the roses, began to chirp with all his little might. The sun streamed in on flowers, bird, and happy child, and no one saw a shadow glide away from the window; no one ever knew that Mr. King had seen and heard the little girls the night before, or dreamed that the rich neighbour had learned a lesson from the poor neighbour.

And Tilly's bird *was* a fairy bird; for by her love and tenderness to the helpless thing, she brought good gifts to herself, happiness to the unknown giver of them, and a faithful little friend who did not fly away, but stayed with her till the snow was gone, making summer for her in the winter-time.

WHAT THE BELLS SAID AND SAW

"Bells ring others to church, but go not in themselves."

1867

NO ONE SAW THE SPIRITS OF THE BELLS up there in the old steeple at midnight on Christmas Eve. Six quaint figures, each wrapped in a shadowy cloak and wearing a bell-shaped cap. All were gray-headed, for they were among the oldest bell-spirits of the city, and "the light of other days" shone in their thoughtful eyes. Silently they sat, looking down on the snow-covered roofs glittering in the moonlight, and the quiet streets deserted by all but the watchmen on their chilly rounds, and such poor souls as wandered shelterless in the winter night. Presently one of the spirits said, in a tone, which, low as it was, filled the belfry with reverberating echoes,—

"Well, brothers, are your reports ready of the year that now lies dying?"

All bowed their heads, and one of the oldest answered in a sonorous voice:—

"My report isn't all I could wish. You know I look down on the commercial part of our city and have fine opportunities for seeing what goes on there. It's my business to watch the business men, and upon my word I'm heartily ashamed of them sometimes. During the war they did nobly, giving their time and money, their sons and selves to the good cause, and I was proud of them. But now too many of them have fallen back into the old ways, and their motto seems to be, 'Every one for himself, and the devil take the hindmost.' Cheating, lying and stealing are hard words, and I don't mean to apply them to *all* who swarm about below there like ants on an ant-hill— *they* have other names for these things, but I'm old-fashioned and use plain words. There's a deal too much dishonesty in the world, and business seems to have become a game of hazard in which luck, not labor, wins the prize. When I was young, men were years making moderate fortunes, and were satisfied with them. They built them on sure foundations, knew how to enjoy them while they lived, and to leave a good name behind them when they died.

"Now it's anything for money; health, happiness, honor, life itself, are flung down on that great gaming-table, and they forget everything else in the excitement of success or the desperation of defeat. Nobody seems satisfied either, for those who win have little time or taste to enjoy their prosperity, and those who lose have little courage or patience to support them in adversity. They don't even fail as they used to. In my day when a merchant found himself embarrassed he didn't ruin others in order to save himself, but honestly confessed the truth, gave up everything, and began again. But now-a-days after all manner of dishonorable shifts there comes a grand crash; many suffer, but by some hocus-pocus the merchant saves enough to retire upon and live comfortably here or abroad. It's very evident that honor and honesty don't mean now what they used to mean in the days of old May, Higginson and Lawrence.

"They preach below here, and very well too sometimes, for I often slide down the rope to peep and listen during service. But, bless you! they don't seem to lay either sermon, psalm or prayer to heart, for while the minister is doing his best, the congregation, tired with the breathless hurry of the week, sleep peacefully, calculate their chances for the morrow, or wonder which of their neighbors will lose or win in the great game. Don't tell me! I've seen them do it, and if I dared I'd have startled every soul of them with a rousing peal. Ah, they don't dream whose eye is on them, they never guess what secrets the telegraph wires tell as the messages fly by, and little know what a report I give to the winds of heaven as I ring out above them morning, noon, and night." And the old spirit shook his head till the tassel on his cap jangled like a little bell.

"There are some, however, whom I love and honor," he said, in a benignant tone, "who honestly earn their bread, who deserve all the success that comes to them, and always keep a warm corner in their noble hearts for those less blest than they. These are the men who serve the city in times of peace, save it in times of war, deserve the highest honors in its gift, and leave behind them a record that keeps their memories green. For such an one we lately tolled a knell, my brothers; and as our united voices pealed over the city, in all grateful hearts, sweeter and more solemn than any chime, rung the words that made him so beloved,—

"'Treat our dead boys tenderly, and send them home to me.'"

He ceased, and all the spirits reverently uncovered their gray heads as a strain of music floated up from the sleeping city and died among the stars.

"Like yours, my report is not satisfactory in all respects," began the second spirit, who wore a very pointed cap and a finely-ornamented cloak. But, though his dress was fresh and youthful, his face was old, and he had nodded several times during his brother's speech. "My greatest affliction during the past year has been the terrible extravagance which prevails. My post, as you know, is at the court end of the city, and I see all the fashionable vices and follies. It is a marvel to me how so many of these immortal creatures, with such opportunities for usefulness, self-improvement and genuine happiness can be content to go round and round in one narrow circle of unprofitable and unsatisfactory pursuits. I do my best to warn them; Sunday after Sunday I chime in their ears the beautiful old hymns that sweetly chide or cheer the hearts that truly listen and believe; Sunday after Sunday I look down on them as they pass in, hoping to see that my words have not fallen upon deaf ears; and Sunday after Sunday they listen to words that should teach them much, yet seem to go by them like the wind. They are told to love their neighbor, yet too many hate him because he possesses more of this world's goods or honors than they; they are told that a rich man cannot enter the kingdom of heaven, yet they go on laying up perishable wealth, and though often warned that moth and rust will corrupt, they fail to believe it till the worm that destroys enters and mars their own chapel of ease. Being a spirit, I see below external splendor and find much poverty of heart and soul under the velvet and the ermine which should cover rich and royal natures. Our city saints walk abroad in threadbare suits, and under quiet bonnets shine the eyes that make sunshine in the shady places. Often as I watch the glittering procession passing to and fro below me, I wonder if, with all our progress, there is to-day as much real piety as in the times when our fathers, poorly clad, with weapon in one hand and Bible in the other, came weary distances to worship in the wilderness with fervent faith unquenched by danger, suffering and solitude.

"Yet in spite of my fault-finding I love my children, as I call them, for all are not butterflies. Many find wealth no temptation to forgetfulness of duty or hardness of heart. Many give freely of their abundance, pity the poor, comfort the afflicted, and make our city loved and honored in other lands as in our own. They have their cares, losses, and heartaches as well as the poor; it isn't all sunshine with them, and they learn, poor souls, that

'Into each life some rain must fall,
Some days must be dark and dreary.'

"But I've hopes of them, and lately they have had a teacher so genial, so gifted, so well-beloved that all who listen to him must be better for the lessons of charity, good-will and cheerfulness which he brings home to them by the magic of tears and smiles. We know him, we love him, we always remember him as the year comes round, and the blithest song our brazen tongues utter is a Christmas carol to the Father of 'The Chimes!'"

As the spirit spoke his voice grew cheery, his old face shone, and in a burst of hearty enthusiasm he flung up his cap and cheered like a boy. So did the others, and as the fairy shout echoed through the belfry a troop of shadowy figures, with faces lovely or grotesque, tragical or gay, sailed by on the wings of the wintry wind and waved their hands to the spirits of the bells.

As the excitement subsided and the spirits reseated themselves, looking ten years younger for that burst, another spoke. A venerable brother in a dingy mantle, with a tuneful voice, and eyes that seemed to have grown sad with looking on much misery.

"He loves the poor, the man we've just hurrahed for, and he makes others love and remember them, bless him!" said the spirit. "I hope he'll touch the hearts of those who listen to him here and beguile them to open their hands to my unhappy children over yonder. If I could set some of the forlorn souls in my parish beside the happier creatures who weep over imaginary woes as they are painted by his eloquent lips, that brilliant scene would be better than any sermon. Day and night I look down on lives as full of sin, self-sacrifice and suffering as any in those famous books. Day and night I try to comfort the poor by my cheery voice, and to make their wants known by proclaiming them with all my might. But people seem to be so intent on business, pleasure or home duties that they have no time to hear and answer my appeal. There's a deal of charity in this good city, and when the people do wake up they work with a will; but I can't help thinking that if some of the money lavished on luxuries was spent on necessaries for the poor, there would be fewer tragedies like that which ended yesterday. It's a short story, easy to tell, though long and hard to live; listen to it.

"Down yonder in the garret of one of the squalid houses at the foot of my tower, a little girl has lived for a year, fighting silently and single-handed a good fight against poverty and sin. I saw her when she first came, a hopeful, cheerful, brave-hearted little soul, alone, yet not afraid. She used to sit all day sewing at her window, and her lamp burnt far into the night, for she was very poor, and all she earned would barely give her food and shelter. I watched her feed the doves, who seemed to be her only friends; she never forgot them, and daily gave them the few crumbs that fell from her meagre table. But there was no kind hand to feed and foster the little human dove, and so she starved.

"For a while she worked bravely, but the poor three dollars a week would not clothe and feed and warm her, though the things her busy fingers made sold for enough to keep her comfortably if she had received it. I saw the pretty color fade from her cheeks; her eyes grew hollow, her voice lost its cheery ring, her step its elasticity, and her face began to wear the haggard, anxious look that made its youth doubly pathetic. Her poor little gowns grew shabby, her shawl so thin she shivered when the pitiless wind smote her, and her feet were almost bare. Rain and snow beat on the patient little figure going to and fro, each morning with hope and courage faintly shining, each evening with the shadow of despair gathering darker round her. It was a hard time for all, desperately hard for her, and in her poverty, sin and pleasure tempted her. She resisted, but as another bitter winter came she feared that in her misery she might yield, for body and soul were weakened now by the long struggle. She knew not where to turn for help; there seemed to be no place for her at any safe and happy fireside; life's hard aspect daunted her, and she turned to death, saying confidingly, 'Take me while I'm innocent and not afraid to go.'

"I saw it all! I saw how she sold everything that would bring money and paid her little debts to the utmost penny; how she set her poor room in order for the last time; how she tenderly bade the doves good-by, and lay down on her bed to die. At nine o'clock last night as my bell rang over the city, I tried to tell what was going on in the garret where the light was dying out so fast. I cried to them with all my strength,—

"'Kind souls, below there! a fellow-creature is perishing for lack of charity! Oh, help her before it is too late! Mothers, with little daughters on your knees, stretch out your hands and take her in! Happy women, in the safe shelter of home, think of her desolation! Rich men, who grind the faces of the poor, remember that this soul will one day be required of you! Dear Lord, let not this little sparrow fall to the ground! Help, Christian men and women, in the name of Him whose birthday blessed the world!'

"Ah me! I rang, and clashed, and cried in vain. The passers-by only said, as they hurried home, laden with Christmas cheer: 'The old bell is merry to-night, as it should be at this blithe season, bless it!'

"As the clocks struck ten, the poor child lay down, saying, as she drank the last bitter draught life could give her, 'It's very cold, but soon I shall not feel it;' and with her quiet eyes fixed on the cross that glimmered in the moonlight above me, she lay waiting for the sleep that needs no lullaby.

"As the clock struck eleven, pain and poverty for her were over. It was bitter cold, but she no longer felt it. She lay serenely sleeping, with tired heart and hands, at rest forever. As the clocks struck twelve, the dear Lord remembered her, and with fatherly hand led her into the home where there is room for all. To-day I rung her knell, and though my heart was heavy, yet my soul was glad; for in spite of all her human woe and weakness, I am sure that little girl will keep a joyful Christmas up in heaven."

In the silence which the spirits for a moment kept, a breath of softer air than any from the snowy world below swept through the steeple and seemed to whisper, "Yes!"

"Avast there! fond as I am of salt water, I don't like this kind," cried the breezy voice of the fourth spirit, who had a tiny ship instead of a tassel on his cap, and who wiped his wet eyes with the sleeve of his rough blue cloak. "It won't take me long to spin my yarn; for things are pretty taut and ship-shape aboard our craft. Captain Taylor is an experienced sailor, and has brought many a ship safely into port in spite of wind and tide, and the devil's own whirlpools and hurricanes. If you want to see earnestness come aboard some Sunday when the Captain's on the quarter-deck, and take an observation. No danger of falling asleep there, no more than there is up aloft, 'when the stormy winds do blow.' Consciences get raked fore and aft, sins are blown clean out of the water, false colors are hauled down and true ones run up to the masthead, and many an immortal soul is warned to steer off in time from the pirates, rocks and quicksands of temptation. He's a regular revolving light, is the Captain,—a beacon always burning and saying plainly, 'Here are life-boats, ready to put off in all weathers and bring the shipwrecked into quiet waters.' He comes but seldom now, being laid up in the home dock, tranquilly waiting till his turn comes to go out with the tide and safely ride at anchor in the great harbor of the Lord. Our crew varies a good deal. Some of 'em have rather rough voyages, and come into port pretty well battered; land-sharks full foul of a good many, and do a deal of damage; but most of 'em carry brave and tender hearts under the blue jackets, for their rough nurse, the sea, manages to keep something of the child alive in the grayest old tar that makes the world his picture-book. We try to supply 'em with life-preservers while at sea, and make 'em feel sure of a hearty welcome when ashore, and I believe the year

'67 will sail away into eternity with a satisfactory cargo. Brother North-End made me pipe my eye; so I'll make him laugh to pay for it, by telling a clerical joke I heard the other day. Bell-ows didn't make it, though he might have done so, as he's a connection of ours, and knows how to use his tongue as well as any of us. Speaking of the bells of a certain town, a reverend gentleman affirmed that each bell uttered an appropriate remark so plainly, that the words were audible to all. The Baptist bell cried, briskly, 'Come up and be dipped! come up and be dipped!' The Episcopal bell slowly said, 'Apos-tol-ic suc-cess-ion! apos-tol-ic suc-cess-ion!' The Orthodox bell solemnly pronounced, 'Eternal damnation! eternal damnation!' and the Methodist shouted, invitingly, 'Room for all! room for all!'"

As the spirit imitated the various calls, as only a jovial bell-sprite could, the others gave him a chime of laughter, and vowed they would each adopt some tune-ful summons, which should reach human ears and draw human feet more willingly to church.

"Faith, brother, you've kept your word and got the laugh out of us," cried a stout, sleek spirit, with a kindly face, and a row of little saints round his cap and a rosary at his side. "It's very well we are doing this year; the cathedral is full, the flock increasing, and the true faith holding its own entirely. Ye may shake your heads if you will and fear there'll be trouble, but I doubt it. We've warm hearts of our own, and the best of us don't forget that when we were starving, America—the saints bless the jewel!—sent us bread; when we were dying for lack of work, America opened her arms and took us in, and now helps us to build churches, homes and schools by giving us a share of the riches all men work for and win. It's a generous nation ye are, and a brave one, and we showed our gratitude by fighting for ye in the day of trouble and giving ye our Phil, and many another broth of a boy. The land is wide enough for us both, and while we work and fight and grow together, each may learn something from the other. I'm free to confess that your religion looks a bit cold and hard to me, even here in the good city where each man may ride his own hobby to death, and hoot at his neighbors as much as he will. You seem to keep your piety shut up all the week in your bare, white churches, and only let it out on Sundays, just a trifle musty with disuse. You set your rich, warm and soft to the fore, and leave the poor shivering at the door. You give your people bare walls to look upon, commonplace music to listen to, dull sermons to put them asleep, and then wonder why they stay away, or take no interest when they come.

"We leave our doors open day and night; our lamps are always burning, and we may come into our Father's house at any hour. We let rich and poor kneel together, all being equal there. With us abroad you'll see prince and peasant side by side, school-boy and bishop, market-woman and noble lady, saint and sinner, praying to the Holy Mary, whose motherly arms are open to high and low. We make our churches inviting with immortal music, pictures by the world's great masters, and rites that are splendid symbols of the faith we hold. Call it mummery if ye like, but let me ask you why so many of your sheep stray into our fold? It's because they miss the warmth, the hearty, the maternal tenderness which all souls love and long for, and fail to find in your stern, Puritanical belief. By Saint Peter! I've seen many a lukewarm worshipper, who for years has nodded in your cushioned pews, wake and glow with something akin to genuine piety while kneeling on the stone pavement of one of our cathedrals, with Raphael's angels before his eyes, with strains of magnificent music in his ears, and all about him, in shapes of power or beauty, the saints and martyrs who have saved the world, and whose presence inspires him to follow their divine example. It's not complaining of ye I am, but just reminding ye that men are but children after all, and need more tempting to virtue than they do to vice, which last comes easy to 'em since the Fall. Do your best in your own ways to get the poor souls into bliss, and good luck to ye. But remember, there's room in the Holy Mother Church for all, and when your own priests send ye to the divil, come straight to us and we'll take ye in."

"A truly Catholic welcome, bull and all," said the sixth spirit, who, in spite of his old-fashioned garments, had a youthful face, earnest, fearless eyes, and an energetic voice that woke the echoes with its vigorous tones. "I've a hopeful report, brothers, for the reforms of the day are wheeling into rank and marching on. The war isn't over nor rebeldom conquered yet, but the Old Guard has been 'up and at 'em' through the year. There has been some hard fighting, rivers of ink have flowed, and the Washington dawdlers have signalized themselves by a 'masterly inactivity.' The political campaign has been an anxious one; some of the leaders have deserted; some been mustered out; some have fallen gallantly, and as yet have received no monuments. But at the Grand Review the Cross of the Legion of Honor will surely shine on many a brave breast that won no decoration but its virtue here; for the world's fanatics make heaven's heroes, poets say.

"The flock of Nightingales that flew South during the 'winter of our discontent' are all at home again, some here and some in Heaven. But the music of their womanly heroism still lingers in the nation's memory, and makes a tender minor-chord in the battle-hymn of freedom.

"The reform in literature isn't as vigorous as I could wish; but a sharp attack of mental and moral dyspepsia will soon teach our people that French confectionery and the bad pastry of Wood, Braddon, Yates & Co. is not the best diet for the rising generation.

"Speaking of the rising generation reminds me of the schools. They are doing well; they always are, and we are justly proud of them. There may be a slight tendency toward placing too much value upon book-learning; too little upon home culture. Our girls are acknowledged to be uncommonly pretty, witty and wise, but some of us wish they had more health and less excitement, more domestic accomplishments and fewer ologies and isms, and were contented with simple pleasures and the old-fashioned virtues, and not quite so fond of the fast, frivolous life that makes them old so soon. I am fond of our girls and boys. I love to ring for their christenings and marriages, to toll proudly for the brave lads in blue, and tenderly for the innocent creatures whose seats are empty under my old roof. I want to see them anxious to make Young America a model of virtue, strength and beauty, and I believe they will in time.

"There have been some important revivals in religion; for the world won't stand still, and we must keep pace or be left behind to fossilize. A free nation must have a religion broad enough to embrace all mankind, deep enough to fathom and fill the human soul, high enough to reach the source of all love and wisdom, and pure enough to satisfy the wisest and the best. Alarm bells have been rung, anathemas pronounced, and Christians, forgetful of their creed, have abused one another heartily. But the truth always triumphs in the end, and whoever sincerely believes, works and waits for it, by whatever name he calls it, will surely find his own faith blessed to him in proportion to his charity for the faith of others.

"But look!—the first red streaks of dawn are in the East. Our vigil is over, and we must fly home to welcome in the holidays. Before we part, join with me, brothers, in resolving that through the coming year we will with all our hearts and tongues,—

> 'Ring out the old, ring in the new,
> Ring out the false, ring in the true;
> Ring in the valiant man and free,
> Ring in the Christ that is to be.'"

Then hand in hand the spirits of the bells floated away, singing in the hush of dawn the sweet song the stars sung over Bethlehem,—"Peace on earth, good will to men

A COUNTRY CHRISTMAS

1882

DEAR EMILY,—I have a brilliant idea, and at once hasten to share it with you. Three weeks ago I came up here to the wilds of Vermont to visit my old aunt, also to get a little quiet and distance in which to survey certain new prospects which have opened before me, and to decide whether I will marry a millionnaire and become a queen of society, or remain 'the charming Miss Vaughan' and wait till the conquering hero comes.

"Aunt Plumy begs me to stay over Christmas, and I have consented, as I always dread the formal dinner with which my guardian celebrates the day.

"My brilliant idea is this. I'm going to make it a real old-fashioned frolic, and won't you come and help me? You will enjoy it immensely I am sure, for Aunt is a character, Cousin Saul worth seeing, and Ruth a far prettier girl than any of the city rose-buds coming out this season. Bring Leonard Randal along with you to take notes for his new book; then it will be fresher and truer than the last, clever as it was.

"The air is delicious up here, society amusing, this old farmhouse full of treasures, and your bosom friend pining to embrace you. Just telegraph yes or no, and we will expect you on Tuesday.

"Ever yours,
"SOPHIE VAUGHAN."

"They will both come, for they are as tired of city life and as fond of change as I am," said the writer of the above, as she folded her letter and went to get it posted without delay.

Aunt Plumy was in the great kitchen making pies; a jolly old soul, with a face as ruddy as a winter apple, a cheery voice, and the kindest heart that ever beat under a gingham gown. Pretty Ruth was chopping the mince, and singing so gaily as she worked that the four-and-twenty immortal blackbirds could not have put more music into a pie than she did. Saul was piling wood into the big oven, and Sophie paused a moment on the threshold to look at him, for she always enjoyed the sight of this stalwart cousin, whom she likened to a

Norse viking, with his fair hair and beard, keen blue eyes, and six feet of manly height, with shoulders that looked broad and strong enough to bear any burden.

His back was toward her, but he saw her first, and turned his flushed face to meet her, with the sudden lighting up it always showed when she approached.

"I've done it, Aunt; and now I want Saul to post the letter, so we can get a speedy answer."

"Just as soon as I can hitch up, cousin;" and Saul pitched in his last log, looking ready to put a girdle round the earth in less than forty minutes.

"Well, dear, I ain't the least mite of objection, as long as it pleases you. I guess we can stan' it ef your city folks can. I presume to say things will look kind of sing'lar to 'em, but I s'pose that's what they come for. Idle folks do dreadful queer things to amuse 'em;" and Aunt Plumy leaned on the rolling-pin to smile and nod with a shrewd twinkle of her eye, as if she enjoyed the prospect as much as Sophie did.

"I shall be afraid of 'em, but I'll try not to make you ashamed of me," said Ruth, who loved her charming cousin even more than she admired her.

"No fear of that, dear. They will be the awkward ones, and you must set them at ease by just being your simple selves, and treating them as if they were everyday people. Nell is very nice and jolly when she drops her city ways, as she must here. She will enter into the spirit of the fun at once, and I know you'll all like her. Mr. Randal is rather the worse for too much praise and petting, as successful people are apt to be, so a little plain talk and rough work will do him good. He is a true gentleman in spite of his airs and elegance, and he will take it all in good part, if you treat him like a man and not a lion."

"I'll see to him," said Saul, who had listened with great interest to the latter part of Sophie's speech, evidently suspecting a lover, and enjoying the idea of supplying him with a liberal amount of "plain talk and rough work."

"I'll keep 'em busy if that's what they need, for there will be a sight to do, and we can't get help easy up here. Our darters don't hire out much. Work to home till they marry, and don't go gaddin' 'round gettin' their heads full of foolish notions, and forgettin' all the useful things their mothers taught 'em."

Aunt Plumy glanced at Ruth as she spoke, and a sudden color in the girl's cheeks proved that the words hit certain ambitious fancies of this pretty daughter of the house of Basset.

"They shall do their parts and not be a trouble; I'll see to that, for you certainly are the dearest aunt in the world to let me take possession of you and yours in this way," cried Sophie, embracing the old lady with warmth.

Saul wished the embrace could be returned by proxy, as his mother's hands were too floury to do more than hover affectionately round the delicate face that looked so fresh and young beside her wrinkled one. As it could not be done, he fled temptation and "hitched up" without delay.

The three women laid their heads together in his absence, and Sophie's plan grew apace, for Ruth longed to see a real novelist and a fine lady, and Aunt Plumy, having plans of her own to further, said "Yes, dear," to every suggestion.

Great was the arranging and adorning that went on that day in the old farmhouse, for Sophie wanted her friends to enjoy this taste of country pleasures, and knew just what additions would be indispensable to their comfort; what simple ornaments would be in keeping with the rustic stage on which she meant to play the part of prima donna.

Next day a telegram arrived accepting the invitation, for both the lady and the lion. They would arrive that afternoon, as little preparation was needed for this impromptu journey, the novelty of which was its chief charm to these *blasé* people.

Saul wanted to get out the double sleigh and span, for he prided himself on his horses, and a fall of snow came most opportunely to beautify the landscape and add a new pleasure to Christmas festivities.

But Sophie declared that the old yellow sleigh, with Punch, the farm-horse, must be used, as she wished everything to be in keeping; and Saul obeyed, thinking he had never seen anything prettier than his cousin when she appeared in his mother's old-fashioned camlet cloak and blue silk pumpkin hood. He looked remarkably well himself in his fur coat, with hair and beard brushed till they shone like spun gold, a fresh color in his cheek, and the sparkle of amusement in his eyes, while excitement gave his usually grave face the animation it needed to be handsome.

Away they jogged in the creaking old sleigh, leaving Ruth to make herself pretty, with a fluttering heart, and Aunt Plumy to dish up a late dinner fit to tempt the most fastidious appetite.

"She has not come for us, and there is not even a stage to take us up. There must be some mistake," said Emily Herrick, as she looked about the shabby little station where they were set down.

"That is the never-to-be-forgotten face of our fair friend, but the bonnet of her grandmother, if my eyes do not deceive me," answered Randal, turning to survey the couple approaching in the rear.

"Sophie Vaughan, what do you mean by making such a guy of yourself?" exclaimed Emily, as she kissed the smiling face in the hood and stared at the quaint cloak.

"I'm dressed for my part, and I intend to keep it up. This is our host, my cousin, Saul Basset. Come to the sleigh at once, he will see to your luggage," said Sophie, painfully conscious of the antiquity of her array as her eyes rested on Emily's pretty hat and mantle, and the masculine elegance of Randal's wraps.

They were hardly tucked in when Saul appeared with a valise in one hand and a large trunk on his shoulder, swinging both on to a wood-sled that stood near by as easily as if they had been hand-bags.

"That is your hero, is it? Well, he looks it, calm and comely, taciturn and tall," said Emily, in a tone of approbation.

"He should have been named Samson or Goliath; though I believe it was the small man who slung things about and turned out the hero in the end," added Randal, surveying the performance with interest and a touch of envy, for much pen work had made his own hands as delicate as a woman's.

"Saul doesn't live in a glass house, so stones won't hurt him. Remember sarcasm is forbidden and sincerity the order of the day. You are country folks now, and it will do you good to try their simple, honest ways for a few days."

Sophie had no time to say more, for Saul came up and drove off with the brief remark that the baggage would "be along right away."

Being hungry, cold and tired, the guests were rather silent during the short drive, but Aunt Plumy's hospitable welcome, and the savory fumes of the dinner awaiting them, thawed the ice and won their hearts at once.

"Isn't it nice? Aren't you glad you came?" asked Sophie, as she led her friends into the parlor, which she had redeemed from its primness by putting bright chintz curtains to the windows, hemlock boughs over the old portraits, a china bowl of flowers on the table, and a splendid fire on the wide hearth.

"It is perfectly jolly, and this is the way I begin to enjoy myself," answered Emily, sitting down upon the home-made rug, whose red flannel roses bloomed in a blue list basket.

"If I may add a little smoke to your glorious fire, it will be quite perfect. Won't Samson join me?" asked Randal, waiting for permission, cigar-case in hand.

"He has no small vices, but you may indulge yours," answered Sophie, from the depths of a grandmotherly chair.

Emily glanced up at her friend as if she caught a new tone in her voice, then turned to the fire again with a wise little nod, as if confiding some secret to the reflection of herself in the bright brass andiron.

"His Delilah does not take this form. I wait with interest to discover if he has one. What a daisy the sister is. Does she ever speak?" asked Randal, trying to lounge on the haircloth sofa, where he was slipping uncomfortably about.

"Oh yes, and sings like a bird. You shall hear her when she gets over her shyness. But no trifling, mind you, for it is a jealously guarded daisy and not to be picked by any idle hand," said Sophie warningly, as she recalled Ruth's blushes and Randal's compliments at dinner.

"I should expect to be annihilated by the big brother if I attempted any but the 'sincerest' admiration and respect. Have no fears on that score, but tell us what is to follow this superb dinner. An apple bee, spinning match, husking party, or primitive pastime of some sort, I have no doubt."

"As you are new to our ways I am going to let you rest this evening. We will sit about the fire and tell stories. Aunt is a master hand at that, and Saul has reminiscences of the war that are well worth hearing if we can only get him to tell them."

"Ah, he was there, was he?"

"Yes, all through it, and is Major Basset, though he likes his plain name best. He fought splendidly and had several wounds, though only a mere boy when he earned his scars and bars. I'm very proud of him for that," and Sophie looked so as she glanced at the photograph of a stripling in uniform set in the place of honor on the high mantel-piece.

"We must stir him up and hear these martial memories. I want some new incidents, and shall book all I can get, if I may."

Here Randal was interrupted by Saul himself, who came in with an armful of wood for the fire.

"Anything more I can do for you, cousin?" he asked, surveying the scene with a rather wistful look.

"Only come and sit with us and talk over war times with Mr. Randal."

"When I've foddered the cattle and done my chores I'd be pleased to. What regiment were you in?" asked Saul, looking down from his lofty height upon the slender gentleman, who answered briefly,—

"In none. I was abroad at the time."

"Sick?"

"No, busy with a novel."

"Took four years to write it?"

"I was obliged to travel and study before I could finish it. These things take more time to work up than outsiders would believe."

"Seems to me our war was a finer story than any you could find in Europe, and the best way to study it would be to fight it out. If you want heroes and heroines you'd have found plenty of 'em there."

"I have no doubt of it, and shall be glad to atone for my seeming neglect of them by hearing about your own exploits, Major."

Randal hoped to turn the conversation gracefully; but Saul was not to be caught, and left the room, saying, with a gleam of fun in his eye,—

"I can't stop now; heroes can wait, pigs can't."

The girls laughed at this sudden descent from the sublime to the ridiculous, and Randal joined them, feeling his condescension had not been unobserved.

As if drawn by the merry sound Aunt Plumy appeared, and being established in the rocking-chair fell to talking as easily as if she had known her guests for years.

"Laugh away, young folks, that's better for digestion than any of the messes people use. Are you troubled with dyspepsy, dear? You didn't seem to take your vittles very hearty, so I mistrusted you was delicate," she said, looking at Emily, whose pale cheeks and weary eyes told the story of late hours and a gay life.

"I haven't eaten so much for years, I assure you, Mrs. Basset; but it was impossible to taste all your good things. I am not dyspeptic, thank you, but a little seedy and tired, for I've been working rather hard lately."

"Be you a teacher? or have you a 'perfessun,' as they call a trade nowadays?" asked the old lady in a tone of kindly interest, which

~ 72 ~

prevented a laugh at the idea of Emily's being anything but a beauty and a belle. The others kept their countenances with difficulty, and she answered demurely,—

"I have no trade as yet, but I dare say I should be happier if I had."

"Not a doubt on't, my dear."

"What would you recommend, ma'am?"

"I should say dressmakin' was rather in your line, ain't it. Your clothes is dreadful tasty, and do you credit if you made 'em yourself," and Aunt Plumy surveyed with feminine interest the simple elegance of the travelling dress which was the masterpiece of a French modiste.

"No, ma'am, I don't make my own things, I'm too lazy. It takes so much time and trouble to select them that I have only strength left to wear them."

"Housekeepin' used to be the favorite perfessun in my day. It ain't fashionable now, but it needs a sight of trainin' to be perfect in all that's required, and I've an idee it would be a sight healthier and usefuller than the paintin' and music and fancy work young women do nowadays."

"But every one wants some beauty in their lives, and each one has a different sphere to fill, if one can only find it."

"'Pears to me there's no call for so much art when nater is full of beauty for them that can see and love it. As for 'spears' and so on, I've a notion if each of us did up our own little chores smart and thorough we needn't go wanderin' round to set the world to rights. That's the Lord's job, and I presume to say He can do it without any advice of ourn."

Something in the homely but true words seemed to rebuke the three listeners for wasted lives, and for a moment there was no sound but the crackle of the fire, the brisk click of the old lady's knitting needles, and Ruth's voice singing overhead as she made ready to join the party below.

"To judge by that sweet sound you have done one of your 'chores' very beautifully, Mrs. Basset, and in spite of the follies of our day, succeeded in keeping one girl healthy, happy and unspoiled," said Emily, looking up into the peaceful old face with her own lovely one full of respect and envy.

"I do hope so, for she's my ewe lamb, the last of four dear little girls; all the rest are in the burying ground 'side of father. I don't expect to keep her long, and don't ought to regret when I lose her, for Saul is the best of sons; but daughters is more to mothers somehow, and I always yearn over girls that is left without a broodin' wing to keep 'em safe and warm in this world of tribulation."

Aunt Plumy laid her hand on Sophie's head as she spoke, with such a motherly look that both girls drew nearer, and Randal resolved to put her in a book without delay.

Presently Saul returned with little Ruth hanging on his arm and shyly nestling near him as he took the three-cornered leathern chair in the chimney nook, while she sat on a stool close by.

"Now the circle is complete and the picture perfect. Don't light the lamps yet, please, but talk away and let me make a mental study of you. I seldom find so charming a scene to paint," said Randal, beginning to enjoy himself immensely, with a true artist's taste for novelty and effect.

"Tell us about your book, for we have been reading it as it comes out in the magazine, and are much exercised about how it's going to end," began Saul, gallantly throwing himself into the breach, for a momentary embarrassment fell upon the women at the idea of sitting for their portraits before they were ready.

"Do you really read my poor serial up here, and do me the honor to like it?" asked the novelist, both flattered and amused, for his work was of the æsthetic sort, microscopic studies of character, and careful pictures of modern life.

"Sakes alive, why shouldn't we," cried Aunt Plumy. "We have some eddication, though we ain't very genteel. We've got a town libry, kep up by the women mostly, with fairs and tea parties and so on. We have all the magazines reg'lar, and Saul reads out the pieces while Ruth sews and I knit, my eyes bein' poor. Our winter is long and evenins would be kinder lonesome if we didn't have novils and newspapers to cheer 'em up."

"I am very glad I can help to beguile them for you. Now tell me what you honestly think of my work? Criticism is always valuable, and I should really like yours, Mrs. Basset," said Randal, wondering what the good woman would make of the delicate analysis and worldly wisdom on which he prided himself.

Short work, as Aunt Plumy soon showed him, for she rather enjoyed freeing her mind at all times, and decidedly resented the insinuation that country folk could not appreciate light literature as well as city people.

"I ain't no great of a jedge about anything but nat'ralness of books, and it really does seem as if some of your men and women was dreadful uncomfortable creaters. 'Pears to me it ain't wise to be always pickin' ourselves to pieces and pryin' into things that ought to come gradual by way of experience and the visitations of Providence. Flowers won't blow worth a cent ef you pull 'em open. Better wait and see what they can do alone. I do relish the smart sayins, the odd ways of furrin parts, and the sarcastic slaps at folkses weak spots. But, massy knows, we can't live on spice-cake and Charlotte Ruche, and I do feel as if books was more sustainin' ef they was full of every-day people and things, like good bread and butter. Them that goes to the heart and ain't soon forgotten is the kind I hanker for. Mis Terry's books now, and Mis Stowe's, and Dickens's Christmas pieces,—them is real sweet and cheerin', to my mind."

As the blunt old lady paused it was evident she had produced a sensation, for Saul smiled at the fire, Ruth looked dismayed at this assault upon one of her idols, and the young ladies were both astonished and amused at the keenness of the new critic who dared express what they had often felt. Randal, however, was quite composed and laughed good-naturedly, though secretly feeling as if a pail of cold water had been poured over him.

"Many thanks, madam; you have discovered my weak point with surprising accuracy. But you see I cannot help 'picking folks to pieces,' as you have expressed it; that is my gift, and it has its attractions, as the sale of my books will testify. People like the 'spice-bread,' and as that is the only sort my oven will bake, I must keep on in order to make my living."

"So rumsellers say, but it ain't a good trade to foller, and I'd chop wood 'fore I'd earn my livin' harmin' my feller man. 'Pears to me I'd let my oven cool a spell, and hunt up some homely, happy folks to write about; folks that don't borrer trouble and go lookin' for holes in their neighbors' coats, but take their lives brave and cheerful; and rememberin' we are all human, have pity on the weak, and try to be as full of mercy, patience and lovin' kindness as Him who made us. That sort of a book would do a heap of good; be real warmin' and strengthenin', and make them that read it love the man that wrote it, and remember him when he was dead and gone."

"I wish I could!" and Randal meant what he said, for he was as tired of his own style, as a watch-maker might be of the magnifying glass through which he strains his eyes all day. He knew that the heart was left out of his work, and that both mind and soul were growing morbid with dwelling on the faulty, absurd and metaphysical phases of life and character. He often threw down his pen and vowed he would write no more; but he loved ease and the books brought money readily; he was accustomed to the stimulant of praise and missed it as the toper misses his wine, so that which had once been a pleasure to himself and others was fast becoming a burden and a disappointment.

The brief pause which followed his involuntary betrayal of discontent was broken by Ruth, who exclaimed, with a girlish enthusiasm that overpowered girlish bashfulness,—

"*I* think all the novels are splendid! I hope you will write hundreds more, and I shall live to read 'em."

"Bravo, my gentle champion! I promise that I will write one more at least, and have a heroine in it whom your mother will both admire and love," answered Randal, surprised to find how grateful he was for the girl's approval, and how rapidly his trained fancy began to paint the background on which he hoped to copy this fresh, human daisy.

Abashed by her involuntary outburst, Ruth tried to efface herself behind Saul's broad shoulder, and he brought the conversation back to its starting-point by saying in a tone of the most sincere interest,—

"Speaking of the serial, I am very anxious to know how your hero comes out. He is a fine fellow, and I can't decide whether he is going to spoil his life marrying that silly woman, or do something grand and generous, and not be made a fool of."

"Upon my soul, I don't know myself. It is very hard to find new finales. Can't you suggest something, Major? then I shall not be obliged to leave my story without an end, as people complain I am rather fond of doing."

"Well, no, I don't think I've anything to offer. Seems to me it isn't the sensational exploits that show the hero best, but some great sacrifice quietly made by a common sort of man who is noble without knowing it. I saw a good many such during the war, and often wish I could write them down, for it is surprising how much courage, goodness and real piety is stowed away in common folks ready to show when the right time comes."

"Tell us one of them, and I'll bless you for a hint. No one knows the anguish of an author's spirit when he can't ring down the curtain on an effective tableau," said Randal, with a glance at his friends to ask their aid in eliciting an anecdote or reminiscence.

"Tell about the splendid fellow who held the bridge, like Horatius, till help came up. That was a thrilling story, I assure you," answered Sophie, with an inviting smile.

But Saul would not be his own hero, and said briefly:

"Any man can be brave when the battle-fever is on him, and it only takes a little physical courage to dash ahead." He paused a moment, with his eyes on the snowy landscape without, where twilight was deepening; then, as if constrained by the memory that winter scene evoked, he slowly continued,—

"One of the bravest things I ever knew was done by a poor fellow who has been a hero to me ever since, though I only met him that night. It was after one of the big battles of that last winter, and I was knocked over with a broken leg and two or three bullets here and there. Night was coming on, snow falling, and a sharp wind blew over the field where a lot of us lay, dead and alive, waiting for the ambulance to come and pick us up. There was skirmishing going on not far off, and our prospects were rather poor between frost and fire. I was calculating how I'd manage, when I found two poor chaps close by who were worse off, so I braced up and did what I could for them. One had an arm blown away, and kept up a dreadful groaning. The other was shot bad, and bleeding to death for want of help, but never complained. He was nearest, and I liked his pluck, for he spoke cheerful and made me ashamed to growl. Such times make dreadful brutes of men if they haven't something to hold on to, and all three of us were most wild with pain and cold and hunger, for we'd fought all day fasting, when we heard a rumble in the road below, and saw lanterns bobbing round. That meant life to us, and we all tried to holler; two of us, were pretty faint, but I managed a good yell, and they heard it.

"'Room for one more. Hard luck, old boys, but we are full and must save the worst wounded first. Take a drink, and hold on till we come back,' says one of them with the stretcher.

"'Here's the one to go,' I says, pointin' out my man, for I saw by the light that he was hard hit.

"'No, that one. He's got more chances than I, or this one; he's young and got a mother; I'll wait,' said the good feller, touchin' my arm, for he'd heard me mutterin' to myself about this dear old lady. We always want mother when we are down, you know."

Saul's eyes turned to the beloved face with a glance of tenderest affection, and Aunt Plumy answered with a dismal groan at the recollection of his need that night, and her absence.

"Well, to be short, the groaning chap was taken, and my man left. I was mad, but there was no time for talk, and the selfish one went off and left that poor feller to run his one chance. I had my rifle, and guessed I could hobble up to use it if need be; so we settled back to wait without much hope of help, everything being in a muddle. And wait we did till morning, for that ambulance did not come back till next day, when most of us were past needing it.

"I'll never forget that night. I dream it all over again as plain as if it was real. Snow, cold, darkness, hunger, thirst, pain, and all round us cries and cursing growing less and less, till at last only the wind went moaning over that meadow. It was awful! so lonesome, helpless, and seemingly God-forsaken. Hour after hour we lay there side by side under one coat, waiting to be saved or die, for the wind grew strong and we grew weak."

Saul drew a long breath, and held his hands to the fire as if he felt again the sharp suffering of that night.

"And the man?" asked Emily, softly, as if reluctant to break the silence.

"He *was* a man! In times like that men talk like brothers and show what they are. Lying there, slowly freezing, Joe Cummings told me about his wife and babies, his old folks waiting for him, all depending on him, yet all ready to give him up when he was needed. A plain man, but honest and true, and loving as a woman; I soon saw that as he went on talking, half to me and half to himself, for sometimes he wandered a little toward the end. I've read books, heard sermons, and seen good folks, but nothing ever came so close or did me so much good as seeing this man die. He had one chance and gave it cheerfully. He longed for those he loved, and let 'em go with a good-by they couldn't hear. He suffered all the pains we most shrink from without a murmur, and kept my heart warm while his own was growing cold. It's no use trying to tell that part of it; but I heard prayers that night that meant something, and I saw how faith could hold a soul up when everything was gone but God."

Saul stopped there with a sudden huskiness in his deep voice, and when he went on it was in the tone of one who speaks of a dear friend.

"Joe grew still by and by, and I thought he was asleep, for I felt his breath when I tucked him up, and his hand held on to mine. The cold sort of numbed me, and I dropped off, too weak and stupid to think or feel. I never should have waked up if it hadn't been for Joe. When I came to, it was morning, and I thought I was dead, for all I could see was that great field of white mounds, like graves, and a splendid sky above. Then I looked for Joe, remembering; but he had put my coat back over me, and lay stiff and still under the snow that covered him like a shroud, all except his face. A bit of my cape had blown over it, and when I took it off and the sun shone on his dead face, I declare to you it was so full of heavenly peace I felt as if that common man had been glorified by God's light, and rewarded by God's 'Well done.' That's all."

No one spoke for a moment, while the women wiped their eyes, and Saul dropped his as if to hide something softer than tears.

"It was very noble, very touching. And you? how did you get off at last?" asked Randal, with real admiration and respect in his usually languid face.

"Crawled off," answered Saul, relapsing into his former brevity of speech.

"Why not before, and save yourself all that misery?"

"Couldn't leave Joe."

"Ah, I see; there were two heroes that night."

"Dozens, I've no doubt. Those were times that made heroes of men, and women, too."

"Tell us more;" begged Emily, looking up with an expression none of her admirers ever brought to her face by their softest compliments or wiliest gossip.

"I've done my part. It's Mr. Randal's turn now;" and Saul drew himself out of the ruddy circle of firelight, as if ashamed of the prominent part he was playing.

Sophie and her friend had often heard Randal talk, for he was an accomplished *raconteur*, but that night he exerted himself, and was unusually brilliant and entertaining, as if upon his mettle. The Bassets were charmed. They sat late and were very merry, for Aunt Plumy got up a little supper for them, and her cider was as exhilarating as champagne. When they parted for the night and Sophie kissed her aunt, Emily did the same, saying heartily,—

"It seems as if I'd known you all my life, and this is certainly the most enchanting old place that ever was."

"Glad you like it, dear. But it ain't all fun, as you'll find out to-morrow when you go to work, for Sophie says you must," answered Mrs. Basset, as her guests trooped away, rashly promising to like everything.

They found it difficult to keep their word when they were called at half past six next morning. Their rooms were warm, however, and they managed to scramble down in time for breakfast, guided by the fragrance of coffee and Aunt Plumy's shrill voice singing the good old hymn—

"Lord, in the morning Thou shalt hear
My voice ascending high."

An open fire blazed on the hearth, for the cooking was done in the lean-to, and the spacious, sunny kitchen was kept in all its old-fashioned perfection, with the wooden settle in a warm nook, the tall clock behind the door, copper and pewter utensils shining on the dresser, old china in the corner closet and a little spinning wheel rescued from the garret by Sophie to adorn the deep window, full of scarlet geraniums, Christmas roses, and white chrysanthemums.

The young lady, in a checked apron and mob-cap, greeted her friends with a dish of buckwheats in one hand, and a pair of cheeks that proved she had been learning to fry these delectable cakes.

"You do 'keep it up' in earnest, upon my word; and very becoming it is, dear. But won't you ruin your complexion and roughen your hands if you do so much of this new fancy-work?" asked Emily, much amazed at this novel freak.

"I like it, and really believe I've found my proper sphere at last. Domestic life seems so pleasant to me that I feel as if I'd better keep it up for the rest of my life," answered Sophie, making a pretty picture of herself as she cut great slices of brown bread, with the early sunshine touching her happy face.

"The charming Miss Vaughan in the rôle of a farmer's wife. I find it difficult to imagine, and shrink from the thought of the wide-spread dismay such a fate will produce among her adorers," added Randal, as he basked in the glow of the hospitable fire.

"She might do worse; but come to breakfast and do honor to my handiwork," said Sophie, thinking of her worn-out millionnaire, and rather nettled by the satiric smile on Randal's lips.

"What an appetite early rising gives one. I feel equal to almost anything, so let me help wash cups," said Emily, with unusual energy, when the hearty meal was over and Sophie began to pick up the dishes as if it was her usual work.

Ruth went to the window to water the flowers, and Randal followed to make himself agreeable, remembering her defence of him last night. He was used to admiration from feminine eyes, and flattery from soft lips, but found something new and charming in the innocent delight which showed itself at his approach in blushes more eloquent than words, and shy glances from eyes full of hero-worship.

"I hope you are going to spare me a posy for to-morrow night, since I can be fine in no other way to do honor to the dance Miss Sophie proposes for us," he said, leaning in the bay window to look down on the little girl, with the devoted air he usually wore for pretty women.

"Anything you like! I should be so glad to have you wear my flowers. There will be enough for all, and I've nothing else to give to people who have made me as happy as cousin Sophie and you," answered Ruth, half drowning her great calla as she spoke with grateful warmth.

"You must make her happy by accepting the invitation to go home with her which I heard given last night. A peep at the world would do you good, and be a pleasant change, I think."

"Oh, very pleasant! but would it do me good?" and Ruth looked up with sudden seriousness in her blue eyes, as a child questions an elder, eager, yet wistful.

"Why not?" asked Randal, wondering at the hesitation.

"I might grow discontented with things here if I saw splendid houses and fine people. I am very happy now, and it would break my heart to lose that happiness, or ever learn to be ashamed of home."

"But don't you long for more pleasure, new scenes and other friends than these?" asked the man, touched by the little creature's loyalty to the things she knew and loved.

"Very often, but mother says when I'm ready they will come, so I wait and try not to be impatient." But Ruth's eyes looked out over the green leaves as if the longing was very strong within her to see more of the unknown world lying beyond the mountains that hemmed her in.

"It is natural for birds to hop out of the nest, so I shall expect to see you over there before long, and ask you how you enjoy your first flight," said Randal, in a paternal tone that had a curious effect on Ruth.

To his surprise, she laughed, then blushed like one of her own roses, and answered with a demure dignity that was very pretty to see.

"I intend to hop soon, but it won't be a very long flight or very far from mother. She can't spare me, and nobody in the world can fill her place to me."

"Bless the child, does she think I'm going to make love to her," thought Randal, much amused, but quite mistaken. Wiser women had thought so when he assumed the caressing air with which he beguiled them into the little revelations of character he liked to use, as the south wind makes flowers open their hearts to give up their odor, then leaves them to carry it elsewhere, the more welcome for the stolen sweetness.

"Perhaps you are right. The maternal wing is a safe shelter for confiding little souls like you, Miss Ruth. You will be as comfortable here as your flowers in this sunny window," he said, carelessly pinching geranium leaves, and ruffling the roses till the pink petals of the largest fluttered to the floor.

As if she instinctively felt and resented something in the man which his act symbolized, the girl answered quietly, as she went on with her work, "Yes, if the frost does not touch me, or careless people spoil me too soon."

Before Randal could reply Aunt Plumy approached like a maternal hen who sees her chicken in danger.

"Saul is goin' to haul wood after he's done his chores, mebbe you'd like to go along? The view is good, the roads well broke, and the day uncommon fine."

"Thanks; it will be delightful, I dare say," politely responded the lion, with a secret shudder at the idea of a rural promenade at 8 A.M. in the winter.

"Come on, then; we'll feed the stock, and then I'll show you how to yoke oxen," said Saul, with a twinkle in his eye as he led the way, when his new aide had muffled himself up as if for a polar voyage.

"Now, that's too bad of Saul! He did it on purpose, just to please you, Sophie," cried Ruth presently, and the girls ran to the window to behold Randal bravely following his host with a pail of pigs' food in each hand, and an expression of resigned disgust upon his aristocratic face.

"To what base uses may we come," quoted Emily, as they all nodded and smiled upon the victim as he looked back from the barn-yard, where he was clamorously welcomed by his new charges.

"It is rather a shock at first, but it will do him good, and Saul won't be too hard upon him, I'm sure," said Sophie, going back to her work, while Ruth turned her best buds to the sun that they might be ready for a peace-offering to-morrow.

There was a merry clatter in the big kitchen for an hour; then Aunt Plumy and her daughter shut themselves up in the pantry to perform some culinary rites, and the young ladies went to inspect certain antique costumes laid forth in Sophie's room.

"You see, Em, I thought it would be appropriate to the house and season to have an old-fashioned dance. Aunt has quantities of ancient finery stowed away, for great-grandfather Basset was a fine old gentleman and his family lived in state. Take your choice of the crimson, blue or silver-gray damask. Ruth is to wear the worked muslin and quilted white satin skirt, with that coquettish hat."

"Being dark, I'll take the red and trim it up with this fine lace. You must wear the blue and primrose, with the distracting high-heeled shoes. Have you any suits for the men?" asked Emily, throwing herself at once into the all-absorbing matter of costume.

"A claret velvet coat and vest, silk stockings, cocked hat and snuff-box for Randal. Nothing large enough for Saul, so he must wear his uniform. Won't Aunt Plumy be superb in this plum-colored satin and immense cap?"

A delightful morning was spent in adapting the faded finery of the past to the blooming beauty of the present, and time and tongues flew till the toot of a horn called them down to dinner.

The girls were amazed to see Randal come whistling up the road with his trousers tucked into his boots, blue mittens on his hands, and an unusual amount of energy in his whole figure, as he drove the oxen, while Saul laughed at his vain attempts to guide the bewildered beasts.

"It's immense! The view from the hill is well worth seeing, for the snow glorifies the landscape and reminds one of Switzerland. I'm going to make a sketch of it this afternoon; better come and enjoy the delicious freshness, young ladies."

Randal was eating with such an appetite that he did not see the glances the girls exchanged as they promised to go.

"Bring home some more winter-green, I want things to be real nice, and we haven't enough for the kitchen," said Ruth, dimpling with girlish delight as she imagined herself dancing under the green garlands in her grandmother's wedding gown.

It was very lovely on the hill, for far as the eye could reach lay the wintry landscape sparkling with the brief beauty of sunshine on virgin snow. Pines sighed overhead, hardy birds flitted to and fro, and in all the trodden spots rose the little spires of evergreen ready for its Christmas duty. Deeper in the wood sounded the measured ring of axes, the crash of falling trees, while the red shirts of the men added color to the scene, and a fresh wind brought the aromatic breath of newly cloven hemlock and pine.

"How beautiful it is! I never knew before what winter woods were like. Did you, Sophie?" asked Emily, sitting on a stump to enjoy the novel pleasure at her ease.

"I've found out lately; Saul lets me come as often as I like, and this fine air seems to make a new creature of me," answered Sophie, looking about her with sparkling eyes, as if this was a kingdom where she reigned supreme.

"Something is making a new creature of you, that is very evident. I haven't yet discovered whether it is the air or some magic herb among that green stuff you are gathering so diligently;" and Emily laughed to see the color deepen beautifully in her friend's half-averted face.

"Scarlet is the only wear just now, I find. If we are lost like babes in the woods there are plenty of Red-breasts to cover us with leaves," and Randal joined Emily's laugh, with a glance at Saul, who had just pulled his coat off.

"You wanted to see this tree go down, so stand from under and I'll show you how it's done," said the farmer, taking up his axe, not unwilling to gratify his guests and display his manly accomplishments at the same time.

It was a fine sight, the stalwart man swinging his axe with magnificent strength and skill, each blow sending a thrill through the stately tree, till its heart was reached and it tottered to its fall. Never pausing for breath Saul shook his yellow mane out of his eyes, and hewed away, while the drops stood on his forehead and his arm ached, as bent on distinguishing himself as if he had been a knight tilting against his rival for his lady's favor.

"I don't know which to admire most, the man or his muscle. One doesn't often see such vigor, size and comeliness in these degenerate days," said Randal, mentally booking the fine figure in the red shirt.

"I think we have discovered a rough diamond. I only wonder if Sophie is going to try and polish it," answered Emily, glancing at her friend, who stood a little apart, watching the rise and fall of the axe as intently as if her fate depended on it.

Down rushed the tree at last, and, leaving them to examine a crow's nest in its branches, Saul went off to his men, as if he found the praises of his prowess rather too much for him.

Randal fell to sketching, the girls to their garland-making, and for a little while the sunny woodland nook was full of lively chat and pleasant laughter, for the air exhilarated them all like wine. Suddenly a man came running from the wood, pale and anxious, saying, as he hastened by for help, "Blasted tree fell on him! Bleed to death before the doctor comes!"

"Who? who?" cried the startled trio.

But the man ran on, with some breathless reply, in which only a name was audible—"Basset."

"The deuce it is!" and Randal dropped his pencil, while the girls sprang up in dismay. Then, with one impulse, they hastened to the distant group, half visible behind the fallen trees and corded wood.

Sophie was there first, and forcing her way through the little crowd of men, saw a red-shirted figure on the ground, crushed and bleeding, and threw herself down beside it with a cry that pierced the hearts of those who heard it. In the act she saw it was not Saul, and covered her bewildered face as if to hide its joy. A strong arm lifted her, and the familiar voice said cheeringly,—

"I'm all right, dear. Poor Bruce is hurt, but we've sent for help. Better go right home and forget all about it."

"Yes, I will, if I can do nothing;" and Sophie meekly returned to her friends who stood outside the circle over which Saul's head towered, assuring them of his safety.

Hoping they had not seen her agitation, she led Emily away, leaving Randal to give what aid he could and bring them news of the poor wood-chopper's state.

Aunt Plumy produced the "camphire" the moment she saw Sophie's pale face, and made her lie down, while the brave old lady trudged briskly off with bandages and brandy to the scene of action. On her return she brought comfortable news of the man, so the little flurry blew over and was forgotten by all but Sophie, who remained pale and quiet all the evening, tying evergreen as if her life depended on it.

"A good night's sleep will set her up. She ain't used to such things, dear child, and needs cossetin'," said Aunt Plumy, purring over her until she was in her bed, with a hot stone at her feet and a bowl of herb tea to quiet her nerves.

An hour later, when Emily went up, she peeped in to see if Sophie was sleeping nicely, and was surprised to find the invalid wrapped in a dressing-gown writing busily.

"Last will and testament, or sudden inspiration, dear? How are you? faint or feverish, delirious or in the dumps! Saul looks so anxious, and Mrs. Basset hushes us all up so, I came to bed, leaving Randal to entertain Ruth."

As she spoke Emily saw the papers disappear in a portfolio, and Sophie rose with a yawn.

~ *85* ~

"I was writing letters, but I'm sleepy now. Quite over my foolish fright, thank you. Go and get your beauty sleep that you may dazzle the natives to-morrow."

"So glad, good night;" and Emily went away, saying to herself, "Something is going on, and I must find out what it is before I leave. Sophie can't blind *me*."

But Sophie did all the next day, being delightfully gay at the dinner, and devoting herself to the young minister who was invited to meet the distinguished novelist, and evidently being afraid of him, gladly basked in the smiles of his charming neighbor. A dashing sleigh-ride occupied the afternoon, and then great was the fun and excitement over the costumes.

Aunt Plumy laughed till the tears rolled down her cheeks as the girls compressed her into the plum-colored gown with its short waist, leg-of-mutton sleeves, and narrow skirt. But a worked scarf hid all deficiencies, and the towering cap struck awe into the soul of the most frivolous observer.

"Keep an eye on me, girls, for I shall certainly split somewheres or lose my head-piece off when I'm trottin' round. What would my blessed mother say if she could see me rigged out in her best things?" and with a smile and a sigh the old lady departed to look after "the boys," and see that the supper was all right.

Three prettier damsels never tripped down the wide staircase than the brilliant brunette in crimson brocade, the pensive blonde in blue, or the rosy little bride in old muslin and white satin.

A gallant court gentleman met them in the hall with a superb bow, and escorted them to the parlor, where Grandma Basset's ghost was discovered dancing with a modern major in full uniform.

Mutual admiration and many compliments followed, till other ancient ladies and gentlemen arrived in all manner of queer costumes, and the old house seemed to wake from its humdrum quietude to sudden music and merriment, as if a past generation had returned to keep its Christmas there.

The village fiddler soon struck up the good old tunes, and then the strangers saw dancing that filled them with mingled mirth and envy; it was so droll, yet so hearty. The young men, unusually awkward in their grandfathers' knee-breeches, flapping vests, and swallow-tail coats, footed it bravely with the buxom girls who were the prettier for their quaintness, and danced with such vigor that their high combs stood awry, their furbelows waved wildly, and their cheeks were as red as their breast-knots, or hose.

It was impossible to stand still, and one after the other the city folk yielded to the spell, Randal leading off with Ruth, Sophie swept away by Saul, and Emily being taken possession of by a young giant of eighteen, who spun her around with a boyish impetuosity that took her breath away. Even Aunt Plumy was discovered jigging it alone in the pantry, as if the music was too much for her, and the plates and glasses jingled gaily on the shelves in time to Money Musk and Fishers' Hornpipe.

A pause came at last, however, and fans fluttered, heated brows were wiped, jokes were made, lovers exchanged confidences, and every nook and corner held a man and maid carrying on the sweet game which is never out of fashion. There was a glitter of gold lace in the back entry, and a train of blue and primrose shone in the dim light. There was a richer crimson than that of the geraniums in the deep window, and a dainty shoe tapped the bare floor impatiently as the brilliant black eyes looked everywhere for the court gentleman, while their owner listened to the gruff prattle of an enamored boy. But in the upper hall walked a little white ghost as if waiting for some shadowy companion, and when a dark form appeared ran to take its arm, saying, in a tone of soft satisfaction,—

"I was so afraid you wouldn't come!"

"Why did you leave me, Ruth?" answered a manly voice in a tone of surprise, though the small hand slipping from the velvet coat-sleeve was replaced as if it was pleasant to feel it there.

A pause, and then the other voice answered demurely,—

"Because I was afraid my head would be turned by the fine things you were saying."

"It is impossible to help saying what one feels to such an artless little creature as you are. It does me good to admire anything so fresh and sweet, and won't harm you."

"It might if—"

"If what, my daisy?"

"I believed it," and a laugh seemed to finish the broken sentence better than the words.

"You may, Ruth, for I do sincerely admire the most genuine girl I have seen for a long time. And walking here with you in your bridal white I was just asking myself if I should not be a happier man with a home of my own and a little wife hanging on my arm than drifting about the world as I do now with only myself to care for."

"I know you would!" and Ruth spoke so earnestly that Randal was both touched and startled, fearing he had ventured too far in a mood of unwonted sentiment, born of the romance of the hour and the sweet frankness of his companion.

"Then you don't think it would be rash for some sweet woman to take me in hand and make me happy, since fame is a failure?"

"Oh, no; it would be easy work if she loved you. I know some one—if I only dared to tell her name."

"Upon my soul, this is cool," and Randal looked down, wondering if the audacious lady on his arm could be shy Ruth.

If he had seen the malicious merriment in her eyes he would have been more humiliated still, but they were modestly averted, and the face under the little hat was full of a soft agitation rather dangerous even to a man of the world.

"She is a captivating little creature, but it is too soon for anything but a mild flirtation. I must delay further innocent revelations or I shall do something rash."

While making this excellent resolution Randal had been pressing the hand upon his arm and gently pacing down the dimly lighted hall with the sound of music in his ears, Ruth's sweetest roses in his button-hole, and a loving little girl beside him, as he thought.

"You shall tell me by and by when we are in town. I am sure you will come, and meanwhile don't forget me."

"I am going in the spring, but I shall not be with Sophie," answered Ruth, in a whisper.

"With whom then? I shall long to see you."

"With my husband. I am to be married in May."

"The deuce you are!" escaped Randal, as he stopped short to stare at his companion, sure she was not in earnest.

But she was, for as he looked the sound of steps coming up the back stairs made her whole face flush and brighten with the unmistakable glow of happy love, and she completed Randal's astonishment by running into the arms of the young minister, saying with an irrepressible laugh, "Oh! John, why didn't you come before?"

The court gentleman was all right in a moment, and the coolest of the three as he offered his congratulations and gracefully retired, leaving the lovers to enjoy the tryst he had delayed. But as he went down stairs his brows were knit, and he slapped the broad railing smartly with his cocked hat as if some irritation must find vent in a more energetic way than merely saying, "Confound the little baggage!" under his breath.

Such an amazing supper came from Aunt Plumy's big pantry that the city guests could not eat for laughing at the queer dishes circulating through the rooms, and copiously partaken of by the hearty young folks.

Doughnuts and cheese, pie and pickles, cider and tea, baked beans and custards, cake and cold turkey, bread and butter, plum pudding and French bonbons, Sophie's contribution.

"May I offer you the native delicacies, and share your plate. Both are very good, but the china has run short, and after such vigorous exercise as you have had you must need refreshment. I'm sure I do!" said Randal, bowing before Emily with a great blue platter laden with two doughnuts, two wedges of pumpkin pie and two spoons.

The smile with which she welcomed him, the alacrity with which she made room beside her and seemed to enjoy the supper he brought, was so soothing to his ruffled spirit that he soon began to feel that there is no friend like an old friend, that it would not be difficult to name a sweet woman who would take him in hand and would make him happy if he cared to ask her, and he began to think he would by and by, it was so pleasant to sit in that green corner with waves of crimson brocade flowing over his feet, and a fine face softening beautifully under his eyes.

The supper was not romantic, but the situation was, and Emily found that pie ambrosial food eaten with the man she loved, whose eyes talked more eloquently than the tongue just then busy with a doughnut. Ruth kept away, but glanced at them as she served her company, and her own happy experience helped her to see that all was going well in that quarter. Saul and Sophie emerged from the back entry with shining countenances, but carefully avoided each other for the rest of the evening. No one observed this but Aunt Plumy from the recesses of her pantry, and she folded her hands as if well content, as she murmured fervently over a pan full of crullers, "Bless the dears! Now I can die happy."

Every one thought Sophie's old-fashioned dress immensely becoming, and several of his former men said to Saul with blunt admiration, "Major, you look to-night as you used to after we'd gained a big battle."

"I feel as if I had," answered the splendid Major, with eyes much brighter than his buttons, and a heart under them infinitely prouder than when he was promoted on the field of honor, for his Waterloo was won.

There was more dancing, followed by games, in which Aunt Plumy shone pre-eminent, for the supper was off her mind and she could enjoy herself. There were shouts of merriment as the blithe old lady twirled the platter, hunted the squirrel, and went to Jerusalem like a girl of sixteen; her cap in a ruinous condition, and every seam of the purple dress straining like sails in a gale. It was great fun, but at midnight it came to an end, and the young folks, still bubbling over with innocent jollity, went jingling away along the snowy hills, unanimously pronouncing Mrs. Basset's party the best of the season.

"Never had such a good time in my life!" exclaimed Sophie, as the family stood together in the kitchen where the candles among the wreaths were going out, and the floor was strewn with wrecks of past joy.

"I'm proper glad, dear. Now you all go to bed and lay as late as you like to-morrow. I'm so kinder worked up I couldn't sleep, so Saul and me will put things to rights without a mite of noise to disturb you;" and Aunt Plumy sent them off with a smile that was a benediction, Sophie thought.

"The dear old soul speaks as if midnight was an unheard-of hour for Christians to be up. What would she say if she knew how we seldom go to bed till dawn in the ball season? I'm so wide awake I've half a mind to pack a little. Randal must go at two, he says, and we shall want his escort," said Emily, as the girls laid away their brocades in the great press in Sophie's room.

"I'm not going. Aunt can't spare me, and there is nothing to go for yet," answered Sophie, beginning to take the white chrysanthemums out of her pretty hair.

"My dear child, you will die of ennui up here. Very nice for a week or so, but frightful for a winter. We are going to be very gay, and cannot get on without you," cried Emily, dismayed at the suggestion.

"You will have to, for I'm not coming. I am very happy here, and so tired of the frivolous life I lead in town, that I have decided to try a better one," and Sophie's mirror reflected a face full of the sweetest content.

"Have you lost your mind? experienced religion? or any other dreadful thing? You always were odd, but this last freak is the strangest of all. What will your guardian say, and the world?" added Emily in the awe-stricken tone of one who stood in fear of the omnipotent Mrs. Grundy.

"Guardy will be glad to be rid of me, and I don't care that for the world," cried Sophie, snapping her fingers with a joyful sort of recklessness which completed Emily's bewilderment.

"But Mr. Hammond? Are you going to throw away millions, lose your chance of making the best match in the city, and driving the girls of our set out of their wits with envy?"

Sophie laughed at her friend's despairing cry, and turning round said quietly,—

"I wrote to Mr. Hammond last night, and this evening received my reward for being an honest girl. Saul and I are to be married in the spring when Ruth is."

Emily fell prone upon the bed as if the announcement was too much for her, but was up again in an instant to declare with prophetic solemnity,—

"I knew something was going on, but hoped to get you away before you were lost. Sophie, you will repent. Be warned, and forget this sad delusion."

"Too late for that. The pang I suffered yesterday when I thought Saul was dead showed me how well I loved him. To-night he asked me to stay, and no power in the world can part us. Oh! Emily, it is all so sweet, so beautiful, that *everything* is possible, and I know I shall be happy in this dear old home, full of love and peace and honest hearts. I only hope you may find as true and tender a man to live for as my Saul."

Sophie's face was more eloquent than her fervent words, and Emily beautifully illustrated the inconsistency of her sex by suddenly embracing her friend, with the incoherent exclamation, "I think I have, dear! Your brave Saul is worth a dozen old Hammonds, and I do believe you are right."

It is unnecessary to tell how, as if drawn by the irresistible magic of sympathy, Ruth and her mother crept in one by one to join the midnight conference and add their smiles and tears, tender hopes and proud delight to the joys of that memorable hour. Nor how Saul, unable to sleep, mounted guard below, and meeting Randal prowling down to soothe his nerves with a surreptitious cigar found it impossible to help confiding to his attentive ear the happiness that would break bounds and overflow in unusual eloquence.

Peace fell upon the old house at last, and all slept as if some magic herb had touched their eyelids, bringing blissful dreams and a glad awakening.

"Can't we persuade you to come with us, Miss Sophie?" asked Randal next day, as they made their adieux.

"I'm under orders now, and dare not disobey my superior officer," answered Sophie, handing her Major his driving gloves, with a look which plainly showed that she had joined the great army of devoted women who enlist for life and ask no pay but love.

"I shall depend on being invited to your wedding, then, and yours, too, Miss Ruth," added Randal, shaking hands with "the little baggage," as if he had quite forgiven her mockery and forgotten his own brief lapse into sentiment.

Before she could reply Aunt Plumy said, in a tone of calm conviction, that made them all laugh, and some of them look conscious,—

"Spring is a good time for weddin's, and I shouldn't wonder if there was quite a number."

"Nor I;" and Saul and Sophie smiled at one another as they saw how carefully Randal arranged Emily's wraps.

Then with kisses, thanks and all the good wishes that happy hearts could imagine, the guests drove away, to remember long and gratefully that pleasant country Christmas.

ROSA'S TALE

1879

"NOW, I BELIEVE EVERY ONE has had a christmas present and a good time. Nobody has been forgotten, not even the cat," said Mrs. Ward to her daughter, as she looked at Pobbylinda, purring on the rug, with a new ribbon round her neck and the remains of a chicken bone between her paws.

It was very late, for the Christmas-tree was stripped, the little folks abed, the baskets and bundles left at poor neighbors' doors, and everything ready for the happy day which would begin as the clock struck twelve. They were resting after their labors, while the yule log burned down; but the mother's words reminded Belinda of one good friend who had received no gift that night.

"We've forgotten Rosa! Her mistress is away, but she *shall* have a present nevertheless. Late asit is, she will like some apples and cake and a Merry Christmas from the family."

Belinda jumped up as she spoke, and, having collected such remnants of the feast as a horse would relish, she put on her hood, lighted a lantern, and trotted off to the barn.

As she opened the door of the loose box in which Rosa was kept, she saw her eyes shining in the dark as she lifted her head with a startled air. Then, recognizing a friend, she rose and came rustling through the straw to greet her late visitor. She was evidently much pleased with the attention, and rubbed her nose against Miss Belinda gratefully, but seemed rather dainty, and poked over the contents of the basket, as if a little suspicious, though apples were her favorite treat.

Knowing that she would enjoy the little feast more if she had company while she ate it, for Rosa was a very social beast, Miss Belinda hung up the lantern, and, sitting down on an inverted bucket, watched her as she munched contentedly.

"Now really," said Miss Belinda, when telling her story afterwards, "I am not sure whether I took a nap and dreamed what follows, or whether it actually happened, for strange things do occur at Christmas time, as every one knows.

"As I sat there the town clock struck twelve, and the sound reminded me of the legend which affirms that all dumb animals are endowed with speech for one hour after midnight on Christmas eve, in memory of the animals about the manger when the blessed Child was born.

"'I wish the pretty fancy was a fact, and our Rosa could speak, if only for an hour, because I am sure she has an interesting history, and I long to know it.'

"I said this aloud, and to my utter amazement the bay mare stopped eating, fixed her intelligent eyes upon my face, and answered in a language I understood perfectly well,—

"'You shall know it, for whether the legend is true or not I feel as if I could confide in you and tell you all I feel. I was lying awake listening to the fun in the house, thinking of my dear mistress over the sea and feeling very sad, for I heard you say I was to be sold. That nearly broke my heart, for no one has ever been so kind to me as Miss Merry, and nowhere shall I be taken care of, nursed, and loved as I have been since she bought me. I know I am getting old, and stiff in the knees, and my forefoot is lame, and sometimes I'm cross when my shoulder aches; but I do try to be a patient, grateful beast. I've got fat with good living, my work is not hard, I dearly love to carry those who have done so much for me, and I'll tug for them till I die in harness, if they will only keep me.'

"I was so astonished at this address that I tumbled off the pail, and sat among the straw staring up at Rosa, as dumb as if I had lost the power she had gained. She seemed to enjoy my surprise, and added to it by letting me hear a genuine *horse laugh*, hearty, shrill, and clear, as she shook her pretty head, and went on talking rapidly in the language which I now perceived to be a mixture of English and the peculiar dialect of the horse-country Gulliver visited.

"'Thank you for remembering me to-night, and in return for the goodies you bring I'll tell my story as fast as I can, for I have often longed to recount the trials and triumphs of my life. Miss Merry came last Christmas eve to bring me sugar, and I wanted to speak, but it was too early and I could not say a word, though my heart was full.'

"Rosa paused an instant, and her fine eyes dimmed as if with tender tears at the recollection of the happy year which had followed the day she was bought from the drudgery of a livery-stable to be a lady's pet. I stroked her neck as she stooped to sniff affectionately at my hood, and said eagerly,—

"'Tell away, dear, I'm full of interest, and understand every word you say.'

"Thus encouraged, Rosa threw up her head, and began with an air of pride which plainly proved, what we had always suspected, that she belonged to a good family.

"'My father was a famous racer, and I am very like him; the same color, spirit, and grace, and but for the cruelty of man I might have been as renowned as he. I was a very happy colt, petted by my master, tamed by love, and never struck a blow while he lived. I gained one race for him, and promised so well that when he died I brought a great price. I mourned for him, but was glad to be sent to my new owner's racing-stable and made much of, for people predicted that I should be another Goldsmith Maid or Flora Temple. Ah, how ambitious and proud I was in those days! Vain of my good blood, my speed, and my beauty; for indeed I *was* handsome then, though you may find it hard to believe now.' And Rosa sighed regretfully as she stole a look at me, and took the attitude which showed to advantage the fine lines about her head and neck.

"'I do not find it hard, for we have always said you had splendid points about you. Miss Merry saw them, though you were a skeleton, when she bought you; so did the skilful Cornish blacksmith when he shod you. And it is easy to see that you belong to a good family by the way you hold your head without a check-rein and carry your tail like a plume,' I said, with a look of admiration which comforted her as much as if she had been a *passée* belle.

"'I must hurry over this part of my story, because, though brilliant, it was very brief, and ended in a way which made it the bitterest portion of my life,' continued Rosa. 'I won several races, and great fame was predicted for me. You may guess how high my reputation was when I tell you that before my last fatal trial thousands were bet on me, and my rival trembled in his shoes. I was full of spirit, eager to show my speed and sure of success. Alas, how little I knew of the wickedness of human nature then, how dearly I bought the knowledge, and how it has changed my whole life! You do not know much about such matters, of course, and I won't digress to tell you all the tricks of the trade; only beware of jockeys and never bet.

"'I was kept carefully out of every one's way for weeks, and only taken out for exercise by my trainer. Poor Bill! I was fond of him, and he was so good to me that I never have forgotten him, though he broke his neck years ago. A few nights before the great race, as I was getting a good sleep, carefully tucked away in my roomy stall, some one stole in and gave me a warm mash. It was dark, I was half awake, and I ate it like a fool, though I knew by instinct that it was not Bill who fed it to me. I was a confiding creature then, and as all sorts of queer things had been done to prepare me I thought it was all right. But it was not, and that deceit has caused me to be suspicious about my food ever since, for the mash was dosed in some way; it made me very ill, and my enemies nearly triumphed, thanks to this cowardly trick.

"'Bill worked over me day and night, that I might be fit to run. I did my best to seem well and gay, but there was not time for me to regain my lost strength and spirit, and pride alone kept me up. "I'll win for my master if I die in doing it," I said to myself, and when the hour came pranced to my place trying to look as well as ever, though my heart was very heavy and I trembled with excitement. "Courage, my lass, and we'll beat in spite of their black tricks," whispered Bill, as he sprung to his place.

"'I lost the first heat, but won the second, and the sound of the cheering gave me strength to walk away without staggering, though my legs shook under me. What a splendid minute that was when, encouraged and refreshed by my faithful Bill, I came on the track again! I knew my enemies began to fear, for I had borne myself so bravely they fancied I was quite well, and now, excited by that first success, I was mad with impatience to be off and cover myself with glory.'

"Rosa looked as if the 'splendid minute' had come again, for she arched her neck, opened wide her red nostrils, and pawed the straw with one little foot, while her eyes shone with sudden fire, and her ears were pricked up as if to catch again the shouts she heard that day.

"'I wish I had been there to see you!' I exclaimed, quite carried away by her ardor.

"'I wish you had, for I won, I won! The big black horse did his best, but I had vowed to win or die, and I kept my word, for I beat him by a head, and then dropped as if dead. I might as well have died then, people thought, for the poison, the exertion, and the fall ruined me for a racer. My master cared no more for me, and would have had me shot if Bill had not saved my life. I was pronounced good for nothing, and he bought me cheap. I was lame and useless for a long time, but his patient care did wonders, and just as I was able to be of use to him he was killed.

"'A gentleman in want of a saddle-horse purchased me because my easy gait and quiet temper suited him; for I was meek enough now, and my size fitted me to carry his delicate daughter.

"'For more than a year I served little Miss Alice, rejoicing to see how rosy her pale cheeks became, how upright her feeble figure grew, thanks to the hours spent with me; for my canter rocked her as gently as if she were in a cradle, and fresh air was the medicine she needed. She often said she owed her life to me, and I liked to think so, for she made *my* life a very easy one.

"'But somehow my good times never lasted long, and when Miss Alice went West I was sold. I had been so well treated that I *looked* as handsome and gay as ever, though my shoulder never was strong again, and I often had despondent moods, longing for the excitement of the race-course with the instinct of my kind; so I was glad when, attracted by my spirit and beauty, a young army officer bought me and I went to the war. Ah! you never guessed that, did you? Yes, I did my part gallantly and saved my master's life more than once. You have observed how martial music delights me, but you don't know that it is because it reminds me of the proudest hour of my life. I've told you about the saddest; let me relate this also, and give me a pat for the brave action which won my master his promotion, though I got no praise for my part of the achievement.

"'In one of the hottest battles my captain was ordered to lead his men to a most perilous exploit. They hesitated, so did he; for it must cost many lives, and, brave as they were, they paused an instant. But *I* settled the point, for I was wild with the sound of drums, the smell of powder, the excitement of the hour, and, finding myself sharply reined in, I rebelled, took the bit between my teeth, and dashed straight away into the midst of the fight, spite of all my rider could do. The men thought their captain led them on, and with a cheer they followed, carrying all before them.

"'What happened just after that I never could remember, except that I got a wound here in my neck and a cut on my flank; the scar is there still, and I'm proud of it, though buyers always consider it a blemish. But when the battle was won my master was promoted on the field, and I carried him up to the general as he sat among his officers under the torn flags.

"'Both of us were weary and wounded, both were full of pride at what we had done; but *he* got all the praise and the honor, *I* only a careless word and a better supper than usual.

"'I thought no one knew what I had done, and resented the ingratitude of your race; for it was the horse, not the man, who led that forlorn hope, and I did think I should have a rosette at least, when others got stars and bars for far less dangerous deeds. Never mind, my master knew the truth, and thanked me for my help by keeping me always with him till the sad day when he was shot in a skirmish, and lay for hours with none to watch and mourn over him but his faithful horse.

"'Then I knew how much he loved and thanked me, for his hand stroked me while it had the strength, his eye turned to me till it grew too dim for seeing, and when help came, among the last words he whispered to a comrade were these, "Be kind to Rosa and send her safely home; she has earned her rest."

"'I *had* earned it, but I did not get it, for when I was sent home the old mother's heart was broken at the loss of her son, and she did not live long to cherish me. Then my hard times began, for my next owner was a fast young man, who ill used me in many ways, till the spirit of my father rose within me, and I gave my brutal master a grand runaway and smash-up.

"'To tame me down, I was sold for a car horse; and that almost killed me, for it was dreadful drudgery to tug, day after day, over the hard pavement with heavy loads behind me, uncongenial companions beside me, and no affection to cheer my life.

"'I have often longed to ask why Mr. Bergh does not try to prevent such crowds from piling into those cars; and now I beg you to do what you can to stop such an unmerciful abuse.

"'In snow-storms it was awful, and more than one of my mates dropped dead with overwork and discouragement. I used to wish I could do the same, for my poor feet, badly shod, became so lame I could hardly walk at times, and the constant strain on the up grades brought back the old trouble in my shoulder worse than ever.

"'Why they did not kill me I don't know, for I was a miserable creature then; but there must be something attractive about me, I fancy, for people always seem to think me worth saving. What can it be, ma'am?'

"'Now, Rosa, don't be affected; you know you are a very engaging little animal, and if you live to be forty will still have certain pretty ways about you, that win the hearts of women, if not of men. *They* see your weak points, and take a money view of the case; but *we* sympathize with your afflictions, are amused with your coquettish airs, and like your affectionate nature. Now hurry up and finish, for I find it a trifle cold out here.'

"I laughed as I spoke, for Rosa eyed me with a sidelong glance and gently waved the docked tail, which was her delight; for the sly thing liked to be flattered and was as fond of compliments as a girl.

"'Many thanks. I will come now to the most interesting portion of my narrative. As I was saying, instead of knocking me on the head I was packed off to New Hampshire, and had a fine rest among the green hills, with a dozen or so of weary friends. It was during this holiday that I acquired the love of nature which Miss Merry detected and liked in me, when she found me ready to study sunsets with her, to admire new landscapes, and enjoy bright summer weather.

"'In the autumn a livery-stable keeper bought me, and through the winter fed me up till I was quite presentable in the spring. It was a small town, but through the summer many city people visited there, so I was kept on the trot while the season lasted, because ladies could drive me. You, Miss Belinda, were one of the ladies, and I never shall forget, though I have long ago forgiven it, how you laughed at my queer gait the day you hired me.

"'My tender feet and stiff knees made me tread very gingerly, and amble along with short mincing steps, which contrasted oddly, I know, with my proudly waving tail and high-carried head. You liked me nevertheless, because I didn't rattle you down the steep hills, was not afraid of locomotives, and stood patiently while you gathered flowers and enjoyed the lovely prospects.

"'I have always felt a regard for you since you did not whip me, and admired my eyes, which, I may say without vanity, have always been considered unusually fine. But no one ever won my whole heart like Miss Merry, and I never shall forget the happy day when she came to the stable to order a saddle-horse. Her cheery voice made me prick up my ears, and when she said, after looking at several showy beasts, "No, they don't suit me. This one now has the right air; can I ride her?" my heart danced within me and I looked round with a whinny of delight. She understood my welcome, and came right up to me, patted me, peered into my face, rubbed my nose, and looked at my feet with an air of interest and sympathy, that made me feel as if I'd like to carry her round the world.

"'Ah, what rides we had after that! What happy hours trotting gayly through the green woods, galloping over the breezy hills, or pacing slowly along quiet lanes, where I often lunched luxuriously on clover-tops, while Miss Merry took a sketch of some picturesque bit with me in the foreground.

"'I liked that, and we had long chats at such times, for she seemed to understand me perfectly. She was never frightened when I danced for pleasure on the soft turf, never chid me when I snatched a bite from the young trees as we passed through sylvan ways, never thought it a trouble to let me wet my tired feet in babbling brooks, or to dismount and take out the stones that plagued me.

"'Then how well she rode! So firm yet light a seat, so steady a hand, so agile a foot to spring on and off, and such infectious spirits, that no matter how despondent or cross I might be, in five minutes I felt gay and young again when dear Miss Merry was on my back.'

"Here Rosa gave a frisk that sent the straw flying, and made me shrink into a corner, while she pranced about the box with a neigh which waked the big brown colt next door, and set poor Buttercup to lowing for her calf, the loss of which she had forgotten for a little while in sleep.

"'Ah, Miss Merry never ran away from me! She knew my heels were to be trusted, and she let me caper as I would, glad to see me lively. Never mind, Miss Belinda, come out and I'll be sober, as befits my years,' laughed Rosa, composing herself, and adding, so like a woman that I could not help smiling in the dark,—

"'When I say "years" I beg you to understand that I am *not* as old as that base man declared, but just in the prime of life for a horse. Hard usage has made me seem old before my time, and I am good for years of service yet.'

"'Few people have been through as much as you have, Rosa, and you certainly *have* earned the right to rest,' I said consolingly, for her little whims and vanities amused me much.

"'You know what happened next,' she continued; 'but I must seize this opportunity to express my thanks for all the kindness I've received since Miss Merry bought me, in spite of the ridicule and dissuasion of all her friends.

"'I know I didn't look like a good bargain, for I *was* very thin and lame and shabby; but she saw and loved the willing spirit in me, pitied my hard lot, and felt that it would be a good deed to buy me even if she never got much work out of me.

"'I shall always remember that, and whatever happens to me hereafter, I never shall be as proud again as I was the day she put my new saddle and bridle on, and I was led out, sleek, plump, and handsome, with blue rosettes at my ears, my tail cut in the English style, and on my back Miss Merry in her London hat and habit, all ready to head a cavalcade of eighteen horsemen and horsewomen. *We* were the most perfect pair of all, and when the troop caracoled down the wide street six abreast, *my* head was the highest, *my* rider the straightest, and *our* two hearts the friendliest in all the goodly company.

"'Nor is it pride and love alone that binds me to her, it is gratitude as well, for did not she often bathe my feet herself, rub me down, water me, blanket me, and daily come to see me when I was here alone for weeks in the winter time? Didn't she study horses' feet and shoes, that I might be cured if possible? Didn't she write to the famous friend of my race for advice, and drive me seven miles to get a good smith to shoe me well? Have not my poor contracted feet grown much better, thanks to the weeks of rest without shoes which she gave me? Am I not fat and handsome, and, barring the stiff knees, a very presentable horse? If I am, it is all owing to her; and for that reason I want to live and die in her service.

"'*She* doesn't want to sell me, and only bade you do it because you didn't want the care of me while she is gone. Dear Miss Belinda, please keep me! I'll eat as little as I can. I won't ask for a new blanket, though your old army one is very thin and shabby. I'll trot for you all winter, and try not to show it if I am lame. I'll do anything a horse can, no matter how humble, to earn my living, only don't, pray don't send me away among strangers who have neither interest nor pity for me!'

"Rosa had spoken rapidly, feeling that her plea must be made now or never, for before another Christmas she might be far away and speech of no use to win her wish. I was much touched, though she was only a horse; for she was looking earnestly at me as she spoke, and made the last words very eloquent by preparing to bend her stiff knees and lie down at my feet. I stopped her, and answered, with an arm about her neck and her soft nose in my hand,—

"'You shall *not* be sold, Rosa! you shall go and board at Mr. Town's great stable, where you will have pleasant society among the eighty horses who usually pass the winter there. Your shoes shall be taken off, and you shall rest till March at least. The best care will be taken of you, dear, and I will come and see you; and in the spring you shall return to us, even if Miss Merry is not here to welcome you.'

"'Thanks, many, many thanks! But I wish I could do something to earn my board. I hate to be idle, though rest *is* delicious. Is there nothing I can do to repay you, Miss Belinda? Please answer quickly, for I know the hour is almost over,' cried Rosa, stamping with anxiety; for, like all her sex, she wanted the last word.

"'Yes, you can,' I cried, as a sudden idea popped into my head. 'I'll write down what you have told me, and send the little story to a certain paper I know of, and the money I get for it will pay your board. So rest in peace, my dear; you *will* have earned your living, and may feel that your debt is paid.'

"Before she could reply the clock struck one, and a long sigh of satisfaction was all the response in her power. But we understood each other now, and, cutting a lock from her mane for Miss Merry, I gave Rosa a farewell caress and went away, wondering if I had made it all up, or if she had really broken a year's silence and freed her mind.

"However that may be, here is the tale, and the sequel to it is, that the bay mare has really gone to board at a first-class stable," concluded Miss Belinda. "I call occasionally and leave my card in the shape of an apple, finding Madam Rosa living like an independent lady, with her large box and private yard on the sunny side of the barn, a kind ostler to wait upon her, and much genteel society from the city when she is inclined for company.

"What more could any reasonable horse desire?"

A CHRISTMAS TURKEY AND HOW IT CAME

1889

"I KNOW WE COULDN'T DO IT."

"I say we could, if we all helped."

"How can we?"

"I've planned lots of ways; only you mustn't laugh at them, and you must n't say a word to mother. I want it to be all a surprise."

"She 'll find us out."

"No, she won't, if we tell her we won't get into mischief."

"Fire away, then, and let's hear your fine plans."

"We must talk softly, or we shall wake father. He's got a headache."

A curious change came over the faces of the two boys as their sister lowered her voice, with a nod toward a half-opened door. They looked sad and ashamed, and Kitty sighed as she spoke, for all knew that father's headaches always began by his coming home stupid or cross, with only a part of his wages; and mother always cried when she thought they did not see her, and after the long sleep father looked as if he did n't like to meet their eyes, but went off early.

They knew what it meant, but never spoke of it,--only pondered over it, and mourned with mother at the change which was slowly altering their kind industrious father into a moody man, and mother into an anxious over-worked woman.

Kitty was thirteen, and a very capable girl, who helped with the housekeeping, took care of the two little ones, and went to school. Tommy and Sammy looked up to her and thought her a remarkably good sister. Now, as they sat round the stove having "a go-to-bed warm," the three heads were close together; and the boys listened eagerly to Kitty's plans, while the rattle of the sewing-machine in another room went on as tirelessly as it had done all day, for mother's work was more and more needed every month.

"Well!" began Kitty, in an impressive tone, "we all know that there won't be a bit of Christmas in this family if we don't make it. Mother's too busy, and father don't care, so we must see what we can do; for I should be mortified to death to go to school and say I had n't had any turkey or plum-pudding. Don't expect presents; but we *must* have some kind of a decent dinner."

"So I say; I'm tired of fish and potatoes," said Sammy, the younger.

"But where's the dinner coming from?" asked Tommy, who had already taken some of the cares of life on his young shoulders, and knew that Christmas dinners did not walk into people's houses without money.

"We 'll earn it;" and Kitty looked like a small Napoleon planning the passage of the Alps. "You, Tom, must go early to-morrow to Mr. Brisket and offer to carry baskets. He will be dreadfully busy, and want you, I know; and you are so strong you can lug as much as some of the big fellows. He pays well, and if he won't give much money, you can take your wages in things to eat. We want everything."

"What shall I do?" cried Sammy, while Tom sat turning this plan over in his mind.

"Take the old shovel and clear sidewalks. The snow came on purpose to help you."

"It's awful hard work, and the shovel's half gone," began Sammy, who preferred to spend his holiday coasting on an old tea-tray.

"Don't growl, or you won't get any dinner," said Tom, making up his mind to lug baskets for the good of the family, like a manly lad as he was.

"I," continued Kitty, "have taken the hardest part of all; for after my work is done, and the babies safely settled, I 'm going to beg for the leavings of the holly and pine swept out of the church down below, and make some wreaths and sell them."

"If you can," put in Tommy, who had tried pencils, and failed to make a fortune.

"Not in the street?" cried Sam, looking alarmed.

"Yes, at the corner of the Park. I 'm bound to make some money, and don't see any other way. I shall put on an old hood and shawl, and no one will know me. Don't care if they do." And Kitty tried to mean what she said, but in her heart she felt that it would be a trial to her pride if any of her schoolmates should happen to recognize her.

"Don't believe you 'll do it."

"See if I don't; for I *will* have a good dinner one day in the year."

"Well, it does n't seem right for us to do it. Father ought to take care of us, and we only buy some presents with the little bit we earn. He never gives us anything now." And Tommy scowled at the bedroom door, with a strong sense of injury struggling with affection in his boyish heart.

"Hush!" cried Kitty. "Don't blame him. Mother says we never must forget he's our father. I try not to; but when she cries, it's hard to feel as I ought." And a sob made the little girl stop short as she poked the fire to hide the trouble in the face that should have been all smiles.

For a moment the room was very still, as the snow beat on the window, and the fire-light flickered over the six shabby little boots put up on the stove hearth to dry.

Tommy's cheerful voice broke the silence, saying stoutly, "Well, if I 've got to work all day, I guess I 'll go to bed early. Don't fret, Kit. We 'll help all we can, and have a good time; see if we don't."

"I 'll go out real early, and shovel like fury. Maybe I 'll get a dollar. Would that buy a turkey?" asked Sammy, with the air of a millionnaire.

"No, dear; one big enough for us would cost two, I 'm afraid. Perhaps we 'll have one sent us. We belong to the church, though folks don't know how poor we are now, and we can't beg." And Kitty bustled about, clearing up, rather exercised in her mind about going and asking for the much-desired fowl.

Soon all three were fast asleep, and nothing but the whir of the machine broke the quiet that fell upon the house. Then from the inner room a man came and sat over the fire with his head in his hands and his eyes fixed on the ragged little boots left to dry. He had heard the children's talk; and his heart was very heavy as he looked about the shabby room that used to be so neat and pleasant. What he thought no one knows, what he did we shall see by-and-by; but the sorrow and shame and tender silence of his children worked a miracle that night more lasting and lovely than the white beauty which the snow wrought upon the sleeping city.

Bright and early the boys were away to their work; while Kitty sang as she dressed the little sisters, put the house in order, and made her mother smile at the mysterious hints she gave of something splendid which was going to happen. Father was gone, and though all rather dreaded evening, nothing was said; but each worked with a will, feeling that Christmas should be merry in spite of poverty and care.

All day Tommy lugged fat turkeys, roasts of beef, and every sort of vegetable for other people's good dinners on the morrow, wondering meanwhile where his own was coming from. Mr. Brisket had an army of boys trudging here and there, and was too busy to notice any particular lad till the hurry was over, and only a few belated buyers remained to be served. It was late; but the stores kept open, and though so tired he could hardly stand, brave Tommy held on when the other boys left, hoping to earn a trifle more by extra work. He sat down on a barrel to rest during a leisure moment, and presently his weary head nodded sideways into a basket of cranberries, where he slept quietly till the sound of gruff voices roused him.

It was Mr. Brisket scolding because one dinner had been forgotten.

"I told that rascal Beals to be sure and carry it, for the old gentleman will be in a rage if it does n't come, and take away his custom. Every boy gone, and I can't leave the store, nor you either, Pat, with all the clearing up to do."

"Here's a by, sir, slapin illigant forninst the cranberries, bad luck to him!" answered Pat, with a shake that set poor Tom on his legs, wide awake at once.

"*Good* luck to him, you mean. Here, What's-your-name, you take this basket to that number, and I 'll make it worth your while," said Mr. Brisket, much relieved by this unexpected help.

"All right, sir;" and Tommy trudged off as briskly as his tired legs would let him, cheering the long cold walk with visions of the turkey with which his employer might reward him, for there were piles of them, and Pat was to have one for his family.

His brilliant dreams were disappointed, however, for Mr. Brisket naturally supposed Tom's father would attend to that part of the dinner, and generously heaped a basket with vegetables, rosy apples, and a quart of cranberries.

"There, if you ain't too tired, you can take one more load to that number, and a merry Christmas to you!" said the stout man, handing over his gift with the promised dollar.

"Thank you, sir; good-night," answered Tom, shouldering his last load with a grateful smile, and trying not to look longingly at the poultry; for he had set his heart on at least a skinny bird as a surprise to Kit.

Sammy's adventures that day had been more varied and his efforts more successful, as we shall see, in the end, for Sammy was a most engaging little fellow, and no one could look into his blue eyes without wanting to pat his curly yellow head with one hand while the other gave him something. The cares of life had not lessened his confidence in people; and only the most abandoned ruffians had the heart to deceive or disappoint him. His very tribulations usually led to something pleasant, and whatever happened, sunshiny Sam came right side up, lucky and laughing.

Undaunted by the drifts or the cold wind, he marched off with the remains of the old shovel to seek his fortune, and found it at the third house where he called. The first two sidewalks were easy jobs; and he pocketed his ninepences with a growing conviction that this was his chosen work. The third sidewalk was a fine long one, for the house stood on the corner, and two pavements must be cleared.

"It ought to be fifty cents; but perhaps they won't give me so much, I'm such a young one. I'll show 'em I can work, though, like a man;" and Sammy rang the bell with the energy of a telegraph boy.

Before the bell could be answered, a big boy rushed up, exclaiming roughly, "Get out of this! I'm going to have the job. You can't do it. Start, now, or I'll chuck you into a snow-bank."

"I won't!" answered Sammy, indignant at the brutal tone and unjust claim. "I got here first, and it's my job. You let me alone. I ain't afraid of you or your snow-banks either."

The big boy wasted no time in words, for steps were heard inside, but after a brief scuffle hauled Sammy, fighting bravely all the way, down the steps, and tumbled him into a deep drift. Then he ran up the steps, and respectfully asked for the job when a neat maid opened the door. He would have got it if Sam had not roared out, as he floundered in the drift, "I came first. He knocked me down 'cause I'm the smallest. Please let me do it; please!"

Before another word could be said, a little old lady appeared in the hall, trying to look stern, and failing entirely, because she was the picture of a dear fat, cosey grandma.

"Send that *bad* big boy away, Maria, and call in the poor little fellow. I saw the whole thing, and *he* shall have the job if he can do it."

The bully slunk away, and Sammy came panting up the steps, white with snow, a great bruise on his forehead, and a beaming smile on his face, looking so like a jolly little Santa Claus who had taken a "header" out of his sleigh that the maid laughed, and the old lady exclaimed, "Bless the boy! he's dreadfully hurt, and does n't know it. Come in and be brushed and get your breath, child, and tell me how that scamp came to treat you so."

Nothing loath to be comforted, Sammy told his little tale while Maria dusted him off on the mat, and the old lady hovered in the doorway of the dining-room, where a nice breakfast smoked and smelled so deliciously that the boy sniffed the odor of coffee and buckwheats like a hungry hound.

"He 'll get his death if he goes to work till he's dried a bit. Put him over the register, Maria, and I 'll give him a hot drink, for it's bitter cold, poor dear!"

Away trotted the kind old lady, and in a minute came back with coffee and cakes, on which Sammy feasted as he warmed his toes and told Kitty's plans for Christmas, led on by the old lady's questions, and quite unconscious that he was letting all sorts of cats out of the bag.

Mrs. Bryant understood the little story, and made her plans also, for the rosy-faced boy was very like a little grandson who died last year, and her sad old heart was very tender to all other small boys. So she found out where Sammy lived, and nodded and smiled at him most cheerily as he tugged stoutly away at the snow on the long pavements till all was done, and the little workman came for his wages.

A bright silver dollar and a pocketful of gingerbread sent him off a rich and happy boy to shovel and sweep till noon, when he proudly showed his earnings at home, and feasted the babies on the carefully hoarded cake, for Dilly and Dot were the idols of the household.

"Now, Sammy dear, I want you to take my place here this afternoon, for mother will have to take her work home by-and-by, and I must sell my wreaths. I only got enough green for six, and two bunches of holly; but if I can sell them for ten or twelve cents apiece, I shall be glad. Girls never *can* earn as much money as boys somehow," sighed Kitty, surveying the thin wreaths tied up with carpet ravellings, and vainly puzzling her young wits over a sad problem.

"I 'll give you some of my money if you don't get a dollar; then we'll be even. Men always take care of women, you know, and ought to," cried Sammy, setting a fine example to his father, if he had only been there to profit by it.

With thanks Kitty left him to rest on the old sofa, while the happy babies swarmed over him; and putting on the shabby hood and shawl, she slipped away to stand at the Park gate, modestly offering her little wares to the passers-by. A nice old gentleman bought two, and his wife scolded him for getting such bad ones; but the money gave more happiness than any other he spent that day. A child took a ten-cent bunch of holly with its red berries, and there Kitty's market ended. It was very cold, people were in a hurry, bolder hucksters pressed before the timid little girl, and the balloon man told her to "clear out."

Hoping for better luck, she tried several other places; but the short afternoon was soon over, the streets began to thin, the keen wind chilled her to the bone, and her heart was very heavy to think that in all the rich, merry city, where Christmas gifts passed her in every hand, there were none for the dear babies and boys at home, and the Christmas dinner was a failure.

"I must go and get supper anyway; and I'll hang these up in our own rooms, as I can't sell them," said Kitty, wiping a very big tear from her cold cheek, and turning to go away.

A smaller, shabbier girl than herself stood near, looking at the bunch of holly with wistful eyes; and glad to do to others as she wished some one would do to her, Kitty offered the only thing she had to give, saying kindly, "You may have it; merry Christmas!" and ran away before the delighted child could thank her.

I am very sure that one of the spirits who fly about at this season of the year saw the little act, made a note of it, and in about fifteen minutes rewarded Kitty for her sweet remembrance of the golden rule.

As she went sadly homeward she looked up at some of the big houses where every window shone with the festivities of Christmas Eve, and more than one tear fell, for the little girl found life pretty hard just then.

"There don't seem to be any wreaths at these windows; perhaps they'd buy mine. I can't bear to go home with so little for my share," she said, stopping before one of the biggest and brightest of these fairy palaces, where the sound of music was heard, and many little heads peeped from behind the curtains as if watching for some one.

Kitty was just going up the steps to make another trial, when two small boys came racing round the corner, slipped on the icy pavement, and both went down with a crash that would have broken older bones. One was up in a minute, laughing; the other lay squirming and howling, "Oh, my knee! my knee!" till Kitty ran and picked him up with the motherly consolations she had learned to give.

"It's broken; I know it is," wailed the small sufferer as Kitty carried him up the steps, while his friend wildly rang the doorbell.

It was like going into fairy-land, for the house was all astir with a children's Christmas party. Servants flew about with smiling faces; open doors gave ravishing glimpses of a feast in one room and a splendid tree in another; while a crowd of little faces peered over the balusters in the hall above, eager to come down and enjoy the glories prepared for them.

A pretty young girl came to meet Kitty, and listened to her story of the accident, which proved to be less severe than it at first appeared; for Bertie, the injured party, forgot his anguish at sight of the tree, and hopped upstairs so nimbly that every one laughed.

"He said his leg was broken, but I guess he's all right," said Kitty, reluctantly turning from this happy scene to go out into the night again.

"Would you like to see our tree before the children come down?" asked the pretty girl, seeing the wistful look in the child's eyes, and the shine of half-dried tears on her cheek.

"Oh, yes; I never saw anything so lovely. I 'd like to tell the babies all about it;" and Kitty's face beamed at the prospect, as if the kind words had melted all the frost away.

"How many babies are there?" asked the pretty girl, as she led the way into the brilliant room. Kitty told her, adding several other facts, for the friendly atmosphere seemed to make them friends at once.

"I will buy the wreaths, for we have n't any," said the girl in silk, as Kitty told how she was just coming to offer them when the boys fell.

It was pretty to see how carefully the little hostess laid away the shabby garlands and slipped a half-dollar into Kitty's hand; prettier still, to watch the sly way in which she tucked some bonbons, a red ball, a blue whip, two china dolls, two pairs of little mittens, and some gilded nuts into an empty box for "the babies;" and prettiest of all, to see the smiles and tears make April in Kitty's face as she tried to tell her thanks for this beautiful surprise.

The world was all right when she got into the street again and ran home with the precious box hugged close, feeling that at last she had something to make a merry Christmas of.

Shrieks of joy greeted her, for Sammy's nice old lady had sent a basket full of pies, nuts and raisins, oranges and cake, and--oh, happy Sammy!--a sled, all for love of the blue eyes that twinkled so merrily when he told her about the tea-tray. Piled upon this red car of triumph, Dilly and Dot were being dragged about, while the other treasures were set forth on the table.

"I must show mine," cried Kitty; "we 'll look at them to-night, and have them to-morrow;" and amid more cries of rapture *her* box was unpacked, *her* money added to the pile in the middle of the table, where Sammy had laid his handsome contribution toward the turkey.

Before the story of the splendid tree was over, in came Tommy with his substantial offering and his hard-earned dollar.

"I 'm afraid I ought to keep my money for shoes. I 've walked the soles off these to-day, and can't go to school barefooted," he said, bravely trying to put the temptation of skates behind him.

"We 've got a good dinner without a turkey, and perhaps we 'd better not get it," added Kitty, with a sigh, as she surveyed the table, and remembered the blue knit hood marked seventy-five cents that she saw in a shop-window.

"Oh, we *must* have a turkey! we worked so hard for it, and it's so Christmasy," cried Sam, who always felt that pleasant things ought to happen.

"Must have turty," echoed the babies, as they eyed the dolls tenderly.

"You *shall* have a turkey, and there he is," said an unexpected voice, as a noble bird fell upon the table, and lay there kicking up his legs as if enjoying the surprise immensely.

It was father's voice, and there stood father, neither cross nor stupid, but looking as he used to look, kind and happy, and beside him was mother, smiling as they had not seen her smile for months. It was not because the work was well paid for, and more promised, but because she had received a gift that made the world bright, a home happy again,--father's promise to drink no more.

"I 've been working to-day as well as you, and you may keep your money for yourselves. There are shoes for all; and never again, please God, shall my children be ashamed of me, or want a dinner Christmas Day."

As father said this with a choke in his voice, and mother's head went down on his shoulder to hide the happy tears that wet her cheeks, the children did n't know whether to laugh or cry, till Kitty, with the instinct of a loving heart, settled the question by saying, as she held out her hands, "We have n't any tree, so let's dance around our goodies and be merry."

Then the tired feet in the old shoes forgot their weariness, and five happy little souls skipped gayly round the table, where, in the midst of all the treasures earned and given, father's Christmas turkey proudly lay in state.

THE ABBOT'S GHOST: A CHRISTMAS STORY

1867

CHAPTER I.

DRAMATIS PERSONAE

"How goes it, Frank? Down first, as usual."

"The early bird gets the worm, Major."

"Deuced ungallant speech, considering that the lovely Octavia is the worm," and with a significant laugh the major assumed an Englishman's favorite attitude before the fire.

His companion shot a quick glance at him, and an expression of anxiety passed over his face as he replied, with a well-feigned air of indifference, "You are altogether too sharp, Major. I must be on my guard while you are in the house. Any new arrivals? I thought I heard a carriage drive up not long ago."

"It was General Snowdon and his charming wife. Maurice Treherne came while we were out, and I've not seen him yet, poor fellow!"

"Aye, you may well say that; his is a hard case, if what I heard is true. I'm not booked up in the matter, and I should be, lest I make some blunder here, so tell me how things stand, Major. We've a good half hour before dinner. Sir Jasper is never punctual."

"Yes, you've a right to know, if you are going to try your fortune with Octavia."

The major marched through the three drawing rooms to see that no inquisitive servant was eavesdropping, and, finding all deserted, he resumed his place, while young Annon lounged on a couch as he listened with intense interest to the major's story.

"You know it was supposed that old Sir Jasper, being a bachelor, would leave his fortune to his two nephews. But he was an oddity, and as the title *must* go to young Jasper by right, the old man said Maurice should have the money. He was poor, young Jasper rich, and it seemed but just, though Madame Mère was very angry when she learned how the will was made."

"But Maurice didn't get the fortune. How was that?"

"There was some mystery there which I shall discover in time. All went smoothly till that unlucky yachting trip, when the cousins were wrecked. Maurice saved Jasper's life, and almost lost his own in so doing. I fancy he wishes he had, rather than remain the poor cripple he is. Exposure, exertion, and neglect afterward brought on paralysis of the lower limbs, and there he is—a fine, talented, spirited fellow tied to that cursed chair like a decrepit old man."

"How does he bear it?" asked Annon, as the major shook his gray head, with a traitorous huskiness in his last words.

"Like a philosopher or a hero. He is too proud to show his despair at such a sudden end to all his hopes, too generous to complain, for Jasper is desperately cut up about it, and too brave to be daunted by a misfortune which would drive many a man mad."

"Is it true that Sir Jasper, knowing all this, made a new will and left every cent to his namesake?"

"Yes, and there lies the mystery. Not only did he leave it away from poor Maurice, but so tied it up that Jasper cannot transfer it, and at his death it goes to Octavia."

"The old man must have been demented. What in heaven's name did he mean by leaving Maurice helpless and penniless after all his devotion to Jasper? Had he done anything to offend the old party?"

"No one knows; Maurice hasn't the least idea of the cause of this sudden whim, and the old man would give no reason for it. He died soon after, and the instant Jasper came to the title and estate he brought his cousin home, and treats him like a brother. Jasper is a noble fellow, with all his faults, and this act of justice increases my respect for him," said the major heartily.

"What will Maurice do, now that he can't enter the army as he intended?" asked Annon, who now sat erect, so full of interest was he.

"Marry Octavia, and come to his own, I hope."

"An excellent little arrangement, but Miss Treherne may object," said Annon, rising with sudden kindling of the eye.

"I think not, if no one interferes. Pity, with women, is akin to love, and she pities her cousin in the tenderest fashion. No sister could be more devoted, and as Maurice is a handsome, talented fellow, one can easily foresee the end, if, as I said before, no one interferes to disappoint the poor lad again."

"You espouse his cause, I see, and tell me this that I may stand aside. Thanks for the warning, Major; but as Maurice Treherne is a man of unusual power in many ways, I think we are equally matched, in spite of his misfortune. Nay, if anything, he has the advantage of me, for Miss Treherne pities him, and that is a strong ally for my rival.

I'll be as generous as I can, but I'll *not* stand aside and relinquish the woman I love without a trial first."

With an air of determination Annon faced the major, whose keen eyes had read the truth which he had but newly confessed to himself. Major Royston smiled as he listened, and said briefly, as steps approached, "Do your best. Maurice will win."

"We shall see," returned Annon between his teeth.

Here their host entered, and the subject of course was dropped. But the major's words rankled in the young man's mind, and would have been doubly bitter had he known that their confidential conversation had been overheard. On either side of the great fireplace was a door leading to a suite of rooms which had been old Sir Jasper's. These apartments had been given to Maurice Treherne, and he had just returned from London, whither he had been to consult a certain famous physician. Entering quietly, he had taken possession of his rooms, and having rested and dressed for dinner, rolled himself into the library, to which led the curtained door on the right. Sitting idly in his light, wheeled chair, ready to enter when his cousin appeared, he had heard the chat of Annon and the major. As he listened, over his usually impassive face passed varying expressions of anger, pain, bitterness, and defiance, and when the young man uttered his almost fierce "We shall see," Treherne smiled a scornful smile and clenched his pale hand with a gesture which proved that a year of suffering had not conquered the man's spirit, though it had crippled his strong body.

A singular face was Maurice Treherne's; well-cut and somewhat haughty features; a fine brow under the dark locks that carelessly streaked it; and remarkably piercing eyes. Slight in figure and wasted by pain, he still retained the grace as native to him as the stern fortitude which enabled him to hide the deep despair of an ambitious nature from every eye, and bear his affliction with a cheerful philosophy more pathetic than the most entire abandonment to grief. Carefully dressed, and with no hint at invalidism but the chair, he bore himself as easily and calmly as if the doom of lifelong helplessness did not hang over him. A single motion of the hand sent him rolling noiselessly to the curtained door, but as he did so, a voice exclaimed behind him, "Wait for me, cousin." And as he turned, a young girl approached, smiling a glad welcome as she took his hand, adding in a tone of soft reproach, "Home again, and not let me know it, till I heard the good news by accident."

"Was it good news, Octavia?" and Maurice looked up at the frank face with a new expression in those penetrating eyes of his. His cousin's open glance never changed as she stroked the hair off his forehead with the caress one often gives a child, and answered eagerly, "The best to me; the house is dull when you are away, for Jasper always becomes absorbed in horses and hounds, and leaves Mamma and me to mope by ourselves. But tell me, Maurice, what they said to you, since you would not write."

"A little hope, with time and patience. Help me to wait, dear, help me to wait."

His tone was infinitely sad, and as he spoke, he leaned his cheek against the kind hand he held, as if to find support and comfort there. The girl's face brightened beautifully, though her eyes filled, for to her alone did he betray his pain, and in her alone did he seek consolation.

"I will, I will with heart and hand! Thank heaven for the hope, and trust me it shall be fulfilled. You look very tired, Maurice. Why go in to dinner with all those people? Let me make you cozy here," she added anxiously.

"Thanks, I'd rather go in, it does me good; and if I stay away, Jasper feels that he must stay with me. I dressed in haste, am I right, little nurse?"

She gave him a comprehensive glance, daintily settled his cravat, brushed back a truant lock, and, with a maternal air that was charming, said, "My boy is always elegant, and I'm proud of him. Now we'll go in." But with her hand on the curtain she paused, saying quickly, as a voice reached her, "Who is that?"

"Frank Annon. Didn't you know he was coming?" Maurice eyed her keenly.

"No, Jasper never told me. Why did he ask him?"

"To please you."

"Me! When he knows I detest the man. No matter, I've got on the color he hates, so he won't annoy me, and Mrs. Snowdon can amuse herself with him. The general has come, you know?"

Treherne smiled, well pleased, for no sign of maiden shame or pleasure did the girl's face betray, and as he watched her while she peeped, he thought with satisfaction, Annon is right, *I* have the advantage, and I'll keep it at all costs.

"Here is Mamma. We must go in," said Octavia, as a stately old lady made her appearance in the drawing room.

The cousins entered together and Annon watched them covertly, while seemingly intent on paying his respects to Madame Mère, as his hostess was called by her family.

"Handsomer than ever," he muttered, as his eye rested on the blooming girl, looking more like a rose than ever in the peach-colored silk which he had once condemned because a rival admired it. She turned to reply to the major, and Annon glanced at Treherne with an irrepressible frown, for sickness had not marred the charm of that peculiar face, so colorless and thin that it seemed cut in marble; but the keen eyes shone with a wonderful brilliancy, and the whole countenance was alive with a power of intellect and will which made the observer involuntarily exclaim, "That man must suffer a daily martyrdom, so crippled and confined; if it last long he will go mad or die."

"General and Mrs. Snowden," announced the servant, and a sudden pause ensued as everyone looked up to greet the newcomers.

A feeble, white-haired old man entered, leaning on the arm of an indescribably beautiful woman. Not thirty yet, tall and nobly molded, with straight black brows over magnificent eyes; rippling dark hair gathered up in a great knot, and ornamented with a single band of gold. A sweeping dress of wine-colored velvet, set off with a dazzling neck and arms decorated like her stately head with ornaments of Roman gold. At the first glance she seemed a cold, haughty creature, born to dazzle but not to win. A deeper scrutiny detected lines of suffering in that lovely face, and behind the veil of reserve, which pride forced her to wear, appeared the anguish of a strong-willed woman burdened by a heavy cross. No one would dare express pity or offer sympathy, for her whole air repelled it, and in her gloomy eyes sat scorn of herself mingled with defiance of the scorn of others. A strange, almost tragical-looking woman, in spite of beauty, grace, and the cold sweetness of her manner. A faint smile parted her lips as she greeted those about her, and as her husband seated himself beside Lady Treherne, she lifted her head with a long breath, and a singular expression of relief, as if a burden was removed, and for the time being she was free. Sir Jasper was at her side, and as she listened, her eye glanced from face to face.

"Who is with you now?" she asked, in a low, mellow voice that was full of music.

"My sister and my cousin are yonder. You may remember Tavia as a child, she is little more now. Maurice is an invalid, but the finest fellow breathing."

"I understand," and Mrs. Snowdon's eyes softened with a sudden glance of pity for one cousin and admiration for the other, for she knew the facts.

"Major Royston, my father's friend, and Frank Annon, my own. Do you know him?" asked Sir Jasper.

"No."

"Then allow me to make him happy by presenting him, may I?"

"Not now. I'd rather see your cousin."

"Thanks, you are very kind. I'll bring him over."

"Stay, let me go to him," began the lady, with more feeling in face and voice than one would believe her capable of showing.

"Pardon, it will offend him, he will not be pitied, or relinquish any of the duties or privileges of a gentleman which he can possibly perform. He is proud, we can understand the feeling, so let us humor the poor fellow."

Mrs. Snowdon bowed silently, and Sir Jasper called out in his hearty, blunt way, as if nothing was amiss with his cousin, "Maurice, I've an honor for you. Come and receive it."

Divining what it was, Treherne noiselessly crossed the room, and with no sign of self-consciousness or embarrassment, was presented to the handsome woman. Thinking his presence might be a restraint, Sir Jasper went away. The instant his back was turned, a change came over both: an almost grim expression replaced the suavity of Treherne's face, and Mrs. Snowdon's smile faded suddenly, while a deep flush rose to her brow, as her eyes questioned his beseechingly.

"How dared you come?" he asked below his breath.

"The general insisted."

"And you could not change his purpose; poor woman!"

"You will not be pitied, neither will I," and her eyes flashed; then the fire was quenched in tears, and her voice lost all its pride in a pleading tone.

"Forgive me, I longed to see you since your illness, and so I 'dared' to come."

"You shall be gratified; look, quite helpless, crippled for life, perhaps."

The chair was turned from the groups about the fire, and as he spoke, with a bitter laugh Treherne threw back the skin which covered his knees, and showed her the useless limbs once so strong and fleet. She shrank and paled, put out her hand to arrest him, and cried in an indignant whisper, "No, no, not that! You know I never meant such cruel curiosity, such useless pain to both—"

"Be still, someone is coming," he returned inaudibly; adding aloud, as he adjusted the skin and smoothed the rich fur as if speaking of it,

"Yes, it is a very fine one, Jasper gave it to me. He spoils me, like a dear, generous-hearted fellow as he is. Ah, Octavia, what can I do for you?"

"Nothing, thank you. I want to recall myself to Mrs. Snowdon's memory, if she will let me."

"No need of that; I never forget happy faces and pretty pictures. Two years ago I saw you at your first ball, and longed to be a girl again."

As she spoke, Mrs. Snowdon pressed the hand shyly offered, and smiled at the spirited face before her, though the shadow in her own eyes deepened as she met the bright glance of the girl.

"How kind you were that night! I remember you let me chatter away about my family, my cousin, and my foolish little affairs with the sweetest patience, and made me very happy by your interest. I was homesick, and Aunt could never bear to hear of those things. It was before your marriage, and all the kinder, for you were the queen of the night, yet had a word for poor little me."

Mrs. Snowdon was pale to the lips, and Maurice impatiently tapped the arm of his chair, while the girl innocently chatted on.

"I am sorry the general is such an invalid; yet I dare say you find great happiness in taking care of him. It is so pleasant to be of use to those we love." And as she spoke, Octavia leaned over her cousin to hand him the glove he had dropped.

The affectionate smile that accompanied the act made the color deepen again in Mrs. Snowdon's cheek, and lit a spark in her softened eyes. Her lips curled and her voice was sweetly sarcastic as she answered, "Yes, it is charming to devote one's life to these dear invalids, and find one's reward in their gratitude. Youth, beauty, health, and happiness are small sacrifices if one wins a little comfort for the poor sufferers."

The girl felt the sarcasm under the soft words and drew back with a troubled face.

Maurice smiled, and glanced from one to the other, saying significantly, "Well for me that my little nurse loves her labor, and finds no sacrifice in it. I am fortunate in my choice."

"I trust it may prove so—" Mrs. Snowdon got no further, for at that moment dinner was announced, and Sir Jasper took her away. Annon approached with him and offered his arm to Miss Treherne, but with an air of surprise, and a little gesture of refusal, she said coldly:

"My cousin always takes me in to dinner. Be good enough to escort the major." And with her hand on the arm of the chair, she walked away with a mischievous glitter in her eyes.

Annon frowned and fell back, saying sharply, "Come, Major, what are you doing there?"

"Making discoveries."

CHAPTER II.

BYPLAY

A right splendid old dowager was Lady Treherne, in her black velvet and point lace, as she sat erect and stately on a couch by the drawing-room fire, a couch which no one dare occupy in her absence, or share uninvited. The gentlemen were still over their wine, and the three ladies were alone. My lady never dozed in public, Mrs. Snowdon never gossiped, and Octavia never troubled herself to entertain any guests but those of her own age, so long pauses fell, and conversation languished, till Mrs. Snowdon roamed away into the library. As she disappeared, Lady Treherne beckoned to her daughter, who was idly making chords at the grand piano. Seating herself on the ottoman at her mother's feet, the girl took the still handsome hand in her own and amused herself with examining the old-fashioned jewels that covered it, a pretext for occupying her telltale eyes, as she suspected what was coming.

"My dear, I'm not pleased with you, and I tell you so at once, that you may amend your fault," began Madame Mère in a tender tone, for though a haughty, imperious woman, she idolized her children.

"What have I done, Mamma?" asked the girl.

"Say rather, what have you left undone. You have been very rude to Mr. Annon. It must not occur again; not only because he is a guest, but because he is your—brother's friend."

My lady hesitated over the word "lover," and changed it, for to her Octavia still seemed a child, and though anxious for the alliance, she forbore to speak openly, lest the girl should turn willful, as she inherited her mother's high spirit.

"I'm sorry, Mamma. But how can I help it, when he teases me so that I detest him?" said Octavia, petulantly.

"How tease, my love?"

"Why, he follows me about like a dog, puts on a sentimental look when I appear; blushes, and beams, and bows at everything I say, if I am polite; frowns and sighs if I'm not; and glowers tragically at every man I speak to, even poor Maurice. Oh, Mamma, what foolish creatures men are!" And the girl laughed blithely, as she looked up for the first time into her mother's face.

My lady smiled, as she stroked the bright head at her knee, but asked quickly, "Why say 'even poor Maurice,' as if it were impossible for anyone to be jealous of him?"

"But isn't it, Mamma? I thought strong, well men regarded him as one set apart and done with, since his sad misfortune."

"Not entirely; while women pity and pet the poor fellow, his comrades will be jealous, absurd as it is."

"No one pets him but me, and I have a right to do it, for he is my cousin," said the girl, feeling a touch of jealousy herself.

"Rose and Blanche Talbot outdo you, my dear, and there is no cousinship to excuse them."

"Then let Frank Annon be jealous of them, and leave me in peace. They promised to come today; I'm afraid something has happened to prevent them." And Octavia gladly seized upon the new subject. But my lady was not to be eluded.

"They said they could not come till after dinner. They will soon arrive. Before they do so, I must say a few words, Tavia, and I beg you to give heed to them. I desire you to be courteous and amiable to Mr. Annon, and before strangers to be less attentive and affectionate to Maurice. You mean it kindly, but it looks ill, and causes disagreeable remarks."

"Who blames me for being devoted to my cousin? Can I ever do enough to repay him for his devotion? Mamma, you forget he saved your son's life."

Indignant tears filled the girl's eyes, and she spoke passionately, forgetting that Mrs. Snowdon was within earshot of her raised voice. With a frown my lady laid her hand on her daughter's lips, saying coldly, "I do not forget, and I religiously discharge my every obligation by every care and comfort it is in my power to bestow. You are young, romantic, and tender-hearted. You think you must give your time and health, must sacrifice your future happiness to this duty. You are wrong, and unless you learn wisdom in season, you will find that you have done harm, not good."

"God forbid! How can I do that? Tell me, and I will be wise in time."

Turning the earnest face up to her own, Lady Treherne whispered anxiously, "Has Maurice ever looked or hinted anything of love during this year he has been with us, and you his constant companion?"

"Never, Mamma; he is too honorable and too unhappy to speak or think of that. I am his little nurse, sister, and friend, no more, nor ever shall be. Do not suspect us, or put such fears into my mind, else all our comfort will be spoiled."

Flushed and eager was the girl, but her clear eyes betrayed no tender confusion as she spoke, and all her thought seemed to be to clear her cousin from the charge of loving her too well. Lady Treherne looked relieved, paused a moment, then said, seriously but gently, "This is well, but, child, I charge you tell me at once, if ever he forgets himself, for this thing cannot be. Once I hoped it might, now it is impossible; remember that he continue a friend and cousin, nothing more. I warn you in time, but if you neglect the warning, Maurice must go. No more of this; recollect my wish regarding Mr. Annon, and let your cousin amuse himself without you in public."

"Mamma, do you wish me to like Frank Annon?"

The abrupt question rather disturbed my lady, but knowing her daughter's frank, impetuous nature, she felt somewhat relieved by this candor, and answered decidedly, "I do. He is your equal in all respects; he loves you, Jasper desires it, I approve, and you, being heart-whole, can have no just objection to the alliance."

"Has he spoken to you?"

"No, to your brother."

"You wish this much, Mamma?"

"Very much, my child."

"I will try to please you, then." And stifling a sigh, the girl kissed her mother with unwonted meekness in tone and manner.

"Now I am well pleased. Be happy, my love. No one will urge or distress you. Let matters take their course, and if this hope of ours can be fulfilled, I shall be relieved of the chief care of my life."

A sound of girlish voices here broke on their ears, and springing up, Octavia hurried to meet her friends, exclaiming joyfully, "They have come! they have come!"

Two smiling, blooming girls met her at the door, and, being at an enthusiastic age, they gushed in girlish fashion for several minutes, making a pretty group as they stood in each other's arms, all talking at once, with frequent kisses and little bursts of laughter, as vents for their emotion. Madame Mère welcomed them and then went to join Mrs. Snowdon, leaving the trio to gossip unrestrained.

"My dearest creature, I thought we never should get here, for Papa had a tiresome dinner party, and we were obliged to stay, you know," cried Rose, the lively sister, shaking out the pretty dress and glancing at herself in the mirror as she fluttered about the room like a butterfly.

"We were dying to come, and so charmed when you asked us, for we haven't seen you this age, darling," added Blanche, the pensive one, smoothing her blond curls after a fresh embrace.

"I'm sorry the Ulsters couldn't come to keep Christmas with us, for we have no gentlemen but Jasper, Frank Annon, and the major. Sad, isn't it?" said Octavia, with a look of despair, which caused a fresh peal of laughter.

"One apiece, my dear, it might be worse." And Rose privately decided to appropriate Sir Jasper.

"Where is your cousin?" asked Blanche, with a sigh of sentimental interest.

"He is here, of course. I forget him, but he is not on the flirting list, you know. We must amuse him, and not expect him to amuse us, though really, all the capital suggestions and plans for merrymaking always come from him."

"He is better, I hope?" asked both sisters with real sympathy, making their young faces womanly and sweet.

"Yes, and has hopes of entire recovery. At least, they tell him so, though Dr. Ashley said there was no chance of it."

"Dear, dear, how sad! Shall we see him, Tavia?"

"Certainly; he is able to be with us now in the evening, and enjoys society as much as ever. But please take no notice of his infirmity, and make no inquiries beyond the usual 'How do you do.' He is sensitive, and hates to be considered an invalid more than ever."

"How charming it must be to take care of him, he is so accomplished and delightful. I quite envy you," said Blanche pensively.

"Sir Jasper told us that the General and Mrs. Snowdon were coming. I hope they will, for I've a most intense curiosity to see her—" began Rose.

"Hush, she is here with Mamma! Why curious? What is the mystery? For you look as if there was one," questioned Octavia under her breath.

The three charming heads bent toward one another as Rose replied in a whisper, "If I knew, I shouldn't be inquisitive. There was a rumor that she married the old general in a fit of pique, and now repents. I asked Mamma once, but she said such matters were not for young girls to hear, and not a word more would she say. *N'importe*, I have wits of my own, and I can satisfy myself. The gentlemen are coming! Am I all right, dear?" And the three glanced at one another with a swift scrutiny that nothing could escape, then grouped themselves prettily, and waited, with a little flutter of expectation in each young heart.

In came the gentlemen, and instantly a new atmosphere seemed to pervade the drawing room, for with the first words uttered, several romances began. Sir Jasper was taken possession of by Rose, Blanche intended to devote herself to Maurice Treherne, but Annon intercepted her, and Octavia was spared any effort at politeness by this unexpected move on the part of her lover.

"He is angry, and wishes to pique me by devoting himself to Blanche. I wish he would, with all my heart, and leave me in peace. Poor Maurice, he expects me, and I long to go to him, but must obey Mamma." And Octavia went to join the group formed by my lady, Mrs. Snowdon, the general, and the major.

The two young couples flirted in different parts of the room, and Treherne sat alone, watching them all with eyes that pierced below the surface, reading the hidden wishes, hopes, and fears that ruled them. A singular expression sat on his face as he turned from Octavia's clear countenance to Mrs. Snowdon's gloomy one. He leaned his head upon his hand and fell into deep thought, for he was passing through one of those fateful moments which come to us all, and which may make or mar a life. Such moments come when least looked for: an unexpected meeting, a peculiar mood, some trivial circumstance, or careless word produces it, and often it is gone before we realize its presence, leaving aftereffects to show us what we have gained or lost. Treherne was conscious that the present hour, and the acts that filled it, possessed unusual interest, and would exert an unusual influence on his life. Before him was the good and evil genius of his nature in the guise of those two women. Edith Snowdon had already tried her power, and accident only had saved him. Octavia, all unconscious as she was, never failed to rouse and stimulate the noblest attributes of mind and heart. A year spent in her society had done much for him, and he loved her with a strange mingling of passion, reverence, and gratitude. He knew why Edith Snowdon came, he felt that the old fascination had not lost its charm, and though fear was unknown to him, he was ill pleased at the sight of the beautiful, dangerous woman. On the other hand, he saw that Lady Treherne desired her daughter to shun him and smile on Annon; he acknowledged that he had no right to win the young creature, crippled and poor as he was, and a pang of jealous pain wrung his heart as he watched her.

Then a sense of power came to him, for helpless, poor, and seemingly an object of pity, he yet felt that he held the honor, peace, and happiness of nearly every person present in his hands. It was a strong temptation to this man, so full of repressed passion and power, so set apart and shut out from the more stirring duties and pleasures of life. A few words from his lips, and the pity all felt for him would be turned to fear, respect, and admiration. Why not utter them, and enjoy all that was possible? He owed the Trehernes nothing; why suffer injustice, dependence, and the compassion that wounds a proud man deepest? Wealth, love, pleasure might be his with a breath. Why not secure them now?

His pale face flushed, his eye kindled, and his thin hand lay clenched like a vise as these thoughts passed rapidly through his mind. A look, a word at that moment would sway him; he felt it, and leaned forward, waiting in secret suspense for the glance, the speech which should decide him for good or ill. Who shall say what subtle instinct caused Octavia to turn and smile at him with a wistful, friendly look that warmed his heart? He met it with an answering glance, which thrilled her strangely, for love, gratitude, and some mysterious intelligence met and mingled in the brilliant yet soft expression which swiftly shone and faded in her face. What it was she could not tell; she only felt that it filled her with an indescribable emotion never experienced before. In an instant it all passed, Lady Treherne spoke to her, and Blanche Talbot addressed Maurice, wondering, as she did so, if the enchanting smile he wore was meant for her.

"Mr. Annon having mercifully set me free, I came to try to cheer your solitude; but you look as if solitude made you happier than society does the rest of us," she said without her usual affectation, for his manner impressed her.

"You are very kind and very welcome. I do find pleasures to beguile my loneliness, which gayer people would not enjoy, and it is well that I can, else I should turn morose and tyrannical, and doom some unfortunate to entertain me all day long." He answered with a gentle courtesy which was his chief attraction to womankind.

"Pray tell me some of your devices, I'm often alone in spirit, if not so in the flesh, for Rose, though a dear girl, is not congenial, and I find no kindred soul."

A humorous glimmer came to Treherne's eyes, as the sentimental damsel beamed a soft sigh and drooped her long lashes effectively. Ignoring the topic of "kindred souls," he answered coldly, "My favorite amusement is studying the people around me. It may be rude, but tied to my corner, I cannot help watching the figures around me, and discovering their little plots and plans. I'm getting very expert, and really surprise myself sometimes by the depth of my researches."

"I can believe it; your eyes look as if they possessed that gift. Pray don't study *me*." And the girl shrank away with an air of genuine alarm.

Treherne smiled involuntarily, for he had read the secret of that shallow heart long ago, and was too generous to use the knowledge, however flattering it might be to him. In a reassuring tone he said, turning away the keen eyes she feared, "I give you my word I never will, charming as it might be to study the white pages of a maidenly heart. I find plenty of others to read, so rest tranquil, Miss Blanche."

"Who interests you most just now?" asked the girl, coloring with pleasure at his words. "Mrs. Snowdon looks like one who has a romance to be read, if you have the skill."

"I have read it. My lady is my study just now. I thought I knew her well, but of late she puzzles me. Human minds are more full of mysteries than any written book and more changeable than the cloud shapes in the air."

"A fine old lady, but I fear her so intensely I should never dare to try to read her, as you say." Blanche looked toward the object of discussion as she spoke, and added, "Poor Tavia, how forlorn she seems. Let me ask her to join us, may I?"

"With all my heart" was the quick reply.

Blanche glided away but did not return, for my lady kept her as well as her daughter.

"That test satisfies me; well, I submit for a time, but I think I can conquer my aunt yet." And with a patient sigh Treherne turned to observe Mrs. Snowdon.

She now stood by the fire talking with Sir Jasper, a handsome, reckless, generous-hearted young gentleman, who very plainly showed his great admiration for the lady. When he came, she suddenly woke up from her listless mood and became as brilliantly gay as she had been unmistakably melancholy before. As she chatted, she absently pushed to and fro a small antique urn of bronze on the chimneypiece, and in doing so she more than once gave Treherne a quick, significant glance, which he answered at last by a somewhat haughty nod. Then, as if satisfied, she ceased toying with the ornament and became absorbed in Sir Jasper's gallant badinage.

The instant her son approached Mrs. Snowdon, Madame Mère grew anxious, and leaving Octavia to her friends and lover, she watched Jasper. But her surveillance availed little, for she could neither see nor hear anything amiss, yet could not rid herself of the feeling that some mutual understanding existed between them. When the party broke up for the night, she lingered till all were gone but her son and nephew.

"Well, Madame Ma Mère, what troubles you?" asked Sir Jasper, as she looked anxiously into his face before bestowing her good-night kiss.

"I cannot tell, yet I feel ill at ease. Remember, my son, that you are the pride of my heart, and any sin or shame of yours would kill me. Good night, Maurice." And with a stately bow she swept away.

Lounging with both elbows on the low chimneypiece, Sir Jasper smiled at his mother's fears, and said to his cousin, the instant they were alone, "She is worried about E.S. Odd, isn't it, what instinctive antipathies women take to one another?"

"Why did you ask E.S. here?" demanded Treherne.

"My dear fellow, how could I help it? My mother wanted the general, my father's friend, and of course his wife must be asked also. I couldn't tell my mother that the lady had been a most arrant coquette, to put it mildly, and had married the old man in a pet, because my cousin and I declined to be ruined by her."

"You *could* have told her what mischief she makes wherever she goes, and for Octavia's sake have deferred the general's visit for a time. I warn you, Jasper, harm will come of it."

"To whom, you or me?"

"To both, perhaps, certainly to you. She was disappointed once when she lost us both by wavering between your title and my supposed fortune. She is miserable with the old man, and her only hope is in his death, for he is very feeble. You are free, and doubly attractive now, so beware, or she will entangle you before you know it."

"Thanks, Mentor. I've no fear, and shall merely amuse myself for a week—they stay no longer." And with a careless laugh, Sir Jasper strolled away.

"Much mischief may be done in a week, and this is the beginning of it," muttered Treherne, as he raised himself to look under the bronze vase for the note. It was gone!

CHAPTER III.

WHO WAS IT?

Who had taken it? This question tormented Treherne all that sleepless night. He suspected three persons, for only these had approached the fire after the note was hidden. He had kept his eye on it, he thought, till the stir of breaking up. In that moment it must have been removed by the major, Frank Annon, or my lady; Sir Jasper was out of the question, for he never touched an ornament in the drawing room since he had awkwardly demolished a whole *étagère* of costly trifles, to his mother's and sister's great grief. The major evidently suspected something, Annon was jealous, and my lady would be glad of a pretext to remove her daughter from his reach. Trusting to his skill in reading faces, he waited impatiently for morning, resolving to say nothing to anyone but Mrs. Snowdon, and from her merely to inquire what the note contained.

Treherne usually was invisible till lunch, often till dinner; therefore, fearing to excite suspicion by unwonted activity, he did not appear till noon. The mailbag had just been opened, and everyone was busy over their letters, but all looked up to exchange a word with the newcomer, and Octavia impulsively turned to meet him, then checked herself and hid her suddenly crimsoned face behind a newspaper. Treherne's eye took in everything, and saw at once in the unusually late arrival of the mail a pretext for discovering the pilferer of the note.

"All have letters but me, yet I expected one last night. Major, have you got it among yours?" And as he spoke, Treherne fixed his penetrating eyes full on the person he addressed.

With no sign of consciousness, no trace of confusion, the major carefully turned over his pile, and replied in the most natural manner, "Not a trace of it; I wish there was, for nothing annoys me more than any delay or mistake about my letters."

He knows nothing of it, thought Treherne, and turned to Annon, who was deep in a long epistle from some intimate friend, with a talent for imparting news, to judge from the reader's interest.

"Annon, I appeal to you, for I *must* discover who has robbed me of my letter."

"I have but one, read it, if you will, and satisfy yourself" was the brief reply.

"No, thank you. I merely asked in joke; it is doubtless among my lady's. Jasper's letters and mine often get mixed, and my lady takes care of his for him. I think you must have it, Aunt."

Lady Treherne looked up impatiently. "My dear Maurice, what a coil about a letter! We none of us have it, so do not punish us for the sins of your correspondent or the carelessness of the post."

She was not the thief, for she is always intensely polite when she intends to thwart me, thought Treherne, and, apologizing for his rudeness in disturbing them, he rolled himself to his nook in a sunny window and became apparently absorbed in a new magazine.

Mrs. Snowdon was opening the general's letters for him, and, having finished her little task, she roamed away into the library, as if in search of a book. Presently returning with one, she approached Treherne, and, putting it into his hand, said, in her musically distinct voice, "Be so kind as to find for me the passage you spoke of last night. I am curious to see it."

Instantly comprehending her stratagem, he opened it with apparent carelessness, secured the tiny note laid among the leaves, and, selecting a passage at hazard, returned her book and resumed his own. Behind the cover of it he unfolded and read these words:

> I understand, but do not be anxious; the line I left was merely this—"I must see you alone, tell me when and where." No one can make much of it, and I will discover the thief before dinner. Do nothing, but watch to whom I speak first on entering, when we meet in the evening, and beware of that person.

Quietly transferring the note to the fire with the wrapper of the magazine, he dismissed the matter from his mind and left Mrs. Snowdon to play detective as she pleased, while he busied himself about his own affairs.

It was a clear, bright December day, and when the young people separated to prepare for a ride, while the general and the major sunned themselves on the terrace, Lady Treherne said to her nephew, "I am going for an airing in the pony carriage. Will you be my escort, Maurice?"

"With pleasure," replied the young man, well knowing what was in store for him.

My lady was unusually taciturn and grave, yet seemed anxious to say something which she found difficult to utter. Treherne saw this, and ended an awkward pause by dashing boldly into the subject which occupied both.

"I think you want to say something to me about Tavie, Aunt. Am I right?"

"Yes."

"Then let me spare you the pain of beginning, and prove my sincerity by openly stating the truth, as far as I am concerned. I love her very dearly, but I am not mad enough to dream of telling her so. I know that it is impossible, and I relinquish my hopes. Trust me. I will keep silent and see her marry Annon without a word of complaint, if you will it. I see by her altered manner that you have spoken to her, and that my little friend and nurse is to be mine no longer. Perhaps you are wise, but if you do this on my account, it is in vain—the mischief is done, and while I live I shall love my cousin. If you do it to spare her, I am dumb, and will go away rather than cause her a care or pain."

"Do you really mean this, Maurice?" And Lady Treherne looked at him with a changed and softened face.

Turning upon her, Treherne showed her a countenance full of suffering and sincerity, of resignation and resolve, as he said earnestly, "I do mean it; prove me in any way you please. I am not a bad fellow, Aunt, and I desire to be better. Since my misfortune I've had time to test many things, myself among others, and in spite of many faults, I do cherish the wish to keep my soul honest and true, even though my body be a wreck. It is easy to say these things, but in spite of temptation, I think I can stand firm, if you trust me."

"My dear boy, I do trust you, and thank you gratefully for this frankness. I never forget that I owe Jasper's life to you, and never expect to repay that debt. Remember this when I seem cold or unkind, and remember also that I say now, had you been spared this affliction, I would gladly have given you my girl. But—"

"But, Aunt, hear one thing," broke in Treherne. "They tell me that any sudden and violent shock of surprise, joy, or sorrow may do for me what they hope time will achieve. I said nothing of this, for it is but a chance; yet, while there is any hope, need I utterly renounce Octavia?"

"It is hard to refuse, and yet I cannot think it wise to build upon a chance so slight. Once let her have you, and both are made unhappy, if the hope fail. No, Maurice, it is better to be generous, and leave her free to make her own happiness elsewhere. Annon loves her, she is heart-whole, and will soon learn to love him, if you are silent. My poor boy, it seems cruel, but I must say it."

"Shall I go away, Aunt?" was all his answer, very firmly uttered, though his lips were white.

"Not yet, only leave them to themselves, and hide your trouble if you can. Yet, if you prefer, you shall go to town, and Benson shall see that you are comfortable. Your health will be a reason, and I will come, or write often, if you are homesick. It shall depend on you, for I want to be just and kind in this hard case. You shall decide."

"Then I will stay. I can hide my love; and to see them together will soon cease to wound me, if Octavia is happy."

"So let it rest then, for a time. You shall miss your companion as little as possible, for I will try to fill her place. Forgive me, Maurice, and pity a mother's solicitude, for these two are the last of many children, and I am a widow now."

Lady Treherne's voice faltered, and if any selfish hope or plan lingered in her nephew's mind, that appeal banished it and touched his better nature. Pressing her hand he said gently, "Dear Aunt, do not lament over me. I am one set apart for afflictions, yet I will not be conquered by them. Let us forget my youth and be friendly counselors together for the good of the two whom we both love. I must say a word about Jasper, and you will not press me to explain more than I can without breaking my promise."

"Thank you, thank you! It is regarding that woman, I know. Tell me all you can; I will not be importunate, but I disliked her the instant I saw her, beautiful and charming as she seems."

"When my cousin and I were in Paris, just before my illness, we met her. She was with her father then, a gay old man who led a life of pleasure, and was no fit guardian for a lovely daughter. She knew our story and, having fascinated both, paused to decide which she would accept: Jasper, for his title, or me, for my fortune. This was before my uncle changed his will, and I believed myself his heir; but, before she made her choice, something (don't ask me what, if you please) occurred to send us from Paris. On our return voyage we were wrecked, and then came my illness, disinheritance, and helplessness. Edith Dubarry heard the story, but rumor reported it falsely, and she believed both of us had lost the fortune. Her father died penniless, and in a moment of despair she married the general, whose wealth surrounds her with the luxury she loves, and whose failing health will soon restore her liberty—"

"And then, Maurice?" interrupted my lady.

"She hopes to win Jasper, I think."

"Never! We must prevent that at all costs. I had rather see him dead before me, than the husband of such a woman. Why is she permitted to visit homes like mine? I should have been told this sooner," exclaimed my lady angrily.

"I should have told you had I known it, and I reproved Jasper for his neglect. Do not be needlessly troubled, Aunt. There is no blemish on Mrs. Snowdon's name, and, as the wife of a brave and honorable man, she is received without question; for beauty, grace, or tact like hers can make their way anywhere. She stays but a week, and I will devote myself to her; this will save Jasper, and, if necessary, convince Tavie of my indifference—" Then he paused to stifle a sigh.

"But yourself, have you no fears for your own peace, Maurice? You must not sacrifice happiness or honor, for me or mine."

"I am safe; I love my cousin, and that is my shield. Whatever happens remember that I tried to serve you, and sincerely endeavored to forget myself."

"God bless you, my son! Let me call you so, and feel that, though I deny you my daughter, I give you heartily a mother's care and affection."

Lady Treherne was as generous as she was proud, and her nephew had conquered her by confidence and submission. He acted no part, yet, even in relinquishing all, he cherished a hope that he might yet win the heart he coveted. Silently they parted, but from that hour a new and closer bond existed between the two, and exerted an unsuspected influence over the whole household.

* * * * * *

Maurice waited with some impatience for Mrs. Snowdon's entrance, not only because of his curiosity to see if she had discovered the thief, but because of the part he had taken upon himself to play. He was equal to it, and felt a certain pleasure in it for a threefold reason. It would serve his aunt and cousin, would divert his mind from its own cares, and, perhaps by making Octavia jealous, waken love; for, though he had chosen the right, he was but a man, and moreover a lover.

Mrs. Snowdon was late. She always was, for her toilet was elaborate, and she liked to enjoy its effects upon others. The moment she entered Treherne's eye was on her, and to his intense surprise and annoyance she addressed Octavia, saying blandly, "My dear Miss Treherne, I've been admiring your peacocks. Pray let me see you feed them tomorrow. Miss Talbot says it is a charming sight."

"If you are on the terrace just after lunch, you will find them there, and may feed them yourself, if you like" was the cool, civil reply.

"She looks like a peacock herself in that splendid green and gold dress, doesn't she?" whispered Rose to Sir Jasper, with a wicked laugh.

"Faith, so she does. I wish Tavie's birds had voices like Mrs. Snowdon's; their squalling annoys me intensely."

"I rather like it, for it is honest, and no malice or mischief is hidden behind it. I always distrust those smooth, sweet voices; they are insincere. I like a full, clear tone; sharp, if you please, but decided and true."

"Well said, Octavia. I agree with you, and your own is a perfect sample of the kind you describe." And Treherne smiled as he rolled by to join Mrs. Snowdon, who evidently waited for him, while Octavia turned to her brother to defend her pets.

"Are you sure? How did you discover?" said Maurice, affecting to admire the lady's bouquet, as he paused beside her.

"I suspected it the moment I saw her this morning. She is no actress; and dislike, distrust, and contempt were visible in her face when we met. Till you so cleverly told me my note was lost, I fancied she was disturbed about her brother—or you."

A sudden pause and a keen glance followed the last softly uttered word, but Treherne met it with an inscrutable smile and a quiet "Well, what next?"

"The moment I learned that you did not get the note I was sure she had it, and, knowing that she must have seen me put it there, in spite of her apparent innocence, I quietly asked her for it. This surprised her, this robbed the affair of any mystery, and I finished her perplexity by sending it to the major the moment she returned it to me, as if it had been intended for him. She begged pardon, said her brother was thoughtless, and she watched over him lest he should get into mischief; professed to think I meant the line for him, and behaved like a charming simpleton, as she is."

"Quite a tumult about nothing. Poor little Tavie! You doubtlessly frightened her so that we may safely correspond hereafter."

"You may give me an answer, now and here."

"Very well, meet me on the terrace tomorrow morning; the peacocks will make the meeting natural enough. I usually loiter away an hour or two there, in the sunny part of the day."

"But the girl?"

"I'll send her away."

"You speak as if it would be an easy thing to do."

"It will, both easy and pleasant."

"Now you are mysterious or uncomplimentary. You either care nothing for a tête-à-tête with her, or you will gladly send her out of my way. Which is it?"

"You shall decide. Can I have this?"

She looked at him as he touched a rose with a warning glance, for the flower was both an emblem of love and of silence. Did he mean to hint that he recalled the past, or to warn her that someone was near? She leaned from the shadow of the curtain where she sat, and caught a glimpse of a shadow gliding away.

"Who was it?" she asked, below her breath.

"A Rose," he answered, laughing. Then, as if the danger was over, he said, "How will you account to the major for the message you sent him?"

"Easily, by fabricating some interesting perplexity in which I want sage counsel. He will be flattered, and by seeming to take him into my confidence, I can hoodwink the excellent man to my heart's content, for he annoys me by his odd way of mounting guard over me at all times. Now take me in to dinner, and be your former delightful self."

"That is impossible," he said, yet proved that it was not.

CHAPTER IV.

FEEDING THE PEACOCKS

It was indeed a charming sight, the twelve stately birds perched on the broad stone balustrade, or prancing slowly along the terrace, with the sun gleaming on their green and golden necks and the glories of their gorgeous plumes, widespread, or sweeping like rich trains behind them. In pretty contrast to the splendid creatures was their young mistress, in her simple morning dress and fur-trimmed hood and mantle, as she stood feeding the tame pets from her hand, calling their fanciful names, laughing at their pranks, and heartily enjoying the winter sunshine, the fresh wind, and the girlish pastime. As Treherne slowly approached, he watched her with lover's eyes, and found her very sweet and blithe, and dearer in his sight than ever. She had shunned him carefully all the day before, had parted at night with a hasty handshake, and had not come as usual to bid him good-morning in the library. He had taken no notice of the change as yet, but now, remembering his promise to his aunt, he resolved to let the girl know that he fully understood the relation which henceforth was to exist between them.

"Good-morning, cousin. Shall I drive you away, if I take a turn or two here?" he said, in a cheerful tone, but with a half-reproachful glance.

She looked at him an instant, then went to him with extended hand and cheeks rosier than before, while her frank eyes filled, and her voice had a traitorous tremor in it, as she said, impetuously: "I *will* be myself for a moment, in spite of everything. Maurice, don't think me unkind, don't reproach me, or ask my leave to come where I am. There is a reason for the change you see in me; it's not caprice, it is obedience."

"My dear girl, I know it. I meant to speak of it, and show you that I understand. Annon is a good fellow, as worthy of you as any man can be, and I wish you all the happiness you deserve."

"Do you?" And her eyes searched his face keenly.

"Yes; do you doubt it?" And so well did he conceal his love, that neither face, voice, nor manner betrayed a hint of it.

Her eyes fell, a cloud passed over her clear countenance, and she withdrew her hand, as if to caress the hungry bird that gently pecked at the basket she held. As if to change the conversation, she said playfully, "Poor Argus, you have lost your fine feathers, and so all desert you, except kind little Juno, who never forgets her friends. There, take it all, and share between you."

Treherne smiled, and said quickly, "I am a human Argus, and you have been a kind little Juno to me since I lost my plumes. Continue to be so, and you will find me a very faithful friend."

"I will." And as she answered, her old smile came back and her eyes met his again.

"Thanks! Now we shall get on happily. I don't ask or expect the old life—that is impossible. I knew that when lovers came, the friend would fall into the background; and I am content to be second, where I have so long been first. Do not think you neglect me; be happy with your lover, dear, and when you have no pleasanter amusement, come and see old Maurice."

She turned her head away, that he might not see the angry color in her cheeks, the trouble in her eyes, and when she spoke, it was to say petulantly, "I wish Jasper and Mamma would leave me in peace. I hate lovers and want none. If Frank teases, I'll go into a convent and so be rid of him."

Maurice laughed, and turned her face toward himself, saying, in his persuasive voice, "Give him a trial first, to please your mother. It can do no harm and may amuse you. Frank is already lost, and, as you are heart-whole, why not see what you can do for him? I shall have a new study, then, and not miss you so much."

"You are very kind; I'll do my best. I wish Mrs. Snowdon would come, if she is coming; I've an engagement at two, and Frank will look tragical if I'm not ready. He is teaching me billiards, and I really like the game, though I never thought I should."

"That looks well. I hope you'll learn a double lesson, and Annon find a docile pupil in both."

"You are very pale this morning; are you in pain, Maurice?" suddenly asked Octavia, dropping the tone of assumed ease and gaiety under which she had tried to hide her trouble.

"Yes, but it will soon pass. Mrs. Snowdon is coming. I saw her at the hall door a moment ago. I will show her the peacocks, if you want to go. She won't mind the change, I dare say, as you don't like her, and I do."

"No, I am sure of that. It was an arrangement, perhaps? I understand. I will not play Mademoiselle De Trop."

Sudden fire shone in the girl's eyes, sudden contempt curled her lip, and a glance full of meaning went from her cousin to the door, where Mrs. Snowdon appeared, waiting for her maid to bring her some additional wrappings.

"You allude to the note you stole. How came you to play that prank, Tavie?" asked Treherne tranquilly.

"I saw her put it under the urn. I thought it was for Jasper, and I took it," she said boldly.

"Why for Jasper?"

"I remembered his speaking of meeting her long ago, and describing her beauty enthusiastically—and so did you."

"You have a good memory."

"I have for everything concerning those I love. I observed her manner of meeting my brother, his devotion to her, and, when they stood laughing together before the fire, I felt sure that she wished to charm him again."

"Again? Then she did charm him once?" asked Treherne, anxious to know how much Jasper had told his sister.

"He always denied it, and declared that you were the favorite."

"Then why not think the note for me?" he asked.

"I do now" was the sharp answer.

"But she told you it was for the major, and sent it."

"She deceived me; I am not surprised. I am glad Jasper is safe, and I wish you a pleasant tête-à-tête."

Bowing with unwonted dignity, Octavia set down her basket, and walked away in one direction as Mrs. Snowdon approached in another.

"I have done it now," sighed Treherne, turning from the girlish figure to watch the stately creature who came sweeping toward him with noiseless grace.

Brilliancy and splendor became Mrs. Snowdon; she enjoyed luxury, and her beauty made many things becoming which in a plainer woman would have been out of taste, and absurd. She had wrapped herself in a genuine Eastern burnous of scarlet, blue, and gold; the hood drawn over her head framed her fine face in rich hues, and the great gilt tassels shone against her rippling black hair. She wore it with grace, and the barbaric splendor of the garment became her well. The fresh air touched her cheeks with a delicate color; her usually gloomy eyes were brilliant now, and the smile that parted her lips was full of happiness.

"Welcome, Cleopatra!" cried Treherne, with difficulty repressing a laugh, as the peacocks screamed and fled before the rustling amplitude of her drapery.

"I might reply by calling you Thaddeus of Warsaw, for you look very romantic and Polish with your pale, pensive face, and your splendid furs," she answered, as she paused beside him with admiration very visibly expressed in her eyes.

Treherne disliked the look, and rather abruptly said, as he offered her the basket of bread, "I have disposed of my cousin, and offered to do the honors of the peacocks. Here they are—will you feed them?"

"No, thank you—I care nothing for the fowls, as you know; I came to speak to you," she said impatiently.

"I am at your service."

"I wish to ask you a question or two—is it permitted?"

"What man ever refused Mrs. Snowdon a request?"

"Nay, no compliments; from you they are only satirical evasions. I was deceived when abroad, and rashly married that old man. Tell me truly how things stand."

"Jasper has all. I have nothing."

"I am glad of it."

"Many thanks for the hearty speech. You at least speak sincerely," he said bitterly.

"I do, Maurice—I do; let me prove it."

Treherne's chair was close beside the balustrade. Mrs. Snowdon leaned on the carved railing, with her back to the house and her face screened by a tall urn. Looking steadily at him, she said rapidly and low, "You thought I wavered between you and Jasper, when we parted two years ago. I did; but it was not between title and fortune that I hesitated. It was between duty and love. My father, a fond, foolish old man, had set his heart on seeing me a lady. I was his all; my beauty was his delight, and no untitled man was deemed worthy of me. I loved him tenderly. You may doubt this, knowing how selfish, reckless, and vain I am, but I have a heart, and with better training had been a better woman. No matter, it is too late now. Next my father, I loved you. Nay, hear me—I *will* clear myself in your eyes. I mean no wrong to the general. He is kind, indulgent, generous; I respect him—I am grateful, and while he lives, I shall be true to him."

"Then be silent now. Do not recall the past, Edith; let it sleep, for both our sakes," began Treherne; but she checked him imperiously.

"It shall, when I am done. I loved you, Maurice; for, of all the gay, idle, pleasure-seeking men I saw about me, you were the only one who seemed to have a thought beyond the folly of the hour. Under the seeming frivolity of your life lay something noble, heroic, and true. I felt that you had a purpose, that your present mood was but transitory—a young man's holiday, before the real work of his life began. This attracted, this won me; for even in the brief regard you then gave me, there was an earnestness no other man had shown. I wanted your respect; I longed to earn your love, to share your life, and prove that even in my neglected nature slept the power of canceling a frivolous past by a noble future. Oh, Maurice, had you lingered one week more, I never should have been the miserable thing I am!"

There her voice faltered and failed, for all the bitterness of lost love, peace, and happiness sounded in the pathetic passion of that exclamation. She did not weep, for tears seldom dimmed those tragical eyes of hers; but she wrung her hands in mute despair, and looked down into the frost-blighted gardens below, as if she saw there a true symbol of her own ruined life. Treherne uttered not a word, but set his teeth with an almost fierce glance toward the distant figure of Sir Jasper, who was riding gaily away, like one unburdened by a memory or a care.

Hurriedly Mrs. Snowdon went on, "My father begged and commanded me to choose your cousin. I could not break his heart, and asked for time, hoping to soften him. While I waited, that mysterious affair hurried you from Paris, and then came the wreck, the illness, and the rumor that old Sir Jasper had disinherited both nephews. They told me you were dying, and I became a passive instrument in my father's hands. I promised to recall and accept your cousin, but the old man died before it was done, and then I cared not what became of me.

"General Snowdon was my father's friend; he pitied me; he saw my desolate, destitute state, my despair and helplessness. He comforted, sustained, and saved me. I was grateful; and when he offered me his heart and home, I accepted them. He knew I had no love to give; but as a friend, a daughter, I would gladly serve him, and make his declining years as happy as I could. It was all over, when I heard that you were alive, afflicted, and poor. I longed to come and live for you. My new bonds became heavy fetters then, my wealth oppressed me, and I was doubly wretched—for I dared not tell my trouble, and it nearly drove me mad. I have seen you now; I know that you are happy; I read your cousin's love and see a peaceful life in store for you. This must content me, and I must learn to bear it as I can."

She paused, breathless and pale, and walked rapidly along the terrace, as if to hide or control the agitation that possessed her.

Treherne still sat silent, but his heart leaped within him, as he thought, "She sees that Octavia loves me! A woman's eye is quick to detect love in another, and she asserts what I begin to hope. My cousin's manner just now, her dislike of Annon, her new shyness with me; it may be true, and if it is—Heaven help me—what am I saying! I must not hope, nor wish, nor dream; I must renounce and forget."

He leaned his head upon his hand, and sat so still Mrs. Snowdon rejoined him, pale, but calm and self-possessed. As she drew near, she marked his attitude, the bitter sadness of his face, and hope sprang up within her. Perhaps she was mistaken; perhaps he did not love his cousin; perhaps he still remembered the past, and still regretted the loss of the heart she had just laid bare before him. Her husband was failing, and might die any day. And then, free, rich, beautiful, and young, what might she not become to Treherne, helpless, poor, and ambitious? With all her faults, she was generous, and this picture charmed her fancy, warmed her heart, and comforted her pain.

"Maurice," she said softly, pausing again beside him, "if I mistake you and your hopes, it is because I dare ask nothing for myself; but if ever a time shall come when I have liberty to give or help, ask of me *anything*, and it is gladly yours."

He understood her, pitied her, and, seeing that she found consolation in a distant hope, he let her enjoy it while she might. Gravely, yet gratefully, he spoke, and pressed the hand extended to him with an impulsive gesture.

"Generous as ever, Edith, and impetuously frank. Thank you for your sincerity, your kindness, and the affection you once gave me. I say 'once,' for now duty, truth, and honor bar us from each other. My life must be solitary, yet I shall find work to do, and learn to be content. You owe all devotion to the good old man who loves you, and will not fail him, I am sure. Leave the future and the past, but let us make the present what it may be—a time to forgive and forget, to take heart and begin anew. Christmas is a fitting time for such resolves, and the birth of friendship such as ours may be."

Something in his tone and manner struck her, and, eyeing him with soft wonder, she exclaimed, "How changed you are!"

"Need you tell me that?" And he glanced at his helpless limbs with a bitter yet pathetic look of patience.

"No, no—not so! I mean in mind, not body. Once you were gay and careless, eager and fiery, like Jasper; now you are grave and quiet, or cheerful, and so very kind. Yet, in spite of illness and loss, you seem twice the man you were, and something wins respect, as well as admiration—and love."

Her dark eyes filled as the last word left her lips, and the beauty of a touched heart shone in her face. Maurice looked up quickly, asking with sudden earnestness, "Do you see it? Then it is true. Yes, I *am* changed, thank God! And she has done it."

"Who?" demanded his companion jealously.

"Octavia. Unconsciously, yet surely, she has done much for me, and this year of seeming loss and misery has been the happiest, most profitable of my life. I have often heard that afflictions were the best teachers, and I believe it now."

Mrs. Snowdon shook her head sadly.

"Not always; they are tormentors to some. But don't preach, Maurice. I am still a sinner, though you incline to sainthood, and I have one question more to ask. What was it that took you and Jasper so suddenly away from Paris?"

"That I can never tell you."

"I shall discover it for myself, then."

"It is impossible."

"Nothing is impossible to a determined woman."

"You can neither wring, surprise, nor bribe this secret from the two persons who hold it. I beg of you to let it rest," said Treherne earnestly.

"I have a clue, and I shall follow it; for I am convinced that something is wrong, and you are—"

"Dear Mrs. Snowdon, are you so charmed with the birds that you forget your fellow-beings, or so charmed with one fellow-being that you forget the birds?"

As the sudden question startled both, Rose Talbot came along the terrace, with hands full of holly and a face full of merry mischief, adding as she vanished, "I shall tell Tavie that feeding the peacocks is such congenial amusement for lovers, she and Mr. Annon had better try it."

"Saucy gypsy!" muttered Treherne.

But Mrs. Snowdon said, with a smile of double meaning, "Many a true word is spoken in jest."

CHAPTER V.

UNDER THE MISTLETOE

Unusually gay and charming the three young friends looked, dressed alike in fleecy white with holly wreaths in their hair, as they slowly descended the wide oaken stairway arm in arm. A footman was lighting the hall lamps, for the winter dusk gathered early, and the girls were merrily chatting about the evening's festivity when suddenly a loud, long shriek echoed through the hall. A heavy glass shade fell from the man's hand with a crash, and the young ladies clung to one another aghast, for mortal terror was in the cry, and a dead silence followed it.

"What was it, John?" demanded Octavia, very pale, but steady in a moment.

"I'll go and see, miss." And the man hurried away.

"Where did the dreadful scream come from?" asked Rose, collecting her wits as rapidly as possible.

"Above us somewhere. Oh, let us go down among people; I am frightened to death," whispered Blanche, trembling and faint.

Hurrying into the parlor, they found only Annon and the major, both looking startled, and both staring out of the windows.

"Did you hear it? What could it be? Don't go and leave us!" cried the girls in a breath, as they rushed in.

The gentlemen had heard, couldn't explain the cry, and were quite ready to protect the pretty creatures who clustered about them like frightened fawns. John speedily appeared, looking rather wild, and as eager to tell his tale as they to listen.

"It's Patty, one of the maids, miss, in a fit. She went up to the north gallery to see that the fires was right, for it takes a power of wood to warm the gallery even enough for dancing, as you know, miss. Well, it was dark, for the fires was low and her candle went out as she whisked open the door, being flurried, as the maids always is when they go in there. Halfway down the gallery she says she heard a rustling, and stopped. She's the pluckiest of 'em all, and she called out, 'I see you!' thinking it was some of us trying to fright her. Nothing answered, and she went on a bit, when suddenly the fire flared up one flash, and there right before her was the ghost."

"Don't be foolish, John. Tell us what it was," said Octavia sharply, though her face whitened and her heart sank as the last word passed the man's lips.

"It was a tall, black figger, miss, with a dead-white face and a black hood. She see it plain, and turned to go away, but she hadn't gone a dozen steps when there it was again before her, the same tall, dark thing with the dead-white face looking out from the black hood. It lifted its arm as if to hold her, but she gave a spring and dreadful screech, and ran to Mrs. Benson's room, where she dropped in a fit."

"How absurd to be frightened by the shadows of the figures in armor that stand along the gallery!" said Rose, boldly enough, though she would have declined entering the gallery without a light.

"Nay, I don't wonder, it's a ghostly place at night. How is the poor thing?" asked Blanche, still hanging on the major's arm in her best attitude.

"If Mamma knows nothing of it, tell Mrs. Benson to keep it from her, please. She is not well, and such things annoy her very much," said Octavia, adding as the man turned away, "Did anyone look in the gallery after Patty told her tale?"

"No, miss. I'll go and do it myself; I'm not afraid of man, ghost, or devil, saving your presence, ladies," replied John.

"Where is Sir Jasper?" suddenly asked the major.

"Here I am. What a deuce of a noise someone has been making. It disturbed a capital dream. Why, Tavie, what is it?" And Sir Jasper came out of the library with a sleepy face and tumbled hair.

They told him the story, whereat he laughed heartily, and said the maids were a foolish set to be scared by a shadow. While he still laughed and joked, Mrs. Snowdon entered, looking alarmed, and anxious to know the cause of the confusion.

"How interesting! I never knew you kept a ghost. Tell me all about it, Sir Jasper, and soothe our nerves by satisfying our curiosity," she said in her half-persuasive, half-commanding way, as she seated herself on Lady Treherne's sacred sofa.

"There's not much to tell, except that this place used to be an abbey, in fact as well as in name. An ancestor founded it, and for years the monks led a jolly life here, as one may see, for the cellar is twice as large as the chapel, and much better preserved. But another ancestor, a gay and gallant baron, took a fancy to the site for his castle, and, in spite of prayers, anathemas, and excommunication, he turned the poor fellows out, pulled down the abbey, and built this fine old place. Abbot Boniface, as he left his abbey, uttered a heavy curse on all who should live here, and vowed to haunt us till the last Treherne vanished from the face of the earth. With this amiable threat the old party left Baron Roland to his doom, and died as soon as he could in order to begin his cheerful mission."

"Did he haunt the place?" asked Blanche eagerly.

"Yes, most faithfully from that time to this. Some say many of the monks still glide about the older parts of the abbey, for Roland spared the chapel and the north gallery which joined it to the modern building. Poor fellows, they are welcome, and once a year they shall have a chance to warm their ghostly selves by the great fires always kindled at Christmas in the gallery."

"Mrs. Benson once told me that when the ghost walked, it was a sure sign of a coming death in the family. Is that true?" asked Rose, whose curiosity was excited by the expression of Octavia's face, and a certain uneasiness in Sir Jasper's manner in spite of his merry mood.

"There is a stupid superstition of that sort in the family, but no one except the servants believes it, of course. In times of illness some silly maid or croaking old woman can easily fancy they see a phantom, and, if death comes, they are sure of the ghostly warning. Benson saw it before my father died, and old Roger, the night my uncle was seized with apoplexy. Patty will never be made to believe that this warning does not forebode the death of Maurice or myself, for the gallant spirit leaves the ladies of our house to depart in peace. How does it strike you, Cousin?"

Turning as he spoke, Sir Jasper glanced at Treherne, who had entered while he spoke.

"I am quite skeptical and indifferent to the whole affair, but I agree with Octavia that it is best to say nothing to my aunt if she is ignorant of the matter. Her rooms are a long way off, and perhaps she did not hear the confusion."

"You seem to hear everything; you were not with us when I said that." And Octavia looked up with an air of surprise.

Smiling significantly, Treherne answered, "I hear, see, and understand many things that escape others. Jasper, allow me to advise you to smooth the hair which your sleep has disarranged. Mrs. Snowdon, permit me. This rich velvet catches the least speck." And with his handkerchief he delicately brushed away several streaks of white dust which clung to the lady's skirt.

Sir Jasper turned hastily on his heel and went to remake his toilet; Mrs. Snowdon bit her lip, but thanked Treherne sweetly and begged him to fasten her glove. As he did so, she said softly, "Be more careful next time. Octavia has keen eyes, and the major may prove inconvenient."

"I have no fear that *you* will," he whispered back, with a malicious glance.

Here the entrance of my lady put an end to the ghostly episode, for it was evident that she knew nothing of it. Octavia slipped away to question John, and learn that no sign of a phantom was to be seen. Treherne devoted himself to Mrs. Snowdon, and the major entertained my lady, while Sir Jasper and the girls chatted apart.

It was Christmas Eve, and a dance in the great gallery was the yearly festival at the abbey. All had been eager for it, but the maid's story seemed to have lessened their enthusiasm, though no one would own it. This annoyed Sir Jasper, and he exerted himself to clear the atmosphere by affecting gaiety he did not feel. The moment the gentlemen came in after dinner he whispered to his mother, who rose, asked the general for his arm, and led the way to the north gallery, whence the sound of music now proceeded. The rest followed in a merry procession, even Treherne, for two footmen carried him up the great stairway, chair and all.

Nothing could look less ghostly now than the haunted gallery. Fires roared up a wide chimney at either end, long rows of figures clad in armor stood on each side, one mailed hand grasping a lance, the other bearing a lighted candle, a device of Sir Jasper's. Narrow windows pierced in the thick walls let in gleams of wintry moonlight; ivy, holly, and evergreen glistened in the ruddy glow of mingled firelight and candle shine. From the arched stone roof hung tattered banners, and in the midst depended a great bunch of mistletoe. Red-cushioned seats stood in recessed window nooks, and from behind a high-covered screen of oak sounded the blithe air of Sir Roger de Coverley.

With the utmost gravity and stateliness my lady and the general led off the dance, for, according to the good old fashion, the men and maids in their best array joined the gentlefolk and danced with their betters in a high state of pride and bashfulness. Sir Jasper twirled the old housekeeper till her head spun around and around and her decorous skirts rustled stormily; Mrs. Snowdon captivated the gray-haired butler by her condescension; and John was made a proud man by the hand of his young mistress. The major came out strong among the pretty maids, and Rose danced the footmen out of breath long before the music paused.

The merriment increased from that moment, and when the general surprised my lady by gallantly saluting her as she unconsciously stood under the mistletoe, the applause was immense. Everyone followed the old gentleman's example as fast as opportunities occurred, and the young ladies soon had as fine a color as the housemaids. More dancing, games, songs, and all manner of festival devices filled the evening, yet under cover of the gaiety more than one little scene was enacted that night, and in an hour of seeming frivolity the current of several lives was changed.

By a skillful maneuver Annon led Octavia to an isolated recess, as if to rest after a brisk game, and, taking advantage of the auspicious hour, pleaded his suit. She heard him patiently and, when he paused, said slowly, yet decidedly, and with no sign of maiden hesitation, "Thanks for the honor you do me, but I cannot accept it, for I do not love you. I think I never can."

"Have you tried?" he asked eagerly.

"Yes, indeed I have. I like you as a friend, but no more. I know Mamma desires it, that Jasper hopes for it, and I try to please them, but love will not be forced, so what can I do?" And she smiled in spite of herself at her own blunt simplicity.

"No, but it can be cherished, strengthened, and in time won, with patience and devotion. Let me try, Octavia; it is but fair, unless you have already learned from another the lesson I hope to teach. Is it so?"

"No, I think not. I do not understand myself as yet, I am so young, and this so sudden. Give me time, Frank."

She blushed and fluttered now, looked half angry, half beseeching, and altogether lovely.

"How much time shall I give? It cannot take long to read a heart like yours, dear." And fancying her emotion a propitious omen, he assumed the lover in good earnest.

"Give me time till the New Year. I will answer then, and, meantime, leave me free to study both myself and you. We have known each other long, I own, but, still, this changes everything, and makes you seem another person. Be patient, Frank, and I will try to make my duty a pleasure."

"I will. God bless you for the kind hope, Octavia. It has been mine for years, and if I lose it, it will go hardly with me."

Later in the evening General Snowdon stood examining the antique screen. In many places carved oak was pierced quite through, so that voices were audible from behind it. The musicians had gone down to supper, the young folk were quietly busy at the other end of the hall, and as the old gentleman admired the quaint carving, the sound of his own name caught his ear. The housekeeper and butler still remained, though the other servants had gone, and sitting cosily behind the screen chatted in low tones believing themselves secure.

"It *was* Mrs. Snowdon, Adam, as I'm a living woman, though I wouldn't say it to anyone but you. She and Sir Jasper were here wrapped in cloaks, and up to mischief, I'll be bound. She is a beauty, but I don't envy her, and there'll be trouble in the house if she stays long."

"But how do you know, Mrs. Benson, she was here? Where's your proof, mum?" asked the pompous butler.

"Look at this, and then look at the outlandish trimming of the lady's dress. You men are so dull about such matters you'd never observe these little points. Well, I was here first after Patty, and my light shone on this jet ornament lying near where she saw the spirit. No one has any such tasty trifles but Mrs. Snowdon, and these are all over her gown. If that ain't proof, what is?"

"Well, admitting it, I then say what on earth should she and Master be up here for, at such a time?" asked the slow-witted butler.

"Adam, we are old servants of the family, and to you I'll say what tortures shouldn't draw from to another. Master has been wild, as you know, and it's my belief that he loved this lady abroad. There was a talk of some mystery, or misdeed, or misfortune, more than a year ago, and she was in it. I'm loath to say it, but I think Master loves her still, and she him. The general is an old man, she is but young, and so spirited and winsome she can't in reason care for him as for a fine, gallant gentleman like Sir Jasper. There's trouble brewing, Adam, mark my words. There's trouble brewing for the Trehernes."

So low had the voices fallen that the listener could not have caught the words had not his ear been strained to the utmost. He did hear all, and his wasted face flashed with the wrath of a young man, then grew pale and stern as he turned to watch his wife. She stood apart from the others talking to Sir Jasper, who looked unusually handsome and debonair as he fanned her with a devoted air.

Perhaps it is true, thought the old man bitterly. They are well matched, were lovers once, no doubt, and long to be so again. Poor

Edith, I was very blind. And with his gray head bowed upon his breast the general stole away, carrying an arrow in his brave old heart.

"Blanche, come here and rest, you will be ill tomorrow; and I promised Mamma to take care of you." With which elder-sisterly command Rose led the girl to an immense old chair, which held them both. "Now listen to me and follow my advice, for I am wise in my generation, though not yet gray. They are all busy, so leave them alone and let me show you what is to be done."

Rose spoke softly, but with great resolution, and nodded her pretty head so energetically that the holly berries came rolling over her white shoulders.

"We are not as rich as we might be, and must establish ourselves as soon and as well as possible. I intend to be Lady Treherne. You can be the Honorable Mrs. Annon, if you give your mind to it."

"My dear child, are you mad?" whispered Blanche.

"Far from it, but you will be if you waste your time on Maurice. He is poor, and a cripple, though very charming, I admit. He loves Tavie, and she will marry him, I am sure. She can't endure Frank, but tries to because my lady commands it. Nothing will come of it, so try your fascinations and comfort the poor man; sympathy now will foster love hereafter."

"Don't talk so here, Rose, someone will hear us," began her sister, but the other broke in briskly.

"No fear, a crowd is the best place for secrets. Now remember what I say, and make your game while the ball is rolling. Other people are careful not to put their plans into words, but I'm no hypocrite, and say plainly what I mean. Bear my sage counsel in mind and act wisely. Now come and begin."

Treherne was sitting alone by one of the great fires, regarding the gay scene with serious air. For him there was neither dancing nor games; he could only roam about catching glimpses of forbidden pleasures, impossible delights, and youthful hopes forever lost to him. Sad but not morose was his face, and to Octavia it was a mute reproach which she could not long resist. Coming up as if to warm herself, she spoke to him in her usually frank and friendly way, and felt her heart beat fast when she saw how swift a change her cordial manner wrought in him.

"How pretty your holly is! Do you remember how we used to go and gather it for festivals like this, when we were happy children?" he asked, looking up at her with eyes full of tender admiration.

"Yes, I remember. Everyone wears it tonight as a badge, but you have none. Let me get you a bit, I like to have you one of us in all things."

She leaned forward to break a green sprig from the branch over the chimneypiece; the strong draft drew in her fleecy skirt, and in an instant she was enveloped in flames.

"Maurice, save me, help me!" cried a voice of fear and agony, and before anyone could reach her, before he himself knew how the deed was done, Treherne had thrown himself from his chair, wrapped the tiger skin tightly about her, and knelt there clasping her in his arms heedless of fire, pain, or the incoherent expressions of love that broke from his lips.

CHAPTER VI.

MIRACLES

Great was the confusion and alarm which reigned for many minutes, but when the panic subsided two miracles appeared. Octavia was entirely uninjured, and Treherne was standing on his feet, a thing which for months he had not done without crutches. In the excitement of the moment, no one observed the wonder; all were crowding about the girl, who, pale and breathless but now self-possessed, was the first to exclaim, pointing to her cousin, who had drawn himself up, with the help of his chair, and leaned there smiling, with a face full of intense delight.

"Look at Maurice! Oh, Jasper, help him or he'll fall!"

Sir Jasper sprung to his side and put a strong arm about him, while a chorus of wonder, sympathy, and congratulations rose about them.

"Why, lad, what does it mean? Have you been deceiving us all this time?" cried Jasper, as Treherne leaned on him, looking exhausted but truly happy.

"It means that I am not to be a cripple all my life; that they did not deceive me when they said a sudden shock might electrify me with a more potent magnetism than any they could apply. It *has*, and if I am cured I owe it all to you, Octavia."

He stretched his hands to her with a gesture of such passionate gratitude that the girl covered her face to hide its traitorous tenderness, and my lady went to him, saying brokenly, as she embraced him with maternal warmth, "God bless you for this act, Maurice, and reward you with a perfect cure. To you I owe the lives of both my children; how can I thank you as I ought?"

"I dare not tell you yet," he whispered eagerly, then added, "I am growing faint, Aunt. Get me away before I make a scene."

This hint recalled my lady to her usual state of dignified self-possession. Bidding Jasper and the major help Treherne to his room without delay, she begged Rose to comfort her sister, who was sobbing hysterically, and as they all obeyed her, she led her daughter away to her own apartment, for the festivities of the evening were at an end.

At the same time Mrs. Snowdon and Annon bade my lady goodnight, as if they also were about to retire, but as they reached the door of the gallery Mrs. Snowdon paused and beckoned Annon back. They were alone now, and, standing before the fire which had so nearly made that Christmas Eve a tragical one, she turned to him with a face full of interest and sympathy as she said, nodding toward the blackened shreds of Octavia's dress, and the scorched tiger skin which still lay at their feet, "That was both a fortunate and an unfortunate little affair, but I fear Maurice's gain will be your loss. Pardon my frankness for Octavia's sake; she is a fine creature, and I long to see her given to one worthy of her. I am a woman to read faces quickly; I know that your suit does not prosper as you would have it, and I desire to help you. May I?"

"Indeed you may, and command any service of me in return. But to what do I owe this unexpected friendliness?" cried Annon, both grateful and surprised.

"To my regard for the young lady, my wish to save her from an unworthy man."

"Do you mean Treherne?" asked Annon, more and more amazed.

"I do. Octavia must not marry a gambler!"

"My dear lady, you labor under some mistake; Treherne is by no means a gambler. I owe him no goodwill, but I cannot hear him slandered."

"You are generous, but I am not mistaken. Can you, on your honor, assure me that Maurice never played?"

Mrs. Snowdon's keen eyes were on him, and he looked embarrassed for a moment, but answered with some hesitation, "Why, no, I cannot say that, but I can assure you that he is not an habitual gambler. All young men of his rank play more or less, especially abroad. It is merely an amusement with most, and among men is not considered dishonorable or dangerous. Ladies think differently, I believe, at least in England."

At the word "abroad," Mrs. Snowdon's face brightened, and she suddenly dropped her eyes, as if afraid of betraying some secret purpose.

"Indeed we do, and well we may, many of us having suffered from this pernicious habit. I have had special cause to dread and condemn it, and the fear that Octavia should in time suffer what I have suffered as a girl urges me to interfere where otherwise I should be dumb. Mr.

Annon, there was a rumor that Maurice was forced to quit Paris, owing to some dishonorable practices at the gaming table. Is this true?"

"Nay, don't ask me; upon my soul I cannot tell you. I only know that something was amiss, but what I never learned. Various tales were whispered at the clubs, and Sir Jasper indignantly denied them all. The bravery with which Maurice saved his cousin, and the sad affliction which fell upon him, silenced the gossip, and it was soon forgotten."

Mrs. Snowdon remained silent for a moment, with brows knit in deep thought, while Annon uneasily watched her. Suddenly she glanced over her shoulder, drew nearer, and whispered cautiously, "Did the rumors of which you speak charge him with—" and the last word was breathed into Annon's ear almost inaudibily.

He started, as if some new light broke on him, and stared at the speaker with a troubled face for an instant, saying hastily, "No, but now you remind me that when an affair of that sort was discussed the other day Treherne looked very odd, and rolled himself away, as if it didn't interest him. I can't believe it, and yet it may be something of the kind. That would account for old Sir Jasper's whim, and Treherne's steady denial of any knowledge of the cause. How in heaven's name did you learn this?"

"My woman's wit suggested it, and my woman's will shall confirm or destroy the suspicion. My lady and Octavia evidently know nothing, but they shall if there is any danger of the girl's being won by him."

"You would not tell her!" exclaimed Annon.

"I will, unless you do it" was the firm answer.

"Never! To betray a friend, even to gain the woman I love, is a thing I cannot do; my honor forbids it."

Mrs. Snowdon smiled scornfully.

"Men's code of honor is a strong one, and we poor women suffer from it. Leave this to me; do your best, and if all other means fail, you may be glad to try my device to prevent Maurice from marrying his cousin. Gratitude and pity are strong allies, and if he recovers, his strong will will move heaven and earth to gain her. Good night." And leaving her last words to rankle in Annon's mind, Mrs. Snowdon departed to endure sleepless hours full of tormenting memories, newborn hopes, and alternations of determination and despair.

Treherne's prospect of recovery filled the whole house with delight, for his patient courage and unfailing cheerfulness had endeared him to all. It was no transient amendment, for day by day he steadily gained strength and power, passing rapidly from chair to crutches, from crutches to a cane and a friend's arm, which was always ready for him. Pain returned with returning vitality, but he bore it with a fortitude that touched all who witnessed it. At times motion was torture, yet motion was necessary lest the torpidity should return, and Treherne took his daily exercise with unfailing perseverance, saying with a smile, though great drops stood upon his forehead, "I have something dearer even than health to win. Hold me up, Jasper, and let me stagger on, in spite of everything, till my twelve turns are made."

He remembered Lady Treherne's words, "If you were well, I'd gladly give my girl to you." This inspired him with strength, endurance, and a happiness which could not be concealed. It overflowed in looks, words, and acts; it infected everyone, and made these holidays the blithest the old abbey had seen for many a day.

Annon devoted himself to Octavia, and in spite of her command to be left in peace till the New Year, she was very kind—so kind that hope flamed up in his heart, though he saw that something like compassion often shone on him from her frank eyes, and her compliance had no touch of the tender docility which lovers long to see. She still avoided Treherne, but so skillfully that few observed the change but Annon and himself. In public Sir Jasper appeared to worship at the sprightly Rose's shrine, and she fancied her game was prospering well.

But had any one peeped behind the scenes it would have been discovered that during the half hour before dinner, when everyone was in their dressing rooms and the general taking his nap, a pair of ghostly black figures flitted about the haunted gallery, where no servant ventured without orders. The major fancied himself the only one who had made this discovery, for Mrs. Snowdon affected Treherne's society in public, and was assiduous in serving and amusing the "dear convalescent," as she called him. But the general did not sleep; he too watched and waited, longing yet dreading to speak, and hoping that this was but a harmless freak of Edith's, for her caprices were many, and till now he had indulged them freely. This hesitation disgusted the major, who, being a bachelor, knew little of women's ways, and less of their powers of persuasion. The day before New Year he took a sudden resolution, and demanded a private interview with the general.

"I have come on an unpleasant errand, sir," he abruptly began, as the old man received him with an expression which rather daunted the major. "My friendship for Lady Treherne, and my guardianship of her children, makes me jealous of the honor of the family. I fear it is in danger, sir; pardon me for saying it, but your wife is the cause."

"May I trouble you to explain, Major Royston" was all the general's reply, as his old face grew stern and haughty.

"I will, sir, briefly. I happen to know from Jasper that there were love passages between Miss Dubarry and himself a year or more ago in Paris. A whim parted them, and she married. So far no reproach rests upon either, but since she came here it has been evident to others as well as myself that Jasper's affection has revived, and that Mrs. Snowdon does not reject and reprove it as she should. They often meet, and from Jasper's manner I am convinced that mischief is afloat. He is ardent, headstrong, and utterly regardless of the world's opinion in some cases. I have watched them, and what I tell you is true."

"Prove it."

"I will. They meet in the north gallery, wrapped in dark cloaks, and play ghost if anyone comes. I concealed myself behind the screen last evening at dusk, and satisfied myself that my suspicions were correct. I heard little of their conversation, but that little was enough."

"Repeat it, if you please."

"Sir Jasper seemed pleading for some promise which she reluctantly gave, saying, 'While you live I will be true to my word with everyone but him. He will suspect, and it will be useless to keep it from him.'

"'He will shoot me for this if he knows I am the traitor,' expostulated Jasper.

"'He shall not know that; I can hoodwink him easily, and serve my purpose also.'

"'You are mysterious, but I leave all to you and wait for my reward. When shall I have it, Edith?' She laughed, and answered so low I could not hear, for they left the gallery as they spoke. Forgive me, General, for the pain I inflict. You are the only person to whom I have spoken, and you are the only person who can properly and promptly prevent this affair from bringing open shame and scandal on an honorable house. To you I leave it, and will do my part with this infatuated young man if you will withdraw the temptation which will ruin him."

"I will. Thank you, Major. Trust to me, and by tomorrow I will prove that I can act as becomes me."

The grief and misery in the general's face touched the major; he silently wrung his hand and went away, thanking heaven more fervently than ever that no cursed coquette of a woman had it in her power to break his heart.

While this scene was going on above, another was taking place in the library. Treherne sat there alone, thinking happy thoughts evidently, for his eyes shone and his lips smiled as he mused, while watching the splendors of a winter sunset. A soft rustle and the faint scent of violets warned him of Mrs. Snowdon's approach, and a sudden foreboding told him that danger was near. The instant he saw her face his fear was confirmed, for exultation, resolve, and love met and mingled in the expression it wore. Leaning in the window recess, where the red light shone full on her lovely face and queenly figure, she said, softly yet with a ruthless accent below the softness, "Dreaming dreams, Maurice, which will never come to pass, unless I will it. I know your secret, and I shall use it to prevent the fulfillment of the foolish hope you cherish."

"Who told you?" he demanded, with an almost fierce flash of the eye and an angry flush.

"I discovered it, as I warned you I should. My memory is good, I recall the gossip of long ago, I observe the faces, words, and acts of those whom I suspect, and unconscious hints from them give me the truth."

"I doubt it," and Treherne smiled securely.

She stooped and whispered one short sentence into his ear. Whatever it was it caused him to start up with a pale, panic-stricken face, and eye her as if she had pronounced his doom.

"Do you doubt it now?" she asked coldly.

"He told you! Even your skill and craft could not discover it alone," he muttered.

"Nay, I told you nothing was impossible to a determined woman. I needed no help, for I knew more than you think."

He sank down again in a despairing attitude and hid his face, saying mournfully, "I might have known you would hunt me down and dash my hopes when they were surest. How will you use this unhappy secret?"

"I will tell Octavia, and make her duty less hard. It will be kind to both of you, for even with her this memory would mar your happiness; and it saves her from the shame and grief of discovering, when too late, that she has given herself to a—"

"Stop!" he cried, in a tone that made her start and pale, as he rose out of his chair white with a stern indignation which awed her for a moment. "You shall not utter that word—you know but half the truth, and if you wrong me or trouble the girl I will turn traitor also, and tell the general the game you are playing with my cousin. You feign to love me as you feigned before, but his title is the bait now as then, and you fancy that by threatening to mar my hopes you will secure my silence, and gain your end."

"Wrong, quite wrong. Jasper is nothing to me; I use *him* as a tool, not you. If I threaten, it is to keep you from Octavia, who cannot forgive the past and love you for yourself, as I have done all these miserable months. You say I know but half the truth. Tell me the whole and I will spare you."

If ever a man was tempted to betray a trust it was Treherne then. A word, and Octavia might be his; silence, and she might be lost; for this woman was in earnest, and possessed the power to ruin his good name forever. The truth leaped to his lips and would have passed them, had not his eye fallen on the portrait of Jasper's father. This man had loved and sheltered the orphan all his life, had made of him a son, and, dying, urged him to guard and serve and save the rebellious youth he left, when most needing a father's care.

"I promised, and I will keep my promise at all costs," sighed Treherne, and with a gesture full of pathetic patience he waved the fair tempter from him, saying steadily, "I will never tell you, though you rob me of that which is dearer than my life. Go and work your will, but remember that when you might have won the deepest gratitude of the man you profess to love, you chose instead to earn his hatred and contempt."

Waiting for no word of hers, he took refuge in his room, and Edith Snowdon sank down upon the couch, struggling with contending emotions of love and jealousy, remorse and despair. How long she sat there she could not tell; an approaching step recalled her to herself, and looking up she saw Octavia. As the girl approached down the long vista of the drawing rooms, her youth and beauty, innocence and candor touched that fairer and more gifted woman with an envy she had never known before. Something in the girl's face struck her instantly: a look of peace and purity, a sweet serenity more winning than loveliness, more impressive than dignity or grace. With a smile on her lips, yet a half-sad, half-tender light in her eyes, and a cluster of pale winter roses in her hand, she came on till she stood before her rival and, offering the flowers, said, in words as simple as sincere, "Dear Mrs. Snowdon, I cannot let the last sun of the old year set on any misdeeds of mine for which I may atone. I have disliked, distrusted, and misjudged you, and now I come to you in all humility to say forgive me."

With the girlish abandon of her impulsive nature Octavia knelt down before the woman who was plotting to destroy her happiness, laid the roses like a little peace offering on her lap, and with eloquently pleading eyes waited for pardon. For a moment Mrs. Snowdon watched her, fancying it a well-acted ruse to disarm a dangerous rival; but in that sweet face there was no art; one glance showed her that. The words smote her to the heart and won her in spite of pride or passion, as she suddenly took the girl into her arms, weeping repentant tears. Neither spoke, but in the silence each felt the barrier which had stood between them vanishing, and each learned to know the other better in that moment than in a year of common life. Octavia rejoiced that the instinct which had prompted her to make this appeal had not misled her, but assured her that behind the veil of coldness, pride, and levity which this woman wore there was a heart aching for sympathy and help and love. Mrs. Snowdon felt her worser self slip from her, leaving all that was true and noble to make her worthy of the test applied. Art she could meet with equal art, but nature conquered her. For spite of her misspent life and faulty character, the germ of virtue, which lives in the worst, was there, only waiting for the fostering sun and dew of love to strengthen it, even though the harvest be a late one.

"Forgive you!" she cried, brokenly. "It is I who should ask forgiveness of you—I who should atone, confess, and repent. Pardon *me*, pity me, love me, for I am more wretched than you know."

"Dear, I do with heart and soul. Believe it, and let me be your friend" was the soft answer.

"God knows I need one!" sighed the poor woman, still holding fast the only creature who had wholly won her. "Child, I am not good, but not so bad that I dare not look in your innocent face and call you friend. I never had one of my own sex. I never knew my mother; and no one ever saw in me the possibility of goodness, truth, and justice but you. Trust and love and help me, Octavia, and I will reward you with a better life, if I can do no more."

"I will, and the new year shall be happier than the old."

"God bless you for that prophecy; may I be worthy of it."

Then as a bell warned them away, the rivals kissed each other tenderly, and parted friends. As Mrs. Snowdon entered her room, she saw her husband sitting with his gray head in his hands, and heard him murmur despairingly to himself, "My life makes her miserable. But for the sin of it I'd die to free her."

"No, live for me, and teach me to be happy in your love." The clear voice startled him, but not so much as the beautiful changed face of the wife who laid the gray head on her bosom, saying tenderly, "My kind and patient husband, you have been deceived. From me you shall know all the truth, and when you have forgiven my faulty past, you shall see how happy I will try to make your future."

CHAPTER VII.

A GHOSTLY REVEL

"Bless me, how dull we are tonight!" exclaimed Rose, as the younger portion of the party wandered listlessly about the drawing rooms that evening, while my lady and the major played an absorbing game of piquet, and the general dozed peacefully at last.

"It is because Maurice is not here; he always keeps us going, for he is a fellow of infinite resources," replied Sir Jasper, suppressing a yawn.

"Have him out then," said Annon.

"He won't come. The poor lad is blue tonight, in spite of his improvement. Something is amiss, and there is no getting a word from him."

"Sad memories afflict him, perhaps," sighed Blanche.

"Don't be absurd, dear, sad memories are all nonsense; melancholy is always indigestion, and nothing is so sure a cure as fun," said Rose briskly. "I'm going to send in a polite invitation begging him to come and amuse us. He'll accept, I haven't a doubt."

The message was sent, but to Rose's chagrin a polite refusal was returned.

"He *shall* come. Sir Jasper, do you and Mr. Annon go as a deputation from us, and return without him at your peril" was her command.

They went, and while waiting their reappearance the sisters spoke of what all had observed.

"How lovely Mrs. Snowdon looks tonight. I always thought she owed half her charms to her skill in dress, but she never looked so beautiful as in that plain black silk, with those roses in her hair," said Rose.

"What has she done to herself?" replied Blanche. "I see a change, but can't account for it. She and Tavie have made some beautifying discovery, for both look altogether uplifted and angelic all of a sudden."

"Here come the gentlemen, and, as I'm a Talbot, they haven't got him!" cried Rose as the deputation appeared, looking very crestfallen. "Don't come near me," she added, irefully, "you are disloyal cowards, and I doom you to exile till I want you. *I* am infinite in resources as well as this recreant man, and come he shall. Mrs. Snowdon, would you mind asking Mr. Treherne to suggest something to wile away the rest of this evening? We are in despair, and can think of nothing, and you are all-powerful with him."

"I must decline, since he refuses you" was the decided answer, as Mrs. Snowdon moved away.

"Tavie, dear, do go; we *must* have him; he always obeys you, and you would be such a public benefactor, you know."

Without a word Octavia wrote a line and sent it by a servant. Several minutes passed, and the gentlemen began to lay wagers on the success of her trial. "He will not come for me, you may be sure," said Octavia. As the words passed her lips he appeared.

A general laugh greeted him, but, taking no notice of the jests at his expense, he turned to Octavia, saying quietly, "What can I do for you, Cousin?"

His colorless face and weary eyes reproached her for disturbing him, but it was too late for regret, and she answered hastily, "We are in want of some new and amusing occupation to wile away the evening. Can you suggest something appropriate?"

"Why not sit round the hall fire and tell stories, while we wait to see the old year out, as we used to do long ago?" he asked, after a moment's thought.

"I told you so! There it is, just what we want." And Sir Jasper looked triumphant.

"It's capital—let us begin at once. It is after ten now, so we shall not have long to wait," cried Rose, and, taking Sir Jasper's arm, she led the way to the hall.

A great fire always burned there, and in wintertime thick carpets and curtains covered the stone floor and draped the tall windows. Plants blossomed in the warm atmosphere, and chairs and lounges stood about invitingly. The party was soon seated, and Treherne was desired to begin.

"We must have ghost stories, and in order to be properly thrilling and effective, the lights must be put out," said Rose, who sat next him, and spoke first, as usual.

This was soon done, and only a ruddy circle of firelight was left to oppose the rapt gloom that filled the hall, where shadows now seemed to lurk in every corner.

"Don't be very dreadful, or I shall faint away," pleaded Blanche, drawing nearer to Annon, for she had taken her sister's advice, and laid close siege to that gentleman's heart.

"I think your nerves will bear my little tale," replied Treherne. "When I was in India, four years ago, I had a very dear friend in my regiment—a Scotchman; I'm half Scotch myself, you know, and clannish, of course. Gordon was sent up the country on a scouting expedition, and never returned. His men reported that he left them one evening to take a survey, and his horse came home bloody and riderless. We searched, but could not find a trace of him, and I was desperate to discover and avenge his murder. About a month after his disappearance, as I sat in my tent one fearfully hot day, suddenly the canvas door flap was raised and there stood Gordon. I saw him as plainly as I see you, Jasper, and should have sprung to meet him, but something held me back. He was deathly pale, dripping with water, and in his bonny blue eyes was a wild, woeful look that made my blood run cold. I stared dumbly, for it was awful to see my friend so changed and so unearthly. Stretching his arm to me he took my hand, saying solemnly, 'Come!' The touch was like ice; an ominous thrill ran through me; I started up to obey, and he was gone."

"A horrid dream, of course. Is that all?" asked Rose.

With his eyes on the fire and his left hand half extended, Treherne went on as if he had not heard her.

"I thought it was a fancy, and soon recovered myself, for no one had seen or heard anything of Gordon, and my native servant lay just outside my tent. A strange sensation remained in the hand the phantom touched. It was cold, damp, and white. I found it vain to try to forget this apparition; it took strong hold of me; I told Yermid, my man, and he bade me consider it a sign that I was to seek my friend. That night I dreamed I was riding up the country in hot haste; what led me I know not, but I pressed on and on, longing to reach the end. A half-dried river crossed my path, and, riding down the steep bank to ford it, I saw Gordon's body lying in the shallow water looking exactly as the vision looked. I woke in a strange mood, told the story to my commanding officer, and, as nothing was doing just then, easily got leave of absence for a week. Taking Yermid, I set out on my sad quest. I thought it folly, but I could not resist the impulse that drew me on. For seven days I searched, and the strangest part of the story is that all that time I went on exactly as in the dream, seeing what I saw then, and led by the touch of a cold hand on mine. On the seventh day I reached the river, and found my friend's body."

"How horrible! Is it really true?" cried Mrs. Snowdon.

"As true as I am a living man. Nor is that all: this left hand of mine never has been warm since that time. See and feel for yourselves."

He opened both hands, and all satisfied themselves that the left was smaller, paler, and colder than the right.

"Pray someone tell another story to put this out of my mind; it makes me nervous," said Blanche.

"I'll tell one, and you may laugh to quiet your nerves. I want to have mine done with, so that I can enjoy the rest with a free mind." With these words Rose began her tale in the good old fashion.

"Once upon a time, when we were paying a visit to my blessed grandmamma, I saw a ghost in this wise: The dear old lady was ill with a cold and kept her room, leaving us to mope, for it was very dull in the great lonely house. Blanche and I were both homesick, but didn't like to leave till she was better, so we ransacked the library and solaced ourselves with all manner of queer books. One day I found Grandmamma very low and nervous, and evidently with something on her mind. She would say nothing, but the next day was worse, and I insisted on knowing the cause, for the trouble was evidently mental. Charging me to keep it from Blanche, who was, and is, a sad coward, she told me that a spirit had appeared to her two successive nights. 'If it comes a third time, I shall prepare to die,' said the foolish old lady.

"'No, you won't, for I'll come and stay with you and lay your ghost,' I said. With some difficulty I made her yield, and after Blanche was asleep I slipped away to Grandmamma, with a book and candle for a long watch, as the spirit didn't appear till after midnight. She usually slept with her door unlocked, in case of fire or fright, and her maid was close by. That night I locked the door, telling her that spirits could come through the oak if they chose, and I preferred to have a fair trial. Well, I read and chatted and dozed till dawn and nothing appeared, so I laughed at the whole affair, and the old lady pretended to be convinced that it was all a fancy.

"Next night I slept in my own room, and in the morning was told that not only Grandmamma but Janet had seen the spirit. All in white, with streaming hair, a pale face, and a red streak at the throat. It came and parted the bed-curtains, looking in a moment, and then vanished.

Janet had slept with Grandmamma and kept a lamp burning on the chimney, so both saw it.

"I was puzzled, but not frightened; I never am, and I insisted on trying again. The door was left unlocked, as on the previous night, and I lay with Grandmamma, a light burning as before. About two she clutched me as I was dropping off. I looked, and there, peeping in between the dark curtains, was a pale face with long hair all about it, and a red streak at the throat. It was very dim, the light being low, but I saw it, and after one breathless minute sprang up, caught my foot, fell down with a crash, and by the time I was around the bed, not a vestige of the thing appeared. I was angry, and vowed I'd succeed at all hazards, though I'll confess I was just a bit daunted.

"Next time Janet and I sat up in easy chairs, with bright lights burning, and both wide awake with the strongest coffee we could make. As the hour drew near we got nervous, and when the white shape came gliding in Janet hid her face. I didn't, and after one look was on the point of laughing, for the spirit was Blanche walking in her sleep. She wore a coral necklace in those days, and never took it off, and her long hair half hid her face, which had the unnatural, uncanny look somnambulists always wear. I had the sense to keep still and tell Janet what to do, so the poor child went back unwaked, and Grandmamma's spirit never walked again for I took care of that."

"Why did you haunt the old lady?" asked Annon, as the laughter ceased.

"I don't know, unless it was that I wanted to ask leave to go home, and was afraid to do it awake, so tried when asleep. I shall not tell any story, as I was the heroine of this, but will give my turn to you, Mr. Annon," said Blanche, with a soft glance, which was quite thrown away, for the gentleman's eyes were fixed on Octavia, who sat on a low ottoman at Mrs. Snowdon's feet in the full glow of the firelight.

"I've had very small experience in ghosts, and can only recall a little fright I once had when a boy at college. I'd been out to a party, got home tired, couldn't find my matches, and retired in the dark. Toward morning I woke, and glancing up to see if the dim light was dawn or moonshine I was horrified to see a coffin standing at the bed's foot. I rubbed my eyes to be sure I was awake, and looked with all my might. There it was, a long black coffin, and I saw the white plate in the dusk, for the moon was setting and my curtain was not drawn. 'It's some trick of the fellows,' I thought; 'I'll not betray myself, but keep cool.' Easy to say but hard to do, for it suddenly flashed into my mind that I might be in the wrong room. I glanced about, but there were the familiar objects as usual, as far as the indistinct light allowed me to see, and I made sure by feeling on the wall at the bed's head for my watchcase. It was there, and mine beyond a doubt, being peculiar in shape and fabric. Had I been to a college wine party I could have accounted for the vision, but a quiet evening in a grave professor's well-conducted family could produce no ill effects. 'It's an optical illusion, or a prank of my mates; I'll sleep and forget it,' I said, and for a time endeavored to do so, but curiosity overcame my resolve, and soon I peeped again. Judge of my horror when I saw the sharp white outline of a dead face, which seemed to be peeping up from the coffin. It gave me a terrible shock for I was but a lad and had been ill. I hid my face and quaked like a nervous girl, still thinking it some joke and too proud to betray fear lest I should be laughed at. How long I lay there I don't know, but when I looked again the face was farther out and the whole figure seemed rising slowly. The moon was nearly down, I had no lamp, and to be left in the dark with that awesome thing was more than I could bear. Joke or earnest, I must end the panic, and bolting out of my room I roused my neighbor. He told me I was mad or drunk, but lit a lamp and returned with me, to find my horror only a heap of clothes thrown on the table in such a way that, as the moon's pale light shot it, it struck upon my black student's gown, with a white card lying on it, and produced the effect of a coffin and plate. The face was a crumpled handkerchief, and what seemed hair a brown muffler. As the moon sank, these outlines changed and, incredible as it may seem, grew like a face. My friend not having had the fright enjoyed the joke, and 'Coffins' was my sobriquet for a long while."

"You get worse and worse. Sir Jasper, do vary the horrors by a touch of fun, or I shall run away," said Blanche, glancing over her shoulder nervously.

"I'll do my best, and tell a story my uncle used to relate of his young days. I forget the name of the place, but it was some little country town famous among anglers. My uncle often went to fish, and always regretted that a deserted house near the trout stream was not occupied, for the inn was inconveniently distant. Speaking of this one evening as he lounged in the landlady's parlor, he asked why no one took it and let the rooms to strangers in the fishing season. 'For fear of the ghostissess, your honor,' replied the woman, and proceeded to tell, him that three distinct spirits haunted the house. In the garret was heard the hum of a wheel and the tap of high-heeled shoes, as the ghostly spinner went to and fro. In a chamber sounded the sharpening of a knife, followed by groans and the drip of blood. The cellar was made awful by a skeleton sitting on a half-buried box and chuckling fiendishly. It seems a miser lived there once, and was believed to have starved his daughter in the garret, keeping her at work till she died. The second spirit was that of the girl's rejected lover, who cut his throat in the chamber, and the third of the miser who was found dead on the money chest he was too feeble to conceal. My uncle laughed at all this, and offered to lay the ghosts if anyone would take the house.

"This offer got abroad, and a crusty old fellow accepted it, hoping to turn a penny. He had a pretty girl, whose love had been thwarted by the old man, and whose lover was going to sea in despair. My uncle knew this and pitied the young people. He had made acquaintance with a wandering artist, and the two agreed to conquer the prejudices against the house by taking rooms there. They did so, and after satisfying themselves regarding the noises, consulted a wise old woman as to the best means of laying the ghosts. She told them if any young girl would pass a night in each haunted room, praying piously the while, that all would be well. Peggy was asked if she would do it, and being a stouthearted lass she consented, for a round sum, to try it. The first night was in the garret, and Peggy, in spite of the prophecies of the village gossips, came out alive, though listeners at the door heard the weird humming and tapping all night long. The next night all went well, and from that time no more sharpening, groaning, or dripping was heard. The third time she bade her friends good-bye and, wrapped in her red cloak, with a lamp and prayer book, went down into the cellar. Alas for pretty Peggy! When day came she was gone, and with her the miser's empty box, though his bones remained to prove how well she had done her work.

"The town was in an uproar, and the old man furious. Some said the devil had flown away with her, others that the bones were hers, and all agreed that henceforth another ghost would haunt the house. My uncle and the artist did their best to comfort the father, who sorely reproached himself for thwarting the girl's love, and declared that if Jack would find her he should have her. But Jack had sailed, and the old man 'was left lamenting.' The house was freed from its unearthly visitors, however, for no ghost appeared; and when my uncle left, old Martin found money and letter informing him that Peggy had spent her first two nights preparing for flight, and on the third had gone away to marry and sail with Jack. The noises had been produced by the artist, who was a ventriloquist, the skeleton had been smuggled from the surgeons, and the whole thing was a conspiracy to help Peggy and accommodate the fishermen."

"It is evident that roguery is hereditary," laughed Rose as the narrator paused.

"I strongly suspect that Sir Jasper the second was the true hero of that story," added Mrs. Snowdon.

"Think what you like, I've done my part, and leave the stage for you, madam."

"I will come last. It is your turn, dear." As Mrs. Snowdon softly uttered the last word, and Octavia leaned upon her knee with an affectionate glance, Treherne leaned forward to catch a glimpse of the two changed faces, and looked as if bewildered when both smiled at him, as they sat hand in hand while the girl told her story.

"Long ago a famous actress suddenly dropped dead at the close of a splendidly played tragedy. She was carried home, and preparations were made to bury her. The play had been gotten up with great care and expense, and a fine actor was the hero. The public demanded a repetition, and an inferior person was engaged to take the dead lady's part. A day's delay had been necessary, but when the night came the house was crowded. They waited both before and behind the curtain for the debut of the new actress, with much curiosity. She stood waiting for her cue, but as it was given, to the amazement of all, the great tragedienne glided upon the stage. Pale as marble, and with a strange fire in her eyes, strange pathos in her voice, strange power in her acting, she went through her part, and at the close vanished as mysteriously as she came. Great was the excitement that night, and intense the astonishment and horror next day when it was whispered abroad that the dead woman never had revived, but had lain in her coffin before the eyes of watchers all the evening, when hundreds fancied they were applauding her at the theater. The mystery never was cleared up, and Paris was divided by two opinions: one that some person marvelously like Madame Z. had personated her for the sake of a sensation; the other that the ghost of the dead actress, unable to free itself from the old duties so full of fascination to an ambitious and successful woman, had played for the last time the part which had made her famous."

"Where did you find that, Tavie? It's very French, and not bad if you invented it," said Sir Jasper.

"I read it in an old book, where it was much better told. Now, Edith, there is just time for your tale."

As the word "Edith" passed her lips, again Treherne started and eyed them both, and again they smiled, as Mrs. Snowdon caressed the smooth cheek leaning on her knee, and looking full at him began the last recital.

"You have been recounting the pranks of imaginary ghosts; let me show you the workings of some real spirits, evil and good, that haunt every heart and home, making its misery or joy. At Christmastime, in a country house, a party of friends met to keep the holidays, and very happily they might have done so had not one person marred the peace of several. Love, jealousy, deceit, and nobleness were the spirits that played their freaks with these people. The person of whom I speak was more haunted than the rest, and much tormented, being willful, proud, and jealous. Heaven help her, she had had no one to exorcise these ghosts for her, and they goaded her to do much harm. Among these friends there were more than one pair of lovers, and much tangling of plots and plans, for hearts are wayward and mysterious things, and cannot love as duty bids or prudence counsels. This woman held the key to all the secrets of the house, and, having a purpose to gain, she used her power selfishly, for a time. To satisfy a doubt, she feigned a fancy for a gentleman who once did her the honor of admiring her, and, to the great scandal of certain sage persons, permitted him to show his regard for her, knowing that it was but a transient amusement on his part as well as upon hers. In the hands of this woman lay a secret which could make or mar the happiness of the best and dearest of the party. The evil spirits which haunted her urged her to mar their peace and gratify a sinful hope. On the other side, honor, justice, and generosity prompted her to make them happy, and while she wavered there came to her a sweet enchantress who, with a word, banished the tormenting ghosts forever, and gave the haunted woman a talisman to keep her free henceforth."

There the earnest voice faltered, and with a sudden impulse Mrs. Snowdon bent her head and kissed the fair forehead which had bent lower and lower as she went on. Each listener understood the truth, lightly veiled in that hasty fable, and each found in it a different meaning. Sir Jasper frowned and bit his lips, Annon glanced anxiously from face to face, Octavia hid hers, and Treherne's flashed with sudden intelligence, while Rose laughed low to herself, enjoying the scene. Blanche, who was getting sleepy, said, with a stifled gape, "That is a very nice, moral little story, but I wish there had been some real ghosts in it."

"There was. Will you come and see them?"

As she put the question, Mrs. Snowdon rose abruptly, wishing to end the séance, and beckoning them to follow glided up the great stairway. All obeyed, wondering what whim possessed her, and quite ready for any jest in store for them.

CHAPTER VIII.

JASPER

She led them to the north gallery and, pausing at the door, said merrily, "The ghost—or ghosts rather, for there were two—which frightened Patty were Sir Jasper and myself, meeting to discuss certain important matters which concerned Mr. Treherne. If you want to see spirits we will play phantom for you, and convince you of our power."

"Good, let us go and have a ghostly dance, as a proper finale of our revel," answered Rose as they flocked into the long hall.

At that moment the great clock struck twelve, and all paused to bid the old year adieu. Sir Jasper was the first to speak, for, angry with Mrs. Snowdon, yet thankful to her for making a jest to others of what had been earnest to him, he desired to hide his chagrin under a gay manner; and taking Rose around the waist was about to waltz away as she proposed, saying cheerily, "'Come one and all, and dance the new year in,'" when a cry from Octavia arrested him, and turning he saw her stand, pale and trembling, pointing to the far end of the hall.

Eight narrow Gothic windows pierced either wall of the north gallery. A full moon sent her silvery light strongly in upon the eastern side, making broad bars of brightness across the floor. No fires burned there now, and wherever the moonlight did not fall deep shadows lay. As Octavia cried out, all looked, and all distinctly saw a tall, dark figure moving noiselessly across the second bar of light far down the hall.

"Is it some jest of yours?" asked Sir Jasper of Mrs. Snowdon, as the form vanished in the shadow.

"No, upon my honor, I know nothing of it! I only meant to relieve Octavia's superstitious fears by showing her our pranks" was the whispered reply as Mrs. Snowdon's cheek paled, and she drew nearer to Jasper.

"Who is there?" called Treherne in a commanding tone.

No answer, but a faint, cold breath of air seemed to sigh along the arched roof and die away as the dark figure crossed the third streak of moonlight. A strange awe fell upon them all, and no one spoke, but stood watching for the appearance of the shape. Nearer and nearer it came, with soundless steps, and as it reached the sixth window its outlines were distinctly visible. A tall, wasted figure, all in black, with a rosary hanging from the girdle, and a dark beard half concealing the face.

"The Abbot's ghost, and very well got up," said Annon, trying to laugh but failing decidedly, for again the cold breath swept over them, causing a general shudder.

"Hush!" whispered Treherne, drawing Octavia to his side with a protecting gesture.

Once more the phantom appeared and disappeared, and as they waited for it to cross the last bar of light that lay between it and them, Mrs. Snowdon stepped forward to the edge of the shadow in which they stood, as if to confront the apparition alone. Out of the darkness it came, and in the full radiance of the light it paused. Mrs. Snowdon, being nearest, saw the face first, and uttering a faint cry dropped down upon the stone floor, covering up her eyes. Nothing human ever wore a look like that of the ghastly, hollow-eyed, pale-lipped countenance below the hood. All saw it and held their breath as it slowly raised a shadowy arm and pointed a shriveled finger at Sir Jasper.

"Speak, whatever you are, or I'll quickly prove whether you are man or spirit!" cried Jasper fiercely, stepping forward as if to grasp the extended arm that seemed to menace him alone.

An icy gust swept through the hall, and the phantom slowly receded into the shadow. Jasper sprang after it, but nothing crossed the second stream of light, and nothing remained in the shade. Like one possessed by a sudden fancy he rushed down the gallery to find all fast and empty, and to return looking very strangely. Blanche had fainted away and Annon was bearing her out of the hall. Rose was clinging to Mrs. Snowdon, and Octavia leaned against her cousin, saying in a fervent whisper, "Thank God it did not point at you!"

"Am I then dearer than your brother?" he whispered back.

There was no audible reply, but one little hand involuntarily pressed his, though the other was outstretched toward Jasper, who came up white and startled but firm and quiet. Affecting to make light of it, he said, forcing a smile as he raised Mrs. Snowdon, "It is some stupid joke of the servants. Let us think no more of it. Come, Edith, this is not like your usual self."

"It was nothing human, Jasper; you know it as well as I. Oh, why did I bring you here to meet the warning phantom that haunts your house!"

"Nay, if my time is near the spirit would have found me out wherever I might be. I have no faith in that absurd superstition—I laugh at and defy it. Come down and drink my health in wine from the Abbot's own cellar."

But no one had heart for further gaiety, and, finding Lady Treherne already alarmed by Annon, they were forced to tell her all, and find their own bewilderment deepened by her unalterable belief in the evil omen.

At her command the house was searched, the servants cross-questioned, and every effort made to discover the identity of the apparition. All in vain; the house was as usual, and not a man or maid but turned pale at the idea of entering the gallery at midnight. At my lady's request, all promised to say no more upon the mystery, and separated at last to such sleep as they could enjoy.

Very grave were the faces gathered about the breakfast table next morning, and very anxious the glances cast on Sir Jasper as he came in, late as usual, looking uncommonly blithe and well. Nothing serious ever made a deep impression on his mercurial nature. Treherne had more the air of a doomed man, being very pale and worn, in spite of an occasional gleam of happiness as he looked at Octavia. He haunted Jasper like a shadow all the morning, much to that young gentleman's annoyance, for both his mother and sister hung about him with faces of ill-dissembled anxiety. By afternoon his patience gave out, and he openly rebelled against the tender guard kept over him. Ringing for his horse he said decidedly, "I'm bored to death with the solemnity which pervades the house today, so I'm off for a brisk gallop, before I lose my temper and spirits altogether."

"Come with me in the pony carriage, Jasper. I've not had a drive with you for a long while, and should enjoy it so much," said my lady, detaining him.

"Mrs. Snowdon looks as if she needed air to revive her roses, and the pony carriage is just the thing for her, so I will cheerfully resign my seat to her," he answered laughing, as he forced himself from his mother's hand.

"Take the girls in the clarence. We all want a breath of air, and you are the best whip we know. Be gallant and say yes, dear."

"No, thank you, Tavie, that won't do. Rose and Blanche are both asleep, and you are dying to go and do likewise, after your vigils last night. As a man and a brother I beg you'll do so, and let me ride as I like."

"Suppose you ask Annon to join you—" began Treherne with well-assumed indifference; but Sir Jasper frowned and turned sharply on him, saying, half-petulantly, half-jocosely:

"Upon my life I should think I was a boy or a baby, by the manner in which you mount guard over me today. If you think I'm going to live in daily fear of some mishap, you are all much mistaken. Ghost or no ghost, I shall make merry while I can; a short life and a jolly one has always been my motto, you know, so fare you well till dinnertime."

They watched him gallop down the avenue, and then went their different ways, still burdened with a nameless foreboding. Octavia strolled into the conservatory, thinking to refresh herself with the balmy silence which pervaded the place, but Annon soon joined her, full of a lover's hopes and fears.

"Miss Treherne, I have ventured to come for my answer. Is my New Year to be a blissful or a sad one?" he asked eagerly.

"Forgive me if I give you an unwelcome reply, but I must be true, and so regretfully refuse the honor you do me," she said sorrowfully.

"May I ask why?"

"Because I do not love you."

"And you do love your cousin," he cried angrily, pausing to watch her half-averted face.

She turned it fully toward him and answered, with her native sincerity, "Yes, I do, with all my heart, and now my mother will not thwart me, for Maurice has saved my life, and I am free to devote it all to him."

"Happy man, I wish I had been a cripple!" sighed Annon. Then with a manful effort to be just and generous, he added heartily, "Say no more, he deserves you; I want no sacrifice to duty; I yield, and go away, praying heaven to bless you now and always."

He kissed her hand and left her to seek my lady and make his adieus, for no persuasion could keep him. Leaving a note for Sir Jasper, he hurried away, to the great relief of Treherne and the deep regret of Blanche, who, however, lived in hopes of another trial later in the season.

"Here comes Jasper, Mamma, safe and well," cried Octavia an hour or two later, as she joined her mother on the terrace, where my lady had been pacing restlessly to and fro nearly ever since her son rode away.

With a smile of intense relief she waved her handkerchief as he came clattering up the drive, and seeing her he answered with hat and hand. He usually dismounted at the great hall door, but a sudden whim made him ride along the wall that lay below the terrace, for he was a fine horseman, and Mrs. Snowdon was looking from her window. As he approached, the peacocks fled screaming, and one flew up just before the horse's eyes as his master was in the act of dismounting. The spirited creature was startled, sprang partway up the low, broad steps of the terrace, and, being sharply checked, slipped, fell, and man and horse rolled down together.

Never did those who heard it forget the cry that left Lady Treherne's lips as she saw the fall. It brought out both guests and servants, to find Octavia recklessly struggling with the frightened horse, and my lady down upon the stones with her son's bleeding head in her arms.

They bore in the senseless, shattered body, and for hours tried everything that skill and sciences could devise to save the young man's life. But every effort was in vain, and as the sun set Sir Jasper lay dying. Conscious at last, and able to speak, he looked about him with a troubled glance, and seemed struggling with some desire that overmastered pain and held death at bay.

"I want Maurice," he feebly said, at length.

"Dear lad, I'm here," answered his cousin's voice from a seat in the shadow of the half-drawn curtains.

"Always near when I need you. Many a scrape have you helped me out of, but this is beyond your power," and a faint smile passed over Jasper's lips as the past flitted before his mind. But the smile died, and a groan of pain escaped him as he cried suddenly, "Quick! Let me tell it before it is too late! Maurice never will, but bear the shame all his life that my dead name may be untarnished. Bring Edith; she must hear the truth."

She was soon there, and, lying in his mother's arms, one hand in his cousin's, and one on his sister's bent head, Jasper rapidly told the secret which had burdened him for a year.

"I did it; I forged my uncle's name when I had lost so heavily at play that I dared not tell my mother, or squander more of my own fortune. I deceived Maurice, and let him think the check a genuine one; I made him present it and get the money, and when all went well I fancied I was safe. But my uncle discovered it secretly, said nothing, and, believing Maurice the forger, disinherited him. I never knew this till the old man died, and then it was too late. I confessed to Maurice, and he forgave me. He said, 'I am helpless now, shut out from the world, with nothing to lose or gain, and soon to be forgotten by those who once knew me, so let the suspicion of shame, if any such there be, still cling to me, and do you go your way, rich, happy, honorable, and untouched by any shadow on your fame.' Mother, I let him do it, unconscious as he was that many knew the secret sin and fancied him the doer of it."

"Hush, Jasper, let it pass. I can bear it; I promised your dear father to be your staunch friend through life, and I have only kept my word."

"God knows you have, but now my life ends, and I cannot die till you are cleared. Edith, I told you half the truth, and you would have used it against him had not some angel sent this girl to touch your heart. You have done your part to atone for the past, now let me do mine. Mother, Tavie loves him, he has risked life and honor for me. Repay him generously and give him this."

With feeble touch Sir Jasper tried to lay his sister's hand in Treherne's as he spoke; Mrs. Snowdon helped him, and as my lady bowed her head in silent acquiescence, a joyful smile shone on the dying man's face.

"One more confession, and then I am ready," he said, looking up into the face of the woman whom he had loved with all the power of a shallow nature. "It was a jest to you, Edith, but it was bitter earnest to me, for I loved you, sinful as it was. Ask your husband to forgive me, and tell him it was better I should die than live to mar a good man's peace. Kiss me once, and make him happy for my sake."

She touched his cold lips with remorseful tenderness, and in the same breath registered a vow to obey that dying prayer.

"Tavie dear, Maurice, my brother, God bless you both. Good-bye, Mother. He will be a better son than I have been to you." Then, the reckless spirit of the man surviving to the last, Sir Jasper laughed faintly, as he seemed to beckon some invisible shape, and died saying gaily, "Now, Father Abbot, lead on, I'll follow you."

* * * * * *

A year later three weddings were celebrated on the same day and in the same church. Maurice Treherne, a well man, led up his cousin. Frank Annon rewarded Blanche's patient siege by an unconditional surrender, and, to the infinite amusement of Mrs. Grundy, Major Royston publicly confessed himself outgeneraled by merry Rose. The triple wedding feast was celebrated at Treherne Abbey, and no uncanny visitor marred its festivities, for never again was the north gallery haunted by the ghostly Abbot.

LOUISA MAY ALCOTT BIOGRAPHY

Louisa May Alcott (November 29, 1832 – March 6, 1888), an American novelist, short story writer, and poet, is best known for her novel Little Women (1868) and its sequels Little Men (1871) and Jo's Boys (1888). (1886). Abigail May and Amos Bronson Alcott, both transcendentalists, raised her in New England, where she grew up among many well-known intellectuals of the day, including Ralph Waldo Emerson, Nathaniel Hawthorne, Henry David Thoreau, and Henry Wadsworth Longfellow.

Alcott's family struggled financially, and she began working at a young age to help support the family while simultaneously seeking an outlet in writing. In the 1860s, she began to receive critical acclaim for her work. She created filthy short tales and sensation books for adults under pen names such as A. M. Barnard early on in her career, focusing on passion and revenge.

Little Women was published in 1868 and is loosely based on Alcott's childhood experiences with her three sisters, Abigail May Alcott Nieriker, Elizabeth Sewall Alcott, and Anna Alcott Pratt. It is set in the Alcott family home, Orchard House, in Concord, Massachusetts, and is loosely based on Alcott's childhood experiences with her three sisters, Abigail May Alcott Nieriker, Elizabeth Sewall Alcott, and Anna Alcott Pratt. The novel was well-received at the time, and it continues to be popular among children and adults today. It has been adapted for stage, cinema, and television numerous times.

Alcott was a feminist and an abolitionist who stayed single throughout her life. She was a lifelong supporter of reform causes such as temperance and women's suffrage. On March 6, 1888, she died in Boston from a stroke, two days after her father.

Louisa May Alcott (November 29, 1832 – March 6, 1888), an American novelist, short story writer, and poet, is best known for her novel Little Women (1868) and its sequels Little Men (1871) and Jo's Boys (1888). (1886). Abigail May and Amos Bronson Alcott, both transcendentalists, raised her in New England, where she grew up among many well-known intellectuals of the day, including Ralph Waldo Emerson, Nathaniel Hawthorne, Henry David Thoreau, and Henry Wadsworth Longfellow.

Alcott's family struggled financially, and she began working at a young age to help support the family while simultaneously seeking an outlet in writing. In the 1860s, she began to receive critical acclaim for her work. She created filthy short tales and sensation books for adults under pen names such as A. M. Barnard early on in her career, focusing on passion and revenge.

Little Women was published in 1868 and is loosely based on Alcott's childhood experiences with her three sisters, Abigail May Alcott Nieriker, Elizabeth Sewall Alcott, and Anna Alcott Pratt. It is set in the Alcott family home, Orchard House, in Concord, Massachusetts, and is loosely based on Alcott's childhood experiences with her three sisters, Abigail May Alcott Nieriker, Elizabeth Sewall Alcott, and Anna Alcott Pratt. The novel was well-received at the time, and it continues to be popular among children and adults today. It has been adapted for stage, cinema, and television numerous times.

Alcott was a feminist and an abolitionist who stayed single throughout her life. She was a lifelong supporter of reform causes such as temperance and women's suffrage. On March 6, 1888, she died in Boston from a stroke, two days after her father.

Early life

On her father's 33rd birthday, Louisa May Alcott was born on November 29, 1832, in Germantown, Pennsylvania, which is now part of Philadelphia, Pennsylvania. She was the second of four daughters born to Amos Bronson Alcott, a transcendentalist and educator, and Abby May, a social worker. Anna Bronson Alcott was the oldest, while Elizabeth Sewall Alcott and Abigail May Alcott were the two youngest. She was a tomboy as a kid who favoured males' games. In 1834, the family relocated to Boston, where Alcott's father founded an experimental school and became a member of the Transcendental Club, which included Ralph Waldo Emerson and Henry David Thoreau. Bronson Alcott's views on education and child-rearing, as well as his periods of mental instability, moulded a young Alcott's mentality with a desire to achieve perfection, a transcendentalist objective. Bronson Alcott's wife and daughters were at odds with him because of his attitude toward Alcott's wild and independent behaviour, as well as his failure to care for his family. Abigail was enraged by her husband's unwillingness to recognise her sacrifices, and she connected his indifference to the greater issue of gender discrimination. She instilled in Louisa a sense of awareness and a determination to right wrongs against women.

The Alcott family moved to a cottage on 2 acres (0.81 ha) of land along the Sudbury River in Concord, Massachusetts, in 1840, following many setbacks with the school. Their three years in the Hosmer Cottage, which they rented, were hailed as wonderful. For a brief while in 1843–1844, the Alcott family, along with six other members of the Consociate Family, went to the Utopian Fruitlands commune. After the Utopian Fruitlands failed, they relocated into leased quarters until they were able to buy a homestead in Concord with the help of Abigail May Alcott's inheritance and Emerson's financial assistance. On April 1, 1845, they moved into the house they named "Hillside" but by 1852, it had been sold to Nathaniel Hawthorne, who renamed it The Wayside. The Alcotts returned to Concord in 1857 after 22 years away, and moved into Orchard House, a two-story clapboard farmhouse, in the spring of 1858.

Alcott had early instruction from naturalist Henry David Thoreau, who inspired her to write Thoreau's Flute, which was based on her time at Walden Pond. Her father, who was rigorous and believed in "the sweetness of self-denial." provided the most of her education. She also got guidance from family friends Ralph Waldo Emerson, Nathaniel Hawthorne, Margaret Fuller, and Julia Ward Howe, all of whom were writers and educators. In a newspaper drawing titled "Transcendental Wild Oats." she later portrayed these early years. The drawing was reprinted in Silver Pitchers (1876), a book on the family's Fruitlands experience in "plain living and high thinking"

Poverty forced Alcott to labour as a teacher, seamstress, governess, domestic servant, and writer from an early age. Her sisters worked as seamstresses to help support the family, while their mother worked as a social worker among the Irish immigrants. Only Abigail, the youngest, was allowed to attend public school. Because of these demands, Alcott turned to literature as a creative and emotional outlet. Flower Fables (1849) was her debut book, a collection of stories written for Ralph Waldo Emerson's daughter Ellen. "I wish I was rich, I was good, and we were all a happy family this day" Alcott is reported as saying, and he was determined not to remain impoverished throughout his life.

In 1847, she and her family worked as Underground Railroad station mistresses, where they hosted a fugitive slave for a week and met Frederick Douglass. Alcott studied and liked the Seneca Falls Convention's "Declaration of Sentiments" on women's rights, which advocated for women's suffrage, and she became the first woman to register to vote in a school board election in Concord, Massachusetts.

The Alcotts had a difficult time in the 1850s, and Louisa found refuge at the Boston Theatre in 1854, where she penned The Rival Prima Donnas, which she eventually destroyed due to a feud amongst the actresses over who would play whose role. In 1857, when he couldn't find job and was depressed, Alcott considered suicide. She read Elizabeth Gaskell's biography of Charlotte Bront during that year and saw many connections to her own life. Her younger sister Elizabeth died in 1858, and her older sister Anna married John Pratt in 1859. This felt like a dissolution of their sisterhood to Alcott.

Literary success

Alcott was a feminist and an abolitionist as an adult. Alcott began writing for the Atlantic Monthly in 1860. She worked as a nurse in the Union Hospital in Georgetown, DC, for six weeks when the Civil War broke out in 1862–1863. She intended to work as a nurse for three months, but she developed typhoid and became deathly ill halfway through, though she eventually recovered. Her letters home, which were amended and published in the Boston anti-slavery newspaper Commonwealth and compiled in Hospital Sketches (1863, republished with modifications in 1869), earned her critical acclaim for her observations and wit. This was her debut book, and it was inspired by her time in the service. She wrote about hospital mismanagement, as well as the callousness and apathy of some of the physicians she met, as well as her personal desire to witness the battle firsthand. Tribulation Periwinkle, her main character, goes from innocence to maturity and is a "serious and eloquent witness" Her work Moods (1864), which was inspired by her own life, was equally promising.

Alcott's father wrote her a touching poem titled "To Louisa May Alcott" after she finished her stint as a nurse. It came from her father." Her father is proud of her for working as a nurse and aiding injured soldiers, as well as bringing joy and love into their family, according to the poem. He concludes the poem by thanking her for being a selfless and faithful daughter. The volumes Louisa May Alcott: Her Life, Letters, and Journals (1889) and Louisa May Alcott, the Children's Friend, which discuss her upbringing and strong relationship with her father, included this poem.

Alcott anonymously produced at least thirty-three "gothic thrillers" for popular periodicals and journals like The Flag of Our Union between

1863 and 1872; they were finally uncovered in 1975. Under the pen name A. M. Barnard, she produced passionate, fiery novels and sensational stories similar to those of English novelists Wilkie Collins and Mary Elizabeth Braddon in the mid-1860s. A Long Fatal Love Chase and Pauline's Passion and Punishment are two of them. Her heroes, like Collins' and Braddon's (both of whom incorporated feminist characters in their works), are powerful, intelligent, and resolute. She also wrote children's stories, and as they got successful, she stopped writing for adults. Other works include the novelette A Modern Mephistopheles (1875), which some mistakenly believe was written by Julian Hawthorne, and the semi-autobiographical novel Work (1873).

With the 1865 thriller "The Murders in the Rue Morgue" Catherine Ross Nickerson credited Alcott with writing one of the earliest works of detective fiction in American literature, second only to Edgar Allan Poe's "V.V., or Plots and Counterplots." and other Auguste Dupin stories. A Scottish aristocracy tries to prove that a strange woman killed his fiancée and relative in this short fiction written anonymously by Alcott. Antoine Dupres, the detective on the case, is a parody of Poe's Dupin, who is more interested in setting up a means to announce the solution with a dramatic flourish than in discovering the crime.

With the first section of Little Women: or Meg, Jo, Beth, and Amy (1868), a semi-autobiographical chronicle of her childhood in Concord, Massachusetts, published by the Roberts Brothers, Alcott became even more successful. Following her travels in Europe, Alcott returned to Boston and worked as an editor at Merry's Museum magazine. It was here that she met Thomas Niles, who encouraged her to write Part I of the novel and asked her to write a book for young women. Part II, popularly known as Good Wives (1869), followed the March sisters as they grew older and married. Jo's life at the Plumfield School, which she founded with her husband Professor Bhaer at the end of Part Two of Little Women, was chronicled in Little Men (1871). Finally, Jo's Boys (1886) brought the "March Family Saga" to a close.

Alcott modelled her heroine "Jo" on herself in Little Women. However, unlike Jo, who marries at the end of the narrative, Alcott lived her entire life alone. "I am more than half-persuaded that I am a man's soul put into a woman's body by some freak of nature," she said in an interview with Louise Chandler Moulton, "because I have fallen in love with so many pretty girls and never once the least bit with any man." However, while in Europe, Alcott wrote of her affair with Ladislas "Laddie" Wisniewski, a young Polish guy, in her notebooks, which she later deleted before her death. In Little Women, Alcott recognised Laddie as Laurie's model. Similarly, every character appears to be based on persons from Alcott's life in some way, from Beth's death reflecting Lizzie's to Jo's rivalry with the youngest, Amy, mirroring Alcott's conflict with (Abigail) May at points. Though Alcott never married, after May's unexpected death in 1879, she took in May's daughter, Louisa, and raised her for the next eight years.

Several of Alcott's earlier writings, including "The Sisters' Trial," "A Modern Cinderella," and "In the Garret." influenced the development of Little Women, in addition to relying on her personal experiences. In addition to Alcott's own family and personal ties, the characters in these short tales and poems influenced the general themes and bases for many of the characters in Little Women and the author's later works.

Little Women was well-received by critics and audiences alike, who found it to be appropriate for a wide range of ages—a fresh, genuine portrayal of everyday life. It was rated "the very best of books to reach the hearts of the young of any age from six to sixty" by an Eclectic Magazine reviewer. With the success of Little Women, Alcott shied away from the spotlight, and when fans came to her house, she would occasionally behave as a servant.

Alcott was part of a group of female authors throughout the Gilded Age, including Elizabeth Stoddard, Rebecca Harding Davis, Anne Moncure Crane, and others, who tackled women's issues in a modern and forthright manner. Their works were "among the decided 'signs of the times'" as one newspaper columnist put it at the time.

Later years

Alcott was a founding member of the Women's Educational and Industrial Union in Boston in 1877. Louisa took care of her niece Lulu, who was named after her after her youngest sister May died in 1879. In her later years, Alcott suffered from a variety of health issues, including vertigo. Her illness and death were linked to mercury poisoning by her and her early biographers. Alcott developed typhoid disease while serving in the American Civil War and was treated with a mercury-based medication. According to a recent investigation of Alcott's sickness, her chronic health problems may have been caused by an autoimmune disease rather than mercury poisoning. Mercury, on the other hand, is a proven trigger for autoimmune illnesses. Although an 1870 portrait of Alcott shows her cheeks to be flushed, possibly due to the "butterfly rash" over her cheeks and nose that is typically associated with lupus, there is no clear evidence supporting a firm diagnosis.

Alcott died of a stroke on March 6, 1888, in Boston, at the age of 55, two days after her father. "Is it not meningitis?" Louisa's last known words were. She is buried in Concord's Sleepy Hollow Cemetery, near Emerson, Hawthorne, and Thoreau, on a hillside now known as "Authors' Ridge" near Emerson, Hawthorne, and Thoreau. Louisa died when her niece Lulu was only eight years old. Anna Alcott Pratt looked after her until she was reunited with her father in Europe, where she resided until her death in 1976.

In her journals, Louisa frequently mentioned going for lengthy walks and runs. She defied traditional gender stereotypes by pushing her young female readers to run as well.

Orchard House (c. 1650), the Alcotts' Concord, MA home where they resided for 25 years and where Little Women was written and set in 1868, has been a historic house museum since 1912, paying tribute to the Alcotts by focusing on public education and historic preservation. The Boston Women's Heritage Trail includes her Boston home. Louisa May Alcott: The Woman Behind "Little Women," was written by Harriet Reisen and then turned into a PBS programme produced by Nancy Porter. Eden's Outcasts: The Story of Louisa May Alcott and Her Father, by John Matteson, won the Pulitzer Prize for Biography in 2008. The National Women's Hall of Fame inducted Louisa May Alcott in 1996.

The edits and layout of this print version are Copyright © 2022
by Moncreiffe Press

Printed in Great Britain
by Amazon

VALE OF MIST

MICHAEL KILGALLON

Copyright © 2021 Michael Kilgallon
All rights reserved.
Evan Casey Publications
ISBN: 9798767428465

Dedicated to my wife Maureen
A chuisle mo chroí
My partner in life's adventure.

My brilliant children Liam and Katy
Their brilliant partners Sally and Danny

And the undisputed champions of the world of grandchildren Evelyn and Casey.

Thanks to my brother Patrick for help with the chapter on Medugorje.

Thanks to Liam J. Kilgallon for cover design and creative input.

Thanks to the Meanderthals. Meanderthals blogspot. Some, of whom have lent their names to the characters herein.

FOLLOW MICHAEL @
Twitter.com/KilgallonMick

Chapter 1

It was a rare sunny day in old Mayo. Jonjo walked with purpose down to the hollow.

His bacon sandwiches, wrapped in greaseproof paper, nestled against a stone flagon containing a quart of porter and an enamel mug. They weighed heavily in the old khaki bag his dad had given him when he was a boy. It had served him well over the years; a school satchel, a lunch box, a pannier on his bike, a picnic basket.

The ground was hard under his feet, one of the hottest summers he could remember. Walking at a good pace, he soon came to the hollow. It was an old green track worn away by centuries of drovers moving their animals and maybe before that by the animals on their own migrations. The ground had sunk, and the trees grew around, making a green tunnel.

Legend had it that it led to the land of the fairies,

Jonjo knew this was nonsense, but he could never enter without a chill running up his spine.

It was a cool, shady place for his picnic, and he settled down, his back against the spongy bark of a tall tree, his bottom cushioned by thick moss. Biting into the thick bread and tasting the mixture of butter and crisp bacon always delighted him.

Almost everything he ate and drank was not good for him, but he was too old to change now, even if he'd wanted to. The salty bacon gave him a thirst, and he quenched it slowly with the thick porter. Looking at the ancient yew tree, green, thin leaves against the celestial blue, his eyelids grew heavy. Jonjo shuffled down the tree, and now the moss became his pillow.

A yew tree marked the boundary between his land and the Walshes' land. Their farm had been put to pasture decades ago when the whole family had emigrated.

Jonjo's peace had recently been disturbed. One of Paddy Feeney's boys had called a couple of months back to say that a Yank had bought Walshes' place. He and the Foy brothers had the contract to modernise the house, including connecting it to the water main.

"I can connect you up too," said young Sean Feeney.

"No, I've got my well, thanks," answered Jonjo. Seeing Sean's crestfallen look, he added, "And I haven't the money."

"No, it'll cost you nothing, Mr Brennan. I've got more than enough pipes, and taps cost nothing when you are in the trade. The Foys could connect you to the gas, and you'd have all the hot water you'd need and a proper shower and toilet if you want."

"I am'nt an old culchie. I know that there are bills to pay for water and gas."

"Well, look at it this way; consider it payment for looking after our materials when we are off-site. Nobody would stand up to you and your hurley."

Jonjo smiled at this and replied, "The new owner will surely know that he is getting bills for things he doesn't use."

"If there are problems with water bills, the water board sends me to look. If it's problems with the gas, then it's the Foys' job. The Yank will probably only be here for two or three weeks a year. It doesn't seem right he should have the luxury and you none. Anyway, the real reason is that I know how you and Mrs Brennan,

God rest her soul, looked after our family in the bad times and the Foys and many others, no doubt."

At the mention of his late wife, Jonjo acquiesced. For the first time in his long life agreed to be dishonest. Lying under the trees, he thought about that decision. Mary wouldn't have agreed to it. He'd been up to the Walsh place and helped the boys unload their gear. Jonjo was old but strong. Every night, he walked up the boreen and checked on the house, sometimes carrying his hurley.

He thought of Mary, as he did every day, and how lucky he had been to spend his days with her. He drifted for a while between sleeping and waking, thinking of his warm showers his central heating. The boys had done him proud. But he knew it was wrong.

It was so warm that Jonjo took off his jacket and made his pillow even softer. He always wore a suit. This one had served him many years. It had started life as his Sunday best many years ago, and now it was his daily apparel. Warmth, comfort, and a full stomach, the summer smell of the warm grass Jonjo was on the peaceful border between slumber and wakefulness.

"Hello neighbour!" a harsh bellow made Jonjo

spring up like a hare.

At the other end of the hollow, a recumbent figure almost invisible in the shaded, long grass continued "Didn't mean to make you jump."

"Who are you?" queried Jonjo, a question he later regretted.

The interruption was from the Yank. It turned out that this man, the new neighbour was Stubby Walsh, returned to the ancestral home. He talked with an irritating accent telling his life story to Jonjo.

This life story consisted of Walsh making amazing business deals and being the toast of Boston society. Lots of beautiful women had apparently tried to ensnare him, but he had outfoxed them all.

The gist was that Walsh had done much more than Jonjo. He had achieved indeed more than any of their contemporaries. The clear implication was that Jonjo had wasted his life, whereas Walsh had been a success. Jonjo was slow to anger, but Walsh was testing him.

Jonjo took his mind back to seeing the Walsh family off all those years ago they had taken the pony and trap down to Kiltimagh station. Stubby had been overweight then, and the pattern seemed to have stuck because he was still rotund and red-cheeked. He now wore sports clothes that appeared outlandish to Jonjo and carried a silver cane.

"So what you are saying is that you are a lot better off and more successful than I am, Stubby," summarised Jonjo when Walsh drew breath.

"No ... I mean.....," demurred Walsh. "It's Sean, not Stubby," he continued, deflated but annoyed.

"We are both sitting in the same hollow, under the same sun, under the same sky, but you are better off?" asked Jonjo.

"Well, wouldn't you agree that I've done more with my life," whined Walsh shakily.

"I don't know about that, but you are definitely better off than me because you don't have to sit here listening to a big-headed Yank," said Jonjo as he stood up. He walked towards home, trying to dismiss thoughts about giving Walsh a few reminders with his hurley.

As he walked back, Jonjo's bag was lighter, but his heart heavier. He replayed the short conversation in his head and regretted his words. Mary would have scolded him for remarks like that.

He sat on the bench that he had made many years ago and waited. He wanted both to apologise to Walsh and to confess to the shenanigans with the plumbing. Mary's long illness had depleted Jonjo's savings leaving him with only a small pension. He never begrudged a penny; nothing was too much for Mary.

He would block off the pipes from the Walsh house and end the problem. He would be much more at his ease knowing that everything was above board.

Jonjo saw Walsh trudging wearily home. "Stu... Sean," he called. "Could I have a word with you?"

A little fearfully, Walsh walked over and eased his bulk onto the bench. The bench creaked, and Jonjo was afraid it would seesaw.

Before he could make his confession, Walsh got in first. "I need to apologise. First, because of the way I spoke just now. I was always a bit in awe of you in our school days, you were the athlete, and I was the dull bookworm. I was just trying to show off."

Jonjo was dumbstruck. "I'm sorry too about the ruse with the plumbing," continued Walsh.

"What!" gasped Jonjo.

"When I had the survey done for connecting the

services, I asked the Foys and Feeney's boy to connect you up. I thought if I asked, you might say, no."

"But why?"

"When we first went to the States, your Mammy would send us a letter each month with a few dollars. They could ill afford it, but it got us on our feet, and I never forgot. I'm sort of repaying a debt I neglected and should have paid many years ago," answered Walsh.

"I know my Mam was a kind soul, but why would she send your Mammy money?"

"Well, it turned out they were related her gran and my great gran were first cousins," smiled Walsh.

"That makes us.....?"

"Third cousins," completed Walsh.

"Well, come in, cousin this calls for a drink," laughed Jonjo.

Chapter 2

Sun was lighting distant mountains and nearby hills. The air was now beginning to shimmer in the heat. A good to be alive, morning.

A ray of sunlight glared off the window, up the boreen, causing Jonjo to screw up his blue eyes.

He was unsure how he felt about having a neighbour. He heard stirrings in the house, which had been empty for over half a century. A considerate man, Jonjo had refrained from chopping wood until he knew the resident was up and about.

Cutting wood was pointless, now that he had central heating, thanks to Sean, his new neighbour, but old habits die hard. The sound of his axe chopping the logs into kindling reassured him. The dull echo of the sharp hatchet resounding from the hill reminded him of many such mornings.

Lots of things took his mind spinning back down the years. He knew that he spent too much time in the past. Jonjo sometimes wondered what his purpose now was. He thought about the love of his life, his late wife, Mary. He had taught himself a mental trick. Every time he had a sad thought about Mary, he made himself think of two happy memories.

"Hi," called Sean. "What's the wood for?"

"I might light a turf fire in the winter," answered Jonjo nodding toward a stack of peat.

"I remember the smell of peat smoke. There is nothing like it. Come up to the house for a coffee," offered Sean.

Jonjo rarely drank coffee but had to admit that the brew Sean made in his strange metal pot was far superior to any he had tasted before.

Sean explained that he might not make it to the winter because of his poor health. Sean's doughy, lugubrious face gave an impression of ill health, but he voiced no self-pity in his words.

His doctor in the U.S.A had told him that his excess

weight meant that he was morbidly obese, and Sean had decided to come home to spend his remaining time in the land of his birth.

"How old was your doctor?" asked Jonjo.

"Maybe 30... but highly qualified."

"Ara! What would he know, just a boy? You are well over double his age. Morbidly-obese nonsense. All the Walsh men are on the hefty side. Look at your Dad. He was a big man 'God rest his soul' what age did he die?"

"83."

"There you go, not a bad life span though I thought he would have lasted longer. If you were morbidly obese, you would be long gone," admonished Jonjo.

"So, you are a doctor now, are you?"

"No, but I know a quack when I hear about one. There's no way I'm going to let a relative of mine sit here waiting for the Grim Reaper," snapped Jonjo with real gusto. "Be down in my house in twenty minutes."

Jonjo strode home with a spring in his step. He knew now what his purpose was. He said a little prayer of thanks to Mary, who was undoubtedly involved in this somehow from up above.

In the kitchen, he scooped a knob of butter out of

his churn. He melted it into his big frying pan. By the time he heard Sean walking up the path, everything was ready.

"Walk in, family don't knock," he called.

The plate in front of Sean contained; bacon rashers, pork sausages, fried eggs, black pudding, mushrooms and fried bread.

"I've done you a little milkshake instead of tea with the weather so," remarked Jonjo.

"Are you trying to kill me? Think of the cholesterol," whined Sean. His eyes, however, told a different story, and he needed little encouragement to dive in.

"It's alright for you," he continued looking at Jonjo's long, spare physique.

"You get the pots done while I prepare lunch."

Sean couldn't remember when he had last done any washing up but did as he was bid. Meanwhile, Jonjo cut up a crusty loaf and made bacon sandwiches; he went down to the well and brought back a thermos of cool water.

"O.K., diet sorted now for exercise, we will have a walk down to the cemetery."

"I don't think I can make it that far," complained Sean.

"Don't worry, we'll stop for a rest, and we can go through the old tunnel."

Sean thought back to his childhood. He was sure that he remembered the old tunnel had caved in. Perhaps Jonjo was getting forgetful. He said nothing and watched his companion heft his khaki haversack onto his back.

"You've left your keys on the outside of the door," he said, really beginning to doubt Jonjo's mental capacity.

"That's O.K.," the taller man replied. "It stops me losing them, and it lets people know I'm not on the farm. It saves them from looking. If they need to deliver something or leave a message, they can go in."

The two men slowly walked down to the hollow where they had become reacquainted just the day before. Jonjo slowed his long, loping stride to accommodate the gait of his cousin.

They stretched out under the shade of the trees. He noted his cousin was sweating profusely more than the heat, and the gentle walk would have justified. He passed him an enamel mug of cold spring water. Refreshed by the drink, Sean began to prattle on about his achievements in America, just as he'd done before.

After a while, Jonjo said gently, "You don't have to talk all the time. There is value in silence. Listen to the birds; enjoy the warmth and the shade."

"That's what we call mindfulness," said Sean excitedly.

Fearful that he would embark on another monologue, Jonjo cut him short and said that they should just rest and let their breakfast digest. Sean did feel a little weary. The sun, the walk and the large breakfast all played their part. Soon both men were in that strange but comfortable land between wakefulness and sleep.

Sean woke at the sound of Jonjo putting away the thermos. They walked through the shaded hollow towards the tunnel.

"I thought the tunnel through the hill had caved in," ventured Sean.

"No, that was just a tale to stop us going in when we were kids. There were all sorts down there then, poteen, ammunition, boxes of cigarettes- stuff we weren't supposed to know about."

They walked on into the tunnel. It took some time for their eyes to adjust, but the air was cool with only the slightest hint of damp. They studied the walls, which revealed the tool marks of the ancient ones and the more recent initials and dates chiselled by locals.

Soon the two men were out of the tunnel and at the church. Jonjo stood by his wife's headstone removed a beautiful, iridescent, yellow flower from his haversack, placing it in a vase and topping it up with spring water.

Jonjo bent his head, lips moving in silent prayer. Sean feeling, suddenly that he was intruding, moved away and sought out his grandparent's headstone. Jonjo came up silently next to him, produced another flower from his haversack, and placed it on the Walshes' headstone.

Sean's eyes misted at the unexpected and considerate gesture. They walked among the headstones reminiscing about those they knew.

"You can't help working out the age at death from the dates," observed Sean. "Some sad stories here."

"For every sad one, there will be many happy ones. Look at this 150!"

"Who is it?" queried Sean.

"Miles from Dublin," replied Jonjo deadpan.

It took a second for Sean to register then both men laughed, startling a brightly coloured chaffinch.

They ate their lunch in silence, Sean surprised at his appetite after the big breakfast. "I suppose what you are saying is I might as well eat what I want. I've not much time left."

"Nonsense!" said Jonjo. "What would you say if I could promise you at least another full year of life?"

"I'd say that was nonsense."

"Well let's go to the pub, and I'll explain..."

Chapter 3

<u>The Pub</u>

Sean Walsh had been in many an Irish pub in America. He liked them. Sean was a bit of a novelty or a rarity over there, being Irish born. Though he had lost his accent long ago, he could still do a fair approximation of it.

Of the Irish pubs in America, none were like this. The outside looked like a shop. The wooden frame of the window had small metal brackets from which hung a variety of items. Displayed there, were colourful plastic hula hoops, rugby and football shirts on coat hangers, flyaway footballs in plastic netting, and postcards in a white plastic rack. Rolled up windbreaks jostled for space with upended skateboards and cheap hurley sticks against the wall.

Jonjo led Sean past aluminium buckets and mops, yard brushes, spades, garden forks and bags of compost. Through an open set of double outer doors, a small porch led to highly polished inner ones, one of which was held open with a brass hook. Immediately on the right was a handsome, curved staircase in highly polished wood wending upwards.

As Sean eyes adjusted after the bright sunlight, he saw the ground floor was a long narrow space. Behind the counter stretching nearly the length of the room were shelves full of groceries and household goods. There were sweets, chocolate bars, an ice cream freezer and a glass-fronted chiller.

Padded bar stools extended along both sides of the room. The right-hand side had a bar deeper and shorter than the counter, with a great variety of Scottish and Irish whiskeys. The back wall had all manner of objects on shelves or hooks; framed photos, old books, wooden and metal advertising materials from a bygone age. Not themed, it was accumulated.

A tall man emerged from a door behind the bar, "Is it yourself, Jonjo?" he asked.

"Who else would it be? And this is my old school friend Sean Walsh."

By now, Sean had become reaccustomed to his surname being pronounced Welsh.

"Ah, the Yank. Were you in the team?" he asked, taking down a black and white framed photo of Jonjo's all-conquering hurling team.

"His parents took him to America before he had the chance," replied Jonjo.

Sean was grateful for the intervention. Both he and Jonjo knew that Sean had never held a hurley stick in his life.

"Welcome home," said the barman. "These are on me."

The two men settled on stools next to an upturned barrel which served as a table. Sean felt an ache in his legs from the unaccustomed exercise and immediately thought about the enigmatic question Jonjo had recently asked him. "What would you say if I could promise you at least another full year of life?"

"O.K., Jonjo, what's your story about living longer?" asked Sean.

"It's no story more like a legend. It dates back before Christianity came and to the time the ancient ones worshipped Mother Nature. It was told that those concerned about their health should go to the Vale of Mist. Once in the Vale, they would live for exactly one year."

Sean was disappointed and full of questions. "Do you expect me to believe that? It makes no sense. Where is the Vale? What happens after the year?"

Jonjo replied, "I admit it's a leap of faith to a faith that predates ours. The legend is that the Vale appears to those who seek it. There is no limit to the times it can be visited if you can find it."

"Have you seen it?" scoffed Sean.

"No, but then I've never looked. I've been fortunate with my health. A Scotsman once told me they had a similar place called Brigadoon."

"I think I've heard of that one," admitted Sean. "But this is nonsense."

"Maybe so, but cleverer men than me believe it. But it's up to you."

The Mangan Problem

The barman Tommy Clarke, whose family had run the pub for generations, cleared their glasses. Jonjo ordered another couple of pints and went to the bar. Sean, meanwhile, started to chat with some of the other drinkers. He was doing his usual spiel about what a great life he'd had and his achievements. The sad thing was that Sean had lost the ability to listen. He showed no interest in the responses of the others. Sean did not converse. He spoke.

The barman took his time pulling the pints of Guinness, something that was never rushed. "You've a faraway look about you," commented Jonjo.

"Sorry," Tommy replied. "Mangan has been up to his old tricks. It's putting off the visitors. I need the business on these summer days."

"I'll have a think about it. I'll talk it over with Sean and see if we can't come up with something." Noting Tommy's doubtful look, Jonjo continued, "Don't take Sean at first sight despite all the blether he has a very clever brain."

The fellows near Sean had unsurprisingly drifted away. "We'd better make these the last two; this can lie heavy on your stomach, and we've a fair walk home."

"We'll get a taxi," said Sean.

"There are no taxis here," laughed Jonjo. "Who would drive one?"

"Surely it would be a good job for a man from the village."

"Look around you. The men from the town are here now or will be later on," answered Jonjo.

"Don't worry," shouted Tommy from the bar. "Micko is going over to Castlebar. I'm sure he'll drop you at the end of the boreen."

A youngish man with an impressively long, shaggy, red beard nodded assent. Soon Sean was sitting up front with Micko and Jonjo sat behind.

"Have you had a drink?" asked Sean.

"Just 5 or 6 pints of the black stuff," replied Micko. He pronounced stuff as shtuff. That Mayo accent that Sean had all but forgotten. Mayo the Wild Wesht of Ireland.

"Don't worry, I can drive just fine," smiled Micko.

"But aren't you worried about the police?" persevered Sean.

"I amn't. There are no guards around here."

"So you are not worried about losing your licence?"

"What licence would that be?" replied Micko.

The reply stopped Sean in his tracks. The two men thanked Micko for the lift. Jonjo noticed that Sean had struggled to get out of the car.

"This short walk will take some of the stiffness out of your legs," he said. "They'll ache more in the morning. You put the kettle on. I'll go home for my bottle of embrocation. Tommy Clarke has a problem for us to solve."

Jonjo walked back with his trusty bottle. It was his own concoction from his days of hurling as a player and a coach. He told Sean how to apply the liquid then he explained Tommy's difficulty.

"Jonny Mangan has a problem with the drink. He has more than is good for him and drives his pony and trap through the town swearing, and shouting. He goes the wrong side of the road upon pavements. It is only the good sense of the pony that has stopped him from hurting someone. The Garda have warned him about it. When he sobers up, he goes to confession. He promises it won't happen again. But it does. He is such a skinny bag of old bones that no one will thump him for fear of killing him. It is spoiling the tourist trade, and Tommy and other traders need all they can on account of the economy. I have told Tommy that we would have a think about it and that you are a good man for solving a problem."

Sean was nothing if not susceptible to flattery.

"You will need a day off the walking tomorrow. When you are ready in the morning, come round to my house, and we will put our heads together. Don't be surprised if you get some cramps tonight; if your legs are aching, put a pillow under them. When the heat of the day has gone down, boil up some whiskey, sugar and water and then take a couple of aspirins. That will see you right."

"What a loss you were to the medical profession," laughed Sean.

"Goodnight and God Bless," answered Jonjo, who disappeared towards the setting sun.

The Mangan Plot

The next day Jonjo was mopping the stone floor of his cottage when he saw Sean walking up the path.

"You're up and about early this morning," he called

cheerily.

"I had cramp aches and all sorts last night, but whatever was in that embrocation did the trick. I'm as good as new," replied Sean.

"Maybe that you are fitter than you think."

"Shall we walk down to the hollow and see if we can solve the problem?"asked Sean. "I've done us a flask of coffee to fuel our brains."

"Grand. I'll finish the floor. I've got to thank you again for getting the hot water put in. It makes life easier."

"Ara musha," responded Sean.

Jonjo grinned hearing Sean use that multi-purpose Irish phrase. The two walked down to the trees. Sean carried a bright, red cooler bag from which he took a silver thermos flask and two mugs. As the men drank their coffee, he took out a pen and pad.

"O.K.," said Sean. "What is important in Jonny Mangan's life? We'll start from there."

They came up with a solution so quickly that they surprised even themselves. Jonjo walked to town to organise a team and the necessary equipment. It was then only a matter of waiting for the opportunity.

The Mangan Solution

Two nights later, the call came. Regan, an off duty Garda officer, picked up Sean and Jonjo. Tommy Clarke and Micko met them at Mangan's house. Jonny Mangan's snoring could be heard clearly even outside. Directed by Micko, the men dismantled the trap piece by piece. The pony looked serenely on from his stall.

They reassembled the trap in Mangan's backroom. It fitted very snugly. Jonjo, who had a way with animals, led the pony in. The animal made not a sound. Jonjo confidently and quickly adjusted all the tack until the animal was harnessed in place. The pony stood hind legs in the back room forelegs in the kitchen. The five conspirators smiled at a job well done and returned to their homes.

The Mangan Conclusion

It was just gone ten in the morning when Mangan was heard shouting in the street. "The Divil has driven my trap into the house. The pony is stuck; I'll have to knock down my wall."

Officer Regan, resplendent in uniform, went out to

deal with it. He accompanied Mangan to his house. Shaking his head, the policeman said, "I've never seen anything like this. I don't think this is a matter for the police. No crime I can see."

"You can't leave me like this," pleaded Mangan.

The policeman held up his hand like he was stopping traffic. "If I were you, I'd go straight to Church. If ever I saw a sign to mend your ways, this is it. Say as many decades of the rosary as you can and ask Father to hear your confession."

"But my poor pony................"

"Whisht, I'll ask the Yank he was a top engineer, maybe he can help; now off you go."

The team reversed the operation of the night before. Jonjo fed and watered the pony. The men, minus Regan, who was still on duty, went to Clarke's bar to tell the tale. There was much hilarity, and Sean and Jonjo walked home, slightly the worse for drink.

"I've been researching 'The Vale of Mist'," said Sean as a parting shot as the two men went to their respective homes.

"Tomorrow then...," called Jonjo, with a wave.

Chapter 4

The fierceness had gone from the sun. It was still warm but pleasantly, bearably warm. The tranquillity of the morning was enhanced by the sound of birdsong. The blackbirds' voices, redolent of many summers past, produced a feeling of timelessness.

Sean's diagrams were set out on the table, along with the handwritten notes, from his research. A gentle summer breeze brought the pleasant sound of footfall crunching on gravel.

Sean poured the coffee and glanced happily at the map. He had always loved maps. He felt a sense of anticipation. He had thought that this was the final paragraph in his life's story, but maybe, just maybe, he still had one more chapter.

Jonjo eased himself down into the chair, though he

would never tell anyone, his joints were beginning to give him some pain. Sean explained that the maps showed all the recorded watercourses, streams, brooks, loughs, ponds and wells in the area. Jonjo was particularly interested in the aerial photograph, which showed roads and footpaths and the ghosts of ancient dwellings.

"It looks like you've been busy studying Sean, but why?" asked Jonjo.

"Well, you know the story of, The Vale of Mist, you told me..?"

"The one you said was nonsense," interrupted Jonjo.

"Yes, well, I've been studying it. It seems that many races at many different periods of history have had similar myths and legends. In Ireland, we have Tír na nÓg, a land of eternal youth. It is found by different means, entering ancient burial mounds or caves. By journeying through a mist or going underwater. Alternatively by travelling across the sea for three days on an enchanted boat."

"So, you believe in it now!" laughed Jonjo.

"No, I wouldn't go that far. But like you said, it would give purpose to our walks. I've got all the information on water in the area because, of course, mist is formed by water."

Jonjo drank the Italian coffee that Sean had introduced to him.

Sean continued, "Do you know the difference between fog and mist?"

"No, I'm mystified," Jonjo replied.

"Very funny. Will you look at the maps? I have made a flask of coffee and prepared some food for our picnic."

Jonjo planned the route, knowing the area much better than his erstwhile schoolmate. He considered Sean's fitness and came up with a walk through the hollow and over the hill into the town. He knew they would get some shade from the ruins up the hill. They could have lunch in the shadow of the old houses. Then after a good rest, they would have a stroll down to the churchyard.

They could have afternoon coffee on the bench outside the church then a pint at Clarke's. They could walk home from the bar this time.

"There are some ponds on the hilltop," said Jonjo. "The walks a bit steeper than last time and with the walk back from the bar included, a few miles longer."

"I've had a couple of days rest, plus it's not as hot. I think I'll manage," agreed Sean.

The hollow was as good a place as any to start the search for the Vale of Mist. The green tunnel had long been associated with the other world. The tradition of fairies was deep in the Irish psyche, and though everyone scoffed at the idea now, the folklore was still strong. The Irish fairy was not the pleasant creature of other places. They were spirits to be feared, not welcomed. Legend had it that they chose places like this to move between worlds.

The two men sat and chatted amiably. They had become more used to each other's company. Sean could even manage some periods of silence without feeling the need to chatter.

"Would you mind if I gave you some advice?" asked Jonjo.

"Of course not."

"When we were last in the bar, did you know two of the fellows you were talking to had worked in America?"

"No, how would I?" answered Sean.

"Well, don't be offended, but you didn't give them a chance to tell you."

Jonjo, saddened by Sean's crestfallen look, continued gently. "When you've been on your own for a while, it's easy to forget to listen."

"People always saw me as the confident fast-talking businessman. I was far from that. The words just covered my insecurity," conceded Sean. "I got good at it, and it impressed people, but it was just an act. Fake it till you make it is what they call it now!"

"You're home. You can be yourself. I hope I haven't offended you."

"No, I know you are well-meaning. You are a quiet man, but you are sure of yourself. When you speak, people listen. I envy that security, that certainty. I will heed your advice."

Birdsong reached them as they left the trees. It occurred to Jonjo it had been absent in the hollow. He gave an involuntary shiver. They took the winding grassy path up the hill.

Jonjo stopped for Sean to draw breath. They moved up beyond the tree line, and Sean caught a glimpse of the sparkling water of the river. He climbed further up the track until he could see the whole lough below. The blue ribbon of the river created a gentle ripple slightly distorting the reflection of the hills in the water.

Sean sat on a rock, looking at the shimmering colours below. "I never remember it being this beautiful."

"Five minutes to the top, and we'll have lunch," responded Jonjo.

The sun was high when they reached the summit. There was little shade visible. Jonjo led the way off the track pushing briars aside with his feet. Amongst overgrown ferns and bushes, he showed Sean the remains of an old stone house. Two walls, the chimney and part of the roof, were still intact, affording them some respite from the heat.

Jonjo explained that the ruins were a deserted famine village. They could still pick out the ridge and furrow of the potato fields. The failure of the potato crop had caused so much death and misery in the area. The story had been told often by the survivors. The untold stories of those who did not survive would not bear thinking about. The shadow still lay across the land, this lovely yet harsh environment.

The two men sat for a while in silence. Ireland's history of repression, rebellion, starvation playing like a silent film in both of their minds.

"It does not seem right to sit here and eat," said Sean.

"You're right. Let's have a look at the ponds."

The three ponds marked on Sean's map were difficult to spot immediately. One was so covered in duckweed that it was hard to see the water.

The other two, however, were ablaze with colour. The large white petals of the arrowheads with their yellow centres, the tall brooklimes with their blue petals and white middles, even the duckweed was sporting tiny white flowers. The long green stems of water-lilies pushed reluctant yellow petals out of the water.

"It would have been a blessing for the people that lived here had there been a Mist to take them from their suffering," added Sean, head bowed.

The companions walked down the far side of the hill. They found some shade and eased themselves down onto the warm grass, their backs against the ridge. They simultaneously made the Sign of the Cross as they tucked into their meal.

They spoke of lighter things to change the sombre mood. They enjoyed the food. Sean had made it from chunks of braised pork belly and marinated beans. They finished with a slice of a sponge cake covered with chocolate that Sean said was the nearest thing he could get to Boston cream pie.

"I wonder who lived in those houses and what became of them," mused Jonjo.

"It's not that long ago. They may have been our ancestors. It is something we could look into," answered Sean.

"Paddy Keane had his DNA tested. He thought that he would have Viking ancestors and Spanish blood, from the boys, washed up from the Armada," said Jonjo.

"How did it turn out?"

"99.4% Irish," laughed Jonjo

"The rest?" queried Sean

"0.4 Guinness and 0.2 whiskey."

They rested their eyes in the sunshine. Jonjo set his internal clock for one hour and lay back on the hillside. Sean was soon fast asleep. Jonjo, for a while, was in that liminal state where he could still detect the sounds around him. The sounds merged with his waking thoughts and then with his dreams. He woke with a feeling of loss, something from his dream was calling to him, but he was frustrated as he could not bring it to mind.

Jonjo eased himself to his feet. The warmth of the sun, the beauty of the view below and the sky above dismissed the melancholy. He had taught himself to chase every sad thought or memory with two happy ones. He was smiling as he helped Sean up.

"I had a strange dream."

"What about?" said Jonjo.

"I could smell smoke and freshly turned soil. I don't remember, but it seemed so real."

They wound down the grassy path and marvelled at flowers that seemed to spring from rocks. They heard the gentle buzz of bees about their work and watched birds spiralling on the rising heat. Nature asked nothing from them, but they drank it in like a mother's milk.

Jonjo's knees ached more travelling down. He kept an eye on Sean's progress. He seemed to be doing well, and they soon reached the churchyard. Jonjo put a flower on his wife's grave, bowing his head in silent prayer. Sean produced a flower and added it to Jonjo's.

"Do you remember her?" Jonjo asked.

"She was the sweetest girl in the village," he answered.

"That she was."

They had their coffee on the bench then walked on to Clarke's bar.

"Is it yourself Sean?" asked Tommy Clarke.

"It is, and Himself," he added, nodding at Jonjo.

"Sit yourselves down, I'll bring them over," the publican added.

They sat in the little corner room and were glad to find seats with a backrest. The craic was in full swing between four men sitting near the back wall. The men were all retirement age or thereabouts, but Jonjo and Sean could give them a good ten years.

"Hello Jonjo, and yourself Sean," called Seamus Burke.

Jonjo could see that Sean was pleased to be addressed by name. He was also delighted when Sean sat back to listen to the conversation, not butting in or trying to talk over anyone.

The same man called, "We were just talking about

that gobshite, Paddy Murphy."

He held up a hand in apology to Jonjo, remembering that the old fella didn't like coarse language.

"We were just remembering some of the tales he told us," Seamus continued. "We've made a list: he played for Ireland at Rugby, for England at cricket, he dated Marilyn Monroe and taught Frank Sinatra how to sing. Murphy was John Wayne's stunt double, told JFK not to go to Dallas. He was the first man on the Moon because he had to film Neil Armstrong landing."

"You know, though," said Tommy Clarke as he brought over the drinks. "I was in Tipperary years ago, when Ronald Reagan was over discovering his Irish ancestors. I was sitting in a pub watching the Pope making a speech, from the Vatican, on T.V. and Reagan said to me, 'Who's the old feller on the balcony with Paddy Murphy?'"

They all roared laughing. "Have you fellers nothing better to do than come up with these daft tales?" admonished Jonjo in mock indignation.

"I don't think half their lies are true at all," contributed Sean in the same vein.

The laughing continued, and the two men drank

their pints.

"We'll just have the one. We've a walk yet," advised Jonjo

The friends both felt the ache of the walk in their legs as they made their way home.

"I've a feeling we've unfinished business with the famine village," said Sean.

"Me too, but I don't know what."

They said goodbye. As Jonjo walked down his path, he heard the rasping call of a corncrake. He revelled in the beauty of the land and its creatures.

And all you had to do was step out to see them.

Chapter 5

A whole wall of Sean's house was devoted to books. Ceiling to floor, there were hundreds. A shiny, wheeled ladder gave access to the higher ones.

"Have you read all of these?" asked Jonjo.

"I have so," replied Sean.

"You brought them all the way from America."

"I did, and it cost me a small fortune," replied Sean.

"But why, when you've read them?" persisted Jonjo.

"I don't know. I couldn't bear to part with these. Some have sentimental value, like the books I won as school prizes others are valuable. I have books signed by the author, some with a dedication, to me, in them. Maybe they're my equivalent of your sports trophies."

"I think you're right!" said Jonjo. "I understand that

so. I was never one much for the reading."

"I love books, even the smell of them. But I suppose I'll have to think about what to do with them when I'm gone."

"You're going nowhere soon, Sean me-boy, unless it's on our next walk,"

It was the first walk that Sean had planned in their search for the Vale of Mist. He showed Jonjo the route. They'd walk to the hollow and have their first break there. They would then follow the path of an old, dried-up watercourse right down to the lough. On the way, they would cross several small streams and pass three wells, including St. Patrick's Holy Well.

"It's an ambitious walk," commented Jonjo. "It is near enough, twice the distance of the others. Easy enough going down but uphill all the way back."

"We won't need to carry a picnic," countered Sean. "We can have lunch at the cafe, on the lough. We can drink water from the wells too."

"Well, you've thought it through," agreed Jonjo.

They stepped out that midsummer morn, the pleasant warmth inviting them to the new day. The view showed every shade of green, from almost yellow to the virtually brown. The myriad paths appeared each to present an opportunity, each diversion offering a diversion. The sun seemed to lead them in their search.

They walked towards the hollow, unencumbered by any bags. They talked about their school days. Sean remembered that he had clung to his mother's skirts and had had to be dragged in.

Jonjo recalled the occasion he had run full pelt into the knot at the end of a skipping rope. The rope swung with great gusto by, what seemed to him at the time a huge girl, knocked him off his feet. He had cried more because of the sympathy he was receiving than the pain. They had taken him, his eye now closed and trickling with blood, to the head teacher.

The head, Sister Angela took one look at him and said, "You'll be better before you're married." The cold manner in which she spoke silenced Jonjo. He resolved never to show any sign of weakness again at school.

They reminisced about the infant class teacher, another nun, who had a few tricks up her sleeve. She once asked the class to put up their hands if they wanted a chocolate biscuit. She then rapped the fingers of any child who had raised their hand, with a wooden ruler saying, "That's for being greedy!"

Her piece de resistance was her end of the world story. Fortunately, Jonjo's uncle had warned him about this. He had told him that the nun would wait for a dark, stormy day and then begin her tale. She would tell the children that this might be the end of the world. She would frighten them with the thought; you might never see your Mammies and Daddies again.

"I remember that," said Sean. "I'd been warned about her too. At one point, we were the only two in the class, not crying. Then an idea occurred to me. I thought that one day she would be right. Maybe it was today. I sobbed as much as the rest."

They reached the hollow, and seated on the higher ground, looked toward the lough. "How do you feel about those days now?" asked Sean.

"At one time, I'd get annoyed about those things. I used to be angry at a lot of things. I was mad at the British for the famine. Then I realised it wasn't the British, it was the rich. The poor in England, the poor everywhere, suffer. What was the point about getting annoyed about something I could do nothing about?"

"There's no point getting older if you don't get

wiser," agreed Sean

They rested outside the hollow, taking fresh water from a stream.

"How do you really feel about these old tales, like the Vale of Mist?" asked Sean.

"I think it is how the ancient people described things. An old civilisation with a different way of expressing their knowledge of the world. We use the language of science. We speak of atoms and chemicals and all manner of stuff. But is our understanding any greater than theirs?" answered Jonjo. "We are still searching for the same truths."

"You are quite the philosopher."

"I think we've lost something from those times," continued Jonjo. "How many take the time to drink from a stream? To admire the beauty in the land, to pick the wild berries. We can race through life and miss so much. We used so much from nature in our remedies, too. I bet you never went to the doctor when you lived here."

The two men continued their walk down the hillside. Jonjo let Sean take the lead. He made sure they had plenty of stops. He noticed that his friend was slowing and beginning to breathe heavily.

He called a break at St.Patrick's Holy Well. Jonjo wound the crank handle and, eventually, the galvanised bucket appeared. They drank the cool water and rested.

"That lough doesn't seem to be getting much closer," wheezed Sean.

"I'm glad the doctor's not here," replied Jonjo.

"Why?"

"It's best that they tend to the sick and leave the well alone."

"That was an old one when we were young," groaned Sean.

Refreshed by the water and the break, they moved on. Jonjo spoke, more than was his wont, to take his companion's mind off the effort. They traversed the ancient stone bridge over the river and arrived at the lough.

The walk had been worth the effort. The sunlight skipped off the surface of the water producing a diamond sparkle. The patterns were almost geometric yet natural. The energy from the light appeared to imbue the spirits of all that saw it. Strangers smiled at each other in a shared, unspoken appreciation of what they witnessed.

The cousins sat at an outdoor table of the cafe, taking their time over their lunch. A heat haze blurred the edges of the lough. The air tasted cooler and sweeter. It was as if it was taking on the flavour of the freshwater. An iridescent butterfly joined them, alighting momentarily, on their table. Giving benediction to their journey.

The two men stopped to look back at the water. "Don't worry about the journey back. It's never as long as the way going," assured Jonjo. "Even though it's the same."

"I know what you mean," laughed Sean. "Do you want a little puzzle to think about as we walk?"

"Grand," said Jonjo, for although he was no great reader, he had a good memory for facts.

"O.K., I've got ten things, and I want you to tell me what they have in common. If you guess it right, after two items, you get 100 points. After three items, 90 points, and so on down. The more guesses, the fewer points."

"Fine, fire away."

"First two; a sewer in Sardinia and the jungle floor in

Borneo."

"No, other than they're both have a terrible whiff, I don't know."

"The mucous of a catfish," added Sean.

Jonjo thought long and hard. "I've got an idea. Give me one more."

"For 70 points," said Sean, in his best T.V. quizmaster voice. "The skin of a frog."

"Sure, I have it. All are places where medicines, more specifically antibiotics, have been found," answered Jonjo.

Sean was genuinely impressed. "I didn't think you'd get it so quickly!"

The two friends had another rest stop. "I had this idea that the world is some sort of big game," said Sean. "Everything we need is there to be found. The cure for every ailment, the answer to every problem. All we have to do is find it."

"Like our search for the Vale of Mist?" queried Jonjo.

"Do you know I had that very same thought just as I was speaking? I never made that connection before."

"Who has set this great game, this test? Is it God's

path back to the Garden of Eden?"

"I don't know, maybe."

Their discussion and speculation continued and, before long, they were passing the hollow. Reaching home, they were tired, but that good feeling of tiredness, that tiredness borne of achievement. They went their separate ways to recuperate.

As the solstice sun began to set, they reconvened in Sean's garden. Jonjo set a fire going in the chimenea, with kindling and turf. He supplied a bottle of poteen, and Sean produced some bourbon.

They saw the constellations appear in the sky and watched the flames. There was no need for the warmth of a fire, but unwittingly they were following an age-old, unwritten tradition.

"You know Sean; I think it's at night when we really see. The sun blocks our view in the day. At night we see our place in the universe."

They looked up deep in their own thoughts, comfortable and content in silence, thinking of their next adventure.

Chapter 6

The breeze dropped, a pregnant silence then a white electric shock. The boom of thunder echoed from the hill. That familiar three-act play; lightning, thunder, and now the rain. Every storm carried a frisson of excitement, locked somewhere in the primitive part of the brain.

Sean's memory slid back, down the years, to his Mammy's voice, "Jesus, Mary, and Joseph turn off the television. Unplug it! Switch off the lights!"

They never had electricity in Ireland when she was young, and she never got to trust it. Lightning was God's way of telling us not to mess with things we didn't understand. The storm was swift, and the rain, though heavy, was short-lived.

Sean slept well and woke to the most beautiful summer day. The winds had cleansed the air, and the birds sang their appreciation. The sun was a little cooler; shamefaced as if apologising, admitting that it had been overdoing things lately.

It had been well over a week since their last walk, and both were keen to get started. The friends looked at the maps and aerial photos that now had a permanent place on Sean's kitchen table. Jonjo pointed out the route.

They would go around the hill, towards the town, on the opposite side, to the hollow. There were lots of small streams running down the slope. Some joined the river into the lough whilst others disappeared into the ground.

"With the rain last night, and the heat in the ground, it will be a rare old chance to find the Vale of Mist," announced Jonjo enthusiastically.

The deluge had let loose the aromas of the earth. The atmosphere smelled sweet and invigorated their lungs. It was a fine day to be up and about.

Jonjo noted that Sean had a new rucksack and a new

lightweight hiking jacket. He himself wore his third-best suit, the one he used for long walks, and carried the khaki bag that his Dad had given him long ago.

As they walked along the boreen, down to the main road, they chatted amiably. Only half a mile to walk on the road before the pair got back onto the paths. They were glad of this as there were no pavements, and there were some erratic drivers around.

They had only been on the road a couple of minutes when Paddy Regan pulled up in his police car.

"Off in search of The Vale?"

Jonjo nodded.

"Well, could I ask a favour from you?" he continued.

The Garda explained that there had been some unusual sightings in the town last night. He looked at his notebook, smiling. "It seems that a man was seen rising out of his grave. Then carrying his coffin out of the churchyard."

The policeman held up his hand and said, "I know it's nonsense, but I've got to spend the day at court in Castlebar. Will you two look into it for me? If I don't find an explanation, I'll be getting calls at all times of the night. These things can soon get out of hand."

"So, you are making us deputies?" asked Sean, his American accent conjuring up a picture of a Wild West sheriff in the Garda's mind.

"I suppose I am."

"Did any of these sightings happen near Clarke's bar, maybe around closing time?" queried Jonjo.

"You've nearly solved it already!" laughed Paddy as he drove off.

They went over the stile into the field and on to the grassy path.

"Do you remember the 'Graves of the Kings'?" asked Jonjo.

"In the churchyard?"

"No, here on the side of the hill. We used to run over them and scare ourselves when we were kids."

"I don't think I ever did that," answered Sean.

"Let's see, if we can find them, they are around here, somewhere. Take care where you put your feet. Some of the streams are covered by grass."

They walked around the hillside for some time. To Jonjo it felt for all the world, like he was a child, playing out again. For Sean, it was a chance to catch up on the time he'd missed out on as a youngster.

They eventually found the stone slabs virtually invisible in the undergrowth. They looked like large gravestones toppled to the ground. There were no markings on them, no discernible pattern to their position, altogether a mystery. They found six, but Jonjo thought there had been more.

They found some rocks to sit upon. Sean fished out two foam-filled plastic mats that kept out the damp. He could see Jonjo's quizzical look, as if this was some new technology, not entirely to be trusted.

They both realised just how tired they were when they sat down. The duo got down to the serious business of eating. Jonjo with his huge bacon sandwiches while Sean favoured mustard covered corned meat.

Sean marvelled at the amount his friend could eat without putting an ounce on his spare frame. They finished off with their flasks. Jonjo poured a pint of strong tea into his enamel mug. Sean used the metal cup from his thermos for his Italian coffee.

"We'll have to come up with a name for ourselves," said Sean.

"What do you mean?"

"Now that we are detectives," explained Sean.

"Oh, it's detectives, is it?" laughed Jonjo.

"Walsh and Brennan."

" Brennan and Walsh!"

"Walsh and Brennan, stalk the mean streets, of the Wild West, in Mayo 3-2. Book him Jonjo!"

"Well, you are the brains of the outfit. How do we solve the mystery?" conceded Jonjo.

"Scene of the crime that is always the first place they start," offered Sean.

The sun was reaching its height. The rays filtered by the leaves gave the light a soporific quality. The two friends decided there was no rush to get to the scene. Seldom the need to hasten to a cemetery. They listened to the chorus of birdsong and rested their eyes a little longer.

Jonjo was always the first to stir and, the two slowly got to their feet. They continued their hike, discussing what the policeman had told them. Belief in spirits and the old ways was still there. You didn't need to scratch far beneath the surface, figuratively or literally speaking, for the old beliefs to emerge. The two men took their time admiring the views and chatting.

"I'm so grateful you got me out on these walks," said Sean. "After what the doctor had said, I was just waiting for the inevitable."

"Ara musha. Waiting to die isn't living. And living isn't waiting to die," commented Jonjo.

"That's very profound. Did you make that up?"

"No, it sounds far too good for me. I must have heard it somewhere," laughed Jonjo.

Arriving at the cemetery, Jonjo placed a flower on his wife's grave. Sean did the same at his grandparents' headstone. He looked for other family tombs, and as he did so, a reflection caught his eye.

Waiting until Jonjo had finished his devotion, he called to him, "Come and look at this!"

In the long grass, near the wall, was a piece of broken red plastic.

"That's part of a reflector from a pushbike," cried Jonjo. "See this too."

He pointed at a skid mark from a bike tyre on the road next to the graveyard.

"O.K.," said Sean. "Someone has pulled up sharply on their bike, but at that angle there is no way the bicycle would have come over this wall."

"Look," insisted Jonjo. "The flattened grass is about the size of a bike. Maybe someone fell off the bike and threw it over the wall in frustration."

A great smile lit up Sean's face. "You've got it. And maybe that someone then walked through the gate, picked it up over their shoulders. If that person was dressed in black as night fell, that could be our mysterious coffin carrier."

The two nodded and walked around to the presbytery. There, against the wall, stood Fr. Flanagan's' bike. The front wheel was buckled.

They rang the bell, and the priest himself answered. "Jonjo, and this must be Mr. Walsh."

They explained the rumour about an apparition in the graveyard. "Should we tell everyone what had happened?" queried Jonjo.

"Please do," said Father Flanagan. "Otherwise, I'll be getting reports of banshees and spectres of all types. I was coming back from Widow Farrell's. We've been discussing a possible donation to the Church. Perhaps it's better if you don't mention that part. Some of these fellows start vicious rumours. They're worse than women, though we're not supposed to say that nowadays."

"I won't tell them anything other than your fall from the bike. I take it you're not injured," inquired Jonjo.

"Just bruised pride. I hope we might be seeing you at Mass soon, Mr Walsh."

Sean muttered something indistinguishable, and he and Jonjo walked over to Clarke's bar. Jonjo told the tale to Tommy and the regulars, giving most of the credit to Sean.

"He must have been at Widow Farrell's," commented Micko.

Sean and Jonjo kept their own counsel.

The conversation inevitably turned to ghost stories. The men and women had a rare old night frightening themselves with ever more implausible tales.

"Never let the truth spoil a good story," added Paddy Regan as he walked in.

"Is that the new motto of the Garda?" piped up Seamus Burke to general laughter.

"No, it's always been that," countered the policeman, to even greater hilarity.

"Is that Fr. in the cemetery again?" queried Seamus.

"Can't be, I know for a fact that he's gone to Castlebar," stated Regan. "It does look like a..." his words tailed off. "There's a strange mist."

He looked around for Sean and Jonjo, but before he could warn them, the two old friends were through the gate into the graveyard.

Chapter 7

Paddy Regan dashed into the churchyard. The mist had disappeared as rapidly as it had emerged. At first, he couldn't see the two old men, then to his relief, he spied them sitting on the wooden bench. They both looked pale and tense. He'd seen that look before. It was the look of someone about to go into shock.

"How long have we been here?" asked Jonjo, with a quaver in his voice.

Paddy had never heard that tone before from this strong old man.

"No time at all," replied Garda Regan. "You just walked in, then the mist disappeared. Did you see anything?"

"No," answered Jonjo, with a sidelong look at Sean.

Paddy could tell that they were holding something back. "I'll give you two a lift home." He dropped them off at the boreen and said, "Thanks for solving my case today."

He was glad to note, the two men were talking as they walked away. Something had clearly shaken them up. Although he didn't know Sean very well, he had known Jonjo all his life and knew that he was one of the strongest and most resilient men he had ever met.

"We'll talk it through tomorrow," said Jonjo. "I prescribe a drop of the hard stuff to help you to sleep."

"O.K., Dr Brennan," laughed Sean. "There'd be queues at your surgery if you were a doctor."

Sean poured himself a bourbon and sat down at his desk. He wrote his recollection of what happened in the mist. He had always found that writing things down stopped him mulling things over, too much, in his mind.

That night, he did something he had not done in countless years. Sean, not without difficulty, got down on his knees and said his night prayers. Unexpectedly, he slept well.

The following morning he asked Jonjo to write

down what had happened. Jonjo declined, "I'm not one for writing."

"How about you tell me, and I write it?" offered Sean. "It was a strange thing, and I'd like to hear what you thought."

Nodding, Jonjo began his tale, "When we went through the gate, I felt as wet as if I were under the sea. It seemed like I was underwater, but I could breathe right enough. There were currents, some warm and some icy cold. I forgot all about looking for the ghost, and I couldn't see you anywhere. I heard a voice say, 'The Vale of Tears.' I'm not sure if it was a voice or just in my own head." Jonjo shuddered at the recollection, "There was a feeling of despair and longing, something had to be done, but I don't know what."

"Here, read my report," offered Sean.

"No, I'm not much of a one for reading you read it."

"Well, I won't read it. It's nearly the same as yours. The only difference is I said it felt like flying and, my feet weren't on the ground. I heard that same thing, 'The Vale of Tears'. I thought we'd been in there for a long time. Someone wanted us to do something, but I don't know what. It was like something I'd been thinking about just before I'd gone to sleep, and I just couldn't remember it."

The morning sun was dispelling the morning haze. The high clouds were already burning away. Sparrows chirping their optimism brightened the mood.

"Will we walk down to the hollow and decide what to do?" said Jonjo.

Jonjo left his keys on the outside of his door. He left a note too, to say where they were. He had no doubt that Paddy Regan would call at some point. The familiar walk down to the hollow lifted their spirits even more, and they sat on the warm turf, with their backs against the moss-covered banking.

"A strange old day yesterday. A policeman, a priest, and a ghost, all in one day. That's a holy trinity you don't meet often," laughed Jonjo.

"Do you know though that 'Vale of Tears' made me believe more in our search for the Vale of Mist? It's the first supernatural experience I've ever had."

"It seems so hard to believe in the daylight. If you hadn't written it down, I'd be doubting it already. We need to do something. Someone was asking for our help," said Jonjo.

"I think I should ask the priest about the Vale of Tears, I know I've heard it said in prayers, but I don't really know what it means. It must all be to do with the graveyard. I'd like to look at the Church records. The information might be there."

As predicted, Paddy Regan arrived. Sean gave him the account he had written.

"I'll go down and cut the grass in the churchyard. They don't do a proper job. It's straggly, all around the edge. We need a good look at those graves. I'll take my big scythe down," said Jonjo.

Sean caught Paddy's eye, and the two smiled and then began to laugh out loud.

"What's up with ye two?" demanded Jonjo.

"Well," said Paddy. "A town rife with paranormal fear, enter a tall, angular figure, with a scythe, amongst the gravestones. What's wrong with that picture?"

The two started laughing again until there were tears in their eyes.

"I'll scythe the two of you, and don't come running to me with no legs," said Jonjo, joining in the hilarity.

The two friends set off on the familiar route to town. "Do you know?" began Jonjo. "When I was a kid, I thought the bit in the Hail Mary 'Blessed art thou amongst women was,' 'Blessed art thou a monk swimming'. I must not have known what a monk was at the time. Because in my head, I pictured it like a monkey. I would imagine a monkey swimming in a pond. Later I understood the word monk, and my picture changed to a fat man in a brown monk's habit, tied around the waist with a cord. I thought to myself how stupid I had been thinking it was a monkey. I liked the image of the monkey better and would sometimes think of that instead, but that made me feel guilty."

"We were always good at feeling guilty," replied Sean. "Do you remember when we made our first confessions? I couldn't think of anything to tell. So I confessed to telling lies, which was a lie, which made it true."

"You were always a deep thinker," laughed Jonjo.

They met with Fr. Flanagan. Over a cup of tea, he thanked them for sorting out the business with the bike and the supposed apparition. Sean showed the priest his written account of the previous night's incident. The clergyman read it and sat silently for a moment or two.

"I can give you a rational explanation of this. The

stories about ghosts in the pub heightened everyone's expectations, the sudden mist coming down shapes and shadows from the moonlight. People see what they expect to see. Two gentlemen of advancing years rush into the mist and become disorientated."

The priest held up his hand, "However, I believe you. I've felt something is wrong in this cemetery ever since I came to the parish. I've not known what to do. I mean, it's hardly the thing for the priest to go around saying that he thinks the graveyard is a bit spooky," said Fr Flanagan, wryly.

"Well, I'm glad you're on our side," responded Sean. "Can you tell us the meaning of the 'Vale of Tears'?"

"I'm sure it must be an Old Testament phrase, but I can't tell you from where exactly. I know it has come to mean the trials and tribulations we face on the earth before we enter Heaven."

"We've had an idea Fr.," said Jonjo. "Somebody, no, I should say someone or some spirit, is asking for our help. I thought I would tidy up the graveyard, cut back the long grass, and so on. Sean, with your permission, could look through the parish records. Maybe one way or another, we can find out what's going on."

"I'll be glad of the help," responded the cleric. "I have two parishes to run. If the people see you two involved, it might encourage others to join in. All the parish records are in the cupboard in the sacristy. There are garden tools in the shed. Help yourself to tea and biscuits, have the run of the place."

The two friends walked over to the church and into the sacristy.

"Furniture polish, incense, and damp. It smells just the same as it did when I was last here over sixty years ago," marvelled Sean.

"Look," laughed Jonjo. He was pointing at the long wooden candle extinguisher. It had a brass cone, cowl for snuffing candles; this had been the favourite job of all the altar boys in their time. After Mass, once out of sight of the congregation, the altar boys would race for the snuffer.

"I bet it's the same one," they said almost simultaneously.

Fr. Flanagan popped his head through the doorway and asked Sean, "Do you have the Latin? The old records are in Latin, but it's easy enough to follow."

"I'll get by," confirmed Sean.

The priest left and the two friends got the parish records out. "That reminds me, wasn't there talk about you going into the priesthood when you were young?" asked Jonjo.

"That's right; luckily the move to the States put an end to that."

The two spent the afternoon on their respective jobs and then met in Clarke's bar. Jonjo had been seen working in the cemetery and explained what he and Sean were up to. Sean was pleasantly surprised at how readily everyone accepted what they were doing. Nobody questioned the concept that there was someone in the afterlife asking for help.

"So, you're ghostbusters now," piped up Seamus Burke. "Well, did you hear the story of the ghost that visited this pub?"

"No, but I'm sure we are going to," replied Jonjo.

Undaunted, Seamus carried on, "It was many years ago in the time Tommy's granddad, Mihail had the pub. A stormy, Saturday night the windows rattling in the wind. Old Rafferty was sitting, right where you are now, Jonjo. When 'bang' up jumped his dog and pushed Rafferty to the floor. At that same instant, a heavy horse brass fell from the wall. The hound had saved Rafferty's life. Sadly for the dog, the brass hit the animal on the head, killing him outright, and, as a further indignity, a sharp edge of the brass cut off the poor creature's tail.

The pub was closed; Mihail was in bed when he was woken by an unearthly noise. He opened the door, and there was the ghost of the brave dog. It looked at him wistfully and said, 'I've got a place in doggy heaven, but I can't enjoy it properly without my tail, so I've come to get it back.'

Mihail replied, 'I'm sorry it's after 11, and I'm not allowed to retail spirits.'"

There was a mixture of groans and laughter. Someone shouted, "Buy Seamus a drink, to shut him up."

"I would, but I fear it would have the opposite effect," laughed Jonjo, who bought him a pint, nonetheless.

Sean and Jonjo walked home across the fields. "I've made some interesting discoveries in the records," offered Sean.

"Will we talk it over tomorrow?" said Jonjo. "I've

had a letter from America; I'd like you to see, too."

"Of course," said Sean. "I'll see you tomorrow."

Chapter 8

Walking down the boreen on a beautiful summer morning. A skylark sprang from nowhere. Flying and singing, it surprised and delighted the walkers. They watched until it was no more than a speck in the lavender-blue sky.

The lane was bright with colour. The middle of the path long since reclaimed by nature. The grey and white drystone walls decorated with ivy and lichen, suffused with fuchsia, framed the route. Before the boreen reached the road, a stone stile gave access to a little-used footpath.

Sean and Jonjo squeezed between the upright stones. Juggling their bags through the gap, they settled for their morning break.

"I found some interesting stuff in the parish records," began Sean. "All our family records are there. The most unusual was some correspondence from 1847 about extending the cemetery."

"That would be 'Black 47' the worst year of the famine," added Jonjo.

"That's right; it seems that the graveyard was expanded right to the roadside. Room was made for a mass grave so that the famine victims could be buried on consecrated ground."

"That fits in with what I've seen," contributed Jonjo. "The churchyard wall has been altered. It looks as though some layers of stone were taken from the top and used for extending the length. Robbing Peter to pay Paul, my dad used to call it. It accounts for that strange corner that Fr bumped his bike on".

"When I cut the grass yesterday, I could see an outline of what must have been the grave. The ground was sunken. It had a rough edge of stones, small rocks little more than pebbles. A makeshift plot but probably a huge undertaking for those struggling people," continued Jonjo.

"It does all go together. I'm not sure what we can do

next to find out what is troubling the poor soul in the graveyard," asked Sean.

"Well, that's why we are on a marathon of a walk today. We are walking down the river. Then past the mill and down to the stone bridge. Across the bridge, the old warehouse has been converted into a Rest Home. It's there we'll find Bridie Murphy. She's the oldest person in the parish and a local historian. She has a good twenty years, even on us two."

The footpath reminded the two of the hollow. The path lay below the level of the fields, the canopy of trees almost forming a tunnel.

"The tinkers used to come this way, but I've not seen any for a long time," commented Sean. "Great fellers, those tinkers."

"You know Jonjo; you've had your fair share of tribulation in life. How do you stay so cheerful?" asked Sean.

Jonjo thought for a moment. "I've had to work at it since Mary died, but she taught me a lot. I try to say positive things, and if I think something that's not positive, I try not to say it."

"If you've nothing good to say, say nothing at all, my

Mammy used to say," said Sean.

"Then Mary told me that I should remember JOY. It stood for Jesus, others, yourself. She said that was the priority. I told her that I found it difficult to work out what Jesus would want. So she told me that putting others before myself would do the job."

"A clever lady," replied Sean.

"The other things I've taught myself are, if I think of a sad memory, then straight away think of two happy ones. I take pleasure in small things; the smell of bacon frying, the songs of birds. If I think about Mary, God rest her soul, I don't think of her criticising me from above. She knows my failings, and I think of her helping me. The same goes for my Mammy and Daddy, and everyone else I've lost, God rest them."

"That's great, Jonjo. You could write a book about it," said Sean.

"Now, that's something I definitely couldn't do. I'll tell you about that when we stop for our lunch," laughed Jonjo.

Emerging from the narrow footpath, the beauty of the river sparkled before them. A startled duck led her ducklings out of the reeds into the shallow water at the edge. The two friends walked in comfortable silence. Each happy in his own thoughts. The water danced gracefully between the smooth stones in the mainstream.

The river, lower than Jonjo had seen for many years, murmured against the rocks. The occasional leaf or twig caught his eye, riding the current, sometimes temporarily beaching on the pebbles. How many centuries had people been drawn to this river? Hunter-gatherers following animals to their watering hole. Fish and wildfowl to hunt.

Later, fertile ground, easily irrigated. Defence against enemies, transportation, a route to navigate, and a route to navigate by. Coming forward in time the power of the water was harnessed by machinery. A timeless place ever-present yet ever-changing.

Jonjo indicated the place they should stop. There was a clearing in the woods, with four large logs arranged in a rough square, each a couple of feet apart. He explained that the tinkers used this place. They had a fire in the middle with a cast iron pot suspended on a metal tripod. "They would always share anything they had with you," confided Jonjo.

"I'd like you to look at my letter from America, please," asked Jonjo. "I've not a lot of confidence in my reading ever since our schooldays. Do you remember how we used to chant our letters 'a' for apple, 'b' for ball and so on?"

"Of course I do. I remember that day the tinker's lad got into trouble. Sister Teresa said 'x' for xylophone. He said, "What the feck is a xylophone?" She lifted him off his chair by his ear and was going to wash his mouth out with soap. He shook himself free, ran out of school, and we never saw him again. The next day she said 'x' is for xylophone. She looked up and said, 'It's like a glockenspiel.'

I so wanted to say, "What the feck is a glockenspiel?" but I didn't swear, and I was terrified of Sister Teresa."

"We all were," said Jonjo. "I struggled with some of the letters. I could never get 'b' and 'd' the right way round. The letters that didn't sound like their names, like 'x' and 'w' flummoxed me. Worst of all, the letters sometimes seemed to swim around."

"Dyslexia," offered Sean.

"That's what they call it now. Back then it meant you

were thick. Good came from it though, that's what pushed me so much into sport. I used to memorise the books at school too, it helped me have a good memory. Fancy calling it dyslexia, though. It's like they're saying you have trouble reading, so we'll call it a name you can't read."

"But I've seen you read the 'paper," queried Sean.

"I can get by, but I'm not what you'd call a confident reader. If I had anything important or out of the ordinary, Mary would read it. This letter I've had from America is about an inheritance. I am an old culchie, but I know some people play con tricks."

Sean read through the letter. "Does the name Francis Brennan of Chicago mean anything to you?"

"Yes, I had an uncle of that name who went to America in the 1930s, but nobody heard from him. I remember asking my dad about him. He told me that Francis was named after my grandad, Sean Brennan."

"What Francis was named after Sean, that doesn't make sense?"

"That's what I said," replied Jonjo. "It turned out my grandad was Francis Sean. Just about everybody in the family was going by their middle names, and I never knew."

"It's the Irish way. I think we should put this letter in the hands of a solicitor. You are right to be cautious about these things," advised Sean.

"Well, if there is any money, you can have it for putting the water and heating in my house."

"No, I've already explained that I was repaying an old debt. Anyway, when I was in the States, somebody kept my house in good repair. They whitewashed the walls, repaired holes in the roof, kept the place watertight. That was you, right?" queried Sean.

"It was, but it was partly for my own good. I didn't want to be living near a hovel."

"If anyone is in debt, it's me," said Sean firmly.

Jonjo smiled, "We're quits." With that, he felt a weight lifted from his shoulder, for he had never liked the idea of being beholden to anyone.

The two companions enjoyed listening to the river flowing past and were almost reluctant to leave their picnic site. Following the riverbank, they came to the ruins of the old mill, an impressive stone building which, although now in disrepair, still had a certain grandeur.

"What clever people they were. To think of using the power of the water to make bread," said Jonjo.

"You are right," said Sean. "I could spend three lifetimes living by a river and never come up with that idea."

They walked across the bridge and up to the Rest Home. The nursing assistant let them in and directed them to Bridie Murphy's room. "She's in her dotage, but she is in and out of it. Sometimes she's fine," she told them. "She's fiercely independent."

Bridie had her own ensuite room. Her window overlooked the garden, which was neatly lawned and had a chicken run. Bridie herself was sitting with her back to the window, head down, engrossed in a book.

"Good afternoon Mrs Murphy," said Jonjo.

Squinting up at him, she replied, "Jonjo Brennan, and this must be the Walsh boy, back home. I've heard about the graveyard. Is that what you've come about?"

"You're very well informed," said Sean.

"She has a network better than MI5," laughed Jonjo.

"I've been thinking it over," said Bridie. "You two are the last in your bloodlines. I think the spirit will be somehow related to you. It is clearly trying to tell you something. Pass me that book will you, Jonjo?"

Jonjo passed her a heavy tome from her bookshelf. It was a volume of collected local newspapers from the 19th century. "I don't know what that message is, but you'll probably find some clues in there. Take that book with you and bring it back when you've solved the mystery."

The three spoke together, for some time, about the village and the past. They took their leave. Jonjo said, cheerfully, "It's never as far going back."

"That's one mystery I know the answer to," said Bridie. "When you set off, you carry the weight of the journey back, in your mind. You have only half that weight on your return."

Sean and Jonjo headed home, already making plans for their next steps.

Chapter 9

The sleek, chirpy creature danced on the grass. The song of the blackbird brought him round from that region between sleep and wakefulness. He whistled back, imitating the call. They kept up the repartee for a minute or two. "Hello, old friend," it seemed to say.

Other birds joined in the chorus, which became a lullaby. Jonjo had that nice comfortable feeling knowing he had only to turn over, to be soundly asleep again. He woke once more, at dawn, and this time, swung his legs out of bed.

The luxury of a shower was still a novelty. The water, as hot as he could bear, Jonjo breathed in the steam. The tiredness of yesterday's walk was still in his legs. He hoped that Sean was O.K. He made breakfast and did his housework. Mary had taught him well, and he did it to the best of his ability, thinking of her.

Jonjo sat on his bench outside and studied the verdant countryside. He had known this view his whole life yet never tired of it. The days had slowed down as the years sped up. Every day there were changes, a flower emerging from stony ground, a new nest among the trees. A seasonal rhythm; a symphony of weather, flora and fauna. The sounds and aromas varied. The shy deer and rabbits disappeared as the noisy birds emerged. The subtle cadence of life, for those lucky enough to have the time and wit to see.

He walked up to Sean's house and inquired about his health.

"Embrocation and bourbon did the trick," replied Sean.

"Make sure you don't mix the bottles up," warned Jonjo.

"Well, it might wash some of the black marks off my soul," laughed Sean.

"I think you'd need a good scrubbing brush, too," answered Jonjo.

On the big kitchen table were two large, musty-smelling books.

Sean said, "We have a mystery to solve. We need to find anything we can about the man who came down from the hill village. Also, we need to work back through the parish records to find the link to our family trees. The genealogy is more about dates and numbers, so maybe you do that?"

"Didn't I tell you I was no good with numbers too," said Jonjo apologetically.

"No, you did not."

"Well, it's a long story. It goes right back to when we were at school," said Jonjo.

"Is it a 'put the cafetiere on the stove and have a coffee' length of a story?" asked Sean.

"Definitely."

The two friends sat back with their strong brew. The aroma of the coffee had a slightly herbal hint. It blended well with the sweet floral breeze from the garden.

"I could never fathom out multiplication."

"Hang on," said Sean. "We used to chant the times tables every day, over and over. We had a test every week. I'm sure you knew them."

"I did, and I still do. But I didn't understand what it meant. It irritated me that if you had 7, and you multiplied it by 0, it was 0. So, where had that 7 gone? I knew one thing, though; you didn't ask the teachers questions in those days."

"I just never questioned it," admitted Sean. "Did that stuff really bother you?"

"Not so much in the early days. It got worse 'x' kept popping up. You had to find out the value of 'x'. Sometimes I'd get it, and then in the next sum, it was a different number. One slippery feller was 'x'," laughed Jonjo.

"Later he teamed up with 'y' and sometimes even 'z'. There'd be all sorts of problems; a train set of from Dublin with x passengers y got on at Wicklow. If it took x men three hours to dig a ditch. A man filled up a barrel with a hole in it. It was endless and pointless, and most of all, I couldn't do it."

"Dyscalculia," offered Sean.

"Maybe, but back then, again, it just meant you were thick. I got through school because I was good at sport. As long as I turned up for matches, they didn't seem to mind if I went AWOL in the afternoons."

"I didn't know," said Sean, sadly.

"Don't be feeling sorry for me. I had the whole countryside as my playground. Those were rare old times. Look, I'll go through the old newspapers if I find anything you can check it."

Sean nodded and turned his attention to the parish record book. He'd been surprised when Fr. Flanagan suggested that he took it home. He'd been genuinely taken aback at how trusting people were. Something that had, sadly, gone from his American hometown.

The two men got down to their study. Both were wearing reading glasses; on Sean, they sat well, adding gravitas to his already studious features. For Jonjo, they were unwelcome, annoying, like a fly that needed swatting. Sean made notes and diagrams, putting together a family tree, meticulous in every detail.

"I think I've found it!" said Jonjo excitedly.

"Don't tell me yet. I need to do as much of the family tree as I can back to the 1840s, then we'll see if it fits," replied Sean.

"Of course," said Jonjo. He made another pot of strong coffee and continued reading the old newspapers.

"Do you remember that 'x' with a little 2 up in the air?" asked Jonjo.

"What?"

"At school, you know. Did you do that in America?" continued Jonjo.

"Square numbers?"

"That's the one. I never understood," said Jonjo.

"Come on, I'll show you. I need a break from this tree." Sean led Jonjo to the new conservatory. He carefully took all the pieces off his ornate chess set. "What's the smallest square you can see on there?" he inquired.

"One square, just one, on its own," replied Jonjo.

"O.K., how many squares in the next biggest one?"

"Two," said Jonjo, mildly irritated.

"Have a look."

"Oh, two squares would make a rectangle. So it would have to be 4, 2 lots of 2. Then it would be 9, that's 3 lots of 3," said Jonjo.

"Yeh, a square number is just a number that is multiplied by itself," confirmed Sean.

"But it actually makes a square. I never got that. Thanks, Sean."

"We are never too old to learn, or so you keep telling me. Come with me I want to show you something. There used to be a sort of cellar at the back of the house. When I knew I was coming back, I had it dug out and extended. Guess what's down there?" challenged Sean.

"I saw them excavating it, with mini-diggers, a great invention those things. I thought it was just a room, maybe a gym. People go in for those at home now. Too much work, for a wood store, I give in."

"Well, there is some wood down there, but that's just for the racks," replied Sean.

He opened the door, and the lights automatically switched on. Row after row of wine bottles stretched into the recesses. Another wooden door was evident at the far end of the vault.

"There must be hundreds of bottles. Is that another cellar at the far end?" queried Jonjo.

"No, the builders found a tunnel. I asked them to close it off."

"I wanted to show you this cellar because, well, I'm ashamed of it."

They went back upstairs and sat on the comfortable

armchairs. Jonjo cradled his coffee cup, in his big hands, as Sean told his tale. "I made a lot of money, rags to riches, the American dream. My parents were proud of me. I made their life a lot easier, I was proud of myself. I loved and had the love of a beautiful girl, Lucia. She was Italian-American, lovely, and so cheerful. We went to the same church, our families got on well, it was written in the stars."

"What happened?" asked Jonjo.

"I was promoted. It meant a lot of travelling, weekends away. I gave little thought and less time to Lucia and my parents. Lucia and I split up, and she married someone else. I got my own place, and I kept making more and more money. I bought properties. I remember my Dad saying that you could only sleep in one bed. I took no notice making money became my passion."

"Well, so you were good at your job," said Jonjo.

"Ever hear the saying, 'He knew the price of everything and the value of nothing', well that was me, that is me. I blamed it on everyone but myself. We'd had no money when I was a child; I claimed that had made me insecure. The reality was that when I was a child, I never knew we were poor. I was loved, and that was all that mattered. I didn't see that then. I'm sorry for burdening you with this."

"Ara musha, isn't that what friends are for?"

"That cellar is packed with rare and valuable wines. But what use are they? I just bought things for the sake of it," continued Sean.

"So you became acquisitive, there are worse things,"

"Acquisitive, exactly! What a vocabulary you have for someone who doesn't read," said Sean.

"You show me an Irishman that doesn't love words," laughed Jonjo.

"The thing is I feel I've wasted my life."

"Nonsense," said Jonjo firmly. "Look, I'll meet you down at the hollow in an hour. We'll make a dent in your wine store; fetch a couple of bottles and the family tree. I'll make us some lunch."

"Aren't you forgetting something?" asked Sean, pointing at the book of collected newspapers.

"It's all in here," answered Jonjo, tapping his temple with his index finger.

Together they ate Jonjo's thick sandwiches, ham and onions with homemade butter.

"Well, now that we've exceeded our recommended daily allowance of everything else, time for the wine," laughed Sean.

"Those recommendations aren't for us. We are already well past the 'three score and ten'. We write the recommendations now, not follow them."

"Well, my 'best by ' date has definitely gone. One of these bottles cost $20, one cost $200. I want you to guess which is which."

"Casting pearls before swine," suggested Jonjo.

He duly tried them, doing his best imitation of a wine taster. He picked his favourite, which turned out to be the more expensive one. "I knew I was descended from the kings of Ireland," he smiled.

They shared the two bottles and discussed Sean's worries. Jonjo got him to think about the happier aspects of his life. They talked about the good he might do with his wealth. The warm sunshine, the full stomachs and the wine loosened their tongues

"I asked the butcher if he had a sheep's head," said Sean, laughing "No, it's just the way I part my hair."

Jonjo countered, "Paddy Regan, the Guard, told me his new Inspector said to him, 'If you can guess how many doughnuts are in my bag, you can have them both'."

"O.K.," said Sean. "An Irishman went into a bar every week in Boston and asked for three shots of whiskey. One for himself and one for each of his brothers in Ireland. One day he ordered two. 'Don't tell me something has happened to one of your brothers said the barman'. 'No,' he said, 'it's me I've given up drinking for Lent.'"

The jokes continued until both men were crying with laughter. Jonjo forgot one while telling it and said, "Well, as me Mammy would have said, 'it musht have been a lie.'"

The two took their thoughts back to what they had discovered. The mystery had been solved, but putting things right, would be another matter. They would act tomorrow.

The warm sun, the comfortable grassy bank, the potent wine, a recipe for pleasant slumber.

Chapter 10

The dry stone walls, as old as time, stretched before them. Countless generations contributed to these works. They snaked along at one with the undulations of the land. At a distance, the grey, moss topped boundaries looked as if they had grown from the land, which in a way they had.

The white wind turbines, at first, seemed to be an aberration. Scars on the skyline. Over time, Jonjo had begun to admire their elegance. He liked the fact that they worked with nature, not against it. Men could injure Mother Nature, but it was a fight they would never win, one they should never attempt. Somewhere, sometime, they had made that mistake. Jonjo was optimistic times were changing for the better.

Sitting against the banking near the hollow, he admired the beauty and variety of the primulas as he spoke to Sean. "Paddy Costello, he's our man?" queried Jonjo.

"It fits. I've checked all the historical records, the Griffith's valuation, the Tithe Applopment Books and of course the parish records."

"Applopment? That's a new word for me," commented Jonjo.

"Me too. I had to read it twice. It was a tax assessment in the 19th Century," confirmed Sean. "The maps and the aerial photos all pin it down to that house on the hill. He was a cousin to both of us, 4th cousin to me, and 4th cousin once removed to you. Like us, he was the last of his line."

"I've never really got that 3rd cousin, 4th cousin stuff," said Jonjo.

"I've had to work at it," admitted Sean. "I had to study a chart."

"Well, you've done a grand job, so."

"Thanks. Will you tell me about the newspaper report?" inquired Sean.

"I know it by heart such a sad story. I'll just tell you the facts. Paddy Costello came down to the town in great distress. His wife and child had died from starvation. He'd had to bury them in a potato trench, having barely the strength to cover them in soil. Paddy was consumed with grief for his loss, made worse, by the lack of a proper burial."

"The records show that he ended up in the famine grave in the church," added Sean.

"His love was so strong that he reached beyond the grave to contact us."

"Do you really believe that?" asked Sean.

"What else can it be? Probably, science will be able to explain it in the future. Maybe something in our shared DNA enables messages to be transmitted across time. One generation's superstition is another's science," explained Jonjo.

"Where did you hear that?"

"I don't know. I might have made that one up," laughed Jonjo.

They finished their brews and replaced the flasks in their heavy bags. Jonjo was carrying the two heavy books, and Sean six bottles of wine, for Fr Flanagan.

"Do you know, the extra weight in the bag straightens me up? It feels better somehow," commented Sean. "I'll be happy when we have this sorted out, and we can get back to our search for the Vale of Mist."

"I know, but it's a good thing we are doing. I am sure Fr Flanagan will know what's to be done."

As they approached the tunnel under the hill, Sean got out his mobile 'phone. "I thought you'd already spoken to him," queried Jonjo.

"I have. I'm just switching the torch on."

"Torch? That's your 'phone."

"You can use it as a torch. Look!"

"Well, I wouldn't have believed that if I hadn't seen it!" exclaimed Jonjo.

"You'll be surprised what it can do. I can use it as a clock, an alarm clock, a calculator, send written messages, and check my bank account. You should get one."

"No, I've no need. I only got a normal phone when Mary was ill. To be honest, I feel uncomfortable speaking on that," replied Jonjo. "Anyway, I wouldn't know how to use it."

"I could soon show you. Mind you I'm no expert. I don't know half of the things it does."

"I never got why they call them mobile 'phones. It's not as if you could put them down, and they'd trot along behind you. They're not mobile they're portable," insisted Jonjo.

"Well, we called them cell phones, but don't ask me what that means. Do you know the other day you were making out that you could barely read, now you are discussing the nuance of different words?" laughed Sean.

At the presbytery, they showed their information to Fr Flanagan. They drank tea together and pondered for a short while.

"The ideal answer would be to recover the bones from the hillside and give them a proper burial in the churchyard. However, I'm not sure that would be the best or even feasible," said the cleric.

"Why not, Father?" asked Sean.

"Well, as Jonjo knows, I'm a late vocation to the priesthood. I did my first degree in Archaeology and Ancient History. Digging up bones isn't as straightforward as it looks on TV. Bones, particularly from a shallow grave, will more than likely have been disturbed, scattered and partly devoured by animals. The soil around here can be acidic, so they may be gone altogether. Then there's getting permission to remove the bones."

"So it's a no go," said Sean disappointedly.

"There is an alternative," replied Fr Flanagan brightly. "If the mountain will not come to Muhammad, then Muhammad must go to the mountain. I can conduct a requiem Mass on the hill and bless the area making it hallowed ground. We could have it for next Saturday evening's vigil Mass. If the weather holds there's nothing like an outdoor Mass, what do you think?"

The two readily agreed, and then Fr. Flanagan continued, "I want to show you something. It involves a lot of steps up to the spire. Do you remember when we had that storm a while back? I thought I'd heard something on the roof. Fortunately, there was no damage anyway I'll show you."

The ascent of the spire using the narrow stone steps was tough going, especially for Sean. Reaching the top, they followed Fr Flanagan's pointing finger and gasped at the sight. From the famine village, there was a line of different colours dotting the landscape. Leading right up to the churchyard.

"They're primulas. I've noticed there are a lot about this year, we had such a mild winter. That pattern, it's like a path from the hill to the church. I've never seen anything like it!" exclaimed Jonjo.

"The thing is, down on the ground, you don't notice it. I'm sure someone could come up with an explanation, but there it is. My opinion is it's a message to me and you two," said Fr Flanagan.

"Have you shown anyone else?" asked Sean.

"No, and I'm not going to. Some people blow these things out of proportion. When I was at the seminary in Spain, I remember a donkey stumbling outside the church. Some locals insisted that it had genuflected. They were ready to contact the bishop and organise a fiesta. We know what it is about, and the Mass should sort it out."

All three laughed at the idea of the genuflecting donkey as they made their way down the steps. Fr Flanagan thanked them for the return of the parish records and confirmed he would give Bridie Murphy her book. He asked that the two men spread the word about the Mass and thanked Sean for his gift of the wine.

As they walked into the town, Jonjo stopped abruptly. "I've just remembered something from Bridie's book. The route from the hill to town was part of an old coffin trail. The reporter called it the Sourcut trail."

"O.K.," replied Sean, a little baffled.

"Don't you see it's sabhaircín? It's the Irish word for primrose. It sounds like 'sourcut' in English," persevered Jonjo.

"Well, that's interesting, but I'm not sure what you are getting at."

"Well, the myth of the ancient people was that the primroses led to the other realm, to heaven. I just think it's a clue in our search for the Vale of Mist. You know when you said that life was like a game, and all the answers were there, just ready to be found. I think it is a sign like that," explained Jonjo.

"I see. I didn't know that myth. I remember my Mammy giving us primroses to rub on our gums for toothache."

"It was in all sorts of medicines then. I think they made wine from it too," added Jonjo.

"Well, none of it made its way into my collection," laughed Sean.

The two made their way to Clarke's bar. Sean got the pints and chatted intently to Tommy, the proprietor. Jonjo got the attention of the pub by tapping on a glass. He explained succinctly about their discovery and the Mass for the following Saturday. There was a general agreement about what good work they had done and the need for a wake.

The Mass on the hilltop had a mixed reaction. When Sean announced that an anonymous benefactor had put money behind the bar for the forthcoming Saturday for the funeral-goers, more warmed to the idea.

Seamus restarted one of his tales, having given way to Jonjo. He began, "I saw Timmy and Sean Murphy today working for the Council. Timmy was digging holes, and Sean was following behind him, filling the holes in. I said, Timmy, why do you dig a hole, only to have your Sean, fill it up again?"

Timmy wiped his brow and sighed, 'Well, I suppose it probably looks odd, because we're normally a three-person team. But today, our brother Danny who plants the trees, called in sick.'"

There were more groans than laughter at this. Jonjo and Sean, aware that they still had the walk home ahead of them, left after the one pint.

"The anonymous benefactor is you?" asked Jonjo.

"Yes, I thought it was the right thing to do. Tommy Clarke said he'd put a cap on the free drinks just so nobody went over the top. I told him just to use his own judgement. He also suggested they lay on some food. He was willing to do that out of his own money. I didn't want to see him out of pocket, so I told him I'd pay for that."

"I wish I could go half on this with you," added Jonjo.

"Well, maybe, if anything comes of the American inheritance, you can," laughed Sean. "I'm kidding. I've got more money than I need more than I can spend."

"Well, you are doing a good thing with it," said Jonjo.

"I'm learning a lot from you. You are getting me on the right track," commented Sean.

"I'll tell you what. You can teach me something."

"What's that?" asked Sean

"More about that wine tasting. We'll have a thirst when we get back. I think I've got a real talent for wine tasting."

Chapter 11

The lough, in the distance, was a serene blue. Rowing boats in silent slow-motion crawled across the surface. The river ran into the lake without a ripple. A shimmering heat haze, creating a sense of unreality. The air itself aromatic, imbued with tranquillity. A magical, mystical day.

Fr. Flanagan looked over the mosaic of fields and to the hills beyond. The hot summer had created parch marks in the meadows revealing the outline of buried structures. The priest tried to imagine these places, trying to visualise the lives that had been lived there.

He had great powers of empathy, which were useful for a historian, vital as a priest. This ability helped him join with others in the moments of their greatest happiness and their sadness. The clergyman saw his occupation as a privilege, not work.

"A penny for your thoughts," said Jonjo in his kindly, gentle voice.

"I'd be overcharging you," laughed Fr Flanagan.

Jonjo looked at the same view, his bright blue eyes screwed up in the dazzling sunshine. Despite his years, he still had perfect distance vision. He saw his whole life before him. The house where he had been born and where he still lived. The now derelict school that he had sporadically attended. The fields that he worked, the paths that he walked. The church in which he had married. The sport's ground in which he had excelled. The churchyard where he had buried his beloved Mary. He knew she wasn't there. She was up above, guiding and helping him, as she had always done. He smiled at the thought.

"What do you see when you look out there?" Fr Flanagan asked Sean.

"I think we all see the same thing, but each through our own filters. The filters of our past and present, and maybe, through the hopes of our futures. I see a part of my past there, and perhaps a future better than I had expected," responded Sean.

They left a trestle table covered with an altar cloth at the derelict house in the famine village. Originally they had planned to have an outdoor Mass at the deserted hamlet. On seeing just how inhospitable the place was, Fr Flanagan had opted for a Mass at church, followed by a procession up the hill.

"I've seen a lot more marks in the soil this year," commented Fr Flanagan.

"I know they show the walls underneath, but I've never been sure how that worked," inquired Sean.

"There's a whole variety of reasons, based on the geology. And whether or not the land has been ploughed. The simple explanation is that the plants that grow over the stones have less depth of soil. Their roots are shorter, so they grow upwards more quickly and die off sooner, leaving the lines," summarised the priest.

Bridie Murphy looked upward from the town. Her keen old eyes spotted the three men, dark shapes against the blue sky. An involuntary shiver ran down her spine. This was a special day.

The priest drove them the short distance into the

town. The church was resplendent in the sunshine unusually, both doors wide open. The sacristy door was ajar too, in an attempt to create a through draught, on this stillest of summer's days.

The weather forecast had said that the heat was coming up from Spain. Fr Flanagan even fancied he could smell the dry air of Andalucia. The warmth of the day was beginning to dissipate as Mass time grew close. There was a buzz about the whole town. An excitement created by the temperature for those not used to hot weather.

Some made the Sign of the Cross outside. The older ones talked of the great wind which had once struck the country. The Irish rivalled the English with their discussion of and superstition about the weather.

The church filled up. The congregation had a holiday mood, as much as a Holy Day mood. Yes, this was to be a Requiem Mass, a sad occasion, but it was for a family from so long ago that there was no personal connection.

The Mass was uneventful apart from Sean's loud response, "And also with you".

"Nobody told me that had changed," he muttered to

Jonjo as they left the church. "All the problems the church has had, and that's all they come up with. There must be some brilliant minds working at the Vatican!"

Jonjo smiled, knowing his cousin was trying to cover his embarrassment. "Come on, we have a job to do," he said.

The two men walked directly behind Fr. Flanagan, who led the procession. The priest carried the aspersorium (the holy water bucket) and the aspergillum (the stick used to sprinkle the holy water). The cousins took it in turns to carry a wooden crucifix from the church. It was Jonjo's turn to feel embarrassed he felt unworthy of the task.

The congregation followed, with children occasionally darting off to the side, frustrated at the slow pace. The beauty and variety of the primulas didn't go unnoticed. "I don't remember them flowering this long," someone said. Others remarked about how well the two old men strode up the hill particularly Sean, because of his bulk.

Reaching the top, the congregation formed into rows at a respectful distance from the makeshift altar. Sean began with a Gospel reading then handed over to

Jonjo.

Jonjo said, "I'll read about what happened from a newspaper report written at the time. The words are not mine. I think, in parts, they are very condescending. Nevertheless, they are the only historical record we have."

Jonjo's voice was at the same time quiet yet audible, emotional yet measured, gentle yet authoritative. Sean noticed that his friend never once looked at the book. It was entirely done from memory.

The story of Paddy Costello, his wife Maria, and their son Joseph (little more than a babe in arms) painted a tragic, picture. Irishmen and women are never short of imagination and emotion. Silent tears ran down many faces.

Fr Flanagan spread the holy water around the old field in front of the house. He proceeded to sprinkle it on the congregation. Sean smiled at the youngsters trying to dodge the cold water.

A sudden hush and fingers were pointing skywards. Jonjo looked around. Two pure white doves were ascending; a third emerged over the crest of the hill. The trio circled overhead and disappeared into the blue sky.

"I wouldn't have believed that if I hadn't seen it," whispered Sean.

"The souls of the Costello family free at last," answered Jonjo.

All around was a stunned silence. Somewhere in the crowd, a cheer went up. The spell was broken. Without prompting, people greeted each other, "Peace be with you". This time Sean got the answer right.

Paddy Regan packed the trestle table into his boot and gave the three men a lift down the hill. The crowd parted on the narrow track for the police car. Again a cheer went up, and people clapped the roof of the vehicle as it slowly went through.

"Well, there's another miracle Father," laughed Paddy. "People cheering a police car."

"What about those doves?" said Fr Flanagan. "People might come up with a rational explanation, but what is the truth?"

"We all know it was to do with that poor family. It is a shame that we can't accept things these days. It is as if we are afraid to admit that there are things we don't understand," answered Jonjo.

Paddy dropped them off at the church to return the artefacts that they had taken with them for the ceremony. The three men went to the presbytery and shared a drink of Sean's fine wine.

"Are you going over for the wake Father?" asked Sean.

"I will, but I won't stay for long. I inhibit some of the people in their fun. Others start telling me things better left to the confessional. I'll see how it goes."

By the time they got to Clarke's bar, the wake was in full swing. Tommy had opened the upstairs bar for the occasion. The small downstairs bar was full. The beer garden was packed. A couple of tables had been set up in the street, in front of the pub.

Tommy looked enquiringly at Sean. "The money is no problem," Sean said. "Use your discretion when you think they've had enough or when you've had enough."

"It's the two oldest altar boys in town," called Seamus Burke.

"We're not too old to alter your face," laughed Jonjo, waving his big fist at Seamus.

Seamus, completely unperturbed carried on with his tale. "Well, the Murphy brothers arrived in Florida and went to the swamplands.'I've always wanted a pair of crocodile shoes,' said Paddy. He immediately dived in the water and started wrestling a giant croc. Underwater above water, they thrashed around, creating a great spray. Eventually, Paddy emerged. He had cuts all over him, blood dripping from his hands. 'Did it get away?' asked Mick.' No, I had him, but guess what? He wasn't even wearing any shoes.'"

As always, Seamus's joke was answered with both laughter and shouts of derision. Someone got up on the stage, at the end of the room, and started singing a traditional ballad. Soon guitars and a fiddle appeared, and a jig was in progress.

The wake was still going strong when Tommy's son offered Jonjo and Sean a lift home. They were grateful to go as the day had taken its toll on them.

Fr Flanagan left at the same time saying, "You two are doing a great thing for the parish and the town. You are putting the heart back in the place."

He added unexpectedly, "I've got some information about the Vale of Mist. I think I can get you two back on track."

Chapter 12

A bright, bright morning. The colours accentuated almost magnified by the morning dew. It gave a freshness to the atmosphere that Jonjo breathed in deeply. An overnight drop in temperature had let the plants claim moisture from the air. It would soon be burned off by the powerful sun. The footprints of a dog, or more likely a fox, were still visible on the grass.

Jonjo was excited he had not been to the seaside for years. He waited with his cousin Sean at the end of the boreen. Fr. Francis Flanagan arrived on cue. The roads were quiet, and the three men chatted amiably.

"I didn't think you would approve of our search for the Vale of Mist, let alone help us," said Jonjo.

"Why not?" asked the priest.

"I thought with it being a pagan legend, you wouldn't like it."

"No, I've a great interest in all religions. If you analyse them, they all give the same message. They all boil down to the same thing 'to love one and other'," continued the cleric.

"They've just been interpreted differently over the centuries," agreed Jonjo.

"Some very literal interpretations have made nonsense of the real message," offered Sean.

"Do you know I can remember taking things literally when I was a kid?" replied Fr. Flanagan. "I was once at the railway station in Dublin. My Uncle Pat was waving us off. He said, 'Look at that man Francis, he's a copper. I can smell a copper a mile off.' Now the man was in plain clothes, but I believed my uncle. Uncle Pat certainly had the nose for it, a great big conk. I used to imagine Pat walking around Dublin, constantly smelling policemen, even ones that were out of sight."

Sean and Jonjo laughed. "The way you say things is important too," said Jonjo. "I once heard a vicar giving a talk on the radio, he said, 'Jesus cured lepers and paralysed people.'"

The priest pulled into a layby on a headland overlooking the ocean. "The Wild Atlantic Way," he announced. "I can't remember when they started calling it that, mind you, it doesn't look so wild today."

The three men stood atop the headland with the sun on their backs. They could almost taste the brine in the air as the aroma blew in on a gentle westerly breeze. The beach described a soft curve. The meeting place between land and sea benign on this mild day. Above the gulls mewed and did not screech. Just like the time on the hill, all three looked at the view, the same vista but redolent of different memories.

"Can you see the islands?" asked Fr. Flanagan.

Sean and Jonjo stared out. Both said that they couldn't.

"Nevertheless, they are there," he said.

As they walked down the slope to the beach, he told them the tale of the islands. He began with the story of Hy Brasil, a phantom island in the Atlantic Ocean west of Ireland. In myths it is described as cloaked in mist, except for one day when it becomes visible but still cannot be reached. Different accounts of the inhabitants were recorded, from giant black rabbits to immortal humans.

"Isn't it just a tale, just nonsense?" argued Sean.

"Maybe," said Fr Flanagan. "But it was shown on maps from 1325 for over 500 years. You can still see the maps. By the way, the name has nothing to do with the country of Brazil. It predates it by centuries. Some people call it Ireland's Atlantis."

"Well, I've lived here all my life and never heard of it. A strange tale" commented Jonjo.

By this time, they were walking on the fine, sandy beach. "There are some stranger ones would you like to hear them?" asked the priest.

"Sure," confirmed Sean, in that one word sounding both Irish and American.

"Well, over that way is Inishkea," said Fr Flanagan pointing northwest. There are two islands North and South, both are uninhabited now. A big storm in the 1930s caused the death of a group of fishermen, and the islands were abandoned. The last man who lived through that died only recently, I believe."

"A sad tale but not strange," said Sean.

"That was just background," said Fr Flanagan. "An account from as late as the 19th century says that although the inhabitants were nominally Catholic, they practised idolatry. They had a stone, carefully wrapped up in flannel, brought out at certain periods to be adored by the inhabitants of Inniskea. In times of storm, they asked this heathen god to send a wreck on their coast."

"Another nearby island Inishglora, has an ancient tradition that bodies laid to rest there never decayed. People would go to visit their ancestors going back generations yet still recognisable."

"All over this area, there are tales of St Patrick defeating all manner of monstrous creatures," concluded the cleric.

"What's your point, Father?" queried Jonjo.

"I'm trying to say we don't have the answer to everything. Think about the doves flying up after the blessing on the hill. An ornithologist could come up with a rational explanation, but we know different. It was no coincidence."

"I studied history and archaeology for years, and I am convinced that there have been many civilisations that have gone before us. I believe they may have been more advanced than us in some if not all ways."

They walked on and went for a swim as planned. Jonjo was the first in. He walked swiftly into the sea, and as soon as it was deep enough, dived forward. Sean and Fr. Flanagan were much more cautious.

"Come on, it's grand once you get in," called Jonjo.

Soon all three were swimming.

"The last time I was in the Atlantic was at Cocoa Beach in Florida," reminisced Sean. "The sea was as warm as bathwater. We saw the space shuttle take off from Cape Canaveral. A few seconds after, the sound of the boom of the rocket firing reached us. It was a time I'll never forget."

"Well, this as warm as I can ever remember the sea this side of the Atlantic," said Fr Flanagan.

They swam slowly, making sure they were never out of their depth. Their chatting occasionally being halted when one or other inadvertently took in a mouthful of the salty water.

"So you are thinking we may need to go out to sea on our quest, Father?" asked Jonjo.

"Who knows, I just wanted to introduce you to some of the other legends of our land. Maybe Tír na nÓg is just over the horizon," he laughed.

The three men dried themselves on the beach. Fr Flanagan and Jonjo managed to take off their trunks beneath their towels and replace them discreetly and efficiently. Sean lost his balance and ended up hopping about on one leg before collapsing in a heap on the sand.

He couldn't stop laughing, which made the other two join in. Sean managed to dress himself from a seated position.

"Help me up, guys," he pleaded. "Before Greenpeace send a ship and drag me back into the ocean."

They walked to a bench in the shade of the rocks to eat their packed lunches.

"In all seriousness, you have lost a fair bit of weight," commented Jonjo to Sean.

"I walked up the middle of the stairway at Clarke's bar the other night," replied Sean. "I realised that for years, I've been heaving on the bannister rails to help me. I walk up the middle of the stairs at home now. It's only a little thing, but I feel it's a sort of achievement."

"You're right. It shows your core strength is improving," confirmed Jonjo. "I studied all that stuff when I was training the hurley team. Here's a test for you, you too Father. Put your things down, and stand up from this bench without using your hands."

Fr. Flanagan managed it, but with difficulty. Sean couldn't do it at all. Jonjo did it in one easy movement.

"I can give you both some simple exercises to sort that out," offered Jonjo.

"Sure," said Sean. "I'll give you some books to read in return. What you don't realise is how good your reading is. When you read the passage from the newspaper at the requiem, you pointed out the condescending attitude of the writer. That's a high-level reading skill, not to mention your memorisation of the text."

"Ah but, I'd read it three times," countered Jonjo.

"I couldn't remember something from reading it three times," replied Sean.

"Me, neither I keep having to check the words when I'm saying Mass," said Fr Flanagan. "Sometimes, we have abilities that we don't know are special because we assume everyone else can do them. You can get a lot of pleasure from reading."

"I sometimes used to like it. When we were at

school, they always spoiled it by saying, 'What did the author mean by this. Why did he use this word?' It took the fun out of it," replied Jonjo.

"I know what you mean about fun. Because I studied so much, I got too fast at reading. I could pick out the main point of a page at a glance. I forgot how to enjoy words. I've taught myself to slow down," commented Fr Flanagan.

As they ate their lunch, Jonjo stripped the fat from the bacon in his sandwiches. When they finished, he pulled out a homemade crab line. He attached the fat, and the three men spent a happy couple of hours catching and returning small crabs to the rock pools while chatting.

The return trip, as always, appeared to be much quicker than the outward journey. Back at the car, all three shook out the sand from their shoes. Fr Flanagan dropped them off in town, refusing their offer to join them for a drink in Clarke's bar.

"Some of us still have a job, you know," he joked.

"And a good job you make of it," said Jonjo seriously.

The two friends were ready for a drink. The bar

seemed so dark after the bright sunshine outside. The unmistakable voice of Seamus called, "Well, if it isn't the Beach Boys."

"Sure, I've never heard you sing ' I get a round'," countered Sean.

This brought the house down, leaving even Seamus rocking with laughter and making his way with mock reluctance to the bar.

Walking home across the fields their faces stinging from too much sun, the two men felt the contentment of a day well spent.

"Can you smell that?" asked Sean, his head turned toward a westerly breeze. "Autumn is coming in from the Atlantic."

"Season of mist and mellow fruitfulness," quoted Jonjo.

"This could be our best chance to find the Vale."

Chapter 13

Summer waved a long, reluctant goodbye to Ireland. Autumn moved in seamlessly, bringing with it crisp fresh air. The strong summer colours were muted, adding yellows and browns to nature's palette.

The distant sound of rutting deer and the occasional shriek of a fox took Jonjo's memory back down the years. He loved the reassuring cycle of the seasons. As a child, he had measured his life in hours and minutes. Now he viewed the year as a whole.

He loved autumn. It was a sort of New Year. The sports seasons starting afresh. Youngsters were facing new challenges at schools and colleges. Harvest time nature reaping the benefits of work and nature's bounty.

Sitting on the bench outside his cottage Jonjo was

engrossed in his book.

"Your turn for the bike," called Sean.

"I've already got the weights out for ye," replied Jonjo.

Jonjo had devised a fitness plan for the two of them. He set up a bench and some weights in his shed. He called it his shed, but it was really his old hen hut.

At first, he had supervised Sean on the weights, but now he was confident that his cousin could work safely. Sean had told him that he had been a member of the most exclusive gym in Massachusetts.

It had all the latest, state of the art fitness machines. Sean had gravitated mainly to the Coca Cola and chocolate bar vending machines.

"With weights," Jonjo had told Sean, "if it hurts but you can do it again, then do it again. If it hurts and you can't do it again, stop. If it doesn't hurt, put some more weights on."

"Ridiculous and totally unscientific," Sean had thought. Strangely, this simple strategy was effective, and Sean now positively enjoyed his training sessions. He was still very overweight. But his stomach, which had been like a beach ball emerging under his ribs and dipping back well below a non-existent waistline, had trimmed back.

Instead of being circular, it was barrel-shaped and in line with his rib cage.

Jonjo went on the exercise bike in Sean's conservatory. Sean called it an orangery, which Jonjo kept meaning to, and forgetting to, ask about. Jonjo had heard about high-intensity training on the radio and ever willing for a new challenge took to it. Three times a week, he did an 8-minute session on the bike. This was 2 minutes easy pedalling followed by 20 seconds as fast as he could repeat 3 times followed by 1 minute of easy pedalling.

Jonjo felt really good for the exercise, and his cheeks became as hollow as in his days of sporting glory. Strangely in Ireland, if you weren't at least 20 pounds overweight, people thought you were ill. Jonjo thought that might be a hangover from the days of the famine.

Having showered in their respective houses, the two men sat on Sean's patio eating breakfast. Sean had always liked his food, and the weight training made him positively voracious.

"You see," explained Jonjo. "There are three body

types. One like me, one like you and another I can't remember."

"Very clearly explained," mocked Sean gently.

"You have the benefit of a shorter, more powerful frame. That gives you good strength and explosive speed," continued Jonjo.

"I can't say I've noticed it," smiled Sean.

"While I have longer limbs and probably greater agility and stamina."

"So, what are you saying?"

"I can't be like you, and you can't be like me. However, we can maintain and improve our ability even at our age," concluded Jonjo.

"You know," said Sean. "Scientists have discovered that each of us can have up to 5% Neanderthal DNA."

"They've not been in Clarke's bar, otherwise, they would be revising those numbers up," laughed Jonjo. "Speak of the devil..."

"And he's sure to appear," completed Sean.

Jonjo pointed to a minibus driving down the boreen. "That's the Rest Home minibus. It must be Micko driving."

"I know you've got good eyesight, but how do you

know it's Micko?"

"He's the only one who drives down the boreen. When they were renovating your house, he got a dumper truck stuck there."

"What happened?" asked Sean.

"They had to get a proper driver in. They set Micko on labouring. He's a headstrong fellow, but he has a good heart. I wonder why they call people headstrong when clearly their head is not their strength."

Micko pulled up in the bus.

"You did well avoiding the ditches on the boreen," said Jonjo.

"Ditches...?"

"Never mind," said Jonjo. "You must have smelled the tay come and have a cup."

They went through the Irish ritual of Micko refusing the tea but Jonjo bringing it anyway. When Jonjo finally 'persuaded' Micko to have a bacon sandwich, as well, the custom was complete.

They chatted about the weather, the big tree Jonjo had chopped down, and the work done on Sean's house. The reason for Micko's visit didn't come up. Sean smiled to himself, thinking how different this was from the frenetic pace of his life in the USA.

"I went down the tunnel, you know," confided Micko." The one at the end of the cellar. Nobody else would. It went a long way then split into two. I took the right-hand side, but it dwindled, getting smaller and smaller. I got a bit scared, and then I thought the fellers would lock me in for an hour or two, so I came out."

"What was it like?" asked Sean.

"No lights, of course. I took my mobile. The walls were cut from solid rock, but they were smooth. It must have been dug by the old people. We don't have builders like that now. I could smell fresh air though I'd have been frightened of gas otherwise."

They carried on chatting for a while longer until Micko came back to the reason for his visit. He explained that Bridie Murphy had donated all her books to the two of them. She had explained that she knew she was in and out of her dotage, and therefore had passed her unofficial duty of village elder to them. They tried to refuse the gift, but Micko had strict instructions from Bridie.

The three of them unloaded the bus. There were two bookcases, which they set up in Jonjo's cottage and lots of cardboard boxes full of books.

"Leave them Micko, we'll get them into the house," said Jonjo. "It's good exercise for us."

Sean reappeared with a box of wine, "Take these Micko, for the people in the home. And the sisters as well. Have one yourself when you've finished driving, of course. Tell me, how did you get this job when you've no licence?"

"I've had a licence since I was 17. I was kidding you on the other week."

"Do the nuns have a tipple?" asked Jonjo.

"Well," answered Micko. "Old Sister Maria smelled strongly of wine the other day.

I said to her, 'Have you had a drink, Sister?'

'A glass of water,' she answered.

'It smells like wine,' says I.

'The Good Lord's done it again,' says she.

"And her a nun," concluded Micko shaking his head.

Sean and Jonjo spent the rest of the morning unloading the books and putting them on the shelves. Jonjo told Sean about Micko's difficult childhood. His mother had died when he was young, and his father had taken to the drink. His main skill was driving and tinkering with cars.

"That's given me an idea," said Sean. "I'll think it through first and see what you think."

"It's strange how things change," said Jonjo. "Me with more books than I could read in two lifetimes, and you now the fitness fanatic."

"Fanatic is putting it a bit strongly, but I love exercising now."

"And I love the books."

It was a golden autumn afternoon. A pleasantly warm day, a day to be valued as the colder weeks approached. The two friends had their customary break at the hollow as they walked into town. They discussed their continuing search for the Vale of Mist, the legendary mist that guaranteed another year of life to anyone who found it.

"Well, from what Fr Flanagan tells us, we are in the right place for all sorts of myths and legends," said Sean. "I wouldn't be surprised if we disappeared down a wormhole and..."

"Ara, and how would two grown men fit down a wormhole?" scoffed Jonjo.

"No, a wormhole is....," began Sean.

"A hypothetical tunnel through space-time," interrupted Jonjo smugly.

"O.K., you got me again with the Oirish culchie routine," laughed Sean.

"Years of practice," smiled Jonjo.

"What Micko was saying about the tunnel made me think," said Sean. "About the 'old people' having built it."

"Yes, it all chimes with what Fr Flanagan said about the ancient civilisations."

"It could be the Tuatha de Danaan. I've been researching them. They came to the west coast of Ireland about 4 thousand years ago. Legend has it that they emerged out of a great mist in the sea and that they had been banished from heaven. Eventually, after losing a battle, they were forced to live underground," said Sean.

"Do you believe that?"

"There are myths and legends all over the world about people living underground. Who knows what's true, but the tunnels didn't dig themselves," answered, Sean

They walked down to the graveyard. Jonjo said a

prayer at his wife's gravestone and laid a flower there. Sean did the same at his grandparents' grave, they both put flowers on the famine grave. There was a small trench between the grave and the cemetery wall.

They had their customary break of tea and coffee respectively seated on the bench outside the graveyard.

"I've arranged for a monument to be made for the famine grave," confided Sean. "That'll be what the trench is for."

"That's a good use of your money," approved Jonjo.

The two chatted about legends and myths and the changing seasons. Although it had been a warm day, the strength was disappearing from the sun. Whether it was the topic of their discussion, the graveyard setting, or merely the temperature, both felt a sudden chill.

As they walked into Clarke's bar, Seamus was in full voice. He was using the tone of a newsreader, "A two-seater 'plane crashed into a cemetery outside Dublin police have so far recovered 128 bodies."

Having waited for the varied reactions to his comments to subside, he turned his attention to Jonjo and Sean. "Well, if it isn't Simon and Garfunkle," he began.

"We'd definitely appreciate the Sound of Silence from you," answered Jonjo.

The two walked back across the fields after their drinks. It had been an eventful day. Both men were tired but a pleasant tiredness.

Jonjo was already planning their next adventure.

Chapter 14

A crisp autumn day. The air was so fresh that it made you feel good just to breathe it in. Gossamer sparkled on spiders' webs in the thin morning light. The sky, a pastel blue, seemed somehow clean and healthy.

They were up before dawn for the walk. The forecast was for a fine day, and they set off at first light. Leaving footprints in the dew, they moved briskly.

Jonjo loved being out in the early morning, the whole day stretching out before him. He thought of that Irish greeting, 'Top of the morning to you' and the lesser-known response, 'And the rest of the day to yourself'. The best thing about retirement, 'the rest of the day to yourself'.

Sean was not a morning person. Getting up early always gave him discomfort somewhere between his chest and stomach. It reminded him of waiting in airports. His mind was awake, but his body longed for his comfortable bed. It was a lesser form of jet lag.

The sun was far enough from summer not to burn and not near enough to winter to have lost its heat. A leaf lazily spiralled down into the stream, and Sean pointed excitedly at a brown trout. The colour of the leaves making up for the loss of flowers. He began to appreciate the beauty of the morning.

Jonjo had felt some pangs of regret when he had cut down the big tree. It had been there before he was born, and he had thought it would be there when he was gone. Unfortunately, its time was up, and he had to cut it before it fell and did some damage.

"You know, Sean, I think we could hollow out the trunk and make a boat," Jonjo said.

"Maybe we could just buy one," suggested Sean.

"Where's the fun in that?" replied Jonjo.

"You know the Native Americans used to light a log on fire and scrape out the ashes to make their boats."

"Smart fellows and generous too. The Choctaw tribe sent money to Ireland in the famine even though they had very little themselves. They saved a lot of lives," added Jonjo.

"That is astounding," confirmed Sean. "But why do you want a boat?"

"Not me, us. I know our main aim is to find the Vale of Mist, but I also know that you have become as interested as me in the myths and legends of our country."

"My parents never talked about it much," said Sean. "Just the odd ghost story and tales of leprechauns."

"Mine too, just banshees and the fairy folk were all I knew about."

"Yes, but why the boat?" persevered Sean.

"Well, I thought we could have a three-pronged attack on discovering our culture. First, we have our walks searching for the Vale. Second, we investigate the tunnels and third, we do a bit of sailing or rowing, at least."

"How will we get the boat to the water?" inquired Sean.

"Where there's a will, there's a relative," laughed Jonjo.

The two friends had high hopes of finding the Vale of Mist. The legendary place, that when encountered, guaranteed a year of healthy life. They could already see patches of mist rolling up the fields ahead of them. The tops of the mountains were covered too technically that would be fog, but close enough.

Their early start and brisker pace were needed because they had a long, tough day ahead, and the amount of daylight was diminishing. Sean had come back to Ireland to fade away, his life almost over. Now he was fitter than he had been in years. Sean had been giving away some of his fortune. He was putting others before himself. It made him feel good, and he didn't broadcast his charitable work. The example of his cousin and the beauty of his homeland had worked their magic on him.

The cousins were carrying a bit more than usual. They had their flasks and sandwiches, but also Jonjo had a small gas camping stove and a couple of soup cans. He wanted to maintain their body temperature on this their highest walk. Everything was meticulously packed into his khaki haversack.

Sean was wearing all the latest, top of the range, outdoor clothing. Jonjo wore his third-best suit, the only concession to the weather was a flat cap and a plastic mac folded over the haversack. In light rain, the mac kept the haversack dry. If it came down more heavily, he would drape it over both himself and the bag.

Sean told Jonjo of his plans as they walked towards the hollow.

"You know my old Chevvie?"

"Yes," nodded Jonjo.

"Well, it's just too big for these roads, and it's left-hand drive."

"So, what made you bring it?" asked Jonjo.

"I hired a container for my move, and there was room. It is a classic. I just couldn't let go."

"And now?"

"I thought we could set Micko up as a taxi driver," replied Sean. "He'd drive it okay he knows the roads. I'd organise a proper accountant for him. I'd put some money upfront and tell him to repay us when he started making a profit."

"Repay us?"

"Yeh, I figured if he thinks you've invested in it, he'll make a real go of it. He told me how much you and Mary did for him when he was a kid," explained Sean.

"Could he make a go of it?"

"Sure. I'd make a business plan. There's a need for a taxi in the town, the car will have novelty value. He could maybe do weddings too. Then there's Knock airport, lots of potential."

"You really are the businessman. But why are you doing this?" said Jonjo.

"Well, Micko has had a raw deal. We can even up the playing field. It feels good helping someone else. Maybe I'm a changed man?"

"No, I think you are going back to yourself. You just got led astray by money," said Jonjo.

"Nice of you to say."

"We'll be able to get the taxi back from Clarke's bar," added Jonjo brightly.

"All part of the plan," laughed Sean tapping his nose with his index finger.

A dense mist shrouded the hollow as they approached. When they were within spitting distance, a breeze blew towards them. Inexplicably, the mist swirled and disappeared in the opposite direction.

They carried on in silence until they reached the bench that was their morning break spot.

"What did you make of that?" asked Sean.

"I think it was the Vale of Mist."

"Me, too. There was a really eerie feeling even though it had gone. So disappointing that we were too late," said Sean.

"I think it was there to encourage us. Telling us not to give up."

Drinking their respective tea and coffee, Jonjo enquired, "A drop of the cratur?"

"It certainly warms you up," approved Sean.

They crossed the medieval bridge and started up the steep hill. There was no pavement, and they stuck closely to the dry stone wall in single file. By the time they reached the footpath to the right, Sean was struggling.

Jonjo had to help his cousin sit on a flat rock. "What's the matter?" he asked.

"Hungry," spluttered his cousin.

Jonjo immediately took out one of the bacon sandwiches from his own bag, saying, "Eat this quickly! But make sure you chew it."

As his cousin ate, Jonjo explained. "It is the 'fear gortach' it is a dreadful, hunger that comes on you when you pass the spot where someone has died. Many say it came from the time of the famine."

After a short break, the two set off along the mountain path. They discussed what had happened, and thankfully, Sean was no worse for the ordeal. The trail was long and winding, firm underfoot after the glorious summer. Soon they were level with the famine village over the valley.

Then they wound around to the other side of the mountain. The far valley was brighter, bathed in gentle sunlight. The fields below a tapestry of browns and greens. Where there were clouds, the sun cascaded through, like a scene from a holy picture.

There was a hypnotic rhythm in looking from your feet to the track ahead. Jonjo fell into a meditative state, imagining the people who had trod this path for generations. He kept hearing and sensing a third person walking along with them, but knowing this was nonsense dismissed it from his mind.

Adding stones to a cairn at the top of the mountain, the two men settled down to their food. Jonjo lit the stove and heated up the cans of soup. They were glad of the warmth because the perspiration that built up was chilled by the breeze. They ate heartily and rested before the journey.

A slight fog was blowing across the steeper return route. Sean looked at the shape of the mountainside, so precisely matching the contour lines on the map he had looked at. The way was much rockier than the grassy upland path.

Jonjo stopped abruptly and faced back up the path. Sean followed the direction of his pointing finger. There at the summit stood the figure of a man in the centre of a circular rainbow. Behind the rainbow were clouds, but the figure cast a shadow in front of him.

The man's features were not distinguishable. The rainbow and the man disappeared, and the fog thickened over the mountain.

Sean and Jonjo stood still, unsure.

"Look!" exclaimed Sean.

Ahead of them on the path was an indistinct spectral form. The figure from the mountain top somehow was now in front. The fog was so dense that it seemed to have swallowed the whole landscape, and where birds had once sung was an eerie silence.

Instinctively Jonjo began to move towards the

figure. Sean pulled him back by his haversack." Wait, we can't see where we are going. We can't just follow that."

"You're right. It could be a Jack O' Lantern. I'll lead, but if I fall, use your strength to pull me back."

The two men walked cautiously down the steep path. The wispy figure slowed when they slowed and stopped when they stopped. Sean was so tense that he barely remembered to breathe. The fog was unrelenting. With no landmarks, they lost sense of time, as well as place.

Gradually, they began to relax a little as they trusted the shape in front. Jonjo wondered if it was the cause of the footsteps he had heard on the way up. Maybe, it was nothing more than another walker, sure-footed and familiar with the route. He called to the figure, but there was no response.

As the path wound around the mountain back to their valley, the air cleared. They looked down on the mosaic of roads, rooftops and fields with relief. Glancing back to the track, the mysterious figure had gone. Sean relinquished his grip of Jonjo's haversack, and they carried on walking. Neither was prepared to stop until they left the mountain behind.

As the two entered Clarke's bar Seamus called out, "It's the two musketeers. Have you come for another battle of wits?"

"That wouldn't be fair against an unarmed man," replied Sean.

As the laughter died down, everyone noticed Jonjo and Sean looking a bit the worse for wear. The two got their pints, and Jonjo began to tell them of the day's adventure. There is nothing an Irish barroom likes more than a tale of the supernatural. Micko came in, and Sean sat with him and explained his business proposal.

After Jonjo's tale, Seamus came up with one of his own.

"Paddy Murphy was in a taxi going to Liverpool airport. The driver asked him if he wanted a riddle, 'Sure,' said Paddy. The driver said, 'Brothers and sisters have I none, but this man's father is my father's son. Who am I?'

'Sure, I don't know,' replied Paddy.

'It's me,' laughed the driver.

When he got home, he tried the same riddle on his

brother.

'Sure, I don't know,' replied Mick.

'You eejit," said Paddy."It's a taxi driver in Liverpool.'"

Sean and Jonjo had a lift home from Micko. It had been a full day. For some reason, he couldn't understand Jonjo had kept back the bit about the fear gortach from his story.

Something told him there was a mystery waiting for them.

Chapter 15

The spider's web had captured the petal of a dahlia. It danced elegantly, alternately back and forth like a pendulum, then gyrating round and round. It was an unintended capture that would warn the unwary insects until the breeze would break its bond.

Jonjo was sitting in the porch sheltered from the rain. The smell of the strong coffee was heightened by the damp breeze. He was happy and content. This was hard, pelting rain, big drops that bounced on the earth. The drought of summer being brought into balance.

"Noah wouldn't have gotten much attention around here," observed Sean.

"What do you mean?" replied Jonjo.

"Forty days and forty nights of rain, that's just the weather forecast here, not an impending flood."

"I've never thought of that, but you are right," laughed Jonjo.

"Do you know the more I've studied the myths and legends of Ireland, the more I see the same stories all over the world?"

"What's the difference between myths and legends? Is there one?" inquired Jonjo.

"Legends are based on people and events that have happened. Myths tend to be about gods and explanations of how things have happened, you know, like the beginning of the universe. That's how I understand it, anyway."

"Well, we are held up with the boat building, and it's not fit for walking. Will we look at the tunnel?" asked Jonjo.

"Sure, but we need to do a bit of research. If you look in the books and I use the computer, let's see what we can find out."

Jonjo loved reading now. He devoured books with the appetite of a farmer. He had missed out on them for so many years. With Sean's guidance, he read widely. Sean had started him initially on sporting biographies and autobiographies. He had moved to history and travel writing thence to fiction. Jonjo was amazed that he was almost entranced when he read. He described it to Sean as being able to live other people's lives.

To his surprise, he found that books could alter his mood. He made sure that his bedtime reading was lighthearted. Making up for lost time, he always had two or three books on the go. He had never been one for television. But since Mary's death, he listened to the radio a lot. He was glad to discover he could read and listen simultaneously.

He loved the smell of the print and even the feel of the books. He liked the fact that pages were called leaves and were made from trees. Jonjo smiled at the thought of Mary looking down on him, amazed.

Comfortable at his kitchen table, he pulled up the collar of his cardigan. It gave a pleasant, familiar warmth on his neck. He looked through the collection of local history books that Bridie had given them. In truth, there was very little difference in any of them, which was probably, how it should be.

He had just about given up hope of finding anything useful when he found a reference to an archaeologist. This man had been one of the first to use aerial photography in Ireland. He had suggested that the hill on which the famine village stood was an Iron Age fort. Jonjo looked with renewed enthusiasm through the books and volumes of collected newspapers for any archaeological information.

He came across an article that said many of the small islands on the lough were 'crannogs' artificial islands built thousands of years ago. There were several mentions of tunnels in the area, used by ancient people to protect their livestock. Could the mount really be man-made? It did have a circular look like that which a child would draw if asked to picture a hill.

The tunnel under the hill, the tunnel at Sean's house, could they be linked? Maybe it was something to do with the Tuatha De Danaan. Were they mythical or legendary? He thought back to the large stone slabs on the hillside known locally as the kings' gravestones. Were they part of the puzzle? Jonjo was sure he had heard about underground cities. Could this be one?

He had more questions than answers and felt unsettled. He did what Sean had advised him to do. He wrote everything down and even drew a diagram of the area. Jonjo Brennan making notes from a book. It must be over sixty years since that had happened, if it ever had. Sean was right. Once he had written it down, his mind stopped racing. Putting something down on paper worked. "Well, you are never too old to learn," he thought to himself.

Early next morning, Sean's footsteps on the gravel were quicker than usual. He walked in with a cheerful "Hello."

"I can't wait to show you what I've found!" exclaimed Jonjo.

"I was going to say exactly the same thing," laughed Sean. "You first."

Jonjo read excitedly from his notes.

"I've found similar stuff on the internet and even found some pictures," said Sean. Sensing Jonjo was a little deflated, he added, "That's brilliant work. We need written sources. You can't always trust the net."

Up at Sean's house, they studied the computer. A remarkable website showed an aerial photograph of the whole country displaying every hill fort so far discovered. Additionally, there was a photo of some large slabs identical to those known as the kings' gravestones. In the picture, the stones were in place as the walls and roof of a tunnel.

"O.K., let's get down the tunnel," said Jonjo.

"Well, I've been looking at health and safety in tunnels. We need to check gas levels, make sure our lights don't spark an explosion. We should inform someone where we are going, our route and intended return time. I also think we should tie a rope to the shelves in the cellar to find our way back if our lights go."

"Look," said Jonjo. "Micko went down the tunnel and came out alright." He held up his hand and continued, "O.K. maybe not the best example."

"The tunnels have been there for centuries, maybe millennia. What's the rush?" asked Sean

"We haven't got centuries. If you get officials involved, we'll never get down there. Mind you, I think the rope is a good idea," replied Jonjo.

"O.K., I agree completely. I just didn't want to rush you into it."

So it was that the men were in the cellar not a half-hour later. They had their bags packed as if they were on one of their walks. Jonjo had tied his longest rope to the wine rack. Sean led the way using his mobile phone torch, Jonjo carrying his big, black rubber covered torch in his bag.

They walked slowly. Paying out the rope behind. The tunnel was wide enough for two cows with plenty of headroom. The stonework was meticulously cut, the joints in the slabs almost invisible. It was the precision work of a master mason. Sean glanced, occasionally, at his compass, which showed they were heading north.

Eventually, the rope ran out. The pair were in sight of the junction Micko had told them about. They could smell fresh air ahead. They decided to take the left tunnel as Micko had been down part of the other one.

"We are heading north-north-west," reported Sean as they moved down the tunnel.

The tunnel was identical to the one they had left. Both meant felt suddenly tired but were comfortable enough to sit with backs to the tunnel wall and have their lunch.

"That rope of yours is the longest I've ever seen," commented Sean.

"It's a sort of family heirloom. It has a good story to it, I'll tell you someday," replied Jonjo.

As he stood up from lunch, Sean inadvertently

pointed his torch at an acute angle down the tunnel.

"Look!" called Jonjo.

The torch had illuminated an inscription on the wall. The letters ran vertically and were not recognisable to either of them. The engraving was not in keeping with the quality of the stonework. Like graffiti on a monument, it seemed out of place. Sean took several pictures from different angles.

"I'll show these to Fr. Flanagan when he gets back from his holidays," decided Sean.

"Pilgrimage," corrected Jonjo.

"Whatever," shrugged Sean.

They decided to leave the rope in place and walked back to the cellar. As always, the return journey took no time at all.

Thirsty and tired from their exertions, they 'phoned Micko and booked his taxi down to the town. He told them that business was going well. Particularly since the rain had come.

"I hear you've been giving your friends a lift for free," said Sean, winking at Jonjo.

"No, no, well yes," admitted Micko.

"Listen, the thing to do is to tell them you are in

business, and you can't give them free lifts. Tell them you'll give them mate's rates, then charge them the normal fare. They'll think they are getting a bargain every time," suggested Sean.

"I think that's smart, Mr Walsh," replied Micko.

"When it comes to business, he's always right," confirmed Jonjo.

"How did you know about the free lifts?" asked Jonjo as the taxi pulled away.

"I didn't," laughed Sean.

They went into Clarke's bar, and Seamus called out, "It's the Dynamic Duo."

"Well, that makes you the Joker. Keep smiling while you bring those two pints you owe us," answered Jonjo.

"Don't fret, Seamus. I'll bring them over," said Tommy Clarke. He joined them, drinking a coffee himself. "I've a tale to tell if the Joker doesn't mind."

Seamus took all these things in a good heart.

Tommy continued, "Paddy Murphy was in last night talking to the feller next to him."

'You sound like a Dublin man,' says Paddy.

'I am sure,' he replies.

'I'm from Finglas,' says the man.

'Me too, did you go to St Joseph's school?' asked Paddy.

'Sure I did. When were you there?' asked the feller.

'I think it was about nine o'clock to half three.'

Tommy Clarke continued, "I turned to my wife and said, "It's going to be a long night, the Murphy twins are drunk again'."

The laughter rang around the bar. If the Murphys had been there, they would have joined in. An Irishman prides himself on being able to take a joke.

After a pleasant couple of hours, Jonjo and Sean returned home in Micko's taxi. The two friends insisted on paying full whack and giving him a tip. They decided to do a bit of wine 'tasting' from Sean's collection.

As they looked at the photos from the tunnel, Jonjo's sharp eyes spotted a lintel with a carving, further down the passage. Sean expanded the photo, on the 'phone (which incidentally astounded Jonjo although he kept quiet about it), but they could make nothing of it. Clearly, there was much more to discover. The cousins bade each other good night, having disposed of the wine and planned their next moves.

Jonjo knew his mind was too active for sleep. He

was thinking of the apparition on the mountain and the mystery of the 'fear gortach'. He poured himself a large whiskey, settled in his armchair and covered himself with a thick blanket. He was looking out on inky blackness, which miraculously transformed into a beautiful view of a Los Angeles valley when he picked up the novel featuring his favourite detective.

Chapter 16

It was a 'soft' day in Ireland. The air was full of moisture, although it wasn't raining. Either the mist had spread upwards, or the fog downwards or maybe the two had met and decided to keep each other company. The result was a mass of grey that wet you as soon as you set foot in it.

Sitting on his porch with a pint mug of tea cradled in his big hands, Jonjo smiled. Someone had once told him that the Earth has only one lot of water that it uses and reuses and has done for billions of years. He loved the thought of it. Maybe his tea held water that dinosaurs had splashed about in.

Jonjo and his cousin Sean had been halted in the search for the Vale of Mist by the recent torrential rain.

Now, though the rain had ceased, the mist had come to find them. They had to go. With the limited visibility, they decided on a low-level route. It was a long walk, but they'd done part of it before, so they were confident, and besides, it gave them the chance to complete a couple of errands.

Kitted up for the weather, they set off down the boreen.

"I've sent the pictures to Fr. Flanagan," said Sean. Referring to photos he had taken in the tunnel that ran from Sean's cellar.

"When did you do that?" asked Jonjo puzzled.

"Last night after you'd gone."

"So, where did you post them?" asked Jonjo.

"Post what?"

"The photos or I suppose it was just the negatives," said Jonjo.

"I see," said Sean. "There are no negatives. I sent the pictures directly from my mobile phone to his."

"Well, how does that work?" asked Jonjo, astounded.

"It's called digital photography. The pictures are converted into digits. I send a message to Fr. Flanagan and attach the photos. It's easier if I show you when we get out of the damp."

"Sure," persisted Jonjo. "But how do the photos get to his phone?"

"They get sent to some phone masts and on to his phone."

"Yes, but what if he is not in, or he's out in his car," he continued genuinely, puzzled.

"Well, it is a mobile phone, so they go directly to it."

"So, you're telling me that if he's in his car, these photos chase along after him onto his phone," said Jonjo.

"It's funny when you put it like that, but I guess that's right," laughed Sean. "Don't worry about it I don't think many people understand it, I certainly don't. I used to keep up with technology, then I stopped because I thought I couldn't be bothered. In truth, I just think I can't."

Jonjo started to chuckle, then to laugh out loud. He had a rare old twinkle in his eyes.

"You're laughing about the phone message chasing the car," guessed Sean.

"I can't help it," spluttered Jonjo, barely able to get

the words out. "I have a picture in my mind of your phone, with little wings on it, chasing Father's car tapping on the window."

This was too much for Sean. He joined in the laughter. They had to stop walking, they were laughing so much. Their ribs ached when they stopped, and they had tears in their eyes.

The mist was with them through the field but had thinned a bit as they reached the riverbank.

"No danger of getting lost here, like on the mountain," said Jonjo.

"What or who, do you think was it that guided us down?"

"I don't know, but maybe we'll ask Bridie," replied Jonjo.

They took the long riverside path to the bridge and across to the Rest Home, where Bridie lived. They wanted to thank her for the books she had given them. And, also call at the hardware shop across the street.

The two men enjoyed the walk. The recent rains had curtailed their activity, and they were glad to be outdoors. They stopped at the deserted tinkers' camp and had their morning break. There was no sheltering on a soft day. Wherever you were outside, you got wet.

They talked about their investigation in the tunnel and what Fr. Flanagan, with his archaeology training, would make of it.

Refreshed, the two friends resumed their walk at a good pace on the level path. Jonjo heard the plop of a drop of water from an overhead branch land in the river. He began to think of the journey of that drop. It would join the river and on to the lough. Or maybe, be taken up by the roots of a tree or plant. It could be evaporated into the clouds and be deposited on a mountain top. It could spend millennia in an underground pool or be whisked by the clouds to a distant land. It could be solid ice, liquid rain or gas vapour. The whole course seemed endless and almost eternal. Like the drop of water, he continued his journey downriver.

Sean was thinking about the mobile phone and the photo. Some years ago, he had been to a meeting when phone technology had been explained. Sean remembered there was a microphone in the phone that converted your voice into digits 1 and 0. He knew that the digits were converted to frequencies and sent to the cell towers. He knew the words but had no understanding of the process.

They were thoroughly soaked when they reached the Rest Home. Sister Frances greeted them like long lost friends, "You've come to look at your rooms?" she inquired.

"No, to visit Bridie," answered Jonjo nonplussed.

"Well, she's having her lunch, but you are welcome to wait or join us for lunch."

"Thanks, but no, we have our packed lunches. We are happy to sit here in the foyer," answered Sean.

"Well, let me take your coats and jackets. I'll put them in the drying room," said the nun.

Jonjo was amazed at her friendly attitude. He glanced at his cousin, who was looking decidedly uncomfortable.

When the nun departed, Jonjo looked at his cousin for an explanation. "I made a donation to the Home. I wanted to compensate them for taking Micko away as their driver. And also to help them for the way they look after Bridie and all the others. It is a job I could never do. It was a large donation, and I said it was from both of us." He held up his hand in apology. "I'm sorry, but I didn't think you would ever find out. Well, the nuns took it that it was also payment for rooms here, should we ever need them."

"Why didn't you explain to the nuns that it wasn't for rooms?" asked Jonjo.

"Have you ever tried to convince a nun that she has got something wrong?"

"Point taken," chuckled Jonjo.

The two friends took their time over lunch. The Rest Home was warm, and the seats comfortable. They listened as the clatter of cutlery died away in the dining room. Sister Frances came through and told them that Bridie was ready to see them.

They went into the old lady's room. Both were surprised to see her sitting in her high backed chair, head to one side, mouth open.

"Looks to be asleep. Will we wait a while to see if she wakes?" suggested Jonjo. Sean nodded.

There was absolutely no movement from Bridie. The cousins looked at each other tentatively. "Is she breathing?" whispered Sean.

Jonjo moved closer, and as he put his ear close to her mouth, Bridie exclaimed, "Got you!"

"Jesus, Mary and Joseph!" exclaimed Jonjo as he jumped back, bumping into his cousin.

Bridie started laughing, "I'm sorry, it's a little trick I play now and again."

"Don't be like the boy who cried wolf," admonished Sean.

"Sure, you've not thought that through. The day that happens, I won't be worried about it," laughed the old lady.

"Well, you've got me there," admitted Sean.

"We've come to thank you for the books," began Jonjo.

"And to ask about the apparition on the mountain?" asked Bridie.

"Do you know, I think there's no need for the Internet or mobile phones in Ireland? Everybody knows everything as soon as it happens," commented Sean.

"Well," began Bridie "The same apparition you saw has been seen on The Reek."

"Where's that?" asked Sean.

"It's the local name for Croagh Patrick," answered

Jonjo.

"I'm sure there were photographs in the paper of it. What it tells me," continued Bridie, "is that it is a good spirit. It led you down the mountain because it wants you to keep on with your good work. The Vale of Mist only comes to those who deserve or have earned it in one way or another."

They told her of their investigation of the tunnel, and she expressed no surprise. She explained that she had read about these tunnels all over Europe. She knew there had been stories about the 'old people' building tunnels all over the area. Bridie's eyes began to grow heavy "Good night and God Bless," she whispered and fell asleep in her chair, a contented smile on her lips.

Having bid farewell to the nuns, the cousins crossed the road to the famously well-stocked Kerrigan 's hardware shop.

"I'm after some long rope," said Jonjo.

"How long do you want it?" asked Kerrigan.

"I want to keep it," grinned Jonjo.

"I let you have that one," smiled the shopkeeper. He then went on to tell his two customers of the variety of rope he had in stock. Jonjo was convinced that if he'd asked for a dog kennel, a hot air balloon and an antique doorknob that Kerrigan would find them all within two minutes.

When they explained why they wanted the rope, Kerrigan suggested what they really needed was twine. They weren't using the rope to pull themselves out of the tunnel, merely to find their way. They came out of the shop with six balls of twine, three helmets with attached lights and great respect for Kerrigan's shopkeeping ability.

Sean thought happily to himself. Ireland was probably the only place men of their age could explain they were investigating a tunnel, and no one would bat an eyelid. The Irish were inquisitive, friendly people but believed in 'live and let live'.

The return journey included following the path near Widow Farrell's house. Jonjo asked Sean how he felt about going past the point where he had felt the 'fear gortach', the dreadful hunger that comes on you when you pass a place where someone has died. Sean assured him that he would be O.K. This time, it had no effect on Sean. They did notice, however, that Widow Farrell was watching through her window. She ducked behind the curtain when she saw them.

Down at Clarke's bar, the two men felt they had earned their beer.

"It's the Lone Ranger and Tonto," called Seamus.

"I'll arrange a loan for you to buy those two pints you owe us," responded Jonjo.

Ignoring the response, Seamus went on with one of his tales.

"The Murphy brothers were looking at a catalogue:

Paddy says, "Look at these gorgeous women! The prices are reasonable too."

Mick agrees, "I'm ordering one right now"

3 weeks later, Paddy says to Mick, "Has your woman turned up yet?"

"No," said Mick "but it shouldn't be long now, though. Her clothes arrived yesterday!"

The cousins spent a couple of pleasant hours in the bar. In Micko's taxi, they received a call from Fr Flanagan. He was really excited about their discovery.

"We were right to get the extra helmet," said Sean.

The two men returned to their homes, wondering what the next adventure would bring…

Chapter 17

A beautiful, bright, crisp morning Fr Flanagan walked down the boreen crunching through the carpet of vegetation. Leaves were falling slowly, moving from side to side like boats rocking in a gentle breeze. The air had that lovely smell of moisture too sweet to be called damp. In the distance, he could see steam rising from the rooftops. He smiled, thinking back to when he was a child pretending that his breath was smoke.

"You've brought the good weather with you Father," commented the ever-positive Jonjo.

The priest, Jonjo and his cousin Sean sat around the big table drinking Sean's Italian coffee. They inquired about his pilgrimage to Medjugorje.

"It's not somewhere I know much about," said Sean.

"Well, to cut a long story short, apparitions began nearly 40 years ago, to some youngsters in the town. They had visions of Mary, who gave a series of messages which continue to this day. The place was under communist control in Yugoslavia, and attempts were made to suppress the news.

At first, the Church too was sceptical but has gradually become more accepting. Millions of people visit every year, and there have been countless reports of people being cured physically and mentally," responded Fr Flanagan.

"You go every year, don't you?" asked Jonjo.

"I do. I feel renewed every time. I climb Cross Mountain every day, making the Stations of the Cross. I go up Apparition Hill saying the Rosary and find a quiet place for reflection. Don't imagine that it is a town of dull Holy Joes. It is full of laughter and joy. The Croatian people are friendly, open and generous, a lot like the Irish. Did you never fancy it, Jonjo?"

"I always thought that with us having Knock so near that it was a bit disloyal to go," replied Jonjo.

"What about you, Sean?" asked the priest.

"Well, to be honest, until a couple of months ago, I

would have dismissed it all as nonsense. But now...,
Sean's answer tailed off.

In turn, Sean and Jonjo told Fr. Flanagan of the strange occurrences during his absence. He was intrigued by the apparition story and remembered seeing photographs of a very similar nature on Croagh Patrick. They got down to the business in hand about the tunnel.

"The inscription you showed me is Ogham," said Fr. Flanagan.

"What's that?" asked Sean.

"It's an ancient language, well to be precise, it's an alphabet. It's the earliest form of written Gaelic. Very little of it has survived."

"Can you read it?" asked Jonjo.

"Look," said the priest, pointing at the photo of the writing. "It reads from the bottom upwards. It translates as 'wise and pure'. This writing is from the 4th to the 6th century A.D."

"I got the impression that it was scratched on. It wasn't in keeping with the quality of the tunnel," contributed Sean.

"Let's go and see," said the priest. He carried with

him his toolbox, "I haven't opened this for years. It was in the back of the shed," continued Fr. Flanagan.

Down in the cellar, the priest opened the toolbox and looked nostalgically at the contents. It was all neatly packed but revealed a strange mixture of implements. There was a large trowel taking up one section. Next to it were a variety of wooden sticks, similar to lollipop sticks or coffee stirrers. A row of thin metal tools, each with a different shaped blade took up the next compartment.

There was a collection of small brushes including a toothbrush and small paintbrushes. The bottom of the box held string lines, spirit levels, small plastic bags, tape measures and a metal ruler. In a plastic wallet, a notebook, pencils, pens and a rubber were visible.

The priest began to examine the wine cellar. His experienced eye revealed the 'ghost' of another entrance to the tunnel. It was directly opposite the one Jonjo and Sean had been down. He showed the two older men the faint outline showing through the plasterwork.

"The tunnel must have originally gone right through. The part your family used as a cellar was a section of the tunnel, blocked off at both ends," stated Fr

Flanagan.

Sean and Jonjo were keen to carry on down the tunnel. Fr Flanagan took the more fastidious approach of the professional archaeologist. He made himself busy making notes, taking measurements and photographs. He indicated that the two men should go ahead without him.

The two friends sporting their new helmets walked down the tunnel. They moved more quickly than on their first trip and were soon at the point where the tunnel divided. They went along the right tunnel. It grew narrower and lower as they progressed. It was also sloping gently downhill.

They moved more slowly as Jonjo unravelled the twine they had attached to the long rope left in situ from their first trip. The air seemed still to be fresh, and they looked cautiously at the roof for any sign of cracks.

Jonjo stopped and said, "I can smell moisture."

At that moment, Sean lost his footing and was saved from falling by Jonjo's strong arms pulling him upwards and backwards. In front of them, the passageway disappeared into an abyss. Looking with the light from his helmet lamp, Sean was shocked to see how close he had been to plunging to his death.

The two men sat with their backs to the tunnel wall. Neither was able to speak at first. Jonjo, feeling horrified at what might have happened.

"Thanks," said Sean. "You saved..."

"Ara musha, you'd have done the same," interrupted Jonjo. "We should have our lunch now. It will save us going into shock."

Sean didn't think he would be able to eat anything. But to his surprise, he tucked into his sandwiches. Unusually, the two men ate their food in silence, each wrapped in their own thoughts.

Getting to their feet, they looked at the hole from a safe distance. It was not, as they had thought, a collapse in the tunnel. What they saw was a purpose-built shaft, the walls rounded like a well. Jonjo shuffled towards the edge, then lay flat and peered over. Even with the light from his helmet, he could not see the bottom. He could, however, feel a slight breeze. The draught had a faint but unmistakable smell of water.

To Sean's relief, Jonjo shuffled back. "I don't think it's a well," he said. "There's no mechanism for drawing the water."

"If it's not for getting water in, then maybe it's for draining water out," suggested Sean.

They heard footsteps from the main corridor. "Father, down the right-hand passage," called Jonjo.

There was no response, and the footfall continued for a few seconds, the sound gradually fading away.

"He must have gone the other way," suggested Sean.

The two men returned to the intersection, but the cleric was nowhere to be seen. Jonjo set off down the left passage. "Don't go past where we went last time," warned Sean. "I'll stay here. I've got a funny feeling."

As Jonjo disappeared down the left fork in the passageway, Sean again heard footsteps approaching. He was relieved to see the familiar shape of Fr Flanagan, his headlamp bobbing, creating shadows in the gloom.

"What's the matter, Sean?" he asked immediately aware of the older man's anxiety.

"Did you come down here a minute or two ago?" queried Sean.

"No, why?" asked the priest.

"I'll tell you later. Let's find Jonjo, and whatever you do, don't go down the other passage. It's dangerous!"

The two men walked down the left passageway. "Thank God you are here," said Jonjo to the cleric. "You did well to wait, Sean, if he'd gone the other way..."

Fr Flanagan was perplexed by the conversation. His mind was quickly diverted when he saw the engraved stone lintel illuminated by Jonjo's lamp. He took several photos using his mobile phone.

"I can see you two are a bit shaken up. Let's go and sort things out," said Fr Flanagan.

They returned speedily down the tunnel and were happy to take their helmets off and reconvene around the big kitchen table. Sean and Jonjo explained what they had seen.

"Well, it sounds like not only did Jonjo save your life, Sean, you may well have saved my life because I was going to go down that right-hand tunnel. The footsteps are a mystery. But when I was working in the cellar, I saw a black shape moving across. It moved from the blocked up door through to the tunnel. I put it down to shadows created by the headlamp, but it was eerie," said Fr Flanagan.

The priest went on to summarise what he had

found. He explained that the tunnel had a gentle upward incline and that the stone was superbly and accurately cut. He said that it wasn't possible to date it without specialist equipment. The priest continued that he had some theories about the structure but wanted to do some research before sharing the ideas.

The three men gathered around the image on the mobile. Carved into the lintel were five rectangles. The first rectangle had nothing in it. The second had a small but clearly visible circle or dot. The third rectangle had a star-shaped centre with straight lines radiating from it. The fourth was identical to the second with the single dot. The fifth was identical to the first-empty.

"These are hieroglyphs. Sacred carvings but what they mean I can only guess at," said the priest. "We need time to think things through."

"Well, having so recently escaped sudden death, I'm ready for a pint," said Sean cheerily, lightening the mood.

"Well, as the only one who hasn't saved somebody's life today, I'll drive you two to town and buy you a pint of the black stuff," laughed Fr Flanagan. Leaving his archaeology toolkit in the cellar, the priest led them to the car.

In Clarke's bar, Paddy Regan, the local guard, was entertaining the drinkers." The other night I was on duty. I saw the Murphy brothers driving home from the pub Paddy was driving. Suddenly he started to swerve from side to side.

I pulled him over and said, "What the Hell are ye doing, Paddy?"

"Didn't you see all the trees?" he says." I did well to miss them."

"Trees, you eejit," says I. That's your air freshener swinging about!"

After a drink or three in the bar, Sean and Jonjo decided to walk back in the last light of day. They passed Widow Farrell on the street. She appeared startled when they wished her, 'Good evening'.

"What's that about?" queried Sean.

"I've an inkling, but I hope I'm wrong," answered Jonjo mysteriously.

The two men walked home as the sun set behind the hill.

Chapter 18

The corncrakes had gone, staying longer than any time he could remember. Maybe the hot summer and mild autumn had suited them. It was hard to believe that these noisy yet frail birds could fly all the way, from Ireland to Africa. There had been more of them this year. Not long ago, Jonjo thought they might disappear altogether. It was a cause for optimism. The world was putting itself right.

His thoughts turned to another visiting bird that harbinger of spring the cuckoo. He'd learnt at school how these creatures laid their eggs in other birds' nests. Their large chicks would hatch quickly and throw out the remaining eggs. The baby would be fed by the foster parents, birds that might be six times smaller than their supposed offspring.

As a boy, Jonjo had waged a guerilla campaign against them. He became adept at listening for the cuckoo's call and throwing out their eggs. Mostly this involved climbing trees, but sometimes the eggs were in ground nests.

He started out on his own. But after a while, some of the other boys from school joined him. They spent a couple of glorious weeks tracking through the undergrowth, climbing and occasionally falling from trees.

One early summer evening, his Mammy had taken him to task about this. He thought she was going to warn him about the dangers of tree climbing. But no, it was to explain in the kind but firm way she had that he had no right to destroy the eggs. The unborn life inside, even if it was a cuckoo, had a right to live. She told him that nature must take its course, and it wasn't for him to interfere. His Dad joined in explaining that killing animals for food was fine, but not for sport.

They explained to him in such a kindly way that he felt no resentment. He knew they were right. His parents would literally not hurt a fly. "They're all God's creatures," they would say.

Jonjo was thankful that his parents had not seen the changes in Ireland concerning the sanctity of life.

As always, when his mind strayed to sad thoughts, Jonjo brought to mind happy memories as an antidote. He remembered the rope swings by the river, swinging out further and higher than everyone, doing his Tarzan call. His great reward was bringing a smile to Mary's lips. He used to imagine saving her from lions and tigers, neither of which, were prevalent in the West of Ireland. There weren't even any snakes to rescue her from, thanks to St. Patrick.

All these thoughts flashed rapidly through his mind as he sat in his cousin's orangery, watching the rain bucketing down. Cousin Sean was on his exercise bike doing the high-intensity training that Jonjo had shown him. The fitness regime that Jonjo had devised for his cousin had worked wonderfully well. Sean now looked ten years younger than when he returned from America.

"I've lost so much weight," said Sean, "that I've packed a suitcase full of clothes for the charity shop."

"That's grand," approved Jonjo.

"I have some coats that would fit you. I've never worn them, still in their bags. You are broad in the shoulder, and you could pull in the waist with the belt," offered Sean.

"Thanks," said Jonjo, "but I've me plastic mac."

"Well," Sean laughed. "If you are going for the demobbed in 1945 look, your mac and suit are fine. Look, you are always getting me to try new exercises. Your turn to try something new."

Sean's trousers were obviously too large in the waist and short in the leg for Jonjo. However, some of the coats, jackets and hats were passable. So it was that when they were waiting in the porch for Micko's taxi, Jonjo was wearing a blue raincoat from Boston's finest.

"I think I'll use my third best suit for my scarecrow," said Jonjo.

"Well, don't be upset if it turns you down," laughed Sean.

"Maybe we should use some of your cast-offs, then it would be outstanding in its field," replied Jonjo.

There was no response from Sean.

"Out standing in its field," enunciated Jonjo, "come on."

"That's terrible," chuckled Sean. "Even Seamus Burke wouldn't use that one."

"Seriously though, I wonder what people will think of me in these new clothes," asked Jonjo.

"Seriously, and I mean seriously nobody will be thinking about it. Something I learned in therapy, we worry what other people are thinking about us, when in fact, they are busy thinking about their own lives."

"Therapy, I didn't know you'd been ... er, ill," asked Jonjo.

"Not really there was a real fad. Everybody had a therapist then. It probably never caught on in Ireland because you've got the pub. Everyone in there is eager to tell you about your shortcomings and give you advice whether you want it or not."

There was a lot of truth in what Sean said. However, at that moment, someone was thinking about Jonjo and Sean. Widow Farrell was rapidly processing thoughts about them both.

Micko pulled up in the taxi, and the two men asked him how things were going in the business that Sean was subsidising.

"Good," said Micko, hesitantly, "there's plenty of

work."

"But?" queried Sean.

"Well, I'm not so good at receipts and bookings, and cash and debit and credit cards," lamented Micko.

"You've got the accountant for the money side of things," reminded Sean.

"Yes. Well, it's keeping things in order and remembering petrol receipts. There's more to it than I thought."

"So you need help then?" queried Sean.

"Funnily enough, Widow Farrell came in and asked if I had any work for her big lad, Sonny. When I told her that I would have to ask you two, she said not to bother."

"Would Sonny be able to help?" asked Sean.

"Well, Mr Brennan knows him," he replied. "All I can think of is washing the car. The thing is, I love washing and cleaning the car meself."

"Yes, a fine job you do of it," replied Jonjo.

Micko dropped them off at the charity shop. Sean and Jonjo parted to do various errands. They agreed to meet up in the cafe.

***

Sean opened the cafe door. Something about the smell took him right back to his childhood. Stale tea and wet dogs and boring Sunday afternoons. The front window of the cafe was steamed up. Droplets of water meandered down in slow competition.

Jonjo was already there, a pint mug of tea in hand. His head was buried in his horse racing paper. The only customer.

"Quiet day?" asked Sean.

"Too quiet," replied Mollie Keane. The proprietress of the cafe had a pleasant, smiley face. Her plump figure suggested to Sean that it wasn't only lack of customers that was eating her profits. He dismissed this thought. Knowing that he was feeling a 'holier than thou' attitude because of his own weight loss.

"I've got some of that Italian coffee you like," Mollie continued.

"Sure," said Sean." And a buttered scone, one for you?" he called to Jonjo.

Jonjo grunted.

"I'll take that as a 'yes'," said Sean. "Two buttered

scones, please, never get any sense out of him when he's studying the horses."

"Aye, him and the rest of the men in Ireland," laughed Molly. "I heard you were a businessman in America," she said.

"My last job was as a consultant. I advised businesses on how to increase their profits."

"Was there good money in it?" asked Molly.

"You wouldn't believe how much we asked for what was really a simple job."

"I wouldn't have enough money to hire you," said Molly sadly.

"I'm retired now, so if you give me a pen and a piece of paper, I'll do a free consultation while Jonjo is sorting out his bets."

Sean sipped his coffee, luxuriated in the melting butter from his scone and looked around. After ten minutes, he handed Molly the sheet of paper.

"That's amazing," she said.

Taking the paper back, he said, "Maybe you do some of these already? Short term first. I'd have a table and two chairs outside every day. Even if it's raining, and nobody will sit on them, it is advertising it says, 'I'm open'.

On days like this, have the door open a crack so the windows don't steam. Use a fan to blow baking smells through from the kitchen. Get a small chalkboard, and put different offers on every day. Have a pensioners' discount. Bake your own scones and call them after the town's name."

Sean paused, then continued, "Let other people advertise in your windows, charge them a nominal amount. I'll get the ball rolling with an advert for Micko's taxis. Although it is someone else's business on the advert, it's your window they are looking in. Have some books in here that customers can borrow. You can get them for next to nothing at the charity shop. I'll bring you some of mine down next time I'm in."

"Longer term," said Sean, "use your wall space. If there's a local artist, let them put pictures up for sale on your wall, share the profits. Do it in the tourist season, maybe advertise it as an exhibition. Use your links with the Church and school."

"Thank you so much," said Molly.

"Some of it will work, some won't," answered Sean. "Good luck."

***

Next door, Widow Farrell appeared to be looking in a shop window. In reality, she was studying her own reflection. What she remembered was the tall, willowy, graceful girl that turned all the boys' heads. The chatty, happy young woman who had the world at her feet. What she saw was a middle-aged woman looking older than her years. Her height and weight gave her an almost masculine look. Her hair cropped short, hat plumped firmly down. Clothes heavy, dark and old-fashioned. Her appearance said, 'I don't want to speak, keep away.'

She drew in a deep breath, put on an air of confidence that she didn't feel and walked into the cafe. She ordered a cup of tea and asked Jonjo and Sean if she could join them. She smiled inwardly at their old fashioned courtesy as they stood to greet her.

"I'd like to invite you to afternoon tea at my house tomorrow. I have a business proposition for you," said Mrs Farrell. She was glad to get the words out in an even tone.

"Let me check my diary," said Sean looking at his phone."Well, it seems I'm free ... every day this week."

Jonjo, consulting the piece of paper on which he was writing his bets, added, "Well, unfortunately, I am only available on Sunday, Monday, Tuesday, Wednesday, Thursday, Friday and also Saturday."

"Tomorrow at 4p.m. then," she said with a smile that lit up not only her face but the whole room.

***

The rain was only spitting, so the two men decided to walk home.

"You've forgotten your suitcase," said Jonjo.

"I gave it to the charity shop."

"It looked an expensive one," commented Jonjo.

"It was. I'm finding it easier to part with things now."

"That's grand," said Jonjo.

Passing through the hollow, there was some mist about. The two knew that it wasn't the Vale of Mist. They knew that they had tasks to accomplish before they could enter the Vale.

On reaching their homes, Sean said, "Shall I fetch us a couple of bottles from the cellar to try?"

"Well, O.K.," said Jonjo. "As long as you know, I'm only helping you drink them, to reduce the burden of possessions that is weighing you down."

"Of course," smiled Sean. "What other reason could there be?"

"It doesn't bother you going down in the cellar after what Fr Flanagan saw?"

"Not till you mentioned it," laughed Sean. "No, actually it doesn't. I've been going in that cellar since I was a child."

Sean got two bottles and challenged Jonjo to guess which was the expensive one and which was the super expensive one.

"A nose this size has to have some use," chuckled Jonjo.

They had a convivial afternoon drinking and reminiscing. They talked about the tunnel and the strange carvings. They appreciated Fr Flanagan had a busy life and understood it would take time before he got back to them.

"What's this worry you have about Widow Farrell?"

asked Sean.

"I'll tell you about it on the way up there tomorrow," replied Jonjo, tapping the side of his long nose.

Chapter 19

The sky was a strange colour, streaks of pink and red amongst the blue though it was only an hour past midday. The hairs on the back of his neck stood on end. There was not a breath of air. A preternatural silence created tension in his muscles.

"Strange day!" said Jonjo, "All Hallows Eve."

"I've been reading up on it. It has a long tradition in Ireland going back way beyond Halloween," said Sean. "It originated with the ancient Celtic festival of Samhain when people would light bonfires and wear costumes to ward off ghosts. It didn't become part of the Catholic tradition until the 8th century.

"I thought it was all down to the Yanks with all that trick or treat nonsense. So it started in Ireland," queried Jonjo.

"Yes, today was regarded as the beginning of the dark half of the year. The boundary between the worlds of the living and the dead dissolved on this night," answered Sean.

A shiver went through Jonjo as he walked. He was pleased to note that he no longer had to reduce his pace for his cousin to keep up.

"O.K., what do you know about Widow Farrel?" asked Sean.

"She's been in the town for about three years. She's from a wealthy Wicklow family called Quinn. They have property all over the country. They've owned that house she lives in for generations. It was derelict for years. Do you remember it from when we were kids?"

"No," replied Sean.

"We used to call it the ghostie house," continued Jonjo.

"I remember. I thought that was a much bigger place deep in the woods," answered Sean.

"It was bigger because we were smaller, and it was overgrown. We hacked our way through to it."

"I remember you found a way in through the cellar!"

"That's right, we used to go in there and scare

ourselves silly with ghost stories. Then we'd run home pretending the ghosts were after us," laughed Jonjo.

"I only went the once. I wasn't the outdoor type like you."

"Anyway, back to the widow, she was married to Danny Farrell, the bookmaker. He had bookmaker's pitches at every racecourse in the country. Somewhere along the line, he got involved with some bad people. The rumour was that it was a Far Eastern betting syndicate and that he owed them money. He was last seen dragged into the back of a van in Dublin by two giant bodybuilder types. It was quite a big story in the national press for a while. Anyway, Danny never turned up dead or alive. Eventually, the courts decided that he was legally regarded as dead," said Jonjo.

"How about Mrs Farrell?" asked Sean.

"Well, when she moved here, Guard Regan told me that as far as the police knew, she took no part in his business affairs and that she didn't benefit financially from his death. He also told me that Danny Farrell was involved in some bad things that never made the papers. 'A chancer, a charmer and rotten to the core was how he described him'."

The cousins walked on to the hollow, Sean laughing at Jonjo's complaint that however many pairs of reading glasses he possessed, he could never find them. "I've either got four pairs or none," he moaned."I think they go off on their own they never stay where I leave them!"

Reaching the Hollow, they sat on the grass banking for a break. "So the Widow Farrell is innocent then," said Sean.

"Of her husband's wrongdoings, yes," agreed Jonjo. "But..."

"But what?"

"Well, you know when we went on the walk up the mountain, you felt the 'fear gortach', the strange hunger when you feel when you are near a dead body," answered Jonjo.

"So you are saying that I've found the body of the missing Paddy Farrell and that the Widow Farrell did him in," summarised Sean.

"When you put it bluntly like that, it seems far-fetched, but it is too much of a coincidence. That woman is seriously troubled. She is hiding something."

"You know, when I was a kid in the States, I used to

read superhero comics. I always wanted a superpower, but I never anticipated it being detecting dead bodies," grinned Sean.

"I keep thinking back to what Bridie said. I think we are earning our right to visit the Vale of Mist. I think we have tasks to complete and this might be one of them."

Sean and Jonjo sat back. Both were thinking about the Vale of Mist. The legend, that anyone who entered the Vale would be guaranteed, at least, a year of good health.

"You know if this is the day when the boundary dissolves between the worlds, the hollow could be the place it happens," suggested Jonjo.

"I know it has the weight of history about it. So many people have trod this path over so many generations. They've worn away the land beneath them," added Sean.

"I believe something of their spirit remains in this place. It's hard to explain, but when I'm here, I have this feeling that we are not alone," said Jonjo, and again a shiver ran through him.

"Someone walking on your grave," laughed Sean.

"Yes, probably you using your superpower."

They walked on to the tunnel through the hill. Sean told Jonjo that in ancient times some tunnel entrances were aligned to sunrise at Samhain. They decided to check out, later on, the tunnel under Sean's house to see if that was aligned. It would mean finding the entrance first.

"I think we'll find it," said Jonjo. "But I like to do one thing at a time. We've to sort out this business with the Widow Farrell, understand the mysterious tunnel carvings under your house, and find the exit and entrance to that tunnel. We've also to finish building our boat, help Micko run his taxi business, and find the Vale of Mist."

"Don't forget, the cellar full of fine wines we've to dispose of," added Sean.

"And us, retired gentlemen of leisure," said Jonjo shaking his head in mock resignation.

They continued into the town, where Sean was happy to take his rest in the cafe. He was glad to see that Molly had taken his advice and put a table and chairs outside. Sean opened his haversack and took out the books that he had promised her. He put them on the shelves in the two alcoves. Only he knew that one was a valuable first edition. He was overcoming the mean side of his nature and feeling all the better for it.

Molly poured him a coffee and said, "You won't be needing anything to eat. Widow Farrell has bought all my buns for your afternoon tea."

"Well, that's good for business, though not for my diet," laughed Sean.

He sat looking at one of his old books, drinking his coffee while waiting for Jonjo, next door at the bookies.

"It's good to see you, Mr Brennan," said Liam Casey from behind the counter.

"You too," replied Jonjo. "I just love this time of year when the good jump races are on." He looked at the bank of TV screens showing racing from around the globe. The race meeting from Roscommon was there on the big screen. He could feel the excitement building. It was amazing how these betting shops had improved over the years.

The sky in Roscommon looked ominous too. Some of the horses looked skittish. They could sense the electricity in the air. Jonjo handed in his cash and betting slip and went to sit with Seamus and a few of the other 'boys' from Clarke's bar. They sat on high stools next to a long, tall desk.

"I've heard you are having tea with the Widow Farrell," said Seamus.

"Who needs a newspaper when you've got Molly Keane?" laughed Jonjo. "I'm surprised it didn't get a mention on the evening news."

"Speaking of news," continued Seamus. "Did you know Murphy rang the maternity hospital and said that he'd like an appointment for Mrs Murphy?"

The nurse said, 'Is this her first child?'

'No,' says Murphy, 'it's her husband. I think she's ready to have the baby.'

'Is she dilated?' asks the nurse.

'Oh yes, she's over the moon,' says Murphy."

As usual, Seamus's joke had a mixed reaction from groans to laughter. Jonjo enjoyed the craic in the bookies. He could quite happily have spent the afternoon watching the gee-gees.

"Are you O.K., Jonjo?" asked Seamus

"I've a headache. I always get one about an hour before a big storm," he replied.

"We'd best get to the bar before the rain comes," said Seamus.

"I'd get something to eat from Molly's first," said Jonjo. "It's no good drinking on an empty head. Come on, I'll get you a discount."

So it was that Jonjo took five of the men into the cafe, and Molly cheerfully offered them the pensioners' discount.

Sean and Jonjo set off first of all to the church, where they laid flowers at the graves of; Mary and of Sean's grandparents. Jonjo put a pot of Michaelmas daisies at the foot of the monument to the famine victims.

When they reached the shelter of the stone gateway, the two men were out of breath. The lightning flashed again, illuminating the house. When darkness returned, they saw behind the curtain the silhouette of Widow Farrell holding aloft, a candelabra. The more indistinct lumbering form of Sonny towering over her.

"This is the bit in the movies where you say, 'Nobody would be mad enough to go in there'," laughed Sean. "But they always do!"

"Come on, are you a man or a mouse?" joked Jonjo.

"Pass the cheese," replied Sean. But he belied his words by striding down the path ahead of Jonjo.

Chapter 20

"Come on in, you must be soaking!" said Mrs Farrell. "Sonny, take their coats."

Mrs Farrell using the light from her candelabra led them to the parlour. She ushered them to two high-backed leather chairs near the fireplace. The fire was prepared but unlit. Mrs Farrell disappeared briefly, then returned with a small shovel full of burning embers. She put them on the fire, and soon it was roaring up the chimney.

"Sorry," she said. "I would have had it ready but for the light failure."

She disappeared again and returned with a tea trolley. It was an ornate trolley made from gold-coloured metal with large wheels at the back and small ones at the front. Tea and coffee pots stood on the top shelf along with a single malt, bottle of Scotch and three tumblers. The lower one was replete with sandwiches and buns.

The two men helped themselves to the tea and coffee, and Mrs Farrell sipped at a small Scotch. The cousins worked their way through the sandwiches and onto the buns. They could hear the occasional laugh from Sonny, who was playing with a torch in an adjoining room. The pleasant smell of smoke from the embers that Mrs Farrell had carried in still filled the parlour.

Outside, the wind howled, and rain battered the windows. Mrs Farrell poured them each a drink, a much greater measure than her own. The two men thanked her for the food and listened to her proposal.

"I need a job for Sonny. I know he has a limited capacity, but he is hard working. He loves cars, particularly Micko's taxi. I thought he could wash and clean the car. If you paid him, I could give you the money back. It would do him good. He'd really feel like he had his own money. I would go with him to keep an eye on him."

She looked at Jonjo for an answer.

"Sean's the businessman. We'll let him have a think. Wouldn't it be better, for Sonny, if you just dropped him off and picked him up?" said Jonjo.

"Well, the thing is he's so big and strong, and he doesn't know his own strength. He can get a bit frustrated when people don't understand him," she replied.

In his mind, Jonjo was writing another possible explanation for the disappearance of Danny Farrell.

"Here's my suggestion," began Sean. "Micko needs some help running the admin side of the business, which I'm sure you are more than capable of sorting out. What if we take the both of you on for a couple of days a week? You can run the office, and Micko can show Sonny how he wants the car cleaning and polishing. Who knows, it could lead on to him washing and valeting cars like his own business."

"That would be wonderful," she smiled.

"Don't underestimate Micko," added Jonjo. "He missed a lot of schooling, but I think there's a good brain hiding in there. He needs his confidence boosting as Sean did with me. It's only a couple of months ago I used to ask Sean to read my letters for me and now I stand up and read at Mass."

"I'll bear that in mind. I've had a lot of practice at teaching reading with Sonny, as you can imagine," she replied. "I'm so grateful." Suddenly, tears ran down her face, and she began to sob.

Sonny appeared swiftly and silently from the other room. "Mammy?" he asked.

"I'm happy, Sonny. You've got a job. Say 'thank you' to Mr Walsh and Mr Brennan."

"Thank you, Mr Walsh, thank you, Mr Brennan," said Sonny in the slow, deliberate manner of a child.

Sonny returned to his game with the torch, clearly enjoying the darkness. There was an awkward silence broken by Sean, who said, "This place has the feel of the old Irish 'Big House' at least from what I have read of them."

Looking around the room in the flickering firelight Mrs Farrell smiled. "I've spent a lot of time cleaning and reorganising this place. I've brought most of the best furniture into this room. I've still not unpacked everything even after three years. I'm setting up the library. I'll show you around one day if you like," she ended hesitantly.

"That would be grand," said Jonjo, with Sean nodding agreement. "Sean's a great man for the books."

"We had a huge library at the house in Wicklow. Lots of books from the 'Big House' period. I used to love the Lady Gregory folktales," said Widow Farrell.

"I love the old tales. In the long, long past before the police and before the Church, it was village elders like us, who ran things. You know if something is troubling you, we can help," said Jonjo softly.

"What do you know?" said Mrs Farrell sharply, her anger making her pretty face ugly.

"I don't know anything. But I see a good person who is troubled," said Jonjo. "You can tell us and, I promise, whatever it is. It will go no further."

"I know this seems strange because it is strange to us, too," added Sean. "But we've found ourselves on a mission, a sort of vocation, to help sort things out in the town. We haven't sought this ourselves, but it comes from a good place."

Mrs Farrell didn't answer immediately and instead refilled their glasses and poured a large measure for herself. She studied the two men then made up her mind. Taking a sharp breath in. "This will go no further."

The two men nodded. "You have our word," replied Sean.

"It's a long tale?"

"We are in the company of a lovely young lady. In front of a roaring fire, with a whiskey in hand. Where else would we be?" replied Jonjo.

"Lovely young lady, maybe once," said Mrs Farrell shaking her head sadly.

"Still lovely," said Jonjo firmly.

"I've wanted to explain for so long. I've worried for so long."

"So, I lived in a house far grander even than this. We had land and horses and servants. I have two older brothers, and I was the baby of the family. I had a privileged and almost idyllic childhood, although, of course, I didn't realise it at the time. I had a family that loved me and wanted for nothing."

"My brothers were sent off to boarding school when they were nine and ten years old. They started together, and I was heartbroken when they packed their huge trunks and left. Girls weren't sent to boarding school, at least not in my family, and I was glad of that."

"The house was so quiet without them. My father was away at work in Dublin, and my mother had the house and estate to run. I had good friends at school, but home was lonely without the boys. There were plenty of good times, though, and all sorts of holidays. I was very fortunate."

She topped up the two men's drinks and continued, "I'm talking too much. I'll get to the point. Danny Farrell came on the scene when I was 17. He came to look at one of Dad's horses. He came galloping up on a horse of his own at breakneck speed. I'd never seen anyone handle a horse so well. It made me think of the legends of the ancient people who enticed the fearless young men to ride with them."

"He hopped off the horse and, putting the reins in my hands, said, 'Well, you must be the prettiest stable girl in the whole of Ireland. Can you stable my horse? I've an appointment with Mr Quinn.'"

"Well, Danny Farrell concluded his business with my father, and I brought his horse back up. My father made no attempt to introduce me, which was very unlike him. So I introduced myself, and we laughed about the misunderstanding."

"My father warned me that Farrell had a bad reputation and told me to keep away from him. Of course, this had the opposite effect. In time we were married, and my father set him up in his bookmaking business. The business thrived, and we travelled the country together. We had a safe put in the house because we came home with so much cash."

"When I was pregnant with Sonny, I stopped travelling with Danny. He took on his old school friend as an assistant, a man I didn't trust. Danny started to stay away nights after the race meetings. I won't go into great detail, but things got worse when Sonny was born. It was clear after the first year that Sonny had problems."

"Danny became unpleasant and aggressive. He'd leave home and come back all apologetic. I'd take him back like a fool. In the end, I told him no more. He never came back, took no interest in Sonny. He never paid anything towards his upbringing. When he was legally accepted as dead, I decided to move here, the other side of the country."

Mrs Farrell poured more drinks and went to check

on Sonny.

"A cold, stormy night shortly after we moved here, a night much like this, a knock came at the door. It was Danny back from the dead, so to speak. He was in a terrible state, his clothes torn, his face scratched. He burst in and called me names I won't repeat. He was demanding money and a bed for the night. I stood up to him and left him in no doubt what I thought about him."

"Danny grabbed me by the throat, and there was murder in his eyes. I screamed, and Sonny came in. Danny looked at him in surprise and called him a horrible name. Sonny came over and lifted Danny off his feet as if he weighed no more than a feather. He threw him right across the room, his head cracked against the cabinet. Danny was out cold, and Sonny was sobbing. I calmed Sonny down and sent him to his room."

"I checked on Danny, and he was dead! I felt for a pulse, put a mirror to his mouth, there was nothing. I don't know to this day what actually killed him. Whether it was the bang on the head, the shock, or some other reason. He was thin. His skin had a grey yellowy tinge."

"I thought quickly. I couldn't bear to think of Sonny going to court. I thought I'd say I'd done it in self-defence, but what would happen to Sonny if I wasn't there? These thoughts went through my head in a fraction of a second."

"Before I knew it, I had rolled the mat on which Danny's body had fallen around him. I dragged him down the path and tipped his body into the ditch. I pushed the stones from the wall down. They went very easily. It felt almost like someone was helping me."

"When I got back in, Sonny was waiting. I told Sonny that it was a scarecrow and that I had thrown it away. The state of Danny's clothes and the way Sonny had tossed him across the room had put that image in my head. I don't know what Sonny made of it all. He was upset, but we watched some of his favourite cartoons, and he went to bed as normal."

"You can imagine I spent the night worrying. I expected the police to call any minute, someone must have seen Danny. It was only a matter of time. But nothing happened, no one came, and I grew more anxious, not less as time went on. I've not slept a full night since it happened. I've had nightmares of Danny coming back through the door. One thing about being brought up on a farm was that I understood death. I know he was dead, not just unconscious. Well, that's my tale and a very sad one it is."

After a few moments of silence, Jonjo began, "Speaking for myself and Sean will interrupt if he disagrees. The only thing you are guilty of is being a good mother. There is the letter of the law and the spirit of the law. You have broken the letter of the law but not the spirit. Ours is not to judge that is the province of the Almighty. You have already served three years of a sentence you have imposed on yourself. As an elder of the village, I absolve you from guilt and give you your freedom."

"I totally agree," said Sean.

"I still worry that somehow, someday, the body will be found. I can never be free," replied Mrs Farrell.

"What happened to the rug he was rolled up in?" asked Sean.

"I burned it... there was no blood or anything. It just reminded me, why?" she asked.

"Well, there is nothing to tie you to the body. The

police might think, he stumbled into the ditch, and the rocks fell in on him," said Sean.

"That never....," began Mrs Farrell. The sentence was never completed because at that moment, the lights came on, and Sonny walked in bleary-eyed.

"Thank you so much for everything. I've so much to think about," said Mrs Farrell.

"Too much thinking is not good for you, and thank you for your hospitality," replied Jonjo.

Outside, the air was fresh after the storm. The water was gurgling down the streams feeding the river. Jonjo's torch led the way.

"Clarke's Bar?" said Sean

"No bout a doubt it," laughed, Jonjo

Chapter 21

The stars were bright against the inky black sky. Street lights reflected on the wet pavements, and pools of water became pools of light. The pleasant smell of wood smoke met them as they crossed the bridge. All around, they felt the freshness that comes after a big storm. The river, running quickly seeming to chuckle as the freshwater splashed in from tributaries great and small. The earth was refreshed and renewed.

"We did the right thing," said Sean, sensing Jonjo's doubt.

"I know the past can't be changed, but the future can. Those two will need more help from us, but we have put them on the right path," agreed Jonjo.

"Well, that's enough of doing good for the day!" exclaimed Sean as they entered Clarke's bar.

"So, if it isn't Laurel and Hardy," Seamus Burke called out. He shuffled himself in his seat and began to whistle the Laurel and Hardy theme tune. As he did so, he inadvertently knocked over his pint, soaking the table and his trousers.

Sean looked at Jonjo and smiled, "You?"

"Both together," laughed Jonjo.

"Well, that's another fine mess you've gotten yourself into," said the two men, fiddling with imaginary neckties.

The pub was in roars of laughter at this, much to Seamus's discomfort. Jonjo ever, kind-hearted got him a cloth from the bar and ordered him another pint. "I bet you've got a Murphy joke for us," he added.

"Well," began Seamus as he dried himself. "As a matter of fact, I have. Murphy and his granddad went out hunting. Unfortunately, the old fellow tripped dropped his rifle and shot himself. Murphy rang the emergency services and said, 'My granddad shot himself dead, I think he's dead,' he wailed.

'Don't upset yourself. Make sure he's dead,' replied the lady with a calm voice from the emergency services. She heard a loud gunshot.

'I've made sure he's dead,' said Murphy."

The joke got a good round of laughter from the bar, and Seamus felt a little happier with himself.

Jim Cullen, a robust man with a head of curly, white hair that a sheep would have been proud of, said, "I believe you've been to see Widow Farrell."

"Just a small business deal," replied Sean. "Nothing too interesting we can't tell you about it until we've completed it."

"Tune in to radio Molly Keane tomorrow afternoon," smiled Jonjo.

The two men had a couple of pints and went home in Micko's taxi. They explained the arrangements that they had made with Mrs Farrell and her son. They told Micko he was still the boss and that if he had any problems to contact them.

Jonjo noticed that Micko was looking tired and asked him how things were going. He told them that business was going well and that maybe they should get an extra part-time driver. Sean promised that he would look into the finances and see what he could do.

Arriving home, Jonjo said, "Will we have a fire in the chimenea?"

"Sure," answered Sean.

They soon had the wood blazing, and they added sods of turf. The night was clear, and the two friends gazed skyward.

"What do you think of when you look up there?" asked Sean.

"I think it is reality. During the day, we can't see beyond our world. On a clear night, we get to see our place in the universe," replied Jonjo.

"And what is that place?" persevered Sean.

"If we are talking about the meaning of life, we need 'the water of life'." Jonjo returned with a small wooden barrel. "I've been ageing some whiskey in this. It's time to try it out."

"O.K., purely in the interest of scientific curiosity, I'll try some," agreed Sean.

The whiskey had taken on some of the taste of the wood and was the better for it.

"When I look at the stars, on a night like this, I feel part of something huge. Something beyond my understanding so vast that it renews my faith," said Jonjo.

"For me, it has the opposite effect," said Sean. "It

makes me feel small, inconsequential, insignificant."

"I suppose it depends on how you view things. I try to look on the bright side. You can train yourself to do it. The more positive you are, the better you feel. Your body reacts to your mind. If you keep your mind positive, your body feels good," replied Jonjo.

"I know that's true. I'm envious of your faith, though. You have such certainty."

"What's your view on the big questions?" asked Jonjo. "You know, why are we here, what happens when we die, did God make all this?"

Sean sipped his drink and answered, "We had it drummed into us as kids, 'Who made you?' 'God made me' 'Why did God make you? We knew all the questions and answers, but we never really thought about them. My parents' faith was absolute and unquestioning."

"And what do you believe?" asked Jonjo.

"I drifted away from the Church. Many years ago, I visited the Vatican and was dismayed by the wealth there. I realised it was a multi-national corporation. I was a businessman and saw the Church through a businessman's eyes. As a business, it is phenomenal. It receives lots of money and has lots of tax breaks. It has millions of unpaid employees. Why is that money not going to the poor? The recent history of the Church has been dreadful," answered Sean.

"But somewhere inside," he continued. "I always had an awareness of the good the Church has done. Like any group, the actions of a nasty minority can obliterate the work of the majority. I felt that I was using the failings of the Church as an excuse for my rejection of beliefs. With any organisation, you wonder, can it be fixed from the inside, does it need fixing from the outside, or is it worth fixing?"

"What did you decide?" asked Jonjo.

"I decided it was too big a problem for me to work out," laughed Sean. "Since I've been back here, and with all the strange sights we've witnessed, I can't help but believe there is life after death. But as to what form it takes. I'm none the wiser. There must be a higher force, a supernatural being. As to why we are here, I keep coming back to the thought that we are here to discover things. To learn, to care for one and another. But what the reason for that is, I don't know."

"Well, maybe that is reason enough in itself," said

Jonjo. "Do you remember when we were at school, we were told not to go into any other Churches? The world was Catholic or non-catholic, nothing else mattered."

"That's what we were taught, agreed Sean. "Only Catholics could go to heaven. Even then, it was a pretty remote chance with all the venial and mortal sins and original sin."

"Well, that view seems to have changed. It's because we are made in the image and likeness of God we can live a Christian life without even knowing about Christ," said Jonjo.

"I remember thinking when I was a kid that the thief on the cross next to Jesus wasn't a Catholic, and he got into heaven, answered Sean. "But I didn't dare say it," he laughed.

"Ay, they were strict times. But at least we learnt right from wrong," said Jonjo.

"It didn't stop us doing wrong, but sure as hell made us feel guilty about it," laughed Sean.

Jonjo sipped his whiskey and rolled it around in his mouth to bring out the taste. "I wonder if God was alone, and that's why he made us," he said. "I know it sounds a bit mad, but if we are made in the likeness of

God, then God must be like us."

"Wait, that's just made me think!" exclaimed Sean. "You know the carving in the tunnel, the blank rectangle, the rectangle with the dot and the rectangle with a star shape. Maybe they are an explanation of creation. The first is nothingness, the second is creation, and the third is the Big Bang."

"They must have been a very advanced civilisation," mused Jonjo. "What about the other two rectangles, the dot again and the final blank?"

"Maybe that it is so the message can be read from either end. Left to right or right to left," offered Sean.

"It's definitely a message, a message sent through time. It reminds me of the time capsule on the Voyager spacecraft. We need to find out more from the tunnel. There may be other secrets in there," Jonjo said.

"Well, we are seeing Fr. Flanagan tomorrow," said Sean. "We can do some more exploration."

Something was nagging at Jonjo's mind about the message in the tunnel. He couldn't work out quite what it was.

The two men said goodnight, and as Jonjo walked home, the message in the tunnel suddenly became clear to him.

Chapter 22

Jonjo watched the water vapour rising up from the tarpaulin cover. He pulled back the sheet tipping the rainwater onto his still flowering primulas, some low to the ground, others reaching up on long stems.

The clouds had drifted in during the night, preventing a frost. The sharp, misty morning was gradually being warmed by the pale sun. He breathed in, slowly and deliberately, tasting the air. Autumn 'when every leaf becomes a flower,' someone had said.

He emptied the ash, from last night's fire, onto the vegetable patch. A couple of nails had survived the blaze. He put these in a tin in his shed. He'd straighten them out later. Under the tarpaulin was the canoe that he and Sean were making. It had been mistaken for a horse trough and a raised flower bed by visitors. Now, at last, it was recognisably boat-shaped, though neither of them knew what they were doing.

Inside the boat were a couple of paddles that Jonjo had carved from branches. In truth, they looked more like hurley sticks than paddles. He had engraved the pattern from the tunnel on them. They would definitely work to propel the boat. Jonjo loved to work outdoors.

He said a silent prayer of thanks and thought about his late wife. Today was All Saints Day. Surely, she was in that category. Still, he would pray for her tomorrow as well, on All Souls Day.

On their walk into town, Jonjo explained his theory about the engraving in the tunnel. "I think you are right about the first part meaning nothingness, the second creation, and the third the Big Bang. But I think the next one means that everything returns to a single dot and then to nothingness."

"That's one of the scientific theories, 'The Big Crunch'. When the universe stops expanding, it reverses and collapses," said Sean. "Then it creates another Big Bang, and so it goes on."

"That's disappointing," replied Jonjo.

"How so?"

"I thought, I'd been the first to think it up. At least the first since the people that carved it," laughed Jonjo.

"I've a theory of my own," began Sean." The people that created that message must have been very advanced. It could be the Tuatha de Danann that we've talked about before. They came to the west coast of Ireland about 4 thousand years ago. Legend has it that they emerged out of a great mist in the sea and that they had been banished from heaven. Eventually, after losing a battle, they were forced to live underground," said Sean.

"Yes, I remember you did some research on them," agreed Jonjo.

"Well, in the States, there is a Hall of Fame for just about anything you can think of, baseball, boxing, music, all sorts. When I went around them, my eye was always drawn to the Irish names. They excelled in every sport, every area of the arts and science. It occurred to me what influence the Irish have had all around the world. For example, over 20 of the U.S. presidents have Irish ancestry."

"What's this got to do with the Tuatha de Danaan?"

asked Jonjo.

The two men had reached the hollow, and they stopped for their morning break.

"Just think of the Irish greats of English literature; James Joyce, George Bernard Shaw, Oscar Wilde, Samuel Beckett. Others, like Jonathan Swift, who wrote Gulliver's Travels, and Bram Stoker, who wrote Dracula, who many don't know are Irish," continued Sean.

"I still don't know what you are getting at," replied Jonjo.

"Well, the Tuatha de Danann surpassed everyone with their mental and physical ability. Even their horses were supposed to be superior. I'm just saying that it may account for the exceptional influence Ireland has had on the world."

"Well, I definitely agree about the horses. The Irish thoroughbreds are the best in horse racing. You only have to look at the number of top jockeys that are Irish to confirm they are the best horsemen. Isn't this a bit racist though, are you saying that the Irish are superior?"

"No, racists don't mix with other races. Just look at

how the Irish have mixed across the world. There's an island in the West Indies where the people still have an Irish accent, and surnames like Sweeney and Ryan, and they are all black," added Sean.

"That's grand. I never knew that."

"I'm not saying anything against other races. For the small population, the country has had a tremendous influence on the world. When you add those of Irish descent, it is phenomenal. You wouldn't believe some of the people who link back to the Emerald Isle," concluded Sean.

They resumed their walk and reached the tunnel under the hill.

"I've been thinking about what you said," began Jonjo. "The tale about the ancient people turning into 'the other crowd', you know the little people, might be an allegory. I hope that's the right word."

"What do you think it is an allegory of?"

"I thought it might be to show that the power of the Tuatha de Danann was decreasing. It was getting smaller," replied Jonjo hesitantly.

"That could be right. It might be telling us also their knowledge is still underground, waiting for us to discover it."

They made their way across the lush green fields into town. Sean bought a newspaper and went to the cafe. Jonjo carried on to church. Sean gave the notice he'd had printed to Mollie for the cafe window. The poster had an illustration of Micko's bright yellow taxi, with the heading, 'Luxury transport but normal price'.

"Should I charge for posters?" asked Mollie.

"I'd make it a nominal amount, just so people don't expect you to keep them up forever. I'll get Mrs Farrell to sort it out with you. She's going to be helping Micko out. When you've a quiet moment once you've a few posters up, rearrange them now and again, it keeps people interested."

"Mrs Farrell, I expect a lady like her would be wanting a good wage?" asked Mollie.

"Well, you know business people, like us, never discuss such things."

"Of course," replied Molly at the same time, flattered and disappointed at the reply.

Sean read his newspaper and enjoyed his Italian coffee. He watched the butter melt on his freshly baked scone. He had plenty of things to do but no deadlines.

He luxuriated in tranquillity. After years of chasing the almighty dollar, he was at peace. His time was his own, 'the rest of the day to yourself' was the phrase that came to mind.

***

Sean rang the doorbell at the presbytery and joined Fr Flanagan at the dining room table. They talked over the opinions they had about the carving. Jonjo joined them after chatting to some of the other parishioners after Mass and explained his theory to the cleric.

"That idea about the universe forming and reforming has a long history," replied Fr Flanagan. "The Hindus believe that time is not a straight line but eternal cycles. Universes being created, existing and 'dying', followed by recreation. Existence and death, with no beginning and no end. This is mirrored in the belief in reincarnation. The Ancient Greeks had similar ideas."

"So we are in good company then," laughed Jonjo.

"There's nothing new under the Sun," lamented Sean.

"On the contrary, there is always something new to discover," answered Fr Flanagan. "I've been doing a lot of thinking about the tunnel. The hill that the tunnel runs under can be described as a hill fort. That has become a sort of 'catch-all' term for any ancient enclosed space. It doesn't necessarily mean it was for military defence. If it was for defence, the people wouldn't have spent all their time digging huge ditches and building a man-made hill. They would have set it at the top of the mountain."

"That makes sense," agreed Jonjo.

"So, what do you think it was all for?" asked Sean.

"I think it is all to do with the tunnels. I believe they were used for underground transport and for shelter. To me, it suggests they were protecting themselves from something," said Fr Flanagan.

"If it wasn't military reasons, then maybe protection from a natural disaster," suggested Sean.

"But not from a flood, otherwise up the mountain would be the answer," added Jonjo.

"The only thing to do is further investigation," said Fr Flanagan. "We'll have to get down there again."

***

Sean and Jonjo walked over to Clarke's bar for a pub lunch. They noticed Anthony Donlan taking off his glasses and flat cap and sitting in the seat Seamus Burke used.

"You know that's Seamus's seat," said Jonjo.

"Not when he's not here," answered Anthony logically.

"Yes, but anyone that sits there has to tell a joke," explained Jonjo.

"O.K., give me time to think. I'm always up for a challenge."

Sean and Jonjo ordered their food and took their pints to the table near Anthony.

Anthony began, "I interviewed Murphy for a job last week. I said, to him, 'First, we start with some psychological questions, is that O.K?'

'No,' he says. 'I hafn't got me bike with me.'

"That's O.K.," says I. "I'll say a word, you tell me what comes into your head.'

'Black.'

'Guinness.'

'White.'

'Guinness.'

'Let's change tack,' I said. 'Have you any ambitions?'

'I've always wanted to be an astronaut, like me Dad,' he said.

'I didn't know your dad was an astronaut,' I said.

'He wasn't, but he always wanted to be,' he answered.

'Where would you see yourself in 5 years?'

'That's easy', he says.'In a mirror.'

He got one right, though. I asked, 'Can you tell me two pronouns?'

'Who, me?' he said."

Anthony's tale not only got a laugh but also a round of applause from Jonjo and Sean.

The two friends made their way home. They looked at the hill with incredulity. It was so hard to believe that this was man-made. What had possessed those ancient people to dig those ditches and build this vast structure?

"Che Guevara," said Sean apropos of nothing.

"What about him?" asked Jonjo.

"Irish descent, his family were Lynches from

Galway. His dad said about him, 'the first thing to note is that in my son's veins flowed the blood of the Irish rebels.'"

"That's news to me," said Jonjo.

"It's amazing when you start looking at who has Irish blood," confirmed Sean.

They sat in Sean's orangery, sharing a bottle of his vintage wine. As the sun went down, the hill, drained of colour, took on an ominous look. Jonjo shivered and wondered if they should leave the secrets in the tunnel.

The first stars began to appear, and he realised it was part of their mission.

Chapter 23

Fr Flanagan smiled happily to himself as he drove out of town. Having taken up the exercises, Jonjo had recommended, the priest feeling the best he had in years. The busy main street gave way to quiet roads, with few houses, then to a patchwork of green fields. The sun was coming up over the mountain on this cold dawn. Frosty leaves sparkled in the late autumn light on the hillside.

Fr Flanagan, who was well versed in archaeology and knowledgeable about geology, studied the countryside. There was no doubting the beauty, but it was not as natural as it first appeared. The hill was an earthwork dug by ancient, long-forgotten people. Fields had been cultivated for countless generations. The land had been colonised for cattle and had forced people to scrape a living on hillside farms. Even the river had been diverted.

The priest parked at the end of the boreen. How could he fail to be happy as he crunched across the frozen brown leaves? He was looking forward to exploring the tunnels and meeting up with Jonjo and Sean, two men who had become his friends.

He had known Jonjo for many years and knew him to be the most positive of people. He was optimistic, generous and helpful. The return of his cousin from America had been a catalyst. The two of them had embarked on a series of walks that had turned into a crusade. A quiet, gentle crusade to improve the lives of the people in the town.

The latest fad in town that Sean had started was finding out famous people of Irish descent. Some words from a half-forgotten childhood rhyme came into the cleric's mind. It was about God selecting the chosen race, 'How could he fail to pick the Gael'.

"Over here, Father," called Jonjo. Fr Flanagan had asked both men to call him by his Christian name. Neither could manage it. It was just something that generation could not do.

Jonjo directed him to Sean's orangery, where they were having breakfast. Fr Flanagan was glad he had remembered to restrict himself to a cup of tea before setting off. He knew that he would have a full Irish breakfast with the two men. Jonjo was a stickler for hospitality, and indeed it had rubbed off on Sean too.

"Look at this Fr," said Sean. In a large pot in the corner was a seedling. "I've grown that from an orange pip. Jonjo told me that everything you plant is an investment in the future. When I first came here, I thought I had no future."

"An investment in the future, that's a profound statement, Jonjo," approved Fr Flanagan.

"Ara, it's easy to sound profound."

"You'll have to teach me. It might improve my homilies", laughed Fr Flanagan.

"Your homilies are grand," replied Jonjo. "We had one old priest, God rest him that did the same ones, on the same day, year after year. Still, he was working well beyond retirement age."

"Thanks," said Fr Flanagan. "But you've not told me how to sound profound."

"Sean knows how to do it," answered Jonjo.

"What you do is pick an abstract noun, for example, knowledge. Then you add something vague. For instance, knowledge is not a destination. It is a journey. Or, you can put two abstract nouns together, loyalty is born of maturity, intelligence is best accompanied by integrity. They don't mean anything, but they sound good, and people interpret them in their own way," answered Sean.

"Where did you learn that?" asked the priest.

"I made it up myself, I used to have to do a lot of public speaking, and it helped with sales pitches," replied Sean.

"Originality creates opportunity," laughed Fr Flanagan.

"See, you've picked it up straight away. The other one I used was repetition. Politicians use it all the time. It works well. It is amazing how easy it is to sway an audience even for a moderately good speaker like myself," added Sean modestly.

***

Jonjo led the way through the tunnel, for despite his age; he was the most sure-footed and had the keenest eyesight. At Fr Flanagan's insistence, they walked slowly, shining their torches at every nook and cranny. They followed the rope and twine that they had left in place since their last visit.

They continued to the divide in the tunnel. Sean shuddered at the memory of nearly plummeting into the abyss in the right-hand shaft. At the back of all the men's minds were the mysterious footsteps they had heard on that previous occasion.

They walked the whole way in silence, and despite their slow pace, they soon found themselves at the engravings on the wall. Fr Flanagan took more photos of these messages from the past.

Jonjo picked up the ball of twine they had left last time and continued to unravel it. The three men continued along the precisely cut stone tunnel, taking the utmost care. They checked for any cracks, holes or other potential dangers.

After possibly an hour of uneventful travel, Jonjo stopped abruptly. He indicated to the others, by cupping his hand behind his ear, that they should listen.

They all heard the unmistakable sound of running water. None of them spoke. They had adopted a silent mode without planning to. Maybe, the thought of an avalanche or the feeling that they were in somebody else's territory or a combination of both influenced their behaviour.

Jonjo pointed forward, then back an unspoken question. Sean and Fr Flanagan both said onward, and Jonjo put his thumb up, indicating agreement. Then he raised his index finger to suggest they stop for a break.

The three companions sat with their backs to the tunnel wall and drank from their flasks.

"What do you think?" asked Sean quietly.

"Probably an underground stream running parallel to the tunnel," whispered Fr Flanagan.

Jonjo nodded agreement and said quietly, "Will we walk on for another hour so?"

The three comrades continued, but not ten minutes had passed before they stopped in awe. The tunnel had widened out until it was about 60 feet wide. The dull, grey rock was replaced both, underfoot and above, by bright, white stone. The roof extended upwards in an arch of cathedral-like proportions. Natural light suffused the whole area.

Alongside the tunnel ran a canal of clear water. Steps of white stone thirty or forty feet long terraced down into the water. There were short white posts evidently for tying up boats. In the white stone were ruts clearly caused by wheels. The walls of the extended tunnel had the faded outlines of colourful frescoes. The canal disappeared into a tunnel with no path on either side.

"Well, that's the end of the walk for today," said Sean.

Fr Flanagan photographed everything in sight. He set down rulers and took photos of them. With Jonjo's help, the priest measured everything he could, including the distance between the ruts. Then he tipped out the contents of his water bottle and filled it from the canal.

"This is a major find," said Fr Flanagan excitedly as they returned.

The anticipation of the outward journey was replaced by excitement on the way back. Each man was replaying in his own mind what they had seen. As always, the return journey was much faster than the outward leg.

Sean picked out a couple of bottles from the cellar,

and the trio sat around the kitchen table.

"This is a major discovery," enthused Fr Flanagan. "That will rewrite history. There's nothing like this I've heard of in Europe. Underground tunnels for freshwater have been built for millennia, especially in arid countries, but for transport underground, this is unique. I'm sure there was nothing like this until the 17th century."

"Would you have a drink to celebrate Fr?" asked Sean.

"I would but, I'm driving," he replied. "And I'd really like to study the 'photos of those frescoes. Why don't you come with me? We can eat at the presbytery and have a drink then?"

***

In town, Sean and Jonjo took the water from the underground canal to the pharmacy, whilst the priest took the wine to the presbytery.

Paddy O'Donnell, a tall, imposing man with a Roman nose, took the bottle from them. When they explained it was for Fr Flanagan, he said he would test it himself. The shop was empty, and the chemist took out a water testing kit and dipped some paper into the water, checking the results against a colour chart.

Sean was looking at some bottles of multivitamins. "Don't bother with those," called Paddy. "They're from my, 'More money than sense range', they'll do you no harm but do you no good either. The water's fine, by the way. Tell Fr he can use it for his illegal distilling."

The chemist refused any payment, so Sean and Jonjo returned to the priest's house. He had made them ham and onion sandwiches and opened one of the bottles to let it breathe.

"While I was making the sandwiches, a thought occurred to me," began the cleric. "If we make our discovery known, it will cause you some upheaval. There will be lots of TV reporters and archaeologists, maybe filmmakers. It will be a big thing, and it will disturb your peace."

"That's a good point. I'd never thought of that," said Sean.

"What is your intention for your house when you die?" asked the cleric.

"I've left it to Jonjo. He's my only living relative,"

said Sean uncomfortably, as he hadn't told Jonjo. If he predeceases me, I've arranged for it to be sold and the proceeds, to go to various local charities."

"What about you, Jonjo?"

"Well, I've not made a will. I wasn't expecting an inheritance from Sean. I'm supposed to get one from my late Uncle Francis in America, too. Kind though it is, I'm happy with what I have, and I don't want them."

"You don't want to die intestate. That causes problems," advised Sean.

"That won't happen. I won't go to Testate," laughed Jonjo.

"How about this?"suggested the priest. "You both leave your properties to the town. You put in a proviso that the properties are developed for archaeological research and visitor facilities."

"It would bring some much-needed work to the town," agreed Jonjo.

"I agree," said Sean. "That canal has been there a long time. A few more years won't hurt."

The three men shared a bottle of wine and discussed their discoveries. Fr Flanagan sent the photos to Sean's phone, and they agreed to meet again to discuss their findings.

It was a brisk, bright day, so Jonjo and Sean set off to walk home.

"It's a shame we can't carry on with exploring the tunnel," said Sean.

Jonjo didn't reply because he was smiling at the new plan he had thought up. But maybe this one was a step too far.

Chapter 24

Sunlight filtered between the overhanging leaves highlighting their fallen yellow and brown brethren on the forest floor. The river whispered its way downstream, carrying more foliage. Some greenery chose a submarine path snaking along just under the surface, others surfing.

Roisin Burke squeezed her husband's hand. "You forget what a beautiful place we live in."

Seamus smiled back admiringly. Roisin's long auburn hair was streaked with grey. Her slim figure and face had hardly changed in the forty years they had spent together.

Half the town seemed to have got the bug for walking inspired by Jonjo and Sean. At first, Seamus had resisted this but now enjoyed it. His walks tended to end at the pub. Sometimes Roisin would join him other times, she would go shopping. They would walk home or take a trip in Micko's big, yellow American taxi. Depending on the weather.

"Look at this!" said Seamus, pointing.

Walking along the riverbank towards them were the familiar forms of Jonjo and Sean. Jonjo had something in his hand. As they got nearer, they could see he held a rope. The rope was attached to a boat in the river.

The four of them exchanged pleasantries, then Seamus laughed, "It's people like you give the Irish a bad name, taking a boat for a walk!"

"We are not taking it for a walk. Boats don't walk. They float," answered Sean.

"Taking it for a float ah well now it makes sense," grinned Seamus. "By the way, I believe Anthony Donlan stole my Murphy's interview story."

"He made a grand job of it so," replied Jonjo.

"He missed one of the best lines. The interviewer says,' If there were anyone, living or dead, you could have a meal with, who would you choose?'

Murphy thinks for a while and replies, 'I think the living one'."

Sean and Jonjo laughed along with Seamus, and even the long-suffering Roisin raised a smile.

Earlier that morning.

Drinking a strong, early morning coffee in Sean's orangery was becoming something of a custom. It kick started their day, ready for their exercises. The two men had moved Sean's exercise bike and Jonjo's weights into the garage. They had plenty of room now that Sean's car had become Micko's taxi.

The two friends savoured their Italian coffee whilst watching four coal tits. The birds fed at the garden bird table, their flight rapid and nervous, barely unfurling their wings.

"I thought we might just do a few light exercises," ventured Jonjo. "We could save our energy and try out the canoe on the pond."

"How do you plan to get it there?" asked Sean.

"I thought I'd get the big rope from your cellar, and we could pull the canoe."

"Come with me," said Sean.

He led Jonjo through the house and into the garage.

In the corner was a two-wheeled aluminium trolley.

"It's specially made for moving canoes," said Sean. "I got it because I thought you'd have the two of us breaking rocks to make wheels like the Flintstones."

"It looks great," enthused Jonjo.

They weren't confident enough to make their maiden voyage on fast-moving water. Instead, decided to float it down the river and launch it on the millpond. Balancing the vessel on the trolley was difficult at first. Once underway, the thick rubber wheels gripped well. The only difficulty they had was getting through the stone stile, where they had to lift the canoe separately from the wheels.

They pulled the canoe and trolley along with the long line they had previously used in their tunnel exploration. Jonjo called the rope his family heirloom. As the two took turns in pulling, Jonjo told its story.

"My Grandad fought in the First World War. He served on the frontline in France. He suffered from shell shock, and after a couple of years, he was given a new posting. He had to lead mule trains carrying ammunition to the front. The sergeant, another Irishman, showed him the ropes literally. They led the donkeys with really long lines through the mud. Now, these lines became heavy with the sludge. They became entangled in all sorts of things."

"Well, my Grandad was too caught up in his own mind reliving the horror of war and for weeks said nothing. One day after a particularly gruelling slog, he said to the sergeant,' Why don't you use a shorter rope?' The answer he received was, 'You'll see.'"

"Nothing changed for many weeks."

"One Autumn day slogging through the mud, my Grandad was blown off his feet by a massive explosion. Stunned, he lay on the ground at the edge of a crater. The mules and munitions had been blown off the face of the Earth by an enemy shell. Grandad was left holding the last 6 inches of the smouldering rope. His sergeant came over and mouthed the words because they were both temporarily deaf,' Now you see!' Despite the conditions, both fell into fits of laughter."

"Wow," said Sean. "That's an amazing story."

"They gave him a new rope, and somehow he managed to bring it back home. It has been here ever since," commented Jonjo.

By the time Jonjo had finished his tale, the two men

were at the riverside. They took the trolley right into the water and slid the boat off. It bobbed merrily on in the river.

"We should have had a proper launch, you know. We could have broken a bottle across the bows," said Sean.

"Well, this is only a test run. We can do that when we officially launch," replied Jonjo happily.

Having made sure they could pull the boat successfully, they loaded it with their rucksacks. Taking it in turns to guide the craft, they made their way downstream.

Waving farewell to the Burkes, they walked on. Sean kept having to come up with reasons why Jonjo shouldn't pay half towards the trolley. He said that because he hadn't consulted Jonjo about it, he had no responsibility. The fact that they were using Jonjo's tree for the boat was put forward. Jonjo would have none of this. He was stubborn and steadfast. Sean knew this was an argument he wouldn't win.

They reached the bridge and secured the boat to a tree. Sean went to Kerrigan's to buy two lifejackets, and Jonjo visited Bridie in the Rest Home.

***

Kerrigan's store was immaculate both inside and out.

"Ringo Starr," said Kerrigan to a puzzled Sean. "Irish descent from a Mayo family."

"Well, I knew the other 3 were of Irish extraction, so that's the complete set," replied Sean.

Sean bought the lifejackets, and his eyes were drawn to some plastic letters.

"I suppose I could glue these to the boat to make a name?" he inquired of the shopkeeper.

"Of course, do you know the driver bringing these dropped the box, and they all fell out."

"Did they?" replied Sean.

"Well, that's the word on the street," laughed Kerrigan. "You don't know how long I've been waiting to tell that one."

"Maybe you should have waited a little longer," replied Sean shaking his head.

***

Sean wore his lifejacket as he returned to the river. It was warm and comfortable and somehow strangely reassuring even on land. Jonjo was waiting for him at the canoe.

"Bridie was very tired. I didn't stay long. I told her about the canal, and she said something about an old quay on the river," informed Jonjo.

"We'll have to get the old maps out and check on that," responded Sean.

As they hauled the boat to the pond, Jonjo asked, "What did Kerrigan sell you apart from the lifejackets?"

"The lettering for the name and a splash cover for the canoe, he says that it will fit any size."

"You got away lightly," laughed Jonjo.

***

They manoeuvered the craft down the slipway, near the old Weir cottage, onto the millpond. Sean found it hard to keep his balance, and the canoe rocked as he took his seat. Jonjo managed to push the boat away from the edge and hop effortlessly into his seat at the front.

As Jonjo dipped his paddle into the water, Sean noticed a flash of light. Jonjo's arm tensed and he gave a small gasp.

"You O.K.?" asked Sean.

"Some sort of spasm in my arm. I'm fine."

Sean plunged in his oar, and the light flashed, and it felt as if a bolt of electricity had shot up his arm. "What's going on?" he asked.

They paddled the boat into the pond with ease. It felt as if the oars that Jonjo had carved were doing all the work. They handled the craft with expertise that belied their inexperience. They travelled at speed then slowed down with the paddles. They went forwards' backwards and in zig-zag lines. The craft responded to their every command.

Back on dry land, they tried to rationalise what had happened.

"We were getting some help there," said Sean.

"I've never been in a canoe before, but I felt like I knew just what to do. It seemed like the paddles were doing it themselves," responded Jonjo.

They had been planning to go back in Micko's taxi

with the canoe tied on the roof. The experience in the pond changed their minds, and soon the two friends were launching the craft at the other side of the bridge. They decided to travel back up the river against the current.

The trip upstream was not easy. Jonjo spotted the parts where the flow was at its slowest. The inside of bends in the river and downstream of rocks offered some respite from the current. They concentrated hard all the way, and even with the strange assistance from the paddles, both men were soon sweating profusely.

The return trip on the river had taken at least three times as long as the outward journey. They were delighted to get out and heave the boat up onto its trolley. They examined the paddles before putting them in the boat and wondered.

By the time they reached home, the friends were almost at the point of exhaustion. Jonjo spent a long time under the hot water in the shower, every muscle aching. He worried about how Sean was coping.

Jonjo was relieved to see his cousin had lit the chimenea and flames were licking up into the night sky. "How are you feeling?" called Jonjo.

"Absolutely terrible, you?"

"The same. I think we really overdid it this time. I'd been thinking of taking the canoe down the canal in the tunnel, but I think it might be too much," commented Jonjo.

"Two septuagenarians, taking a boat down an unexplored tunnel. What could possibly go wrong?" laughed Sean.

"I think we need a bit of a break from the tunnel. We've got off track in our search for the Vale of Mist."

"Agreed," said Sean. "Let's have a couple of days off, and then continue our search above ground."

"The canoe is great, though."

"Sure is," said Sean.

They shared a bottle of Sean's vintage wine. Warmed by the fire and the drink, they retired to the homes with heavy limbs and light hearts.

Chapter 25

Spirits soaring, Jonjo raked the leaves off the lawn into the flower bed. The green and brown provided a lovely background for the colourful cyclamen. The musty sweetness of the autumn air filled his lungs; the beauty of the countryside filled his eyes. A gentle breeze whispered through the trees, occasionally disturbed by squabbling starlings. A hint of turf smoke drifted in from afar.

Sean and Jonjo had recovered from their adventures in the canoe but were not yet ready for a long walk. Putting his rake back into the shed, Jonjo walked up to his cousin's house, and the pair sat on the garden bench waiting for Micko's taxi.

"Fine day," ventured Jonjo.

"Shall we walk to the end of the boreen to save

Micko the trouble?" asked Sean.

They arrived at the same time as the big yellow taxi. The two men were surprised. Micko, usually attired in a jumper and jeans, wore instead, a shirt and tie and sported trendy sunglasses. Most surprising of all was that he was clean-shaven.

"I can't remember the last time I saw you without your beard," commented Jonjo.

"True. I've been hiding my fine, looks for a good while," laughed Micko.

"Well, you're looking smart. That's for sure," answered Jonjo.

"Alicia said that it shows respect to the customers in the taxi," continued Micko.

"That's a good point," confirmed Sean. "But who is Alicia?"

"Sure, it's Widow Farrell's first name," supplied Micko.

The three men all fitted in the long front bench seat in the taxi. On the journey to town, Micko told them of recent developments with the taxi business in which Sean had invested both his car and money.

He said that when he was looking at paperwork with

Alicia, she had noticed that he was screwing up his eyes. On her advice, he had an eye test and discovered that he was short-sighted but had exceptional long-distance vision. The optician also recommended polarised glasses for night driving and for protection against damaging sun rays.

Alicia had sorted out the paperwork and reorganised Micko's haphazard booking system.

"How's Sonny doing with the car cleaning?" inquired Sean.

"Fine, he cleaned and polished this himself," replied Micko. "It took him a while to get going, but there's no stopping him now. When I'm out working, Alicia and Sonny have been cleaning my house too. She made me laugh. She said to Sonny, 'the ideas not to transfer all the dirt onto your overalls'."

"You and Alicia are getting on well," observed Sean.

"Truth is, I was a bit wary of her at first. One day she had popped out to the cafe when Sonny and me were washing the car. So the two of us were having a bit of a water fight while she was gone, squirting each other with old washing up liquid bottles. Throwing buckets having a rare old time. Well, she walked back in and saw the two of us full of suds. I thought she would go mad, but she started laughing. She laughed until she cried. Poor old Sonny didn't know what to make of it. Then she turned the cold hose on us straight in the face and ran into the office before we could get her back."

Jonjo and Sean laughed at the tale. The idea of the austere widow soaking the men was hilarious. The fact that Sonny, who had severe learning difficulties, was enjoying life warmed their hearts.

Micko continued, "She's had some ideas for the business and asked if she could speak to you two today."

"Well, I've a busy day ahead," laughed Jonjo. "I've my horses to study, my bets to put on. But I think I could find the time so."

"I'll clear my diary," affirmed Sean smiling.

Arriving at Micko's house, they discovered that the front room was now an office. A table to the side of the window had a desktop computer, a phone and an anglepoise lamp. A comfortable-looking, well-worn leather club chair added a touch of class. On the wall to the right was a large map of the local area with concentric circles, marking price boundaries. A smaller map of the whole of Ireland was pinned next to it. On the wall to the left was a whiteboard. The board had two columns, one for messages and the other for words that made Jonjo smile. The list had the local names for places next to the official ones.

The most extraordinary change was the Widow Farrell. She wore brightly coloured clothes and a little make-up, which enhanced her natural beauty. Her smile was radiant as she welcomed the men in. She was a different person from the troubled soul they had first met.

"Would you make us all a nice cup of coffee, Sonny?" she asked.

As he walked through to the kitchen, she explained that Sonny hadn't quite got the hang of tea yet. Micko went out on another job, and Alicia explained her plan. She wanted to buy a half share in the business, and on the days Sonny was at college, help out with the driving. She had other ideas of buying and renovating cars as well as a car valeting service.

Sean could see that her plans were well thought out but asked for time to consider it. Alicia went on to extol the virtues of Micko and how well he got on with

Sonny.

"Two big kids together," laughed Sean.

"Do you know I think Micko has a genuine affection for him? He really looks out for him," replied Alicia.

"Micko and me going to pub one day," interjected Sonny.

"We'll see," said Alicia.

"You know, Sonny," said Jonjo. "Some people at the pub might say nasty things. Now you are a big man like Mr Walsh and me and Micko. You mustn't hurt them."

Sonny nodded, "Not push people too strong, Mammy says."

Jonjo continued, "Only push people if they hurt you."

"Or hurt Mammy?" asked Sonny.

"Or hurt Mammy," agreed Jonjo.

"Sometimes I get mad," said Sonny.

"Me too," said Jonjo. "But I have a trick that stops me."

Jonjo got out his old brown leather wallet.

"When I feel mad, I rub this wallet, and the madness goes away."

"Is it magic?" asked Sonny.

"It is, and now it's yours," said Jonjo. "A working man needs somewhere to keep his wages."

Jonjo left a 5 euro note in it for Sonny and was about to slide out the small photo of his wife when Sonny saw it.

"Is she an angel?" asked Sonny innocently.

"Yes, she is," answered Jonjo. "She always looked after me. Now she can look after you too."

Sonny walked off happily with his gift.

Alicia had tears in her eyes as she said farewell. "That was a lovely thing to do."

***

The two friends walked up to the main street.

"What do you think of her plans?" asked Jonjo.

"They look fine. Very little outlay or overheads, and I've more than enough to bail them out if they got into trouble. I just wanted to check with Micko. Lovely though Alicia is, she is a strong woman. I'm worried she'd boss Micko about," replied Sean.

"Maybe he wants to be bossed?" ventured Jonjo. "Have you not seen the way they looked at each other?"

"Well, the tough old farmer and sports star is just a soft-centred romantic," laughed Sean.

"True, but don't you be telling anybody," laughed Jonjo shaking his big fist at his friend.

They went their separate ways in the town, Jonjo to the bookies and Sean to the presbytery.

The usual crowd in the bookies welcomed Jonjo. He settled on a stool near the high desk and looked through the form. There was a pleasant hubbub of conversation among the men as they discussed the day's racing. The big screens showed live events from courses around the world. Jonjo wrote out his bets in his neat, careful handwriting.

Liam Casey, behind the counter, took his money and said, "One of my regular punters rang up today. He said, 'My wife's leaving me and taking the children. She says I'm obsessed with horse racing. I can see her now she's at the gate, and they're off.'"

Jonjo laughed, "You had me believing you for a minute there, Liam."

***

At the presbytery, Fr Flanagan had a set of large documents on the table.

"These are the photos from the tunnel. I've had them enhanced, enlarged and printed. Mike Holleran did them for me. He's a bit of an expert at this sort of thing," began Fr Flanagan.

"I know him. That slim fellow who is always flying about on a bike," replied Sean.

"That's him, Mike the Bike. What do you make of these?"

The reproduction of the frescoes had certainly enhanced them. The sharpest images were of a sword and a spear. Next to them were depictions of a stone and a cauldron. These wouldn't have been easily identifiable had Sean not known what to expect. These altogether were known as the four magical treasures of the Tuatha de Danann.

"I can see the four treasures," answered Sean. "The other bits are hard to identify. Maybe maps or a pictorial story, a volcano, stars, a big wheel I'm just guessing, nothing that looks like writing."

"It definitely warrants more study. I have copies of

them for you and Jonjo," said the cleric.

Sean told the priest about their adventures on the river. He then showed him an old map with a small rectangle marked on the bank just downstream from where they had first launched their canoe. A short line was drawn next to the oblong angled away from the river.

"I think," mused Sean. "This is the old quay that Bridie spoke of. Watch this," he continued.

Taking out a ruler and pencil from his bag, he continued the line on the map. It went directly under the hill fort, passing to the left of Sean's house. Getting out the next, chart, he continued at the same angle and the line intersected with the river again past the town centre.

"I think you have found the route of the underground canal. Well done!" exclaimed Fr Flanagan. "Do you know a strange idea occurred to me the other day? You two have had some strange experiences: in the churchyard, the apparition on the mountain and the canoe adventures."

"Don't forget what we saw and heard in the tunnel," added Sean.

"If I were a betting man, I'd wager that tunnel comes out southeast, facing the winter solstice," said the priest.

At that moment in walked a betting man. "Will we go to Molly's cafe for lunch?"

"Yes," replied Sean. "Fr Flanagan has a strange idea he wants to tell us about."

Chapter 26

The sun and the southerly wind had brought out many of the townspeople. Jonjo loved the music of a busy street. Somehow it gave him energy.

The gentle breeze murmured a pleasant melody. Gusts through the bare trees and over the rooftops raised both volume and pitch. Squeaking doors and shop bells added to the mix. Buffeting awnings supplied a soothing beat, with the lyrics coming from the shoppers.

Sean loved being a pedestrian again after so many years in the U.S.A., where everybody drove everywhere. The Irish had their own way of parking too. Treating road signs as suggestions, more than requirements.

Cars double-parked, blocking others in. Nobody seemed to get annoyed. People here had time, time to talk, time to listen, time for each other. More and more, he felt at home.

The main street was full of colour. Houses and shops painted blue, green, yellow, vibrant colours. He remembered this road as rainy, grey and dark in his childhood. The country had come of age exuberant and confident in its own identity.

Fr Flanagan stopped and talked with almost everybody, he was their shepherd. He didn't like that analogy. He didn't think of them as his flock. Each one made in the image of God was more than a herd animal. He thought of beautiful newborn lambs, free spirits running and jumping joyfully. Then the grown sheep, docile, and conditioned. Maybe that's what happened to everyone if they weren't careful.

As they approached Molly's cafe, the smell of baking and coffee reached them.

"It's mild enough to sit outside," suggested the priest. "It reminds me of Spain, cafe culture in Ireland in December, who would believe it?"

"Global warming?" queried Sean.

"An old priest told me that the Earth is getting warmer because Hell is getting bigger," smiled the cleric.

"Well, whatever it is, the Earth will still be here no matter what man does to it," assured Jonjo.

Molly came out to take their order and tried to encourage them to sit inside.

"No, we'll not be cluttering up the place. We are fine here," said Jonjo.

"She's frightened she'll miss a bit of gossip," laughed Sean.

"What's the strange idea you were telling Sean about?" asked Jonjo as he drank from his big mug of tea.

"It's a bit fanciful perhaps, but I wondered if you two could be descendants of the Tuatha de Danann?" queried the priest.

"A bit like the 'Last of the Mohicans'?" chuckled Sean.

"Well, maybe not the last. If the Tuatha de Danaan created the canal and earthwork, it stands to reason that they lived here. You two seem to have some connection with them. That could explain some of the strange things you've seen."

"You're probably right, Fr," confirmed Jonjo. "But

there's no way of knowing."

"I thought we could do a simple experiment. The next time you are in the canoe, I'll try one of the paddles. If it doesn't have the same effect on me, then that would tell us something."

Seamus Burke and the men from the bookies arrived, "Sure, I'm not surprised Mollie makes you three eat outside," he laughed.

"Take a seat, Seamus," said Fr Flanagan "I have a story for ye."

"Not one of your parables. I've heard too many and understood less."

"I was conducting a funeral once in Dublin. The feller was a big man in business. He'd made a fortune. There was much talk of how he was mean and had been a real taskmaster. He had no family, and there didn't seem to be much grieving. I was glad to see someone go up to his coffin and whisper a prayer. I asked him what he had said. The man replied, 'I said to him, 'Who's thinking outside the box NOW?' Not you.'"

"Good man, Father," laughed Seamus." I'll be telling that myself," he continued as he joined his friends in the cafe.

The three companions returned along the colourful main street to the presbytery.

"I just wanted to show you something else on the map," said Sean. "Where I've drawn the line of the canal, it crossed two tumuluses."

"Tumuli," corrected Fr Flanagan.

"Well, so what are they?" asked Jonjo.

"They are artificial hills usually associated with prehistoric tombs," explained the priest.

"I remember. We used to call them the Divil's Humps when we were kids," recalled Jonjo. "Will we walk down to the river and see where the canal starts it's not far?"

The hypnotic murmur of the river was so different from the hubbub of the town. For a while, a cheeky robin hopped along with the three men before losing interest. Reaching the point where they thought the canal started, they found nothing. Lining up with the tumuli, they tried again.

Jonjo, steadied by a grip of Sean's hand, walked carefully down the bank. He stepped back and forth on the gravel at the river's edge, his boots in the shallow water. There was still nothing to be seen until they started to pull him back up.

"Stop, look!" commanded Jonjo.

Almost obscured by the overhanging bank was a large, upright rectangular stone firmly lodged in the river bed. Leaning over precariously, Fr Flanagan and Sean could see it. They hauled Jonjo back up and heard a cheer go up from the bridge downstream. They were unaware that a small crowd had been watching their antics.

"Bifurcation!" exclaimed Fr Flanagan.

"Steady on Father," smiled Sean.

"As you know, that means splitting something into two. I'd guess that the stone is the first of a row leading the water into the canal. The river has probably moved course over the centuries. The stones may have been in the middle of the river when put in place millennia ago," speculated Fr Flanagan.

There was a mixture of cheers and boos as the men got back to the bridge. The crowd was mainly the crew from the bookies with a few children hanging about.

"It's the Three Wise Men," somebody called.

"What's going on?" demanded Jonjo.

"Paddy Regan, the local guard said happily, "I'm moving them on illegal street betting."

"Come off it, Paddy," said Jim Cullen. "You had 2 Euro on Jonjo."

Seamus explained that he had started a book on who would fall in first. Sean had been most popular until Jonjo had climbed down the banking, then he'd moved to odds on favourite.

"Well, sorry to disappoint you," laughed Sean. "You'll have to give the money back."

"There's still the other bet on what ye were doing," said Seamus. "The odds were; 3-1 Fr. Flanagan baptising Sean, 4-1 baptising Jonjo, 10-1 Jonjo or Sean walking on water, 100-1 Fr Flanagan turning the water into porter."

"No luck, boys," said Fr Flanagan. "We were looking for prehistoric remains."

"And sure, they were standing by you all the time," laughed Seamus pointing at Jonjo and Sean.

"I'd be baptising you, with my hurley right now, Seamus Burke, if I had it with me," shouted Jonjo, feigning anger.

Children standing by all joined in the general

laughter, then the crowd dispersed the majority to the pub and the rest to the shops. The three friends went back to the presbytery. They had a cup of tea, fortified with a drop of the cratur, to warm themselves up.

"Well, we know where the canal flows. What we don't know is what it was for," began Sean.

"If anybody does, Fr Flanagan does," affirmed Jonjo.

"Thanks," smiled the cleric. "One of the best tools of the archaeologist is empathy. You put yourself in the place of the people who dug it. Why did they want water diverting? The more I think about the location, the more I think they were preparing for something. I think they were stocking up on things. The fresco of the volcano might be significant maybe they came from a place that had suffered from an eruption. If we study the frescoes and the history, I'm sure we will come up with a solution."

***

"It's Bob Hope and Bing Crosby," called Seamus cheekily as the two men entered the pub.

"Well, that makes you, Dorothy Lamour," replied Jonjo

"Don't trip over your skirt on 'The Road to the Bar'," added Sean.

When the laughter died down, Seamus returned to one of his tales. "I was walking past Murphy's in the summer. His donkey was fast asleep on the lawn. The poor cratur had no shoes on it.

I said, ' That animal has no shoes on!'

'Sure, he's not got up yet,' answered Murphy.

Murphy had an overcoat and a jacket on and was lathered with sweat painting his wall.

'It's boiling. Why are you so dressed up?' I asked.

Pointing at the paint tin, he said, 'You must put two coats on it tells you right there.'"

***

Jonjo and Sean stayed only for a couple of pints and, as there was still daylight left, decided to walk home. They talked about Fr Flanagan's theories and the strange occurrences. As they crossed the damp fields, both began to regret their decision to walk. Their escapades in the canoe had taken even more out of them than they had realised.

The two men walked in silence. They were moving at a snail's pace, and the daylight became gloomier. Eventually, the hollow came into view, and an eerie mist rolled across the fields to meet them there.

Instantly the two had renewed energy. "The Vale of Mist?" asked Sean.

"I think so," agreed Jonjo. "I don't think we got the full dose, though."

"Me too, just enough to get us home, I think."

***

After having their evening meals in their respective homes, the two men sat at Sean's chimenea. The external warmth from the blazing logs and the internal heat supplied by Jonjo's poteen created a feeling of wellbeing. They recapped the events of the day and the strange quest they had found themselves on.

"There must be something significant under the hill," said Sean.

"We seem to have been chosen to find out," agreed

Jonjo.

"Much as it scares me, I feel drawn to the canal under the hill fort," answered Sean.

"Do you ever look at this?" asked Jonjo, pointing at the night sky. "And think there is something we are missing. I'm not talking about God or the universe. I can't explain it, but I feel there is something more."

"Do you mean a scientific explanation of everything?"

"No, something beyond science. I think there is something that is beyond our brains to understand. There is an answer, but I can't even think up the question. It's like that feeling when you can't remember something from a dream. It's like having something on the tip of your tongue, but it's on the tip of your brain. It's frustrating."

"I think I get what you mean. It is a feeling of incompleteness, searching for something, but you don't know what that something is, "replied Sean. "Maybe the answer is in that tunnel."

"Well, let's not think of going down there this side of Christmas," said Jonjo.

"A job for the New Year, God willing," added Sean.

"Amen to that," agreed Jonjo.

Chapter 27

The distinctive clip-clop of hooves blew in on the wind.

Jonjo lifted his nose skyward and inhaled the air. "Can you smell it, Sean?" he called.

"What?"

"Christmas, Christmas in the air," he answered gleefully.

"You are just a big kid," laughed Sean.

"Do you remember when we were altar boys? I loved the Church in Advent. The lead-up to Christmas, lighting a new candle each week."

"It was better than Easter. It was so sad, and Good Friday was a praying marathon. Every Station of the Cross, the story got worse," answered Sean.

"I know what you mean. The nun's convinced us

that we were personally responsible for Jesus' death. Still, it was always great on Easter Sunday," agreed Jonjo.

The clopping of hooves got louder, then became more muffled. A pony and trap emerged from the end of the boreen.

"Is it yourself?" asked Jonjo.

"It is," answered Mangan.

Jonjo held the pony's bridle as Mangan climbed down from the trap. The horse rubbed its muzzle into Jonjo's big hand. Animals always instinctively trusted him. He fetched the creature a bucket of water, then said to Mangan. "I've not seen you about lately."

"I've been staying with my daughter in Westport. I've come to thank you and Sean for getting the pony and trap out of my house. The shock of what happened set me on the right road. I've not touched a drop since."

"Well, you're looking well so," confirmed Jonjo.

"Too well," said Mangan. "I used to be a bag of bones. Now, look at the size of me."

"Well, it's my lucky day," said Sean. "I've just emptied my wardrobe of clothes that are too big for me. I didn't know what to do with them."

"I've not come looking for charity," said Mangan.

"It's not charity. You'd be doing me a favour," countered Sean.

"He's right," confirmed Jonjo. "I've got some of his clothes. They are top quality. It would be a sin to throw them away. I'll get you a cup of tay and a bacon sandwich while Sean fetches them."

Mangan told them of his time in Westport. His daughter had looked after him in her guest house. He dried out from the alcohol and took to riding around the area in his pony and trap. This led to him giving lifts to Croagh Patrick and beyond. He started an unofficial taxi service and made good money from the tourists. Somebody reported him to the council, and they explained that he needed a licence.

Mangan was only too aware that he was taking up a room that his daughter and son-in-law should have rented out. Though they never said anything to him, he felt he was outstaying his welcome and returned home.

"Well, thanks for everything," said Mangan. "If you ever need a lift, just let me know."

"That's given me an idea," said Sean. He heaved the

suitcase full of clothes up onto the seat of the trap. "Keep the case. I do not need it. Would you like a bit of work driving the trap?"

"That I would!"

"I can't promise anything. I'd have to check with the council," said Sean.

Jonjo started singing, 'The Jarvey* was a Leprechaun'. A song made famous by Val Doonican. Sean and Mangan joined in.

"I'm sure you'll do fine as a jarvey, but way too big for a leprechaun," laughed Jonjo.

Mangan tipped his hat and drove off whistling.

***

"Come and see what I found. It has been blocking a hole at the back of the shed for years," said Jonjo

At first, it looked like a pile of sticks joined at odd angles, but then, Sean gasped as he recognised it.

"It's the sledge my Da made for me!" exclaimed Sean. "He carved the runners from a fallen tree. I remember him burning holes for the screws with a white-hot poker."

"Did you ever have a go on it?" queried Jonjo

"No, it didn't snow that year and then we were off to the States."

"We'll get it fixed good as new," enthused Jonjo.

"I could display it in the house as a tribute to my Dad."

"That would be grand," agreed Jonjo. "But we'd have to test drive it first if we get any snow."

"O.K.", laughed Sean. "But don't be carving any patterns in it. We wouldn't want it taking off with us like the canoe."

"Sure. I've learned my lesson on that."

The two friends spent the rest of the day working outside, putting the sledge back together. They worked slowly, taking care appreciating the work that had gone into it. They sanded each piece by hand and varnished it. Some of the slats were cracked, so they made new ones.

Jonjo had a fire burning in the old metal brazier so they could get some warmth. He heated the poker, and Sean burned through the wood.

"No need for a drill," he laughed.

They hung the sledge from a rafter in the shed to let

the varnish dry. Sean brought up a bottle from his wine cellar, and Jonjo replenished the fire.

"What do you think of an early start tomorrow?" asked Jonjo. "We could walk down to the dock on the river."

"To check the alignment with the winter solstice?"

"Exactly."

***

So it was that the two men walked out that morning, Jonjo, torch in hand leading the way. The air was damp and chilling. The water gurgled quietly, the lifeblood of the planet circulating in the river. Neither man spoke inspired to silence by Nature itself.

Jonjo shone his torch at the spot where the dock was on the map. A whiteness among the green of the bank was just visible.

"It looks like the rock in the tunnel," whispered Sean.

Getting closer, they could see water joining the river near the white stone. The two men settled down on the banking, waiting for the sunrise. Jonjo took out the flask from his khaki haversack, and they drank a strong cup of tea.

Shortly after eight o'clock, mist began to roll up from the river. A deep red tinge spread through the clouds over the distant mountains. Then a pink shade appeared. The first yellow-ray of the sun lit the water shining directly onto the white stone, illuminating the course of the long-hidden tributary.

A dull clunk echoed down the watercourse, followed by the gentlest humming sound. Something had sprung to life under the hill fort. The river began to bubble softly as more water streamed into the tributary.

"Look!" gasped Sean.

The mist coming up the river separated into wraith-like figures. They moved in single file, drifting along, drawn by an invisible force toward the hillfort. Silently they moved, and silently, the two men watched. The sunlight became vivid orange, lighting first the sky then the land.

Jonjo and Sean got to their feet, not without difficulty. Completely transfixed by what they had seen, the two had barely moved a muscle while they were sitting. Circulation returning to their frozen limbs, they walked homeward. Again they strode, unspeaking, each trying to process what they had seen.

Back in Sean's kitchen, coffees in hand, they began to talk.

"I think I should write down what we saw, and you check it," began Sean. "Otherwise, we might think we imagined it."

Jonjo read over the account, nodding as he did so. "That's just right, but I still don't know what we saw. It wasn't just mist. All the shapes were identical. They were like a column of soldiers."

Sean said, "This is something we should keep to ourselves. They'll say we're a few fries short of a Happy Meal."

"If that's the same as 'not the full shilling' you are right. Though we can trust Fr Flanagan and Bridie with the story," replied Jonjo.

The two men went to Sean's garage to do their exercises in their homemade gym. Neither spoke, both preoccupied with what they had seen, trying to make sense of it all.

***

Putting another coat of varnish on the repaired sledge, the two men spoke of their Christmas plans. They had several kind invitations to Christmas dinner from; the nuns at the Rest Home (including Mass with Fr Flanagan); Mollie Keane and her family (above the cafe); the Clarke family (upstairs at the bar); Widow Farrell and Sonny (with Micko at the Big House) and surprisingly from Seamus Burke.

"So, is Clarke's bar open on Christmas Day?" asked Sean.

"No, of course not," said Jonjo. "But you can still go in to buy a drink, so."

Sean smiled at the reply. It was an answer that made complete sense in Ireland, but probably in few other places.

"I was thinking," began Sean. "That we should invite Mangan here for Christmas Day. It will be hard for him on his own, especially as he is on the wagon."

"That's a grand idea. We'd have to stay off the booze while he was here too."

"We'll have no trouble making up for that after," laughed Sean.

"It'll save upsetting anyone that's invited us. They'll

understand what we have done. It is a kind and generous thought," added Jonjo.

***

<u>*Christmas Day Morning.*</u>

The most special morning of all had arrived. The years had not diminished Jonjo's love of this day. He had his morning meal on his own, finishing by eight a.m., making sure he had well over an hour's fast before Holy Communion. Then up to Sean's house, he walked, breathing in the Christmas magic.

The two men exchanged Christmas greetings and presents. Sean opened his first. It was an exquisitely bound volume of Irish Folk Tales. The pages were gilt-edged with a silk ribbon bookmark. The inscription from Jonjo read:

To Sean, a kind, generous man who I am proud to call my friend.

The adventures continue...

Sean mumbled his thanks, clearly moved and passed an envelope to Jonjo. Opening it, he was surprised to see a photograph of a racehorse.

He read the description of the three-year-old gelding, which came from excellent breeding stock.

"Now, before you get annoyed at me," warned Sean. "It only cost 50 Euro. It is a one-off payment that entitles you to one 3000th share in the horse for one year. But you get weekly reports from the trainer and the chance to tour the stables."

"That's wonderful. I've always dreamed of owning a horse. It'll train to go over hurdles and maybe go chasing one day," said Sean excitedly.

The two men sat on the pony and trap. Mangan, clean and tidy resplendent in his new clothes, set off heading into what would be the most memorable Christmas.

* Jarvey: the driver of a hackney coach or of a jaunting car.

Chapter 28

The view from the pony and trap took Jonjo's mind back in time. He was 10 years old again, holding on to the big rope atop a cart full of hay. It began as a sad memory of loss but soon switched to happier thoughts of a time gone by.

The pony's thick coat and mane protected it in this winter weather. Its strength came from a broad chest and powerful legs. Steam came from its mouth, and it trotted happily, ears back and relaxed.

The rhythm of its hooves was answered by an echo once they reached the town. Sean joined Jonjo at Mass because it was Christmas Day.

The sight of the tree and the crib made Sean's mind too wander back. He remembered setting up the little crib at home with his mother. On no account could the

Baby Jesus join the other figures until Christmas Day. Sean remembered playing with the Infant, getting him to look through the window of the crib. Once, he tried to balance him on the back of the donkey, but suddenly felt very guilty this was a step too far.

Fr Flanagan, resplendent in his white vestments, spoke well. Sean joined in the prayers and hymns with enthusiasm. He waited in his pew after the service while Jonjo took the collection plate into the sacristy.

By the time Jonjo emerged, the church was empty. They walked to the door surprised to find the whole congregation had dispersed.

"They must all be rushing home for Christmas presents," said Jonjo disappointedly.

Presently the sound of the hooves greeted them, and they hopped on board. They made their way down the main street, which was extremely quiet. On reaching the junction, Mangan turned the pony off the road onto the grass track.

"Taking the scenic route?" inquired Sean.

"This time of year, a lot of the fellers will be drinking. They'll be letting their wives drive, 'tis safer off the roads," answered Mangan.

Sean and Jonjo laughed, neither sure if Mangan was joking.

The journey home was pleasant as they looked at the path they had trodden many times. Going through the Hollow, they felt the wheels dip into the ruts worn by previous generations. The pony's ears shot up. He whinnied and tossed his head.

"Easy boy, easy Arkle," soothed Mangan. "'Tis the little people, he senses them."

As they approached their homes, Sean asked, "Can you hear that?"

Jonjo nodded. The sweet sound of a choir reached their ears. "Thank God," continued Sean. "I thought that my number was up."

"That's no heavenly choir. I can hear Seamus Burke's rumbling voice," laughed Jonjo.

Sean's chimenea and Jonjo's brazier were burning brightly. Around them were the choir and half of the townsfolk singing 'In The Bleak Midwinter', Jonjo's favourite. As the people caught sight of the pony and trap, a great cheer rang out.

Sean and Jonjo were bemused.

Fr Flanagan stepped forward to explain. "These

good folk have got together to thank you for everything the two of you have done for this town."

Sister Frances stepped forward and presented them with a Christmas pudding. "God Bless you for your help at the Rest Home."

Mollie Keane, not to be outdone, gave them a Christmas cake. "Thank you for the ideas for my business and bringing in extra customers."

"To my loyal deputies who solved the mystery of the ghost in the churchyard," began Regan. He gave them a small card. "That's a 'Get Out of Jail Free Card.'"

"Is that genuine?" queried Sean.

"Of course, it's from my Monopoly set," he laughed. "I took it out years ago because I didn't want my kids to think there was such a thing."

"Will it work, though?" laughed Jonjo.

"Let's hope we don't need to find out," replied the policeman.

Roisin Burke stepped forward. "Thanks, Jonjo and Sean, you two have been a great example to the men of the town. You have encouraged them to get out walking in the countryside, showing them there's more to life than the pub and the bookies."

There were some mock jeers at this point.

"I'm sorry about that, gentlemen," apologised Jonjo, grinning.

Then came Tommy Clarke and his son with a keg of beer. "The ceilidh you organised after the Mass on the hill really gave my business a boost. Also, the other idea you came up with worked a treat."

"I hope you've got nothing for us," laughed Jonjo looking at Callaly, the undertaker.

"Not today," he replied genially. "None of the rest of you go dying either I'm wanting a week off. There's Paddy O'Donnell don't be going in his shop for a bit I get most of my customers from him. His motto is, 'We dispense with care'."

There was general laughter at this good-natured banter.

The pharmacist was up to the task and responded. "Callaly's motto is 'You can trust us, but we'll let you down in the end'"

That one took a little while for the joke to click, and again there was more laughter.

Various other people came forward with their stories and contributions. Jonjo noticed that Sean had gone into his house with Alicia and Sonny Farrell along with Micko.

Fr Flanagan reminded everyone of the special Mass on the hill. Also, the new monument to the famine victims in the churchyard. He gave a blessing to the crowd and looked across to Jonjo.

Sean had re-emerged from the house, and along with Jonjo, thanked everyone. Finally, Jonjo said, "We are in for heavy snow before dark, so make sure you get yourselves snug in your home."

"There's a bottle here for every family," said Sean.

The two friends distributed the fine wine with help from Sonny and Micko.

"I'll be off because there's a pub that doesn't need opening because it's Christmas Day," said Tommy Clarke, winking at Guard Regan.

"And sure, I'll check the pubs locked up at the front," confirmed the guard. "The back door is the family house which is beyond my jurisdiction but go steady. I don't want to be called out to any raucous behaviour."

The crowd dispersed the magic of the day firmly in their hearts.

Jonjo brought out the big rope to tether Arkle but give him the run of the field. Mangan went into the house to get warm. Sean, Micko and the Farrells went into the garage, where Sean gave Micko some snow chains for the taxi.

When Jonjo came back, Alicia thanked him and Sean. "I couldn't say anything when everyone was around, but I'd like to thank you from the bottom of my heart. You two have changed everything for me and given me a chance for happiness that I thought had gone."

Jonjo looked cautiously at Micko.

Correctly interpreting Jonjo's look, she continued. "I've told Micko everything." She then welled up with tears and gave each of the old men a peck on the cheek.

"Ara musha," answered Jonjo.

All visitors having departed, Jonjo, Sean and Mangan settled down to their Christmas dinner. They chatted about the great turnout of people that had taken Sean and Jonjo aback.

"I don't know whose idea it was," claimed Mangan. "But it was Fr Flanagan who told me to slow you down on the way back from church."

***

After finishing the Christmas pudding, the three men sat on the comfortable armchairs. Mangan produced a bottle of poteen. "The last one I made and the last I will make," he stated as he opened the bottle.

"Will it not bother you, us having a drink and you on the wagon?" asked Sean.

"No, I'm a new man, and I'll never go back to the old ways."

"Here's to that," said Jonjo and clinked glasses with Sean.

"Slainte," added Mangan, joining the toast with his coffee cup. "This coffee's as good as a drink. I don't know how you do it."

"I'll show you later. I've a spare cafetiere that you can have," said Sean agreeably.

"That's good of you, and thanks to you two, I've got my licence as a jarvey for your taxi business.

"Well, you'll be working for Micko. We don't get involved in the running of it," replied Sean.

"I looked at the contract from the council. It says that Arkle has to have three days a week off, but me, I can work every day," laughed Mangan.

***

Jonjo told Mangan what had been happening in town while he was away. Sean related some of the adventures that he and Jonjo had been involved in. Mangan was intrigued by the stories about the river.

"My Dad told me there was an underground stream. He used it to make his poteen, he said that it was special water, made by the little people. It was so good, the UISCE BEATHA, the water of life, that it was a sin to distil it. Not that it stopped him," said Mangan.

"Where is the stream?" asked Sean.

"It ran under all the wells down from here to the lough," he replied.

"That's interesting. Some of those are Holy Wells. My well has always had its own distinctive taste," offered Jonjo.

***

When Mangan had departed, Sean and Jonjo fired

up the chimenea watching the last of the daylight disappear. They kept the barrel of ale at the other side of the patio away from heat. Dinner digested, they sat happily with their pints and poteen chasers.

The snow fell, as soft as sleep, big lazy flakes that would settle and stay.

Not a theatre in the world could compete with the show Mother Nature presented for them. They clinked their glasses, feeling like the luckiest men alive.

Chapter 29

He relished the physical effort of digging in the cold. His nose was streaming, and his breath was steaming. A real winter's day, he loved it. Yesterday the choir sang 'In the Deep Midwinter'. Today was more of a 'deep and crisp and even' day. Jonjo whistled 'Good King Wenceslas', as he worked.

Jonjo shovelled the embers from the fire and put the ashes on the step. He continued to make a narrow path in the snow. He tipped out the brazier too and extended the track. His snow shovel was already leaning against the shed. He'd had the foresight to get it out the previous day. It had spent many redundant years at the back of the hut. He used it to dig the snow from the shed door. Not without difficulty managed to open it.

He continued the path, banking up the snow on

either side. The footprints of small birds out foraging decorated the white. The deeper, distinctive arrow shape of a heron's prints disappeared towards the pond.

Sean was out on his patio. Adopting Jonjo's idea, he tipped out the contents of the chimenea. He made a path to join up with Jonjo's but using only a hand shovel made slow progress. The two met, and Sean asked, "Do you want a cup of coffee?"

"I'm after having a cup of tea. Ara, go on, I will."

It took a second or two for Sean to decipher that reply. 'After having' meant 'I've had' and, Sean had been out of Ireland long enough to forget. Translated Jonjo, was saying,' No thanks I've had a cup of tea, but I've changed my mind and will have a coffee'.

Sitting on the patio, Sean said, "We had a skinful last night."

"We did and all but, I'm right as rain today, we should still be ossified."

"Do you remember going down to the well and bringing back a bucket of water?" asked Sean.

Jonjo had a vaguely embarrassing memory of walking back from the well singing, 'Jack and Jill went up the hill.'

"I do. I'd come up with a theory about the water, not that I can remember it now."

"You insisted that we both drank two pints of water before we turned in and that it would save us from a hangover. It certainly worked."

"I hope I wasn't blathering on too much," said Jonjo.

"If you were, I didn't notice I was as bad as you."

"It's lucky we'd had all that food onboard. Otherwise, we could have been ill," answered Jonjo.

"Well, there's no fool like an old fool but, I wouldn't have missed that view of the snow coming down."

"True, it was a wondrous sight. I remember watching it coming down so much I felt I was going up. Though that might have been the poteen," laughed Jonjo.

"Still no harm done. We live to fight another day."

"Christmas comes but once a year,"

"Good job," answered Sean. "How were you so sure it was going to snow?"

"Well, on Christmas Eve, there were haloes around the moon with clouds chasing. That's always a sign of rain or snow and, the temperature was around freezing.

We had a hot summer that's usually balanced with a cold winter. I think we'll have a cold winter, the flowers have blossomed long into the winter, and they are growing long stems to keep their heads up."

The two men surveyed the view. The whole countryside was clothed in snow. Featherweight snow balancing on the thinnest of branches heavyweight snow banked up in drifts. The distant mountains and nearby hills uniformly still and white.

It was as if God was saying stop and look at the very least slow down. This is my work. Take time to admire it. This is your life, don't rush through, don't fast forward and miss the best bits. The pristine snow, cleansing and purifying like the rainbow, renewed the promise of old.

***

St Stephen's Day was sometimes an anti-climax after the big day, not this year. Down in the town, excitement was everywhere. Parents and grandparents had been pestered to find sledges put away since the last 'Big Snow'.

Kerrigan was having his best day at the store for ages. He'd sold his entire stock of wellies, even the multi-coloured ones he'd had for years. All his sledges had gone straight away, and people were coming up with more inventive ways of sliding. Every one of his big plastic containers had been sold lids for adults and boxes for little ones. One or two people had come for snow shovels. A gang of kids came begging for empty cardboard boxes.

"Don't come running to me when you've broken your legs," laughed the shopkeeper.

The town was alive with children slipping, sliding and snowballing. Some of the children were trying out their new bikes but finding it impossible in the deep snow.

There was a holiday atmosphere, and even the oldest in town were drawn in. Remembering praying, that snow would settle. Then singing, "Allay allay aster snow, snow faster." They might just get a day off school.

***

If anyone had been foolhardy enough to drive out of town, they would have spotted two dark specks against the snow. As they drew closer, they would have seen two children taking turns on a sledge down the hillside. On closer inspection, they would have seen the figures were far too large to be children. It was fortunate nobody was on the road because they would have been distracted by two old men sledging. The pair, both well stricken in years, were whooping and shouting as they went on ever steeper runs.

"Will we take your sledge for its maiden run?" Jonjo had asked.

Sean was about to make some excuse but changed his mind, "I think it's a case of now or never."

Jonjo took the snow shovel, and they walked up to the top field near the road. Sean pulled the sledge at first, but it was slow in the deep snow, so he carried it underarm.

Jonjo scraped a path in the snow taking off the top layers of the softest stuff. Sean sitting on the sledge at the top of the run began to get nervous. "How do I stop this thing?"

"Hold on to the string. Use your body to change

direction. Turn the sledge into the deep snow, and it will stop," replied Jonjo.

"I'll go flying off."

"It's soft snow. What's the worst that can happen?"

"I could end up with some life-threatening injury. Emergency services unable to reach me with you telling me tales about hurley tactics my final memories of this life," joked Sean.

"It could be the other way around. Me lying here in agony while you explain the intricacy of arbitrage trading and the Dow Jones index. Me praying for blessed release," replied Jonjo.

Despite falling off, the first tentative slide by Sean caused no injuries. The two were encouraged and increased the length and steepness of the course. Using the snow shovel, they extended the track to lead into a gentle curve. This meant they could slow and stop without falling off.

The track became icier and slippier, and the speed increased. Jonjo tried going headfirst but couldn't negotiate the bend. He ploughed straight into the deep snow the sledge came to an abrupt halt. Momentum carried Jonjo across the snow for another few yards. He could barely get up for laughing, which of course, set Sean off. The two men had a good few minutes of uncontrollable laughter.

It was only exhaustion that made them stop. The friends returned home tired but exhilarated,

"Will we keep the sledge in the garage?" said Jonjo."It'll save me having to dig it out from the shed."

"No need for exercise today," laughed Sean looking at their homemade gym in the garage.

The landline was ringing. It was Seamus Burke, "Is Jonjo there?"

"He is so. I'll call him," replied Sean.

"No, it's only a message. Will you tell Jonjo that Liam Casey is snowed in, so the bookies won't be open? The Irish racing is off, but they are racing in England."

"He'll be disappointed there's some big race today, isn't there?" asked Sean.

"He can watch it on the telly. He could bet online if he had a smartphone," replied Seamus.

"He hasn't, but I have. How do you do it?"

Seamus explained, and it sounded straightforward. "Thanks for ringing," said Sean.

"I didn't want him walking all the way down here. You two would be best staying out of that snow."

"Good advice," replied Sean thinking if only he knew.

"You know Murphy was in the cafe the other day. He said to Molly,' That coffee is grand.' She said,' It is all the way from Italy.' He says, 'And sure it's still warm,'" concluded Seamus.

***

Sean found the online betting site on his laptop. The screen, more suitable for his old eyes than the phone. He opened the account in his own name as it was easier. It took him a long time to convince Jonjo to use the account. Jonjo even insisted on giving Sean money in cash that he had deposited.

Once Jonjo looked at the site and the ease with which he could place bets, he was amazed. "This is great," he said. "It is so easy. Maybe too easy it doesn't feel like real money."

"Will we watch them on T.V.," asked Sean. "I know you are not so keen on television."

"Sure, I've nothing against television. I think it is more for old people or those who are not so well."

"You don't think you are old then."

"Not while I can still get about and can still dig. Look at the pair of us this morning. We're not old yet. Maybe, the time will come, and I'll watch it. The racing is a different matter though I watch it at the bookies."

"So, will we watch it?"

"Of course, do you remember at school, they told us that television was the work of the devil? I remember thinking, well, bad fellow that he is; he must be clever inventing television. Not that I knew anybody that had a set."

Sean laughed at the recollection.

"Two things, though," continued Jonjo. "Have a bet yourself on the racing. It's like having an alcohol free beer, otherwise not much fun."

"What's the other thing?"

"Come outside and look."

Jonjo brushed the snow off the patio bench. He helped Sean up on it; the two men stood looking down the hill.

"What are we looking at?" asked Sean.

Jonjo pointed, at regular intervals, a fair distance apart, plumes of mist were rising up.

"I think I know what it is," said Jonjo excitedly. "The Vale of Mist, I know what it is."

Chapter 30

The two stood back, looking at the wall. The left-hand side was devoted to maps and aerial photographs. In the middle were the blown-up images of the frescoes from the tunnel. The right hand had a whiteboard with a series of jottings.

The table in front of the wall piled high with books and internet printouts. Sean's P.C. sat amongst the books; two chairs were pushed up to the table. The garage, which served as their gym, was now also the incident room. Inspired by T.V. detective series, Sean had collated all the information into one place.

***

A couple of days had passed since their adventures

on the sledge. Jonjo had enjoyed watching the racing that day. He was astounded at the clarity of the picture on Sean's large television. Sean had become involved too. He was as much taken with the mathematics of the betting as with the racing itself.

The day after the sledging Jonjo, found that his words about not being old had come back to bite him. His whole body ached, and he could barely move his legs. A long hot shower followed by applying embrocation got him mobile again. He stepped out stiffly, moving like a rusted robot.

The view outside was uplifting. The snow had come down heavily again overnight. The countryside had been flattened out, ditches had disappeared, field walls invisible.

"Earth stood hard as iron,

Water like a stone;

Snow had fallen, snow on snow,

Snow on snow."

The words came to Jonjo, but there was nothing bleak about this midwinter. The weak sun was magnified by reflection in the whiteness. It was as if he had woken up in a new world, bright as a midsummer day.

He put homemade food on the bird table. It was made from lard mixed with porridge oats. The high-fat content was ideal for the creatures at this time of year. Jonjo cleared the snow from his bench. Sitting on his plastic mac drank deeply from his pint mug of tea. Throwing some seed onto the snow, he was rewarded by a chirpy robin landing near him.

Looking across the countryside, he felt content. He believed that he had begun to understand the secret of the Vale of Mist. More pieces of the puzzle were falling into place, and now he felt confident to share his theory with Sean.

Jonjo felt the chill from the ground. Although the sun was shining, it was not strong enough to affect the mass of snow. He saw Sean opening the orangery door but not stepping onto the patio. Jonjo made his way carefully and painfully up the path until he was in hailing distance.

"How are ye feeling?" called Jonjo.

"My head is fine. The rest of me is lagging behind," laughed Sean. "I feel like I've been run over by a snowplough. What about you?"

"I can barely move. It was worth it for that fun on the sledge. I think."

"What sort of day is it?" asked Sean, unable or unwilling to step out.

"It'd be warm if it wasn't cold."

Sean somehow understood this enigmatic reply.

"Will we start our detective work tomorrow?" asked Sean.

Jonjo nodded in agreement.

***

So it was that the friends with coffees in hand sat in the warm garage. Jonjo got to his feet and began to sketch on the whiteboard.

"Do you remember the walk we did to the lough? The one you planned past the wells," asked Jonjo.

"Sure, it was midsummer's day."

"Well, this is a rough sketch of the route. Look your house, my house, the hollow and the track of the old watercourse. These dots are the wells and springs."

"Yes, I can see they are in a straight line," answered Sean.

"When I pointed out that mist coming up, just before we watched the racing, I think it was coming from those springs and wells. I think the water in the tunnel is what makes the Vale of Mist."

"So you mean it flows from there underground to the lough?"

"Some to the lough, and some to the river. I think it comes out as a mist because it is warmed in the tunnel. When we were there last week, we heard that noise from the tunnel."

"Of course, the morning of the winter solstice," agreed Sean.

"I don't know how, but I think the angle of the sun at the solstice set going a machine in the tunnel. Maybe that device underground does something to the water."

"Don't you remember we had the water tested, and it was O.K.?"

"Yes, the test just ruled out anything harmful being in it. If there is something beneficial, it could account for the Vale of Mist. There are lots of tales about the healing properties of the Holy Well, too," added Jonjo.

"You are definitely on to something," enthused Sean. "Are you still thinking it is the work of the Tuatha de Danann?"

"I'd say they're favourites."

"Odds on,"

"No, more like 6-4," laughed Jonjo.

"This is great. Now, all we have to do is prove it," said Sean pointing at the pile of books and maps.

***

The two friends spent the rest of the morning searching for information. Jonjo, with his reading glasses somehow incongruous on his rugged face, and Sean, looking every inch the scholar. They worked methodically, making notes. Sean regularly refilled their coffee cups in the American fashion.

They sat in the main house talking as they ate their lunch and filled in details.

Jonjo began, "I've been looking at the mythical treasures of the Tuatha de Danann. The 'COIRE ANSIC' was a cauldron that never ran out. It was owned by Dagda. He could control life and death. He was the god of the weather and crops, as well as time and the seasons."

"How do you think that fits in?" queried Sean.

"Well, whatever that machine is, it produces this beneficial water. If it is still doing it now, that qualifies as never running out. The control of time and seasons fits with the use of the solstice sun. Controlling the water supply that's clearly the work of a god of crops. It all fits."

"I've been looking at the frescoes from the tunnel," contributed Sean. "Particularly, the one that looks like a wheel. It is circular in the centre, but it has what look like stones hanging around it. I think it is some sort of waterwheel but unbalanced with the weights around it."

"What do you think it is?"

"I checked on the computer, and this is the nearest I can find."

Sean showed him a black and white illustration that he had printed off.

"This is a picture from a 16th-century engraving of a perpetual motion machine," continued Sean. "It says in the article that perpetual motion is impossible because it breaks the laws of physics."

"Well, we've found a lot out, said Jonjo. "But I've had enough bookwork for the day."

"Me too, but I've a bit of archaeology for us to do." Carrying his shovel, he led Jonjo onto the patio. "This is the dig," he laughed. Sean dug through the snow until he uncovered the cask of ale that Tommy Clarke had given them. "I hope this is still fit to drink," said Sean.

"There's only one way to find out," smiled Jonjo.

***

The two friends looked at the beautiful view from the orangery. They basked in the magnified sunshine. The ale had kept well, insulated by the snow against the worst of the frost. Enjoying their first drink since Christmas Day, the two friends relaxed in the warmth. And both dozed for a while.

"What do you make of these ancient Irish gods?" asked Sean.

"Something Fr Flanagan said rang true," he replied. "He said that there have been all sorts of civilisations in the past. There are lots we don't know about them and their technologies. The knowledge has come down to us in stories and myths."

"True, look at the pyramids in Egypt. Nobody can

really explain how they were built. Technologies get lost. The Romans had central heating, but it was lost for centuries, the same with the use of concrete," added Sean.

Jonjo fetched another couple of pints. The conversation generally turned to ghost stories or jokes when they'd had a few. Feeling pleasantly relaxed, Jonjo said, "Did you know Murphy has been in court for bank robbery. The judge said, 'You have been found not guilty.' Murphy said. 'Great, does that mean I can keep the money?'"

Not to be outdone, Sean countered with. "When Murphy got home, Paddy said to him, 'I'm going to get a labrador.' 'Don't do that. Have you seen how many of their owners go blind?'"

"Not bad," laughed Jonjo. "Well, Paddy said to Murphy, 'look at this in the paper, three cliff walkers have fallen to their death.' 'Unbelievable,' says Murphy. 'They all had the same name.'"

The two continued in the same vein until the light began to go down. Jonjo returned home and spent the evening listening to the radio and studying the racing form. There were good cards tomorrow in England and

Wales including, the Welsh Grand National.

As Jonjo settled down to sleep later that night, a thought sprang unbidden into his head. He knew what they needed to do next on their quest.

Chapter 31

The sky was as blue as a robin's egg. Sean sat in the orangery, looking out at the bright winter day. He had that pleasant buzz of contentment from completing his morning workout.

Sipping his fresh orange, he listened to the sound of an engine. The roads were passable in both senses of the word. But the fields were still deep with snow. The noise grew louder, confirming his suspicion that it was Micko in the taxi. The only person who would drive down the boreen in these conditions.

The car drew to a halt, sliding briefly on the snow. Alicia Farrell beckoned him to join them while Sonny and Micko carried bags into Jonjo's. As Sean stepped gingerly along the makeshift path, ashes and salt crackled beneath his feet.

They had brought groceries from town for the two men. Jonjo insisted on paying straight away while insisting there had been no need. He pointed out that he and Sean were quite capable of looking after themselves.

"We are not old fellers yet," he insisted.

"Whist," said Alicia gently. "Nobody's saying you are old. We've been to a few other outlying houses. Only the taxi with the snow chains has been able to take to the roads."

Jonjo's cottage had the lovely sweet smell of peat and fresh wood fire.

Bacon and fried bread smoking in the pan were as warm as Jonjo's hospitality. They did the traditional dance of being offered tea, refusing it, knowing they would be given it anyway. They had to stand firm about being given breakfast, insisting they had already eaten. Jonjo eventually reluctantly relented, letting them get away with just tea and biscuits.

Crowded into the cottage, they discussed the days that had passed since Christmas. Sean was pleased to note that Sonny was joining in with the conversation. He seemed settled and confident in their company.

Jonjo told them about their adventures on the snowy hill.

In no time, they had retrieved the sledge from the garage. The depression in the snow was still visible, and Jonjo uncovered the track they had made. The three visitors all had their turns on the sledge, Alicia slid along fearlessly and elegantly. Sonny was more circumspect but hooted with excitement as he picked up speed.

Micko went for the headfirst approach with the same outcome as Jonjo the previous week. He flew over the top of the sledge, his head ploughing a furrow in the snow. Staggering to his feet, he had a wide grin on his face and a pile of snow on his head.

Alicia laughed, "Everyone warned me you were headstrong."

"You couldn't call me a hothead today," he replied, shaking the snow off.

Even though Sonny didn't understand the wordplay, he caught the mood and laughed loud and long. His laughter encouraged the others, and all five were soon helpless with mirth.

"Come on, it's your turn," said Micko looking at the

older men.

"It's no good getting older if you don't get wiser," responded Jonjo, shaking his head.

"You kids enjoy yourselves," called Sean as the friends returned to his house.

***

Back in the garage, Jonjo pointed to the diagram on the whiteboard.

"Remember when Fr Flanagan suggested we try the canoe with somebody else, paddling?" asked Jonjo.

"Yes, to test his theory that we are descendants of the Tuatha de Danann."

"Well, how about here?" said Jonjo, indicating the point where they thought the underground river entered the lough.

"Sure, we could check if the river comes out there."

"Maybe Micko and Alicia could try the canoe," suggested Jonjo.

"We would have to tell them what it is all about."

"We can trust them. After all, it was Micko who discovered the tunnel," replied Jonjo.

"Do you know, I'd almost forgotten that?"

"We will have to wait for better weather, but I think we could strap the canoe on the taxi roof to get it down there," suggested Jonjo.

***

The two men went into the kitchen and prepared a great pile of ham and onion sandwiches. They let a pan of soup simmer on the stove and watched the fun outside.

Alicia was the first to come in from the cold. Her cheeks were rosy red, and her eyes were laughing as she said, "They were picking on me, teaming up in the snowball fight."

The three of them settled down to the soup.

"It's lovely to see how well they get on," she continued, looking out on Micko and Sonny. "Micko never talks down to him. He just seems to have an instinct."

"Is Sonny's talking getting better?" asked Sean. "He seems to be using complete sentences sometimes."

"Yes, that's well spotted. Sonny has made more

improvements recently. I think it's having someone else to talk to. He loves Micko."

"What about you? How are you and Micko getting on?" asked Jonjo.

"I love him too. I mean, I really love him."

"How does Micko feel?" asked Sean.

"I'm sure it is mutual, but Micko finds it hard to talk about things like that," replied Alicia.

"I can understand that he didn't have the best upbringing," mused Jonjo.

"I want to take things to the next stage," said Alicia. Noticing Jonjo's discomfort, she continued, "By that, I mean engagement and marriage. I'm not sure how I can get Micko to move things on."

"Well, I think we can help with that," assured Jonjo.

"Well, be subtle, don't scare him off," warned Alicia.

The two men came back in, and silence reigned as they made short work of the soup and sandwiches.

Back in the garage, Sean stood at the wall explaining all about the tunnel and the discoveries they had made.

"It's a good job you didn't go any further down there, Micko. There is a huge hole. Jonjo saved me from falling in it. It still scares me when I think about it," said Sean.

"So you two want to find out as much about it as you can. Then you will leave your properties to the town so that it can become an archaeological site," summarised Alicia.

"That's right, so we don't want anyone else knowing about it for now," responded Sean.

"You might want to look at the books at my place. There are lots of local history works. There are even some handwritten records of local stories, myths and legends and so on," added Alicia.

"There was a movement in the 19th Century for collecting folk tales," confirmed Sean.

***

Meanwhile, Jonjo and Sonny washed the pots in the kitchen.

"Micko take me to the pub one day," said Sonny hopefully, as the others returned from the garage.

"I've an idea there," said Sean. "We have a barrel of beer here. Maybe Sonny could have a drink with us, as a sort of practice."

"A pub school that's a novel idea," laughed Alicia. "It's not bad though, we could see how Sonny takes to a drink. Would you like that, Sonny?"

The grin on Sonny's face was an answer in itself.

"The taxi's booked later. I'll do, the trip and you four men can have a drink in peace. Call me when you are ready for a lift," said Alicia. "Look after him."

"I will, Mammy," said Sonny.

This made them all laugh apart from a bemused Sonny.

"You walk your Mammy to the car," said Jonjo." We'll get the pub ready."

When they departed, Jonjo immediately said, "Micko, Alicia wants you to ask her to marry her. What do you think?"

"Very subtle," scoffed Sean.

"I want to marry her, but I wasn't sure that... with her being so posh and me being ...," hesitated Micko.

"Sure, she's just waiting for you to ask," assured Jonjo.

"I don't know how to go about it," Micko said.

"All you need is a ring and a romantic occasion," offered Sean.

"Don't worry, we'll help you out," encouraged Jonjo.

***

Sonny came back in, and they spent a pleasant couple of hours drinking and chatting. Sonny pulled a face at his first taste of beer but then began to enjoy it. They got Sonny to practise ordering and paying for drinks and taught him the idea of buying rounds. They gave him sage advice on not drinking too much.

They told a few jokes. Micko came up with the tale of Murphy at the bar.

"Well, look at that feller on TV. I'll bet you 10 euros he doesn't jump off that bridge," said Murphy

"You're on said the barman."

The man jumped. The barman didn't take the money and said, "I've already seen that it was on the 6 o'clock news."

"I saw it too," said Murphy. "But I didn't think he'd do it again."

Sonny laughed along with the others, but it was clear he didn't follow the jokes. He tried making up his own jokes using the rhythm of the language that the others used. His jokes made no sense but were all the funnier for their absurdity. It was a fine line between laughing with him and laughing at him, so they decided to teach him an easy joke.

After some practice, he perfected the line. "I was going to make a nasty face at Murphy, but I realised he already had one."

Sonny was delighted with himself. Alicia turned up in the taxi and listened to Sonny tell the joke. She laughed at it and gave her big boy a hug.

Sean and Jonjo insisted on giving the sledge to Sonny, who didn't seem any the worse for wear. His big frame clearly could cope with the drink.

"You look as happy as a dog with two tails," said Jonjo to him.

This really tickled Sonny, who kept repeating the phrase. They could still see him mouthing the words as the taxi drew away.

***

"One for the road?" asked Sean.

Back in the orangery, Jonjo said, "We should be able

to get back walking soon."

"I'll be glad to get back to the search for the Vale of Mist. Now we know where the water comes from, we have a better chance," mused Sean.

"I still can't work out whether the mist is a result of a people with superior technology or whether it is supernatural," queried Jonjo.

"We've had so many inexplicable experiences I think it is supernatural."

"Maybe so. We definitely have some path set out for us. Is it fate, or do we have a say in things?" asked Jonjo. "I suppose people have been asking about this from time immemorial."

"I've been having that same thought that you told me about. Somehow we are on the verge of something, finding something important. It is just out of reach."

"God willing, we'll find out," said Jonjo as he walked the slippery slope home.

Chapter 32

"To appreciate the beauty of a snowflake, it is necessary to stand out in the cold."

- ARISTOTLE

Stepping out into the fresh air of a cold, bright morning, the two men were in their element. The snow had almost disappeared, but the ground was hard and icy underfoot. The weather had prevented them from any long-distance hikes, but now they were underway.

"We've been hibernating in Hibernia," laughed Sean.

Jonjo had cut them each a wooden walking stick for the journey. He carried his trusty khaki haversack and was well wrapped up. He had one scarf around his neck and mouth and another around his waist. He had a firm belief in keeping his kidneys warm. He also sported a pair of sunglasses. These at first felt strange, but he had to admit they were practical. They kept the cold from making his blue eyes water and prevented him from having to squint in the icy glare.

Sean's big backpack was bulging. He carried books and bottles along with his packed lunch. He wore the latest outdoor walking gear, yet it was no fashion statement. The long hikes with Jonjo and their fitness routines had transformed him. He strode along like a soldier on a route march, keeping pace with Jonjo's long loping stride.

"I can't believe I used to be exhausted by the time I reached here," said Sean, as they settled for their break at the hollow.

"Well, you used a lot of air for talking then," replied Jonjo.

"I was a real blatherskite," acknowledged Sean.

Jonjo drank his tea from the flask. He said, "I don't think we can find the Vale of Mist. I think it will find us."

"I guess we'll stumble upon it one way or another when the time is right. At least we now have an understanding of what it is."

As they walked on, they continued their discussion about the Tuatha de Danann. All the way, they admired the frosted grass. The bare limbs of the trees with even the tiniest twig encased in ice crystals. The ice mimicking and extending each branch. Puddles had become mirrors, some cracked and crazed.

As they crossed the river, the sun highlighted the remaining chunks of ice in the water. The white clouds and blue sky reflected in the current were framed by the snowy banks. They looked upstream at the point where the river had been partly diverted all those centuries ago. Both were glad of the chance to rest before the last uphill stage to the Farrell's house.

The air had begun to warm up, and the gentlest breeze followed the course of the river. Birdsong floated downwind and with it a feeling of peace and calm. The weather seemed to tell them to slow down, and they finished their walk at a sedate pace. Reaching the stone shelter and gate, Jonjo pointed out some very early daffodils in the grass at the other side of the road.

***

Alicia Farrell made them welcome. She insisted on serving them a full Irish breakfast before they even looked in the library.

"Sonny is at work," she said. "That's something I thought I'd never say. It's thanks to you two."

The two men responded, but neither answer was discernible as both were too busy with their food.

"Nothing like a good long walk for building an appetite," approved Jonjo.

"And it stops you feeling guilty about putting on the pounds," agreed Sean. "I've got to say you are looking very trim, Alicia."

"Nice of you to say," she smiled. Here in her own home, she was comfortable in a pair of jeans and a jumper. Her hair was longer, and she appeared much younger than when they had first visited her.

Sean gave her a couple of books from his own collection and two bottles of his vintage wine. The two men declined the offer of a drink, explaining that they were meeting Fr Flanagan later. Alicia led them through to the library.

Even Sean, who was no stranger to book collections, was staggered. The high ceilinged room was full of books. Sean counted 10 shelves high on all four walls of this rectangular room. There were two windows, one standard height and one recessed at ceiling height.

The window recess revealed the thickness of the walls, which Jonjo estimated as at least two feet. The wooden floor had a rug in the middle. Pushed up to one side was a library ladder. It was an antique version of the one Sean had in his home. Half of one of the bottom shelves held catalogue drawers, identical to those in public libraries.

There was a pleasant odour of polish, the floor gleamed, and the whole place had been freshly dusted. The room, though still had a hint of the smell of musty books that delighted Sean.

"All Sonny's good work," explained Alicia. "He loves cleaning. The books I told you about are here."

She opened an old, brown leather briefcase and took out four volumes. Three were 19th-century pamphlets of collected local stories and songs. The fourth was much older, a handwritten work on parchment. Sean opened it carefully, looking at the Latin script.

"One for Fr Flanagan," said Sean. "Do you have any other local history books?"

"I can't be sure, but you are welcome to look. Those four were in the bag already," answered Alicia.

"Sure, we've plenty to be going on with there," replied Jonjo.

"How are you doing getting Micko to pop the question to me?" asked Alicia.

"Don't ye be worrying, as the poet said, 'In the spring young man's fancy lightly turns to thoughts of love' " replied Jonjo.

***

After paying their respects at the cemetery, the two men met Fr Flanagan in the presbytery. He was intrigued by the books and fascinated by their stories and theories. Deeply involved in the men's quest, they trusted his views.

"What do you think of the wraiths we saw? Are they good or evil?" asked Jonjo directly.

"I can't answer that," said the cleric. "But I can tell you that I believe you saw them. There are so many things in the world that we can't perceive normally. Lots of animals can see a much broader spectrum of light than us. Dogs can hear sounds that are inaudible to us."

"How did we see them, you know the wraith or the spirits?" asked Sean.

"The ancients believed that everything vibrates. Things that appear solid, such as rock vibrate. Humans vibrate at a higher frequency. This has been proved by science Einstein, said, 'Everything in life is a vibration.' It's funny how science always catches up with ancient beliefs," smiled the priest.

"I'm sorry, I don't really understand that," said Jonjo hesitantly.

"We'll do an experiment. Close your eyes and listen. Focus your hearing on the nearest sound and then the furthest sound you can hear," said Fr Flanagan.

The two men did as they were asked. After a minute, Fr Flanagan asked, "What was the nearest sound?"

"My heart beating," answered Jonjo. Sean concurred with a nod.

"That's one of your body's vibrations. What was the furthest sound?"

"An aeroplane in the distance," offered Sean.

"O.K. How did that sound get to you?" asked the

priest.

"Well, it travelled from the 'plane through the air," replied Sean.

"But then it came through the wall and the window by making them vibrate. Even though you couldn't see those vibrations, your ear picked them up," replied Fr Flanagan.

"It's astonishing when you put it like that," said Jonjo.

"I believe that there are other beings on Earth that we can't see because they are at a different frequency to us. I think the winter solstice helped you to see them. Maybe they are at a lower frequency then, and they come into our range. I don't know. Maybe that's why ancient people spent so much time and effort with their stone circles. I can't pretend I know the answers," concluded Fr Flanagan.

"It's given us food for thought," confirmed Sean.

Looking at the manuscript, Fr Flanagan said, "It's time to get the old Latin to English dictionary out."

***

"Clarke's bar?" queried Sean.

"Definitely, I need a drink. The ghostie house followed by a discussion of invisible beings...." shuddered Jonjo.

"'Tis the two Musketeers," called Seamus looking at their sticks. "Ye two been fencing?"

"No wonder your cows keep escaping if you use sticks like these for fencing," replied Jonjo.

"Quick, I'll give you that," laughed Seamus.

They settled in for the drinks, and Seamus continued, "Paddy and Mick went on their first aeroplane flight.

'Do you think if this plane went upside down, we would fall out?' asked Paddy.

'No, we'd still be friends.'"

This drew a groan from the pub.

"Well," continued Seamus. "Once the flight had taken off, the pilot announced:

'Ladies and Gentleman, this is your Captain welcome to flight 33 from Knock to Alicante. The weather ahead is good, so we should have a smooth, uneventful flight, so sit back, relax and... OH, MY GOD!'

A scream then silence followed....

Some moments later, the captain came back on the intercom.

'Ladies and gentlemen, I am sorry if I scared you. While I was talking to you, a flight attendant accidentally spilled a cup of hot coffee in my lap. You should see the front of my pants!'

'Jaysus, you should see the back of mine,' shouted Paddy."

This joke went well, and Seamus smiled smugly. After a couple of pints, Jonjo and Sean set off on their walk home. The two men made good time across the hard ground.

With the hollow just in sight, a strange event occurred. The temperature plummeted and all colour drained from the day. As if a colour television had become black and white all around were different shades of grey.

Surrounding them. The greyness pushed in. The two men were being squashed and squeezed by a mysterious force. Breathing was difficult, and what little they drew in wasn't air. Sean looked at Jonjo, his face reflecting his own feeling of both terror and pain. Then the greyness assumed the pallid, insubstantial terrifying form of wraiths.

Chapter 33

Sean felt the life force leaving him, then he heard a shout. Jonjo had raised his arm and was lashing about with his stick. The stick was singing as he swung it about so swiftly that it was virtually invisible. Sean joined in and began hacking away at the shapes in front of him.

Between them, they created a gap in the surrounding mass of wraiths. Once the space was created, it was as if an electrical circuit had been broken. The creatures instantly disappeared, and Jonjo and Sean were released from the pressure on their bodies. Colour returned to the black and white world.

The two friends marched swiftly towards the hollow. Their brains abuzz with adrenalin, the pair did not stop until they reached home. Jonjo threw a couple of turfs on the embers. They had not spoken a word since the frightening encounter. As the fire began to take hold, they pulled their chairs closer to the flames.

Jonjo poured them both a large whiskey. Sean noticed that his old friend's hands were shaking. He then realised he, too, was trembling. The fear, the exercise, the cold and the adrenalin had combined. He felt out of control.

"Take deep, slow breaths," advised Jonjo.

The external heat of the fire and the internal warmth of the drink began to take effect. It was still some time before the men could reflect upon what had happened.

"I'm going to write it down on the computer," began Sean. "I'll show it to you, and then send a copy to Fr Flanagan."

"We best not tell anyone else they will think we've lost our marbles," replied Jonjo. "Leave your stick. I want to do a bit of work on it. Give me a couple of hours."

Jonjo assembled the materials from his shed and began. Working with his hands always eased his mind. First of all, he whittled all the bark off the sticks. Then he dug a shallow pit in the hard ground and filled it with embers. He rotated the pieces of wood in turn over the heat to dry them out. Jonjo sorted through his old hurley gear and found a couple of grips that would do the job.

Gluing the grips to the sticks, he gave them time to dry. Meanwhile, he cut through some old copper pipe. He shaped the ends so that they fit snugly into the copper. He glued the sticks into the copper and hammered the metal tight. He carved into them the symbols they had discovered in the tunnel. Finally, he coated them both with creosote.

***

Sean, meanwhile, had written up the encounter and prepared a meal. It was one of his favourites, pork pie, mushy peas, and mint sauce. When he had been overweight, this type of food had played havoc with his digestion, but now he could eat it again untroubled. If someone had told him that being fit meant you could eat what you really like, he would have got fit long ago. Jonjo liked it too, with the addition of English mustard to the pork pie.

They sat down to the meal before looking over Sean's account.

"You have a way with words, to be sure," confirmed Jonjo. "That is, exactly, what happened."

Sean sent it to Fr Flanagan, who rang almost straight away.

"Are you two, O.K.?" he inquired.

"Yes," replied Sean. "A bit shaken up, though."

"I'm not surprised. I guess this answers your question about the wraiths being good or evil," replied the cleric.

"I'm not sure what we have done to upset them," answered Sean.

"You will have to be careful."

"Jonjo has devised a secret weapon," laughed Sean. "I don't know what it is, but he sure scared them with just a stick."

"His years with the hurley have paid dividends for sure. I think the speed you were swinging the sticks at might be significant. The singing sound of the stick may have created vibrations which crossed into their realm."

"We are not going to tell anybody other than you," said Sean. "Anyone else would think we had lost the plot."

"Either that or they would try to rationalise it, saying it was marsh gas, even though that is not marshy land."

"We are going to have to work out what to do," said Sean.

"I will get straight on to that Latin text and see if I can find anything," offered Fr Flanagan. "Keep in touch. Let me know if there is anything else I can help with."

Jonjo showed the poles to Sean. The idea had come to him that the symbols might bestow the same power to the sticks that they had to the oars.

When Sean gripped the stick, he felt the surge of power up his arm. He swung the wood experimentally. It was superbly balanced, and he brandished it like a sword. Jonjo did the same, wielding it with a real flourish.

"Only for use against the wraiths," warned Jonjo, with a smile. "Not for walloping Seamus, tempting though it might be."

"We will need to take these on all our walks," said Sean. "I feel better for having it."

"Make sure you use that embrocation. We will be

aching tomorrow. Not only were we battling, but we covered the ground at record pace getting home."

"What are two old fellers like us doing battling evil spirits?" asked Sean.

"Ara, I wouldn't have it any other way," laughed Jonjo. "Keeps life interesting."

***

From his youngest days, Jonjo could recall that same feeling. Even now, he sensed the energy in the air. The same force that drove the flowers and the animals was alive in him.

The gentlest of breezes ushered in the excitement. The air so fresh in from the Atlantic waking the land. Petals poking through the green. Renewal and rebirth. Spring was here.

"Fine morning," he called to his cousin.

"Grand, apart from aching in every muscle in my body," replied Sean. "You?"

"The same. Will we look through the books for clues?"

The two friends sat reading in an area of Sean's

garage. They called it the incident room. Fuelled with cups of coffee, they spent a couple of hours looking at the local history books. They were just about to stop for lunch when Sean said excitedly, "Look at this!"

He read from the pamphlet.

'An old man called Patrick MacBranain sat smoking his pipe in the corner of his cottage. He was the last Seanchaí (shan-a-key) of his generation, the last storyteller. He was famed for his tales of ancient lore and tradition passed down through time. From him, I heard the tale of the wraiths.'

"WHEN THE ANCIENT ONES FIRST WALKED THE LAND, THE WRAITHS STILL HELD SWAY. THEY WERE NOT THEN JUST CREATURES OF THE NIGHT BUT WOULD BOLDLY APPEAR IN THE DAY. JUST FOR SPORT, THEY CHOKED BOTH CATTLE AND MEN.

THE TUATHA WERE BOTH CLEVER AND RESOURCEFUL. THEY KNEW THE SECRET OF THE STONES AND BUILT THE CIRCLES

PROUD AND STRONG. THE WRAITHS WERE DRAINED OF THEIR DAYTIME POWER AND EVEN MUCH OF THEIR DARK TIME. RESENTFUL AT BEING DISMISSED FROM THE LIGHT, THE CREATURES CREATED MORE EVIL IN THE NIGHT.

THE TUATHA BUILT THE WHEELS, AND THEY USED THE POWER OF THE RIVER. THEY DREW IN THE WRAITHS AND DISCHARGED THEM FROM THIS WORLD. NOT ALL WERE CAPTURED. SOME REMAIN TO THIS DAY. A FEW BECAME POOKAS (shapeshifters), OTHERS STILL TRY TO RECLAIM THE LAND.

WHEN THE STONES ARE AT THE WEAKEST THE WRAITHS TRY TO RESTORE THEIR POWER. ONLY THE SONS OF THE TUATHA CAN DEFEAT THEM."

***

"There is so much to take in," said Jonjo.

"I'll send a copy of this to Fr Flanagan. We need to talk it through with him," advised Sean.

"I haven't the energy today."

"Me, neither. What about having our lunch, then helping me get through some wine tasting."

"Now that is a good idea! We can forget about the divils and demons for a while."

***

The two friends sat in the orangery. They drank and told each other jokes to take their minds off the problems.

Jonjo

"Murphy's grandad had a medical. He went with his wife for the results.

The doctor said, 'Paddy, you are fortunate apart from your eyesight, you are in great shape for a man of your age.'

Paddy replies, 'God knows I have poor eyesight, so He's fixed it so when I get up in the middle of the night to go to the bathroom, poof!

The light goes on. When I'm done, poof! The light goes off.'

'Wow, that's incredible,' the doctor says.

'You eejit you've been peeing in the fridge,' said Mrs Murphy."

Sean

"Paddy went to the doctor's today and said, 'Do you treat alcoholics?'

The doctor replied, 'Of course we do'.

Paddy said, 'Great, get your coat on. I'm skint.'"

Jonjo

"The barman says to Murphy, 'Your glass is empty, fancy another one?'

Looking puzzled Murphy, says, 'Why would I be needing two empty glasses?'"

Sean

"Paddy says, 'Murphy, if you were stranded on a desert island, who would you like most to be with you?'

'My uncle Mick,' replies Murphy.

'What's so special about him?' asks Paddy.

'He's got a boat,' says Murphy."

Jonjo

"Murphy was in a line up at the police station suspected of bank robbery.

The bank manager was brought in.

'That's him. He's the one that saw me,' shouts Murphy."

***

Jonjo walked the short way home with many thoughts spinning in his head. Holding his stick aloft, he drew himself to his full height and shouted, "Just come and try it!"

There was no response from the empty fields. He knew they were out there. He knew they were not scared, but neither was he.

Chapter 34

A beautiful spring morning, the air fresh and the day unrolling before them. The untamed flowers and new growth completely covered the dry stone walls. The boreen looked like an avenue from the imagination of an artist.

Over the last few days, two men had recovered physically from their encounter with the wraiths. They carried the sticks diagonally across their backs under the straps of their backpacks, like swords ready to be drawn.

They carried too their own thoughts. Jonjo had a quiet yet irrepressible enthusiasm. The beauty of the wildflowers was not wasted on him, and he gloried in the sounds of spring. Robins, blackbirds and thrushes had sung to him before dawn. Wrens, sparrows and wood pigeons had joined the chorus. As he walked, he thought of the week to come.

It was one of his favourite weeks of the year. Not only was it was the week of St Patrick's Day, but it was the week of the Cheltenham Festival. This was four days of the best horse racing and a traditional and good-natured rivalry between the Irish and British. Jonjo loved this, the highlight of his betting year.

Sean too admired the beauty of the day. He wondered why his parents had swapped this beautiful country for the concrete and smoke of the States. He already knew, of course, generations of Irish had been forced to move. Religion, politics, famine had all conspired, 'the luck of the Irish'.

"We are soon here," said Sean as they reached the end of the path.

"A good companion shortens the road," laughed Jonjo.

The taxi drew up, and Micko sprang out with a cheery, "How ye doing?"

As they drove to town, he told them how well Mangan was doing with his pony and trap. Sonny helped to look after Arkle, the pony. And Mangan was in his element, showing off the town to visitors.

"Is it time you popped the question to Alicia?" inquired Jonjo.

"I don't know what to say. Even the thought of it makes me tongue-tied," replied Micko.

"But you've the 'gift of the gab'," insisted Sean.

"Maybe, but not in this," said Micko.

"Well," began Jonjo. "You need to plan it. It is a day the two of you will look back on for years to come. Set a date, plan out the place and decide what you are going to say."

By the time they had reached the town, the three had come up with a plan. The day was to be the 21st of March, the equinox, a magical date. The place would be the bridge on the lough (Alicia's favourite place). Mangan would take them in his pony and trap, and Sean and Jonjo would look after Sonny. Micko would take with him Sean's posh wicker picnic hamper. Along with the picnic, he would have a bunch of flowers and an engagement ring. Micko, meanwhile, would practise what to say.

"Thanks, boys," said Micko. "You've set my mind at rest. Now I've got a definite date in mind."

***

Seated around the long table in the priest's house, Fr Flanagan discussed the extract that Sean had sent him. "It's fascinating stuff," he began. "The idea that the Tuatha built stone circles to ward off the wraiths is brand new. I've never heard that before."

"Do you think it is true?" asked Sean.

"Well, I don't know. But all around the world are massive stone structures. Ancient people went to an enormous effort to build them. I know experts have suggested they are astronomical calendars. However, did they really need to be that big? Could they have made them from wood? What springs into your mind when I say, the Stone Age?"

"I think of a caveman wearing an animal skin, maybe carrying a club," laughed Jonjo.

"That's what we were taught," agreed Fr Flanagan. "What we need to remember is that the Stone Age lasted over 3 million years and these people were just as intelligent as us. Modern archaeologists have discovered large cities from those times. They have found that trading occurred over great distances," continued the cleric.

"So they were more sophisticated than we thought. It is possible then, the technology based on stone could have been used in a way that we don't know about," suggested Sean.

"I agree," said Fr Flanagan. "But alternatively, the whole story might be an attempt to try and explain the tunnel and the wheel."

"A myth based on a story from someone else that has been down the tunnel," suggested Jonjo.

"Yes and the name of that storyteller, Patrick MacBranain. Do you recognise that?" asked the priest.

Both men shook their heads.

"It is an old form of 'Brennan', probably one of your ancestors," suggested Fr Flanagan.

"Could be," conceded Jonjo.

"I still don't know why the wraiths attacked us. That bit is no myth. I don't know what we should do next. I don't know what it is all about," complained Sean.

"Look at that line," said Fr Flanagan, pointing at the extract.

WHEN THE STONES ARE AT THE WEAKEST, THE WRAITHS TRY TO RESTORE

THEIR POWER. ONLY THE SONS OF THE TUATHA CAN DEFEAT THEM.

To me, it suggests that the stones might be at their weakest around the winter solstice. I interpret it to mean that the only thing to prevent them from regaining their power is the sons of the Tuatha."

"Down to us two," summarised Sean.

"I have had a look at the Latin document, cursory glance really," said the priest.

"I know you have so much work in the parishes," said Jonjo.

"Well, it strikes me that it is the work of a monk from the Middle Ages. It is about mythological traditions, especially those dealing with the pre-Christian notion of the otherworld. There may be something in it that can help you."

"I hope you find something," pleaded Sean.

"Have faith. You have had a lot of help already. Think back to when you were lost on the mountain. Meanwhile, I'll be trying to find the answers in the book."

"Thanks, Fr Flanagan. I know we can rely on you,"

said Jonjo wholeheartedly.

***

Lunch at Molly's cafe filled their stomachs with food and overfilled their heads with the local gossip. The two men went to Clarke's bar.

"Well, if it is not Abbot and Costello," exclaimed Seamus Burke as they entered.

"So we must be meeting..." began Jonjo.

"Frankenstein," suggested Sean.

"The Mummy," said Callaly.

"Dr Jekyll," offered Donlan

"Not forgetting Mr Hyde," added Cullen.

"The Invisible Man," came the ghostly voice of Tommy Clarke, who had ducked down behind the bar.

"Very funny," acknowledged Seamus wryly.

Jonjo and most of the men in the pub settled down to discussing the forthcoming horseracing. The depth of knowledge about the horses, jockeys and trainers they displayed surprised Sean. Not being involved, he drifted over to the bar to chat with Callaly, the funeral director.

The undertaker remarked, "You have lost a little over 3 stones since you returned to Ireland."

"45 pounds," confirmed Sean, slightly dumbfounded.

"Sorry for being so personal," apologised Callaly. "Occupational hazard, I can't help sizing people up."

"No problem, I feel so much better for losing the weight."

"Yes, you've slid down the list."

"What list would that be?" asked Sean.

"I have a list in my head of who my next customer will be. Just a sort of rough plan, nothing scientific."

"Well, I'm glad I'm down the list," answered Sean, uncomfortably. "How about Jonjo?"

"He's not much further up than me. I don't think that man has a day's illness in his life."

***

Seamus was beginning one of his stories.

"Murphy was muttering, 'Dopey, Sleepy, Dublin... no Doc, Sleepy, and Dublin..., no I can 'remember.'

'What's the matter?' says Paddy.

'I can't remember my password.'

'Why not?'

'It's the seven dwarfs then Dublin.'

'Does it have to be so long?'

'Of course ye eejit, it has to be seven characters and a capital.'"

The joke got the reaction it deserved which did nothing to discourage Seamus.

***

Jonjo and Sean set off homeward. They had decided to have only a couple of whiskeys. Jonjo reasoned that stout would slow them down, but whiskey would put fire in their bellies. The friends thought they might well face the wraiths again. They were determined not to let the creatures prevent them from walking the land.

They chatted as they walked. However, the conversation became stilted as the two approached the point of the last encounter. Moving along, engrossed in his thoughts, Sean was startled by a cry from Jonjo.

"Scampeen!"

A brown and white collie dog was trotting happily

towards Jonjo. Thinking back on what happened next; Sean saw it in his memory thus. He sprinted across to Jonjo, simultaneously drawing his stick like a knight of old. Pushing his friend aside, he brought the weapon to the nose of the animal. The creature disappeared, revealing itself as a wraith, leaving behind only its sulphurous stench.

Sean played it as a slow-motion cinematic event in his mind. In reality, the events were not quite so elegantly choreographed. Nevertheless, it was both quick thinking and brave, so let Sean have his moment of glory.

"I could have sworn it was my old dog," said Jonjo shakily.

"A Pooka, a shape-shifter," said Sean.

"You saved my life!"

"Well, that makes us even," replied Sean graciously.

"How did you know what it was?"

"I don't know, just instinct."

***

Later in the evening, the two men sat around the chimenea. Both were still shaken by the events of the afternoon. Determined not to be defeated by the wraiths, they were at a loss what to do next.

"We need a miracle," said Jonjo.

As luck would have it, a miracle was on its way.

Chapter 35

A sudden shower briefly interrupted the spring sunshine. The rain sparkled until the sun regained the upper hand. Moisture heightened the fragrance of the flowers. A goldfinch happily picked at a silver ragwort as its partner looked on. The profusion of fresh colour and long remembered birdsong stirred his soul.

He wondered how the wraith had conjured up the image of his old pet. He reasoned that the picture must somehow have come from his own mind. That tilt of the head and one ear curled down it was Scampeen who had faithfully followed him on his childhood adventures. He had let his guard down, but Sean had been there.

At that precise moment, he heard his cousin call, "Look at this, Jonjo!"

From the vantage point of Sean's patio, Jonjo could understand the excitement. All the way down to the hollow was a path of primroses. A yellow trail had emerged overnight. The miracle they had been looking for.

"What was it that you found out about primroses?" asked Jonjo.

"There are a few ancient traditions about them. The most relevant one here is that they give protection from the other world," answered Sean.

"So we have a safe path, at least to the hollow."

"I have some primulas in pots. They are more or less the same thing. The legends say that if you put them on your doorstep, they stop spirits getting into your house," added Sean.

"I'll have to take the whiskey through the back door," laughed Jonjo.

***

The two men set off down the path, St. Patrick's Day and the first day of Cheltenham races. It was a day they weren't going to be staying home.

"Do the pubs open on St. Patrick's Day now?" inquired Sean.

"I'd almost forgotten that they didn't at one time," answered Jonjo.

"My memory of St.Patrick's Day, when we were kids, is having shamrocks pinned to my jacket and walking in a parade. It was always raining and freezing cold," said Sean.

"Sure, it's more of a holiday now. Better fun, ye know."

"It's a big deal in the States. They dye the river green in Chicago. There are huge parades and marching bands," added Sean.

"Why not? It's a good thing to remember your roots."

From a distance, the path appeared like a yellow carpet. Close up, it was predominantly grass, but the brightness of the flowers subdued the green. The two companions stopped at the hollow to drink from their flasks of tea and coffee.

Sean told Jonjo about a legend he had read. St Patrick had been troubled by demons that changed shape. They had become blackbirds. Patrick rang his bell so loudly that it could be heard all over Ireland. He then threw the bell with such force at these demon birds that it cracked, and all the birds disappeared.

"It might be worth a prayer to St Patrick at Mass this morning," speculated Jonjo.

"Do you know, I might join you," replied Sean. "We need all the help we can get."

The two men approached the point where they had encountered the wraiths. They had taken out their sticks like the warriors they had become. Fortunately, they were able to continue untroubled. The primroses became few and far between. Yet, there was the outline of a pathway right through to the town.

Jonjo had never tired of the view of his hometown. Bathed in the spring sunlight, it was forever familiar and welcoming. There had been few changes in his lifetime. It was as if the builders had put away their trowels long ago, happy with what they had done.

The two men paid their respects in the cemetery. They were pleased to see flowers on the famine monument. The town came to life, and people young and old came to morning Mass. Fr Flanagan's homily was his usual assured performance linking the Gospel to the life of the parishioners. He always had an element of humour to put across a serious message.

Jonjo, Sean and the priest met in the presbytery.

"I've been studying the Latin document you brought," began the cleric. "I didn't realise how rusty my language skills were. It's medieval rather than classical Latin."

"What have you discovered?" queried Sean.

"I've been skimming through slowly if that's not a contradiction. I've been searching for something about the wraiths. From what I've read, it seems they appear now and again. It is connected to the wheel in the tunnel that we have seen on the frescoes."

At this point, Fr Flanagan got out the photos from the tunnel.

"That's the wheel. You likened it to an illustration of a perpetual motion machine, Sean."

"That's right."

"According to the myths, the Tuatha maintain the machine. The wheel works using magnetite to power it. The wheel, of course, is what the Tuatha used to dismiss the wraiths from this world."

"What is magnetite?" queried Jonjo.

"I've got a definition of it here," said the cleric.

'Magnetite is a common iron oxide mineral. Magnetite is attracted to a magnet, but some specimens are automagnetized. They can attract small pieces of iron, magnetite, and other magnetic objects. This form of magnetite is known as lodestone.'

"I've heard of lodestones," confirmed Sean. "They are supposed to be the first compasses."

"That's right," said Fr Flanagan.

"So what you are saying is that this wheel needs to be repaired to get rid of the wraiths?" asked Jonjo.

"I think so," said the priest. "I'm guessing the magnetite might need replacing. There may be something else that needs fixing, I don't know."

"You've done grand. It's clever to have found out so much. Thank you," said Jonjo.

"I tell you what else I've discovered. The wraiths can't cross water. That's why the ancient people built their stilt houses on the lough."

"But we saw them coming up the river on the morning of the winter solstice," argued Sean.

"Yes, but that is when they were being drawn in by the wheel," countered Fr Flanagan.

"Of course. It all fits in with the idea of the Tuatha de Danann having a technology based on stone," agreed Sean.

"I tell you what else the legend says, and you will like this Jonjo. The Tuatha were great hurley players. They beat the Firbolg (a race that preceded the Tuatha) in a game that was played until death."

"All these things we didn't know about our ancestors," mused Jonjo.

"There's a lot more to uncover in the document. It is like being an armchair detective," said the priest.

"Now that's an easy job," said Jonjo.

"What do you mean?" asked the cleric.

"Detecting armchairs. There's two in here and loads in the furniture shop," laughed Jonjo.

The other two men groaned. "That's poor even by your low standards," added Sean.

"Even Seamus would reject that one," confirmed the priest.

***

Jonjo went off to Casey's bookies and Sean to Molly's cafe. She served him one of his Italian coffees and whispered, "That feller used to be an art teacher in Castlebar."

"O.K.," answered Sean quizzically.

"I thought you might tell him about your idea of exhibiting paintings in the cafe."

"Why don't you?"

"I don't like. You see, he taught me years ago. He mightn't remember, but anyway, I wasn't his favourite pupil."

"Talking in class too much?"

"How did you know?" asked Molly.

"Lucky guess," laughed Sean.

Sean introduced himself to the former teacher and pitched the idea.

"Well, I've lots of canvasses stacked up," replied Frank Jennings.

As Frank lived out on the road to Castlebar, he suggested that Sean look at the paintings. They would select the most suitable ones. Sean could see Frank weighing up the wall space and looking at the light. Sean gave Molly an affirmative nod and smile. He left the cafe, agreeing to phone the artist to sort out a suitable time.

Going across to Clarke's bar Jonjo was already there, and Seamus was in full flow.

"Murphy and his wife were sitting on their patio watching the sunset. He said, 'I love you'. His wife asked, 'Is that you talking, or is that your beer talking?' Murphy replied, 'I'm talking to my beer.'"

Paddy Regan, the local Garda, sat at the bar drinking orange juice. "I saw an old-timer at the station today. He said,' "When I was a boy, my mother would send me with £1 to the corner shop. I'd come back with 5 potatoes, 2 loaves of bread, 3 bottles of milk, a hunk of cheese, a box of tea and a dozen eggs. You just can't do that today...too many security cameras.'"

Seamus, not to be outdone, replied. "Murphy said, 'When I die, I want it to be peaceful in my sleep like my Grandad. Not terrified and screaming like the passengers on the bus.'"

***

Micko took Sean and Jonjo home in the taxi. They sat on the settee watching the recording of the first day of Cheltenham races. Jonjo cheered home the Irish trained winner of the Champion Hurdle. It was all the much sweeter because he had a bet on it.

Looking out from the orangery, the friends mused on what Fr Flanagan had told them.

"There's a job to be done. We will need to plan it thoroughly," said Sean.

"True," agreed Jonjo. "But we mustn't forget Micko and his proposal. We've that to sort out first."

"Goodnight and God bless," said Sean. It was the phrase his mother had used, and it surprised him. He had never said those words before himself. It felt strange, as if someone else had spoken.

Chapter 36

Officially today was the first day of spring. But spring had already sprung. Micko pulled up in the taxi. This formerly shaggy-haired hirsute man was shaved to within an inch of his life. He was as spruced up and neat as Jonjo had ever seen him.

Sean had lent him the luxurious wicker hamper. It held a check picnic rug for the alfresco outing. All the crockery and cutlery were neatly stowed inside, along with one of Sean's best wines. Everything was ready. Even the weather had played its part. The next step was to pick up the food order from Molly Keane's cafe.

"Special occasion?" inquired Molly.

"That's right," confirmed Micko.

Frustrated at receiving no further information, Molly was gracious enough to pack the hamper.

"There you go," she said, admiring her handiwork. "Some jobs are best done by a woman."

"A lovely job too, thanks, Molly," replied Micko.

They drove down to Micko's house and placed the hamper on the seat of the pony and trap. Sonny was brushing the pony, and Mangan was sitting aloft ready. Excitement was contagious, and all the men felt it.

"Remember to smile," advised Jonjo.

"Enjoy the moment," added Sean.

Alicia walked out. She looked lovelier each time they saw her. Smiling radiantly at the men, she looked at Sonny and said, "Now you be good going gallivanting."

"Yes, Mammy," was his dutiful response.

Micko gallantly helped Alicia onto the trap, and off they went.

***

Although Sean was a reasonable height, he felt dwarfed between Sonny and Jonjo.

"I feel like I've got bodyguards on either side of me. Like some mob boss," he commented.

"Ara, you can look after yourself," laughed Jonjo,

indicating Sean's stick.

The three went to Molly's for lunch. She was pleased to see them because they were all big eaters. She liked to see her food appreciated, and they did just that.

"Your Mammy not here?" she asked Sonny.

He looked around and replied seriously, "No."

"Gone out somewhere nice?" she persevered.

"Yes," nodded Sonny.

She gave up her line of inquiry.

"Me, Mr Brennan, Mr Walsh, go to pub," beamed Sonny.

"You keep those two out of mischief," laughed Molly.

"I do," said Sonny. "Don't go in mischief!" Sonny added firmly.

The words triggered Molly's brain. 'I do.'

"Alicia and Micko, could it be?"

***

Meanwhile, Micko was sitting happily in the trap. He smiled at Alicia, and she smiled back. Immediately, he relaxed and felt the tension drain from him. Mangan was whistling tunefully in time with the rhythm of the pony's hoofs.

Micko marvelled at the view of the town from the trap. He'd seen the road countless times but never before seen the beauty of the path before him. To describe the wildflowers as jewels would be undervaluing them. 'Enjoy the moment,' Sean had said. It couldn't have been more perfect. Then Alicia put her head on his shoulder, and it was.

They travelled on, a comfortable silence between them. The hypnotic clip-clop, the birdsong on the gentlest of warm breezes and the fresh spring air lulled them and excited them simultaneously.

The trap rolled to a stop, and Mangan held Alicia's hand as she climbed down. Micko carefully carried the wicker basket and set it down on the ground. Mangan saluted and drove smartly off, singing a cheery song. The pony Arkle whinnied something, which to a fanciful mind sounded like 'goodbye'.

Micko spread the blanket on the grass and walked over to Alicia. Bending on one knee, he said the words that he had been practising. "Will you do me the honour of being my wife?"

"Yes," answered Alicia, who promptly burst into tears of joy.

Anybody closely observing might have noticed, Micko brushing his own eye.

***

In Clarke's bar, someone else was rolling out a phrase he had practised but never used.

"Three pints of the black stuff, please," said Sonny very precisely.

"Have a seat, and I will bring them over," replied Tommy Clarke.

Sonny proudly took out the wallet Jonjo had given him and handed over the money. He walked across the pub, his face beaming with pleasure.

"You look like the cat that got the cream," commented Seamus.

"Not cat, dog with two tails," said Sonny. He then laughed so much at his own comment that it was infectious. Everyone around was laughing. Jonjo was pleased to see they were laughing with the young man and not at him.

Seamus began one of his tales. "Murphy came home drunk every evening toward midnight, staggering across the countryside. This really annoyed his wife.

At her wit's end, one night, she hid in the graveyard, intent on scaring some sense into him. As her husband stumbled by, up from behind a tombstone, she jumped. All done up in a red devil costume, she wailed, 'PADRAIG MURPHY GIVE UP THE DRINK' Undaunted, he swayed defiantly and demanded, 'Who the blazes are you?'

'I'm the divil, ya old fool!'

To which Murphy replied, 'Pleased to meet you, Sir. I'm married to yer daughter.'"

Jonjo noticed that Sonny joined in with the laughter. He knew that he had not understood the joke, but he had enjoyed the merriment. They were on their second pint when Micko came in. He indicated that he wanted a word with Sonny and the two went outside.

"I've never seen Micko look so happy," commented Seamus.

"If there was a sand boy here, he'd be looking sad in comparison," confirmed Jonjo.

"True," added Sean. "Even if Larry were here, he'd

only look mildly pleased in contrast."

"What are you two talking about?" demanded Seamus.

At that moment, Micko rang the bell at the bar. "I'm pleased to announce that Alicia Farrell and I are engaged to be married."

There were some shouts of congratulations and muted applause.

"Drinks on the house!" called Tommy Clarke. This had a much noisier roar of approval. A careful observer might have noticed a slight nod from Tommy to Sean, Sean was footing the bill. He liked to put his fortune to good use and preferred to do it anonymously.

Micko joined them at the table. Sonny was delighted about what was happening. He had got it into his head that Micko was now his dad. He was convinced that either Jonjo or Sean was his grandad.

"Well, you can have two grandads," confirmed Micko.

"But, we are not...," began Sean.

"Ara musha, we'll be honorary grandads," agreed Jonjo. "One thing Micko, you will hear more about wedding arrangements than you ever thought possible.

There will be more planning for this than the D Day landings. It will be worth it in the end."

Micko sensibly had only the one drink and took Sonny to find Alicia. Alicia had meanwhile told Molly about the engagement, thus ensuring the word would spread through the town.

***

Jonjo and Sean set off walking home. The primrose trail was still visible, but there was a difference. The path where the wraiths had attacked was singed at the edges.

"The creatures have been testing their luck," commented Jonjo.

"I think we are running out of time," added Sean.

"We need to plan everything out thoroughly," replied Jonjo.

"I've promised to see Frank Jennings about the paintings for Molly's cafe tomorrow," said Sean.

"I would like to come," said Jonjo, fingering the handle of the wooden stick.

"I'd appreciate it."

"Then after that, it is planning," said Jonjo

"Then action!" said Sean far more confidently than he felt.

***

Beneath the setting sun was a strange sky. An orange band above earth-brown clouds. Then yellow ochre clouds tinged with pure white light. Above the horizon, a stripe of lemon yellow.

Higher than the sun, green and muddy brown and highest of all an ink blue.

The two friends chatted, taking heat from the chimenea.

"Fr Flanagan called to say that he had found a reference to say that the Tuatha knew the power of magnetism. They had harnessed the power of volcanoes and used it on a solar wind," reported Sean.

"I've no idea what any of that means," confessed Jonjo.

"Me neither," replied Sean. "I suppose he is just giving us all the information he can.

They talked over the day. The delight on Sonny's

face matched only by the grin on Micko's. It gave them a warm feeling, and they drank the health of Micko's new family as the sun went down.

"In Ireland, the other world is never far away," said Sean. "I think W.B. Yeats," said that.

"Let's think of the good things from today. I don't want those creatures haunting my dreams," said Jonjo.

"'Tread softly because you tread on my dreams' that was definitely Yeats", added Sean.

Chapter 37

The light spring shower produced a pleasant, earthy smell. Walking along the verge was agreeable, if not ideal. The grass had not been cut for some time, and the ground was uneven. At times, there was no pathway, and they had to cross the road. Occasionally, they had to walk the edge of the highway itself.

A mild, almost balmy day. It was not their idea of a perfect trek, but they enjoyed the view of the low hills. The different coloured crops and the ancient farm walls added to the beauty of the countryside. They passed hedgerows and solitary trees shaped by the wind.

Frank Jennings house stood alone at the end of a short drive. It was screened from the road by a hedge of fuchsias, holly and pyracantha. The house was of modern rendered brick that occupied the site of previous dwellings. The stone outhouses were the remnants of old farmhouse buildings.

The main house was painted a pastel blue and had dark green ornamental wooden shutters. Between the main house and the outbuildings was a cobbled yard. The surface was a mixture of old stones, stone flags, and slates. It had been bedded down to make a rough yet level paved area.

Two large olive jars stood among a host of terracotta pots and a variety of plants. The mixture of feathery foliage and bright flowers pleased the eye. A mosaic topped outdoor table had four chairs tipped against it, reminiscent of a cafe at closing time.

"We could be in Tuscany," enthused Sean.

Sinead Jennings had seen them and opened the front door silently.

"That's what it's meant to look like, thank you!" she exclaimed. Sinead had a local accent, albeit a slightly refined version.

The two men introduced themselves.

"Ah, the art experts," she smiled.

Jonjo felt a little uncomfortable. His knowledge of

art could have been written on the back of a postage stamp, leaving plenty of room for his appreciation of opera and ballet.

Frank came out to join them. He had a full head of white hair, a little on the long side for a man in his sixties. His face was dominated by a large nose, but his ready grin and lively eyes welcomed them.

"Cup of tea," he commanded. "You must be parched after your walk."

They sat at the garden table, and in no time, the four were chatting, drinking tea and eating ham and onion sandwiches.

"I've canvasses all over the place," continued Frank. "I reckon four large ones, two medium and four small ones would do for the cafe without overwhelming the space."

"She's done well for herself with that cafe, has Molly," commented Sinead. "I didn't think she would have the nous to run a business."

"You know her, too?" asked Sean.

"We both had the pleasure of teaching her," answered Sinead "She was Molly Kane back then."

"Just added one letter to her name when she got

married," laughed Frank.

"She's done well for herself with that cafe," repeated Sinead.

They went indoors and admired a large oil painting over the fireplace. It was a view of the famine village in the foreground with a beautiful backdrop of the countryside below. There were a couple of smaller canvases of the local area. Even to Jonjo's untutored eye, these did not match the quality of the big painting.

"Our children's work," said Frank, proudly indicating the smaller pictures.

Sean thought it admirable that Frank was so proud of these works. They were not up to the standard of his own.

***

Two easels set up in the conservatory to the back of the house.

"There's a picture that paints itself," commented Frank indicating Thornhill looming up through the clouds.

"Will we go and look at the paintings out in the

studio?" asked Frank.

Jonjo would prefer to have captured an escaped bull than venture his opinion on works of art. He was half hoping an enraged beast would appear to excuse him from the task.

"Yer man's the expert," said Jonjo indicating Sean. Sean smiled, always susceptible to a bit of flattery.

"Well, so, me and you can do a bit of painting," said Mary to Jonjo.

This turn of events happened too fast for Jonjo. With neither divine nor bovine intervention in sight, Jonjo stood unwillingly at the easel as Sinead began to instruct him.

"Paintings not as hard as you might think," she began. "These are acrylic paints which dry quickly. It's easy to cover up mistakes. We can do a seascape. We'll start with the sky. What colour do you want to make it?"

Jonjo looked at the assembled paints. He spotted the word cerulean on one of the tubes.

"That's the one," he said, more confidently than he felt.

"Good," said Sinead. "Remember, the sky is always

lighter than you think."

Under her instructions, he put a thin masking tape horizontally across the canvas. She gave him a large brush that he would have associated more with painting a skirting board than an artistic composition.

Jonjo became engrossed. Sinead showed him how to mix in white to lighten the sky. Under her guidance, using a painter's knife, Jonjo produced an ultramarine blue and titanium white sea. Drying the canvas with a hairdryer, Sinead showed him how to add further detail to his masterpiece.

By the time Sean and Frank had come back, Jonjo had completed the painting. He had added himself in his canoe heading out into the sea. On the horizon was the suggestion of a distant island, and looming towards the foreground was an eerie mist.

Jonjo listened to Sean and Frank's conversation as they entered. It was pleasing to hear Sean listening and responding to Frank's words. He had come a long way from the self-centered man who had returned from America less than a year ago.

They congratulated Jonjo on his work.

"All due to the excellent teaching," he commented

graciously. Truth be told, he was inordinately proud of what he had accomplished.

Sean and Frank spread out the canvasses they had chosen. Jonjo's immediate reaction was to realise how good they were compared to his own effort, which now seemed flat and lifeless. The overwhelming response, however, was one of understanding. The pictures spoke to him without words. He recognised the location of some of them, but he could also sense the mood. It wasn't just the mood of the day but also the emotion of the artist that painted them.

He had heard discussions about art and not understood or had any interest in them. It was as though he suddenly had an insight into a whole new world.

They put all the canvasses in Frank's car, including Jonjo's, as he had offered them a lift home. Sinead was stopped in her tracks as she passed Sean his walking stick.

"Look, Frank!" she called excitedly, as she showed him the engravings on the stick.

"I've seen those symbols before," said Frank. "Will you wait while I show you something?"

They sat down, and Frank returned with a dusty cardboard portfolio. It had black ribbons on three sides and must have measured a foot by a foot and a half. Frank carefully brushed the dust from the top, under Sinead's watchful eye, then placed it on the table.

He opened the cover to reveal a vibrantly coloured page reproducing the frescoes that Sean and Jonjo had seen in the tunnel.

The picture underneath was even more astounding. It had been divided into nine equal rectangles, three rows of three. It depicted two men in a boat paddling along a river. The following picture showed them tying their canoe to a bollard and loading something onto it.

It was clear to Jonjo and Sean that this was nothing less than an instruction manual. These were the directions on how to maintain the machine in the tunnel. The means to keep the wraiths at bay.

"Where did you get these?" asked Sean.

"Handed down through the family. They are what got me interested in art when I was a child. I used to copy them, but I was always told they were precious and had to be looked after," answered Frank.

"How old are they?" asked Jonjo.

"I've no idea," admitted Frank." The story was they were from the MacBranain side of the family. But I know nothing about the MacBranains or any of the pictures."

"Is it O.K., if I take a photo of them?" asked Sean.

"Sure," replied Frank.

"I can tell they mean something to you," said Sinead. "What is it?"

Sean looked over at Jonjo for approval.

"Are you two in the mood for a story? It's quite a long and quite a strange tale?"

"Sure, we've all the time in the world."

Chapter 38

Fr Flanagan had spread the illustrations out on his dining table.

"This is wonderful," he commented.

Sean and Jonjo nodded their agreement. Sunlight streaming through the window lit motes of dust rising from the ancient documents. It was as though the sun itself was helping them uncover the secret.

"So," said Sean. "How do you read it, Father?"

"It seems that you need to take the canoe to the tunnel. It looks like the blocks of magnetite are there. You load the block onto the canoe and take it through to the wheel," said the priest.

"One block, it looks like," agreed Jonjo.

"The boat looks like it is still tied to the bollard on

the next picture. The block is unloaded in that tunnel within a tunnel next to the wheel," said Sean. "That's the bit we couldn't get to on foot."

"At the side of the wheel, there's what looks like a lever. The picture shows it being turned through ninety degrees. I guess that is to stop the wheel while you remove the old magnetite," said the cleric.

They pored over the remaining pictures working out their strategy. Compiling a list of tools and equipment, they sat back with a cup of tea.

"How are we going to get the canoe down there?" queried Sean.

"There's no way it will go down the steps and through the cellar," confirmed Jonjo.

"We'll find a way," said Fr Flanagan confidently.

***

Frank Jennings had hung his paintings in the cafe. Molly was uncharacteristically demure in the presence of her former teacher.

They agreed to a fifty-fifty split on any sales. Sean had advised Frank on pricing, telling him to account for the cost of material and the time it had taken to paint them.

"I've never seen the cafe look so beautiful!" exclaimed Molly.

Frank heard the emotion in her voice. He felt a lump in his throat, seeing his work displayed.

Sinead had painted posters advertising the exhibition. Her chosen style was influenced by Toulouse Lautrec, whom both she and Frank had admired since their student days. The notices lent a continental air to the town and created great interest.

Frank had tried to get Sinead to put some of her own work in the exhibition.

"We'll see," she replied.

From experience, Frank knew this meant, 'No'. Nevertheless, he loved to see her enthusiasm in producing the posters. Frank felt these practical pieces of art were more valuable than his own. He determined to collect them up once the exhibition was over.

The encounter with Jonjo and Sean had given the two of them a fresh lease of life.

***

Fr Flanagan drove into the end of the boreen. He pulled up close to Frank Jennings' car. Parking bumper to bumper, he made sure he wasn't blocking the road.

The three men caught a sickly, sweet smell as they walked towards the house. The canoe bright with the Tuatha de Danann symbols was receiving its final coat of varnish. Sinead had made two padded seat covers.

They had reproduced the patterns from the ancient documents onto the canoe. It now looked just like the illustrations.

"Ye've done a grand job," complimented Jonjo.

"Leave it out here for the afternoon. It will give it time to cure," advised Frank.

"The seat covers are detachable," confirmed Sinead.

The two artists waved their new friends a fond farewell.

Having admired the canoe, Sean, Jonjo and the priest went into the garage.

This was their headquarters. Here they had all the information regarding the tunnel. Fr Flanagan located the aerial photograph of the area.

"This is my idea," he began. "We know the route of the underground river from where it is diverted from the main course."

He pointed this out. "We can't go in from that end. We would be on the wrong side of the wheel. So logically, our only choice is to go from the other end."

"Well, we know where to start," agreed Sean. "But is it navigable?"

They studied the photo under a magnifying glass. Jonjo's sharp eyes spotted some disturbance in the stream. "They are probably rocks. We need to go down there and look at this close up," he said.

"We could take the big rope and a crowbar. We might be able to make a passage through. The more manpower we have, the better," contributed Sean.

"Horsepower as well," added Jonjo. "If we can get up here with Arkle, he'll make a formidable team with Sonny and Micko."

"When will we do it?" asked Sean.

"Time is running short. We will try for first thing tomorrow," urged Jonjo.

***

Mangan arrived the next day along with Sonny and Micko. There was no way that the jarvey would let his beloved Arkle out of his sight. They all squashed into Jonjo's cottage, where he insisted on filling them up with bacon sandwiches and mugs of tea.

"I want to thank you for what you did with my pony and trap," said Mangan. "I know you two were involved."

He got no response. "I worked out that you had taken the trap apart and put it back together in my kitchen. It gave me the fright of my life, seeing Arkle there in the house," he continued.

"When did you realise what we had done?" asked Sean.

"While I was drying out, at my daughter's. You got me off the booze. You saved me from killing myself, or God forbid someone else," his voice cracked a little as he spoke.

"Wisht that's done with now. It will make for a good tale someday," said Jonjo.

Arkle, unhitched from his trap, stood steaming in

the morning sun. He lapped water loudly and contentedly from a bucket. Jonjo gave him an apple, and Sonny brushed the pony's hair.

"Don't be making a pet of him," barked Mangan. "He's a working animal." This gruff manner fooled nobody; they all knew how much he loved the creature.

The canoe was resplendent in its shiny varnish. Frank and Sinead had done a great job. It reminded Sean of a picture of a war canoe from some remote Pacific island. The patterns looked like eyes, and the boat seemed to have taken on a personality. It was almost a living entity. Sean shook his head and laughed internally. It hadn't taken him long to get back his Irish imagination.

There was still a hint of varnish in the air of the garage as the men studied the aerial photo. They discussed how to tie the big rope to Arkle's harness and what tools they would need. Mangan explained that he could take all they needed in the trap. He showed them the route he would take to the start of the river cutting. He couldn't take the shortcut because of the narrow path.

"If we can clear a way today," said Jonjo, "then we

can take the canoe there tomorrow. Time is running out."

Sonny was leaning over, looking at the photo and becoming agitated. "Boat, tunnel, rocks," he repeated.

"What do you mean?" asked Micko. "Say it slowly, big feller."

Sonny raised his index finger to his lips. Then he pointed at the photo. "Boat." he said. Indicating where the water went underground. "Tunnel," he continued drawing his finger along the route of the river cutting, "Not rocks."

The men looked at each other blankly. Jonjo sensed Sonny was becoming irritated. "Take your time Sonny," he said. "Tell us again."

This time Sonny drew his finger along and said, "Not rocks." Then pointing at the tunnel entrance, "Water, boat!" he exclaimed.

"Of course!" said Jonjo joyfully. "It's obvious now." He clapped Sonny on the back, and the two big men began to laugh.

"Tell us," demanded Sean.

"We have all been looking at how to get the boat past all the rocks. Sonny has said we carry the boat to the tunnel entrance and put it in the water there. There's no need to navigate that section at all," explained Jonjo.

"He is always studying the maps in the taxi office. I never knew he understood them," said Micko.

They all congratulated the beaming Sonny.

"Like a dog with two tails," he laughed. It was impossible not to join in with his laughter.

***

Mangan hitched up Arkle and set off to town. Squeezing through the stone stile at the end of the boreen, the other four set off on their search. There was no clear path across the field to where they estimated the tunnel went underground. They followed the compass bearing, and before, long they had to use their sticks to cut through the undergrowth.

They came to a line of trees that seemed to track the course of the river cutting. There were rabbit holes and tree roots which made the walking difficult. A small clearing came into view under the thick canopy of two ancient yew trees. The air was cooler here, but it was not the temperature that made Jonjo shiver. Instinctively he knew this was the place. He knew Sean sensed it too.

The sound of running water confirmed their suspicions. Between the two trees was a path. Steps had been cut into the banking. The roots of the yew tree provided handholds, and all four clambered down to the bank.

They sat on a mossy mound, the shape of an upturned boat and took stock.

"We can tie the rope to the yew then lower it down to the water," said Jonjo. As he spoke, he became a little lightheaded and overcome with the strangest feeling of déjà vu. It felt as if he had tied that rope to that tree many times before.

"Well," began Sean. "We can pull the canoe on the trailer as far as the treeline tomorrow. Then we will have to manhandle it down through the branches. If we bring our backpacks with our equipment in, we should be fine."

"Sonny and me, could go instead of you," offered Micko.

"If you help get us here and launch us, that will be

fine," said Jonjo. "It has to be us."

***

They went back to the house. The return journey seemingly taking no time. Plans were made for the morning, and Alicia came and picked up the boys in the taxi.

"You should be proud of that young man," said Sean, indicating Sonny. "He has the clearest brain of us all."

"I'm always proud of him," replied Alicia, as she listened to Micko's explanation of what had happened.

***

Taking in the afternoon sun on the bench outside Jonjo's house, Sean said, "I've put my affairs in order. I've left a letter on my desk for Alicia about what to do if we don't come back."

"I know the final pictures on the document don't look good, and it is a dangerous trip. I've been having a recurring dream that Mary is calling to me. I've got to get the canoe out to sea to find her. Will you promise to help me launch it if we get back?" asked Jonjo.

"Of course. I'll come with you," said Sean.

"No, this is a one-way trip, and it's not your time yet."

Chapter 39

Condensation dripped. Sean wiped the pane with his cuff, mist pushed against the windows. Grey intangible shapes waited. Malevolent nebulous forms that were the wraiths.

He recognised the sound of his old car coming down the boreen. The noise was deadened by the atmosphere. The engine stopped, and Sean stepped outside, whirling his stick overhead. Jonjo emerged from the fog, mirroring his actions.

The two men kept the evil at bay until the six guests decanted from the big American car and into the house. Sonny and Micko looked fine, the other four shaken.

Seated around the big kitchen table, Fr Flanagan began to pray. Only he and Jonjo were practising

Catholics, but all had been brought up in the faith. The words normally almost automatic had a real relevance today. The 'Our Father', 'Hail Mary', and the 'Glory Be' were spoken.

Sinead Jennings took her husband's hand, and almost immediately, everyone was holding hands in a circle. The prayers relaxed the gathering a little.

"Nobody has to do this, and nobody will think the less of any of you who changes their mind," said Jonjo in his quiet yet authoritative way.

"We have survived Micko's driving in the fog," laughed Sinead. "We can do anything."

The laughter, although tinged with nerves, further relaxed the group.

"You take the high road...," sang Frank as they split into their allotted duties.

***

It was a battle. Whirling their sticks to create the sound waves that kept the wraiths at bay was exhausting. At every opportunity, the evil creatures forced themselves in. The choking pressure they put on the men's bodies was draining. The four plugged on resolutely.

It had been their plan to take turns in dragging the canoe on its trolley. In practice, only Sonny could manage both to pull the boat and wave his stick. They fought on up the boreen sweat forming rivulets on their bodies, moisture from the fog blinding them.

They detached the trolley to lift the canoe through the stone style.

"Do this!" commanded Jonjo.

They lowered the boat over their heads and crouched as low as they could.

"The symbols on the boat are warding them off," explained Jonjo.

They abandoned the trolley and moved on. Two men held the boat overhead while two used their weapons to keep the creatures at arm's length. Progress across the field was painstakingly slow. The stops to rest under the boat became more frequent.

Jonjo worried about how they would be able to continue through the trees. Manoeuvring the boat amongst the branches and trunks while stepping over the roots. Simultaneously battling the evil ones. Still, they had not reached the trees.

"One step at a time," thought Jonjo figuratively, and maybe soon literally.

***

Sinead sat alone at the table, back in Sean's house. She was in charge of communications. That was how Sean had described it. The four men with the boat were to ring her with any messages.

She felt like she had drawn the short straw. Sinead would have preferred to be with the group in the tunnel. Fr Flanagan had to go, having been down there before. Alicia was admittedly younger and sturdier than she. Frank, who loved to roam the countryside, was slim and athletic for his years.

It made sense she could see the logic. Still, she felt like she was the last to be picked for netball. She settled diligently at her post, looking at the phone. Occasionally, she looked over her shoulder out the window. There was no sign of the wraiths, but she had seen enough horror films. There was no way she was going to set foot outside.

***

Fr Flanagan led the way through the tunnel. They walked three abreast along the smooth passageways. For some reason, the cavernous space made them speak in hushed tones.

"Who could have built this?" asked Alicia rhetorically.

The priest reminded them for the umpteenth time about the danger of the other tunnel. Frank shivered at the thought of the abyss that had nearly been the end of Sean. It was a long walk until they reached the point where the tunnel widened out. Their eyes adjusted to the brightness of the white stone in this section.

The elegance and grandeur of this whole space took their breath away. Frank was already composing a painting in his mind. The faded frescoes on the wall brought his mind back to the job at hand. Alicia tied one end of the rope to one of the bollards. It fitted neatly into ancient grooves.

They began their search for the magnetite blocks. A small alcove next to the frescoed wall was the storage area. The magnetite had been deposited in individual carved spaces. For Fr Flanagan, it was eerily reminiscent of catacombs.

The magnetite gave a silvery lustrous glow. The heavy block now in place on the dock edge, the rope tied, they waited. All three were tired from the walk in this underworld. All three of them thought about how their comrades were faring above ground.

***

The battle across the field was torturous. When they hit the treeline, it became almost impossible. Threading the boat through the branches while swinging the sticks within the gap between the trees slowed them further.

Every muscle in Jonjo's body ached, yet he kept encouraging the others on. Blood dripped from Sean's hands, his skin torn by the effort of carrying the boat. Micko had been physically sick and was bent and bowed with exertion.

Only Sonny seemed able to cope. He lowered the boat on the others fighting single-handedly against the demons. Then pulling up the canoe, he called, "Trees, water."

The two yew trees were only yards ahead. In unison, the men surged forward and collapsed in a heap. They were in the patch of earth under the canopy of the two trees. The patch of ground where nothing could grow.

The four gathered their wits and took up their sticks. But there was no onslaught. The wraiths surrounded them but did not step into the shade of the poisonous trees. Slowly the men recovered their equilibrium and took stock.

"It's the yew trees. They were always planted in cemeteries," began Sean. "It was believed that it was to stop animals from digging around and prevent the ground from being grazed. Maybe, it was to keep out the wraiths."

Checking their belongings, they assessed what they had. Only Sonny still had his backpack, and one mobile remained in Micko's pocket. The helmets and torches were gone, so too the lifejackets. Both paddles had survived firmly attached under the seats.

"We are surrounded," said Micko. "We can't lower the boat down through them."

"Remember the sledge," said Jonjo excitedly.

"No, we can't do that. There is no snow," objected

Sean.

"A soft landing in the river. No wraiths in the water," countered Jonjo. "Slide down lean to the left ride the boat into the river."

"There's no other way," admitted Sean. "Just like being on a sledge," he continued unconvincingly.

Sonny manoeuvred the boat between the two trees. Jonjo and Sean squeezed themselves as low as they could onto the bottom of the canoe. They used the seats as handholds.

The craft seesawed as it balanced at the top of the bank. Sonny gave the boat such a mighty shove that it covered the first few feet out of contact with the ground. It careered forward at such a pace that the two men were pinned back.

They were heading for a fatal headlong plunge into the water. At the last moment, the canoe hit the mossy mound. This both slowed them down and spun them almost parallel to the stream. They hit the water with a resounding slap.

"Are ye O.K.?" shouted Micko.

"Grand," replied Jonjo, with more conviction than he felt.

Feeling the power from the oars strengthening their arms, the two men cautiously paddled forward. The current pushed gently against them as they entered the tunnel. The space was suffused with a yellow light that was strangely comforting. The phrase 'and let perpetual light shine upon them' came unbidden into Sean's mind.

The water was clean and clear. The roof of the tunnel had no joins or cracks. There was no plant life, yet the shaft seemed almost organic as if it had grown inside the hill. Their aches and pains from the journey were forgotten in the serenity of their surroundings.

It felt as though time stood still. The two paddled in perfect unison, unspeaking each in his own thoughts. The reverie was brought to an end by the sight of the white stones. Shouts of welcome from their three allies brought them back to the task at hand.

Jonjo steered the craft onto the landing stage. Alicia deftly threw the rope to Sean, who tied it onto the canoe.

"How are the boys?" she asked.

"Surrounded by wraiths, but safe for now," replied Jonjo.

"Are you two alright?" asked Fr Flanagan.

"Battered and bruised. We lost most of our stuff getting away from the creatures," answered Sean.

Frank passed them tea from his flask. "Are you stopping for a rest?" he asked.

"No time," replied Jonjo, as he and Sean took the magnetite block on board.

They set off for the tunnel again, heading for the wheel. Keeping the boat tied Alicia, paid out the rope as they moved on. The canoe was lower in the water with the magnetite on board. Jonjo looked cautiously at the waterline. Suddenly, he was dazzled by an explosion of light.

They were at the wheel.

It was much taller than they had anticipated. At each side were banks of crystal brighter than diamonds. They reminded Jonjo of the solar panels that had been springing up on rooftops. The wheel itself had razor-thin blades of black stone. The apparatus was turning very slowly, propelled by water diverted from the river.

The water hit the blades at the top of the wheel. The large stones hanging from the wheel helped increase this power. The crystals formed part of the mechanism.

There was nowhere to tie their boat. Jonjo kneeling up on the seat took hold of the lever. To his surprise, this was also cold and crystalline to the touch. It was not the wooden lever they had assumed it to be. The entire apparatus was constructed from stone.

The lever moved smoothly and clicked into its new position. As it did so, it ejected the existing magnetite block into the water, splashing the boat. By kneeling on the other seat facing Jonjo, Sean and his companion lifted the magnetite block into place.

As they sat back in the canoe, the wheel went into overdrive. It was spinning so fast that it was churning up the water. The boat was forced down the tunnel. The water became higher; the rope tying the canoe to the bollard was pulling it under.

With great presence of mind, Alicia cut the rope. The boat flew down the channel like a cork from a bottle.

***

"Run," shouted Fr Flanagan.

They needed no invitation. The tidal wave that had

swept the boat away was threatening them too. The trio ran as fast as they could down the tunnel, the water getting progressively higher. The initial sprint turned into a jog. Progress became more difficult as the water deepened. Clothing became heavy, and they had to take increasingly higher steps.

All were frightened of being swept off their feet. The tunnel that led to the abyss was clearly intended as a drain. They did not want to be sucked down. By the time they reached the junction, the water was over shoulder height.

Fr Flanagan stopped to shepherd the other two past the intersection. As he did so, a wave took him off his feet. Frank and Alicia grabbed him and pulled him up.

The drain took away the water. The three adventurers trudged the remainder of the journey, sopping wet. Their hearts were heavy with worry about the two old men in the boat.

"The wheel turned the wrong way," said Fr Flanagan. "Instead of sucking in the wraiths, it is sending water down the river."

"Of course, that was what the drawings were telling us," exclaimed Frank. "The ones we didn't understand.

The wheel rotates the other way to power up. Then it deals with the wraiths."

Sean and Jonjo flattened themselves to the boards. Powerless against the might of the water, Sean found himself saying prayers at as fast a rate as the boat was travelling.

Emerging from the tunnel, the power of the water dissipated. They were like surfers cresting a wave. Suddenly the water dropped, and the boat span upside down. They were thrown out into the water. The canoe floated on, beaching itself upside down on the bank.

Jonjo and Sean swam, walked and scrambled to the bank. Their hearing was assailed by a high pitched keening sound.

"Look!" exclaimed Sean, pointing at the river.

The water was being pulled the other way, and with it the wraiths.

***

Micko and Sonny scrambled, and half fell down the bank to meet them. All four broke into uncontrollable laughter. As soon as one tried to speak, the others laughed. How long this hysteria lasted was hard to say.

They pulled themselves up the banking using the big rope. Micko had tied it around one of the yew trees.

"I had the strangest feeling when I tied that rope," said Micko.

"I know," said Jonjo.

***

They trudged their weary way home.

Phoning Sinead, Micko said, "We are all safe. The job's done."

"True," smiled Jonjo. In his mind, he knew there was one last act for him to play out.

Chapter 40

It was a rare sunny day in old Mayo. Jonjo walked with purpose down to the hollow. He had his bacon sandwiches, wrapped in greaseproof paper, nestled against a stone flagon containing a quart of porter and an enamel mug. They weighed heavily in the old khaki bag; his dad had given him when he was a boy. It had served him well over the years; a school satchel, a lunch box, a pannier on his bike, a picnic basket.

After the adventures in the tunnel, both he and Sean were bruised and battered. They had shortened their walks but enjoyed them just as much. A few weeks had passed since the battle with the wraiths. With their backs resting against the tree trunks, they recapped recent events.

The art exhibition had been a roaring success. Frank

Jennings' paintings had sold rapidly now the tourist season was here. He had already replenished the stock in Molly's cafe. And would shortly have to do so again.

Sinead's posters had attracted attention from a prestigious gallery on the eastern seabord of the U.S.A. Jonjo suspected that Sean had a hand in this. His cousin had kept his cards close to his chest, preferring anonymity for his good deeds.

Whether it was just his imagination or not, Jonjo had sensed a change in the town. People seemed brighter and happier. The whole place was somehow more optimistic.

The eight people who defeated the wraiths had met in Sean's house. They had all recounted their version of events and discussed what to do next.

The boat and other belongings had been recovered. They decided to build a boat in the tunnel to be left for use in future battles. Micko volunteered for this, and the Jenningses would do the artwork. They hoped this would not be needed for years, perhaps centuries to come.

The two artists would update the diagrams of how to change the magnetite block. The missing piece of information to return the lever to its original position was added. This omission had caused the near-disaster of Jonjo and Sean's trip.

The group of eight had decided that they would not reveal to anyone what had happened. For a start, they thought most would not believe them. They needed to ensure the message would pass down the generations to prevent a future disaster.

Fr Flanagan, although disappointed about the missed archaeological opportunities, agreed. He had found out about a secret Vatican repository where he lodged a copy of the information about the tunnel. The knowledge would be kept safe and unopened until if and when it was needed. The document would only be opened if there were reports of problems in the locality of the tunnel. To his surprise, he had been told that the Papal State had many such documents.

To preclude the need for outside involvement, Sean had changed his will. He left his house to Micko and Alicia. They would keep the secret and pass it down.

"You know, it's not too late for you to have descendants," said Alicia.

Micko blushed in the extravagant way that only a

red-haired person can.

Jonjo bequeathed his house to Sonny. He would be near enough to his Mammy so that she could care for him. He would also be able to develop some independence. Alicia decided when she moved home, she would give her big house to the town. She hoped that it could be used for the benefit of the community.

***

Jonjo began to slumber in the sunshine. Sean tried to sleep, but his mind continued to whirr. He was trying to nod off, but unbidden thoughts would not let him.

Jonjo had described to him a recurring vision. His late wife Mary had appeared to him. She had told him to be prepared to join her. The dream was crystal clear. He had to set out from the coast in his canoe and paddle out to the Veil of Mist. The day was imminent. Jonjo believed so faithfully that he had recruited his friends. On Jonjo's say-so, the canoe would be strapped to the roof of the big, old taxi. He would be driven to the coast and set off.

***

Jonjo slept and dreamed, but it was not the vision of his beautiful wife. He was in the tunnel again. The boat had been lifted up to the cavern roof his chest was being pressed against it. Then the wraiths were squeezing the life from him.

He woke with a start. The dream had ended, but the pain had not.

"It is time!"

Sean saw his friend's pain. He rang for Micko and the taxi. Jonjo resolutely refused the offer of a call for an ambulance. Slowly the men retraced their steps. Jonjo stopping intermittently, gripped by the pain.

By the time they approached the house, Micko was there. The canoe was already loaded. Micko and Sonny ran out to Jonjo. They half walked, half carried him the rest of the way.

Micko drove the car as only he could. Alicia and Sean supported the silent Jonjo in the back seat.

Driving the taxi right down onto the sand, Micko and Sonny jumped out. They had the canoe in the water; in the time it took Alicia and Sean to help Jonjo to the water's edge.

They lifted the old man into the craft.

Interpreting Sean's look, Jonjo said, "Just me this time, old friend."

They pushed the boat into the water. At first, the strength from the paddle helped Jonjo, and he made some progress. Then a breaker caught the craft and spun it broadside. Sean ran out into the water. He tried to get into the boat but was unable, weighed down by his sodden clothes.

Sonny walked resolutely into the sea and picked up the solid figure of Sean without any effort. He placed him gently down on the seat and just as he had done on the riverbank, he gave the boat a mighty push.

Sean paddled furiously. Jonjo slumped unmoving in the front.

"Look!" cried Alicia.

A gentle mist rolled across the sea and caressed the boat. When the cloud lifted, there was no sign of the two friends.

Yet on the horizon was the distinct shape of an island where no island should be.

ABOUT THE AUTHOR

Michael Kilgallon was born in Leeds and is the youngest of a large County Mayo family. A retired teacher and head teacher, he spent most of his career in Preston. He now lives in Bispham on the west coast of England. Michael is married with two grown up children and two grandchildren. He enjoys spending time with his family, reading, writing, competing with his wife at Scrabble and chess, and following Leeds United and the Republic of Ireland football teams.

Printed in Great Britain
by Amazon